PRAISE] O

"*The Legacy of Us* is a sweet story about love,
family secrets, and the notion that everyone deserves a
few secrets that don't have to be shared."
—National bestseller KRIS RADISH,
author of *The Year of Necessary Lies*

"Contino unlocks a treasure-trove of emotion
in her multigenerational debut! Richly-layered and
unique, *The Legacy of Us* is a tale of family, forgiveness, and
finding love where (and when) you least expect it."
—JESSICA TOPPER, author of *Deeper Than Dreams*

"I don't know what I liked more about Kristin Contino's
debut—the double dose of romance and intrigue
spanning 100 years, the relatable, inspiring characters
or the fact that the book takes place in my hometown.
What I do know is that this sparkling novel delivers,
so don't miss it!"
—ELISE MILLER, author of *Star Craving Mad*

"*The Legacy of Us* is a heartfelt story about the
bonds of family and the strength of real love through
the generations. A moving and beautiful tale,
as classic as your grandmother's cameo necklace."
—ANDEE REILLY, author of *Satisfaction*

the legacy of us

the legacy of us

a novel

KRISTIN CONTINO

SparkPress, A BookSparks Imprint
A Division of SparkPoint Studio, LLC

Published by SparkPress, a BookSparks imprint,
A division of SparkPoint Studio, LLC
Tempe, Arizona, USA, 85281
www.gosparkpress.com

Published 2015
Printed in the United States of America
ISBN: 978-1-940716-17-6 (pbk)
ISBN: 978-1-940716-16-9 (e-bk)

Library of Congress Control Number: 2015940043

Cover design © Julie Metz, Ltd./metzdesign.com
Cover Art © Trevillion Images

Dedication

TO ALL THE
MOTHERS AND
GRANDMOTHERS OUT THERE—
ESPECIALLY MY OWN.

CHAPTER 1

LIZ

*M*Y GRANDMA DIED in the middle of *House Hunters International.* There I was, Googling properties in Europe like I inevitably do during every episode, when the phone rang. One minute I was busy calculating how much money I'd need to move to a remote village in Tuscany; the next I was sobbing uncontrollably on my hand-me-down floral couch.

I don't know why I felt so shocked. Nan was no spring chicken at ninety years old. But still, she'd never had any major health issues, and half the time when I called her she was out and about, volunteering at the animal shelter or at church. She'd even learned how to use Facebook over the summer. Just two weeks earlier we had gone to Linvilla Orchards and picked apples for fresh pies and she had told me how she'd "met a cutie" at the Lower Merion Senior Center. Then just like that, she was gone: "Natural causes," the doctor said.

Later that week, I pulled up to her classic Tudor on Philadelphia's Main Line, home of old money, exclusive prep schools, and La Bella, the restaurant Nan and Pop had built from the ground up. My parents and younger sister, Cate, were carrying empty cardboard boxes and plastic storage bins inside while Gracie, the baby of the family, sat on the front step, crying and blowing her nose so loudly it sounded like a trumpet.

Walking through Nan's front door to silence just felt wrong; I expected her to come out of the kitchen with a tray of cookies, offering to take everyone's coats and enveloping us in warm hugs. When that didn't happen, the devastation washed over me, as fresh as it had been on the night when I'd heard the news. I'd never have Sunday dinner with Nan again, or take a "just us" trip to see a Broadway show. No more breakfasts at the hole-in-the-wall diner down the street, no more nightly heart-to-heart phone calls. Her house had been my second home, the one place where I could always go no matter what. I'd even lived with her my senior year of high school after teenage angst made it impossible to get along with my mother.

It would never be the same.

I fingered the heavy brocade of the curtains and the somewhat gaudy figurines on the coffee table, trying to remember every detail. I let the tears fall as I snapped Instagram photos of the mural of Venice on the living room wall (yes, we're *that* Italian), the carefully stacked china in the cabinet, and the pencil marks noting her grandkids' heights inside the pantry door. "Liz" was written in my wobbly five-year-old handwriting toward the bottom, progressing to an only slightly neater cursive next to the highest line, when I turned eighteen.

"Liz?" Mom called out. "Where are you? I need a favor."

"Yeah? What?" I asked, wiping away a stray tear and slamming the pantry door. Why couldn't she just leave me alone for a second?

"I know you're taking this really hard, but can you please rein in the attitude?" she said, hand on hip. "You're not the only one grieving here. She was my mother, you know."

Resentment shone through in Mom's tone, and for the first time I noticed the dark circles around her eyes and the tension in her shoulders. She gave me that same pained look I always got when Nan and I shared an inside joke or told a story she didn't know. Like a third wheel pretending to be part of the bike. To be fair, it was the same look I probably gave her when she laughed with Cate, or took her out for yet another girls' day without me.

I sighed and looked at the ground. "Sorry."

"I brought your good camera because we need some pictures for the real estate listing. And you know, just to have for memories. Can you take care of that?"

I nodded and took the heavy old Nikon, the camera Nan had given me when I took up high school photography classes, and slipped the frayed strap around my neck.

As I snapped away, Gracie, our resident drama queen, remained curled in a ball on the plastic-covered couch. She sobbed with increased vigor every time someone walked into the room and then reverted to texting her friends and admiring her new sequined Uggs whenever she thought no one was looking. I shook my head at her not-so-subtle attempt to get out of cleaning.

Cate, also known as "Beep" due to her propensity for making odd beeping sounds when she laughed, helped my Dad carry things out of the kitchen and box them up, not speaking unless spoken to. Being a seriously preppy Villanova student and president of her sorority, she was dressed as usual in cords and a bright-green Lilly Pulitzer V-neck with a printed floral shirt underneath, her dark hair pulled back with a matching green patent-leather headband.

Although we didn't always get along when we were younger, Cate and I had become much closer once she got out of the moody teen years. Now she was almost halfway through her senior year of college, which made me feel ancient.

"Cate, you okay?" I asked, handing her a glass.

She looked at me like I was an alien and shook her head no, pushing her headband back into place and continuing to pack the boxes in silence. Everyone grieves in a different way, but Cate was seriously worrying me, especially because we came from a family of criers.

You know how some people refer to their families— "We're big sports people," or "We're drinkers"—well, the Moretti family, we're criers.

I grew up in a home where it was perfectly normal for someone to be in front of the TV sobbing because of a talk show or even a Hallmark commercial. My cousin famously cried at an episode of the game show *Supermarket Sweep* because she was "just so happy for the winners." Rightly, Cate's lack of tears concerned me.

She wasn't talking, so about two hours into the whole production, I gave up and headed upstairs to Nan's bedroom to take a break and have some time alone. The staircase was one of those grand old curving ones you'd expect to see in a Southern mansion and had served as the backdrop for many a family photo over the years.

The best part of the staircase, though, was the vase at the bottom. Nan had a penchant for antiques, and her pride and joy was a gigantic Japanese porcelain vase that stood about four feet tall. We used to climb up to the third floor and have a contest to see who could drop (insert random object here) into the vase. Cate and I preferred Ping-Pong balls, but according to Nan, balled-up paper, Matchbox cars, and other small toys had been favorites over the years. Thinking about what on earth sat inside the vase made me laugh for the first time that week.

I climbed up to the third floor in slow motion, my pink Converse squeaking against the shiny wood. Finally I pushed open the door to Nan's bedroom and took a deep breath. It smelled exactly the same: Chanel No. 5.

The oil paintings she and Pop had acquired on their travels over the years, along with some original art by a family friend in Italy, had already been taken down and were spread out on the huge canopy bed with bright yellow Post-its indicating to whom they'd been left in the will. Otherwise, the rest of the room looked exactly the same, all warm golds, browns, and cherry furniture. The vanity still had scratch marks on the edge from when Gracie brought over our cat, Smokey, and he went on a rampage through Nan's house.

I took some photos and walked around absorbing the details, stopping to open and close the heavy, painted lid of a ceramic trinket box on her dresser while the tune of "Greensleeves" tinkled through the room.

Memories of playing that music box as a child flooded over me, and I sunk to the ground, staring at the walls and just remembering. Twirling through her room in my tutu the night of my first dance recital; sleepovers at Nan's when we would watch episodes of *I Love Lucy* and sip hot chocolate together; countless Christmases snooping in the closet to see where the presents were (behind the hat boxes on the top shelf, as always).

After at least ten minutes of uncontrollable sobbing, I managed to hoist myself off the carpet and pull it together. That was, until my elbow whacked into the little porcelain box as I turned to face the dresser, sending it toppling. Athleticism has never been my strength, so it was no surprise my attempt at catching it was futile and the box smashed into three large pieces on the floor. As if I didn't already have enough to cry about.

As I started to pick up the pieces and think of what to tell my mother, I stopped. Lying on the carpet next to a small brass key and a hundred-lire coin was a pair of emerald-cut diamond studs. *Ah, Cate's earrings,* I thought, picking them up and placing them on the dresser. She'd been left this particular pair of diamonds in Nan's will, and I had to admit I thought I'd be the one who would inherit them. Nan had worn those earrings almost every day of my entire life, whether we were going to a black-tie wedding or digging up weeds in the backyard. I guess she figured Cate's classic style was a bit closer to hers, which was true, since I usually wore my own designs, anyway.

Along with the money she'd set up in a special account (that I was forbidden to touch until I was ready to buy a house), Nan had left me her scratched-up old desk in the will. Although it was presumably to use for my jewelry making, I didn't have any special connection to it, and wondered how I'd even get the massive piece of oak inside the elevator to my apartment. But then I saw the key, and remembered the desk had a locked drawer. I replayed the reading of the will in my head.

I hope you'll use the desk to make lots of beautiful pieces for LM Designs, and it has plenty of drawers to keep your materials and secrets inside, too.

I pursed my lips, staring at the key on the floor. Might as well have a look.

I popped my head into Nan's office, which over the

years had served as her sewing room-slash-library-slash-personal escape. As kids, we weren't allowed to go in there unless she went with us, and even Pop wasn't permitted in her office. As a little girl it was annoying, but as an adult, I didn't blame her for wanting a place of her own.

There was nothing special about the room; it smelled kind of like mothballs, had hideous sixties-style daisy wallpaper and equally hideous furniture to match the maroon, yellow, and green color scheme. Four large bookshelves, painted a deep green, lined the walls, along with a sewing table, her desk, and a comfy plaid recliner. A small window, framed with eyelet curtains Nan had made, looked into the backyard, and she would open it up in the summer so she could keep part of an eye on the kids playing.

As outdated and tacky as it was, the office always had a sort of mythical quality to it, and the few times I'd been granted entrance, it had felt like being admitted to a secret club. As a five-year-old, being allowed to watch Nan put the finishing touches on a sewing project was thrilling stuff. Being there by myself as an adult, however, wasn't quite as exciting.

I sat down on the small wooden chair in front of her desk and slid the tarnished key into the top drawer's lock. The drawer wobbled a bit, but finally I heard a soft click. I slowly pulled it open to reveal a mess of paper, craft supplies, instruction manuals, and who knows what. Disappointment set in as I realized it was probably just a junk drawer that happened to have a lock.

I grabbed a stack of papers and fanned them out on the worn shag carpet. There were some old greeting cards that made me smile, mostly from Pop, and a note from my mom asking permission to have a sleepover (yes or no, circle one), signed "Your favorite daughter, Lily." After sorting through the rest of the first pile, I went back into the drawer and fished around for anything interesting, pulling out nothing more exciting than a book of stamps from back when they cost twenty-five cents.

And then I spotted the box. It was a fairly nondescript little pink jewelry box, like the type you'd get at a department store with a heart-shaped charm for your mother's birthday. It opened with a creak to reveal an old cameo necklace sitting on top of a folded piece of cream notepaper. Was this for me?

I unfolded the thick paper and smiled at Nan's familiar, loopy handwriting, even though it hurt my heart to know it was the last new note I'd ever get from her.

> *My dear Lizzie, Wear this in good health and happiness.*
> *I trust you'll know what to do with it! Keep shining brightly,*
> *and remember I love you always.*
> *xoxo Nan*

I read the note again, and then looked down at the cameo. What on earth would I do with it, other than wear it?

I picked the necklace up and examined it closely, realizing it was actually a locket. The shell was a pretty reddish-orange hue, and it had a raised silhouette of a woman with a ponytail, a puff-sleeved blouse, and a pronounced nose. At her neck was a tiny diamond chip, making it look like she was wearing a pendant. I could tell it was an antique and probably worth something. Gently prying the locket open, I squinted to read the phrase engraved inside. Suddenly, I knew why it had been tucked inside the drawer for so long.

The cameo had an inscription, and although it was a

bit worn, there was no mistaking what it said.

Marry me, Ella. Yours, Joseph

Joseph? Who the hell was Joseph?

I read it over again, making sure I got it right. Unless Pop had randomly decided to change his name to Harry, his first name was certainly not Joseph. They say there are things you only learn about people after they're dead, but this was crazy. Nan and I used to talk for hours about guys; I thought I knew every story of hers, and she definitely knew mine. Nan never even dated until late in her twenties, and her first-ever kiss was with my grandfather after a date at the ice cream parlor. Could she have lied to me? Had she been engaged to another man before Pop?

On the other hand, I knew my great-grandmother had been named Gabriella and nicknamed Ella, which Nan hated because everyone confused them. Maybe this was another case of confusing the Ellas; it very well could've been Nonni Gabriella's necklace. But my great-grandpa's name was Angelo, so that definitely didn't explain things, either.

What was she trying to tell me? I was supposed to "know what to do with it," but instead felt more confused than ever. I sighed and went back into Nan's bedroom, stepping in front of the vanity. I pulled my mousy brown hair up into a half-assed bun, admiring the cameo against the oh-so-glamorous Philadelphia Eagles hoodie I'd thrown on over my vintage pink slip dress. The diamond sparkled in the light and I pictured Nan in one of her floral 1950s-style dresses, twirling in front of the same mirror. I wanted to run down and ask my mom about the necklace, but for some reason I plopped myself back on the floor instead. Asking Mom if she knew about a secret fiancé would probably just make her more upset.

Of course, I could've asked Nan's sister, Aunt Mary.

She surely would've known if Nan had received a proposal from this Joseph. Sisters tell each other everything, right? Thinking about my ill-fated trip to Cancún senior year and what Cate and Gracie didn't know about a particular night at Señor Frogs answered that question in about a second.

The bigger question was whether to share the cameo with my own sisters. Cate I could trust, but with Gracie I was more than apprehensive due to her propensity for tattling and being, well, fifteen.

As if she'd been reading my mind, Cate poked her head into Nan's bedroom and announced everyone was going out to get some dinner.

"You look weird," she said, and suddenly I didn't feel like talking. I tucked the necklace into my sweatshirt pocket before she could see it.

"I broke Nan's trinket box. Mom's gonna kill me," I said, placing the rest of the pieces of broken ceramic on top of the dresser. "But on the bright side, I did find the earrings she gave you."

Cate's face lit up and she instantly put the earrings on. "Thanks. I'm never going to take these off. And at this point, I'm sure Mom will just shrug and tell you not to worry about the box. Take advantage of it while you can."

Cate was right. I had gone to my parents' house for dinner earlier in the week, and while juggling a carafe of wine in one hand and a stack of plates in another, one of the plates had slipped out of my hands and smashed on the kitchen's tile floor.

Normally this would have elicited screeching and/ or crying from my mother about her heirloom dishes, but she'd simply put her hand on my shoulder and said, "These things happen, hon. It's just a plate," while the rest of us looked at her like she was nuts.

"Good point," I said. "Let's go before I break something else."

I figured I'd wait until things calmed down to tell her about the cameo and in the meantime possibly dig up some information. Maybe something was hiding in the house that could tell me more about the story behind the necklace; I knew Nan used to keep a diary, and maybe there were even some letters or other trinkets from this Joseph guy. Who knows, they might've been hiding in the desk, just like the cameo.

I followed Cate down the hall and took one last look at the mess I'd made in the office. "I'll be right down," I said, before gathering the pile of crap on the floor, taking the cameo out of my pocket and putting it in its box, and placing everything back in the drawer. Finally, I turned the key and slipped it into my hoodie . . . just in case.

I headed downstairs to join everyone for dinner, wishing we could just go to La Bella with Nan like old times instead of grabbing pizza around the corner. But I guessed it was time to discover a new normal.

Over the next few days I tried to convince my family to go back to Nan's house to continue getting things in order, but my mother was avoiding it at all costs. The first trip had been, understandably, an emotional experience, and she came up with every excuse in the book not to go back again.

Finally, on Wednesday morning, I decided to look for more clues about the cameo myself. It was my day off, and since everyone else was at school or work, I knew I wouldn't have any interruptions on my little fact-finding mission. Sometimes working retail had its benefits.

As I drove down Lancaster Avenue, I passed La Bella and waved in the direction of the building, a tradition Cate and I had formed when we were kids and never gave up, even after Nan sold the restaurant. I still couldn't believe that my grandmother could have had another fiancé. The stories of Nan and my Pop were legendary; they were the ultimate husband/wife team, running La Bella together in addition to Nan's special project, a high-end bakery. It's hard to imagine a grandparent having a love life, but it was permanently inscribed in the cameo: this Joseph character had asked Nan, or her mother, to marry him. Either way, it was weird.

I started coming up with wild stories in my head: Joseph went off to war, or Nan found him in bed with another woman. Anything could have happened to break them up, but I had no way to find out the truth.

As I walked into Nan's house, my cell buzzed. "Hey, Kaycee," I said, happy to hear my friend's (and boss's) voice. Stepping into silence was just too depressing.

"I know you have a lot on your plate right now, but are you free to take over Clare's shift this afternoon? She just called out sick and was supposed to be here in half an hour."

I grimaced. Extra hours at Plaid, the trendy boutique where I worked, would normally be a good thing. But I needed to find some information on Nan's past, and my mother would kill me if I bailed on our family dinner later.

"I'm really sorry, you know normally I would, but I'm in the 'burbs doing some stuff at my grandma's house, and then I have plans with my parents."

"Totally understand. I can call one of the other girls. By the way, your last two pairs of earrings sold today. Can you make some more of the blue sparkly ones, those purple beaded hoops, and then the green chandeliers?"

I pumped my fist as I walked up the steps. Despite the

upcoming holiday season, I hadn't sold any of my jewelry pieces at the boutique in weeks, and orders from my Etsy site were borderline pathetic. It felt like I'd knocked on every boutique door in Philadelphia and had them all shut in my face, so I was thankful for any orders Kaycee placed.

I ended the call just as I stepped into Nan's office, tossing my phone on top of the desk.

"Can you give me a sign?" I said, wondering if Nan could hear me out there. "Anything?"

The only response was the sound of the neighbor's dog barking next door. So much for signs, because Nan definitely wasn't a dog person.

I pondered some new jewelry designs as I sorted through the endless brochures, office supplies, and other miscellaneous stuff in the desk. After emptying all of the smaller drawers and about half of the locked one, all I had was a bag of trash, a huge pile of things on the floor, and a seriously sore back. Letting out a deep sigh, I picked some of the papers off the carpet, ready to shove them back inside the desk. But something in the back of the drawer made me stop.

Underneath the mess of items still inside sat a slim book of faded red leather. Inscribed on the cover in gold was the word "Diary."

CHAPTER 2

ELLA

September 10, 1957

I can't stand my mother. I hate the way she barks orders at everyone, how she gives unsolicited parenting advice, and the ridiculous way she dresses. She drinks too much, buys the kids over-the-top gifts, and is just plain rude most of the time. Did I mention how she unapologetically favors my brothers and sister over me?

I guess that's the beauty of having a diary . . . you can go about saying things you'd never dare to admit out loud.

As a child, I guess I thought it was just a matter of my being a little girl and she an authority figure, and that we'd grow closer in time. Now I'm in my mid-thirties, and I've realized it isn't going to happen. The worst part is Mom isn't doing too well, and now I'm the one who has to take care of her.

We all think about losing our parents, but I feel like it's almost an abstract thought; it's something that happens to other people and will happen to you eventually, but not for a long time. Now that day seems like it's around the corner, always lurking.

I was telling the neighbors over coffee the other day how fast it went from minor things like forgetfulness to her falling down the stairs and starting a minor fire trying to cook rice. I have no idea what possessed her to do that in the first place, considering she had a chef, but that's neither here nor there. Since Harry is about the only person Mom will take advice from, he finally convinced her to leave that big old house. And now here she is, living with us. She's my mother, and of course I feel horrible about the situation, but now I'm put in the position of caregiver for a woman who has rarely shown me any affection my whole life.

I don't know what else to do. We can't leave her alone, and let's be honest, it's not like any of her other children are going to take her in. I only wish Lessie was still with us, because not only did she always know the right thing to do, she probably would've moved in with Mom. I'm going to have to take some time off from the restaurant and stay home until this has all been figured out.

The kids are thrilled to have their Nonni in the house, and luckily, they don't sense it's actually for a bad reason.

I've been spending more and more time in my office these days, even if it's just to shut the door and cry for fifteen minutes. I keep thinking about my idea to open a bakery, but it feels like a distant and impossible dream, and that makes me feel even lower. I should've thought of it before we had kids . . . how could I possibly handle all of that work now? And with Harry being in the process of unveiling a new menu, I can't burden him with even more to think about.

Between trying to deal with my mother, the kids, and the restaurant, I feel like I'm going batty. Harry suggested I start a journal to help get my feelings out, so here I am . . .

Ella closed her diary and slipped it into the locked drawer of her new desk, turning the shiny key with a quick click. Harry was out back with the kids playing ball, and she had a project to finish before they came inside.

Lily's birthday was just days away, and Ella wanted to finish her daughter's party dress as soon as possible. She admired the Vogue pattern she'd just picked up earlier in the week; it had a pin-tucked bodice and small puffed sleeves. It was the perfect birthday dress for Lily, the quintessential girl's girl. After the dress was done, she'd start working on the elaborate three-tiered pink cake with fondant roses. A sketch of the cake sat next to the pattern on her sewing table, with Ella's initials in curly script at the bottom.

"Maybe the birthday party will help Lily," she told Harry earlier that morning. "She's so jealous when it comes to the twins lately, and then with my mother moving in and everything at work, perhaps she just needs some special attention."

Carol and Harry Jr. were in full-fledged toddler mode, and now that they were on the move, Ella had to watch them constantly or face yet another broken vase or figurine. Playing dolls or reading Lily's favorite stories sometimes took a backseat to running after sweaty two-year-olds. This resulted in frequent tantrums from Lily, and earlier in the week a framed photo of the twins mysteriously wound up in the trash. Ella hoped the excitement of a party and a pretty new dress would distract Lily for a day or two, at least.

Today, Harry was able to coax Lily outside, and Ella hoped she would relax and have fun like a normal little girl. Lily was definitely five going on thirty, and preferred to spend her time chatting with adults or trying on her favorite dresses while the neighborhood kids played outside. Like grandmother, like granddaughter, Ella thought with a sigh.

The Indian summer breeze blew in through the open window, sending Ella's loose brown curls floating in front of her face. She could hear Harry Jr. laughing, Carol crying, and Lily screeching. Who knew what was going on in the yard, but trying to concentrate on her sewing project was proving to be impossible. How was she ever going to complete the dress, let alone bake a huge cake? She felt like a fool to even think opening her own bakery would be a good idea.

A loud knock sounded and Ella threw her fabric down in defeat. "It's your darling mother," came the voice from the other side of the door.

Ella rested her head on the sewing table for a few seconds before taking a deep breath, straightening her skirt, and opening the door. Her mother was dressed in a bright-purple floral blouse and matching skirt with dime-sized pearls around her neck. Gabriella's makeup and perfectly coiffed hair could've given a Hollywood starlet a run for her money, even though she'd told Ella earlier she had no plans of leaving the house.

"Ella, be a dear and get me some lunch, will you? I don't know what kind of restaurant you're running if you can't even feed your own family on a regular schedule."

Ella forced her lips into a tight smile. "Sure, Mother. What would you like?" she asked.

"Surprise me."

If times had been different, Ella would've snapped, but since her mom's health was declining, she was trying as best she could to be nice. Still, Ella's temper got the best of her sometimes, like the day before, when she'd told Gabriella that she could go find her own dinner if she didn't like the meatloaf.

"I'll get lunch ready in a few minutes," Ella said. Gabriella simply nodded, marching away as fast as she could muster with her cane.

Their personalities had never quite meshed. The fact that Gabriella had been born in a time period when women were supposed to be seen and not heard meant little; she'd grown up very, very rich in her family's huge villa in Florence, moving to New York when she was a young girl to an even more ostentatious home. She generally mouthed off and did whatever she wanted, and Ella remembered her grandma telling her how pleased she was to see Ella hadn't turned out "spoiled and crass" like Gabriella.

Ella always thought she and her mother should've switched lives; she definitely would've fit in better back in her mother's day than her own. While her older siblings were deep into the jazz scene, dancing on tables at speakeasies and drinking until dawn, Ella was sitting in her room reading or begging their cook to teach her a new recipe.

Most people would have thought she was a dream child: she listened to her parents, made the honor roll, and never missed curfew. But Ella knew her mother wondered how she'd wound up with a daughter who was so . . . boring. She had told Ella she'd never find a husband, considering she spent most days up to her elbows in flour or at the sewing table instead of attending parties with the rest of New York society girls her age.

Despite their differences, Ella was making a concerted effort to try and get to know her mother better now that she was going to be living in their house. Since Gabriella was getting on in years and clearly slowing down, Ella had become aware how little time she had left, and she believed she owed it to the kids to at least make nice.

As Ella walked into the kitchen, she was greeted by the sound of little feet hitting the tile at full speed along with various shouts of "Hey," "Stop," and "MOMMA!"

She bent down and lifted up a crying Carol, shooing Lily and Harry Jr. to go back into the yard to play with their father.

With the toddler on one hip, she quickly fixed six tuna sandwiches and glasses of milk and called out for her mother to come into the kitchen. Gabriella hobbled into the sunny room, taking longer than usual to take a seat at the table.

She narrowed her eyes at the lunch in front of her. "Tuna, eh? Some chef."

Carol's cries grew louder, and Ella reached her breaking point. "Please just eat it, or feel free to make your own lunch. I don't have time for this today."

She threw a checkered dishtowel on the counter and stuck her head out the window to call for the others to come inside.

Gabriella took a bite of the sandwich, making a point to wrinkle her nose and comment on the texture and flavor every so often. Once the kids joined her at the table, she not-so-subtly suggested they ask their mom for something more interesting to serve for lunch tomorrow. This elicited nothing more than an eye roll from Harry, but Ella refused to keep quiet.

"Mother, please don't rile them up," she said, reaching over to break up a fight between Harry Jr. and Lily. "And you know we don't have time to make elaborate meals when we're not at the restaurant. If you don't like it, order out."

"Well, that's your role, isn't it?"

Ella pursed her lips. "Oh yes, I forgot. My only job in life is to cook gourmet meals for my mother, ignoring three kids, La Bella, cleaning, medical bills . . ."

"You'll be sorry when I'm dead," Gabriella said with a huff.

Ella looked at her mom and nodded. "I know I will."

Harry Jr. began sobbing again and Ella sighed, carrying the kicking and screaming child into the playroom. He wiped his face against her shoulder, smearing snot and pieces of mashed-up tuna all over her crisp white blouse while simultaneously knocking a miniature Eiffel Tower on the floor.

"Auntie Mary will be angry if you break this," Ella said, setting the figurine on the table. *And thanks for the reminder that my sister's off traveling the world while I'm here with a house full of hooligans.*

Harry Jr. stopped crying for a minute and said "Sowwee," hanging his head in shame. God forbid anyone disappoint Mary.

"How about I tell you a quick story?" Ella said, eager to distract him but not quite willing to reread one of the sticky, worn children's books they requested every day.

"NO! No story!"

Ella was just on the brink of tears as Harry came in and picked his son up in one swift motion. "Time to finish lunch, champ!" he said, carrying him back into the kitchen.

Relief flowed through her veins as Ella sunk to the floor, taking a moment to compose herself. A few deep breaths and a swipe of red lipstick from her apron pocket, and she was back in the mothering mindset. Almost.

"Harry? Mother?" she called into the kitchen. "Can you keep an eye on the kids for a few moments? I need to make a quick phone call."

She trotted up the wide, curvy steps and headed into the master bedroom, shutting the door behind her.

Trudy, Ella's neighbor and close friend, was one of the few people she could commiserate with at a time like this.

"Is everything okay?" Trudy asked. "I thought Harry was home this afternoon."

"I could just use a chat with a girlfriend, that's all. I guess it's hard for me to believe I was complaining about my destiny as a spinster with a bunch of cats not so long ago. Maybe the single life was easier, huh?"

Trudy laughed. "And if you were still single, you'd be complaining about never finding a beau."

Ella smiled, twisting and untwisting the phone cord around her wrist. "I suppose. It's always 'What next?' After how long we struggled with becoming parents, and hearing from everyone and their brother, 'When are you starting a family?' now I should feel complete. But I don't."

"What else is there? The kids are great, Harry's great and the restaurant's thriving. Ella, dear, I think you're being too hard on yourself."

"I know. But I've been thinking about the bakery idea again. Going to culinary school is out of the question for me at this point, and it's great having my cakes on the menu at La Bella, but wouldn't it be keen to have something of my own?"

"That sounds wonderful," Trudy said. "But with the kids and taking care of the house, wouldn't it be a burden? You already have a restaurant. How can you run a bakery, too?"

Ella paused. Why hadn't she thought of this before? "Actually, you're on to something. I hadn't considered attaching a cake shop to the restaurant, but it could work."

"Do you think Harry would go for it?"

"I don't know," Ella said. "I don't want to bring it up when he's been working until all hours of the morning.

And I just don't see how any of this is possible with my mother, and the kids have been terrors lately . . ."

She was about to launch into the whole story when Gabriella's voice carried up the staircase. "Ella? Can you come down here and help your poor sap of a husband with this mess?"

She sighed and said goodbye to Trudy, running downstairs to find Harry Jr. wailing next to a pile of vomit. Being a spinster surrounded by cats didn't seem so bad at that moment, after all.

CHAPTER 3

LIZ

*N*AN WAS STILL dealing with pukey toddlers and a pain-in-the-butt mother when a text from my friend Lucy interrupted my little diary-reading session.

You're still coming out for the big T-giving eve get together, right??

It was the Wednesday before Thanksgiving, otherwise known to twenty-somethings as the biggest party night of the year. With Nan and the cameo and everything else going on, I had nearly forgotten about meeting my next-door neighbor and her friends at a local Irish bar. After a rough November, I didn't feel much like celebrating, but I'd promised Lucy weeks ago I'd be there . . . and deep down, I knew she was right about me moping around the house constantly. It would probably be good to get out and let off some steam.

I checked the time on my phone. If I wanted to make it to the bar on time and still have dinner with my parents, I'd be cutting it close.

I sighed and closed the diary, slipping it into my brown cross-body bag. So far there was nothing about the cameo, and after a quick flip through the book, I saw there was still a year's worth of lengthy entries to read. I didn't know why Nan had only left one diary in the desk, but it had to be important if the rest she'd kept over the years were MIA.

I dialed my best friend's number as I walked out to the car.

"Addie! Hey, I forgot to ask earlier, but what are your plans tonight? I have that Thanksgiving Eve thing with Lucy at O'Connell's. You should come with us."

"Sorry, I'm supposed to barhop with Renee and Caitlin in Rittenhouse," she said. "And by the way, I figured you would've given up on trying to get those girls to like me by now."

"I'm sure they all like you, your personalities are just a bit different, that's all."

Okay, that might've been a slight falsification, but I wanted Addie to come.

"We can just hang with Lucy if you want," I added, even though this was probably not the best motivator. Addie and Lucy were friendly enough when we all got together, but I think they mostly tolerated each other because of me.

"Lucy's kind of a weirdo, and I mean that in the most affectionate way possible."

"Just because she's an artist doesn't make her a weirdo."

I could picture Addie rolling her eyes. "Anyway," she said, "why don't you just hang out with us? You know it would be more fun."

"I can't bail on them, and Lucy would probably just drag me out of the apartment if I backed out last minute. She's been really worried about me the past few weeks."

She let out a loud sigh. "So have I. Fine. I'll meet you there, but I'm not gonna stay too long." *Click.*

I tossed the phone in my purse, annoyed but not

surprised at Addie's reaction, and drove over to my parents' house. Addie tended to be a bit dramatic and opinionated, not surprising considering her career as a lawyer. This has rubbed more than one of my friends the wrong way, as she's shared her thoughts on everything from religion (atheist) to Tom Cruise (totally not weird, and still hot). Hopefully, she'd behave tonight.

After a quick dinner and a not-so-quick drive in holiday traffic on I-76, I finally ran into my building, giving the doorman a hasty wave. My leisurely "going out" prep routine was replaced by a thirty-second shower and haphazard makeup job. I pulled my hair up in a ponytail and slipped into a pair of jeans, a new polka-dot sweater I'd bought at Plaid with my employee discount, and a pair of tall brown boots, before clasping the cameo around my neck, grabbing my bright-green pea coat, and dashing out the door. Not my greatest look, but the temperature had dropped to about thirty degrees, and the plan wasn't to go out trolling for guys, anyway.

I took a cab over to O'Connell's, an Irish pub popular with the "let's get wasted and sing Journey songs at the top of our lungs" crowd. Even at twenty-seven, I was pushing the acceptable age range to be there, which appeared blatantly obvious as a group of college-age girls piled out of the car in front of me, stilettos clacking against the concrete and bare shoulders exposed to the night's bitter chill. I practically felt like a nun in my winter getup.

Luckily, Addie was waiting outside for me, similarly clad in a black cashmere turtleneck, faded (albeit skintight) jeans, and her favorite cowboy boots. I threw my arms around her neck.

"Did we go out looking like that when we were in college? It's freezing!" I said.

She laughed. "God forbid they cover up their halter tops with a coat. And in case you haven't noticed, I'm not pulling out my A-game tonight. At least not for this joint."

"Um, yeah, I can tell." Her short red hair, usually styled to perfection, was tucked into a glittery black knit beret, and random pieces were sticking out the back.

"How are you holding up, by the way?" she asked.

"I'm all right. Thanksgiving and Christmas are going to be rough since we always spent them at Nan's house."

Addie nodded, patting my arm. "It'll be okay. The holidays usually suck anyway, dead relative or not. Too much drama."

"This coming from the drama queen of the Northeast," I said, rolling my eyes. "Let's go see if the girls are here."

We spotted Lucy and her friends at a high-topped table in the corner of the dimly lit bar and made our way through the shoulder-to-shoulder crowd of pink-polo-wearing types. An old Madonna song blasted while a group of guys wearing "Smith's Bachelor Party" shirts crowded around the dark wood bar doing shots of tequila.

"Remind me why we agreed to come here?" Addie asked, wrinkling her nose. "The whole place reeks of wood and stale beer."

"Don't forget desperation," I said, as one of the guys from the bachelor party leered at us, making a lewd gesture involving his hand and an oversized beer glass. I mentally calculated how many trips to Starbucks I owed Addie for tagging along with me.

"You made it!" Lucy said, sliding out of her seat and running over to give me a tight hug. She'd moved in next door the year before, and despite her being five years older, we'd found a kinship in watching *The Bachelor,* and even had exchanged keys to each other's apartments. She turned to Addie and kissed her on the cheek. "Good to see you too, *chica*."

Three of Lucy's friends from the art gallery where she worked nursed red wine in the corner, and Addie gave me a "see what I'm talking about" look.

"Seems like an odd choice of bar for you guys," she said. "I even feel too old to be here."

Lucy smirked. "No kidding. My brother's bartending tonight, so I told him we'd support him. He just started, so I think he's pretty nervous."

Four Miller Lites later, the atmosphere had somewhat improved, and even the gossip about people from Lucy's job seemed interesting. Addie managed to only get into one political debate, so overall I would have called the night a win.

Sometime around twelve thirty, the group started to disperse. Lucy was meeting her fiancé back at their apartment to pack for an early-morning flight to see his parents, and the others wanted to head to a new bar. Addie offered to drive me home, and I was about to grab my coat when my heart dropped into my stomach.

Of course he would be here.

It was like one of those movie scenes where the rest of the room blurs slightly out of focus and all you see is the guy standing there with a big smile. I thought that only happened in cheesy rom-coms, but what did I know?

"Are you freaking kidding me?" Addie whispered, her expression turning sour. "Adam's here."

Adam Shipman . . . what would I even have called him? My college boyfriend? My almost-fiancé? He had moved to Chicago for a dream job four years earlier, and distance and my cold feet had meant the end of us. Since then, Adam had dropped totally off the grid, but the pain in my heart never totally did.

I hadn't allowed myself to think about him for a long time. Okay, I might have looked him up on Facebook and Googled him every so often . . . but that's beside the point. What mattered was he was standing in front of me and I had no idea what to say, except for, "What the hell are *you* doing here?"

He laughed, revealing deep dimples. "Good to see you too, Lizzie."

"Sorry, I just thought you still lived in Chicago, but duh. It's Thanksgiving. I guess you're here to see your parents?"

"Nope. Back in Philly permanently now. I quit the agency and I'm doing freelance design again. Tutoring some inner-city kids on Photoshop, too, which is cool."

Behind his shoulder, I could see Addie's horrified expression; she was mouthing, "Do you need to go to the bathroom?" That had always been our signal to get out of unwanted bar conversations. I shook my head no.

"So what have you been up to?" he asked. "It's been forever."

Four years had felt like forever, yet my life post-Adam was hardly any different than it was when we broke up. I wished I could tell him I'd made it big and the latest It Girls were wearing my designs, but the truth was I'd given myself a deadline. If my jewelry career didn't take off within one more year, I'd get a "real" job in an office or something. I smiled and gave him my best PR answer instead.

"I'm still making jewelry, and I work at a really cool boutique in Old City to help pay the bills. It's not so bad because they carry some of my designs, and I get a great discount on clothes, too."

Adam put his hand on my shoulder. "That's awesome. You gotta start somewhere. Do you have a website? I could help you with a logo or anything like that you might need."

As usual, Adam went from zero to sixty, which was why we'd broken up in the first place. This time I didn't mind as much, considering my business needed the help, but still.

"I have a logo, but it's not the best," I said. "Just something I did myself in Photoshop with my initials. I haven't had time to do much with my website or Etsy shop."

His eyes lit up. "Perfect, I can totally pull something together for you. I wouldn't charge you, obviously. I'd just want to use it for my freelance portfolio."

I smiled back, part of me thinking it would be great since Adam was a talented designer, but also that this favor might come with strings attached. Did I really want him in my life again?

"Hey, do you want another beer?" he asked. "I'm going up to get one."

"Why not?" I said, feeling my heart race and wishing I could just leave those feelings in the past.

While Adam pushed through the crowd, I turned back to Addie. "That was weird."

"Clearly," she said. "Considering you haven't talked to him in years. Now suddenly he wants to help you with your business?"

"I know. What the hell am I supposed to say? 'Nah, it's cool that you dumped me. And then I dumped you. No big deal.'"

I looked over at Adam, who was leaning against the bar. His dirty-blond hair was much shorter now, but the surfer look I loved still shone through with his pairing of a striped button-up shirt with super-faded, hole-in-the-knee jeans. He'd shown up at almost every important moment in my life: the first day of college, my graduation. Of course he'd turn up when Nan died, too.

"Liz? Hellooo? Snap out of it," Addie said, breaking my trance. "If you're going to stay here to hang out with that ass, then I'm leaving. There's still time to meet up with Caitlin and Renee, and I'm not in the mood to be a third wheel here. You coming?"

I looked back and forth between her and Adam, who was now approaching our table. "I think I'll stay for a bit. I'm curious to see what's up with him."

Addie threw her hands up. "Do what you want, but if you need me, just call."

"I'll ask Adam to drive me home or I'll just take a cab. Don't worry about me, okay?"

"The cab's probably a good idea. I don't know that he's in any better shape to drive than you are," she said. "In any case, just try not to get your hopes up because I'm not sure I can take another breakup."

I tried to push Addie's concerns out of my head after she left, which wasn't hard, considering the five beers and two shots I'd consumed. Adam and I caught up for a few minutes, but then he asked about my family.

"So what's your Nan up to these days? Still ruling over the senior center crowd? She always cracked me up."

I took a deep breath, trying to remain cool. "Actually, she passed away a few weeks ago."

"Oh my God, I'm so sorry," he said, touching my arm. "What happened?"

"Thanks," I said, the tears welling up faster than I expected. "It was just her time, I guess."

I bit my tongue, I clenched my teeth, but it was no

use. The waterworks began flowing and before I knew it, I was officially "ugly crying." Choking, sobbing, sputtering, you name it. In public. In front of Adam.

He grabbed my wrist and looked me (very intensely, I thought) in the eyes. "Okay, you're going to breathe in through the nose, out through the mouth. In through the nose, that's it . . . out through the mouth."

I felt the tears slow down and tried to focus on his face, which felt both warm and familiar yet foreign at the same time. After about five deep breaths I was feeling better, but still in a somewhat incoherent state. The fact that Adam's eyes were a startling shade of green may or may not have had something to do with it.

"You all right?" he asked. His eyes crinkled with concern, but I struggled to tell if we'd finally crossed into the friend zone or if he had other intentions.

I nodded and wiped my nose with my sleeve. Very attractive.

"Tell your family I send my condolences. She was always nice to me. Well, for the most part."

I laughed and wiped away a stray tear. "One time, after you graduated, Nan told me she ran into you at the grocery store and wanted to plow you down with the cart. But she said, 'I told him I had every expectation he'd figure things out and come to his senses about his choices in life because he was, deep down, a very nice young man.'" I said this in Nan's lecturing voice and almost felt her there, looking on with approval.

"That sounds about right," Adam said, shaking his head. "I was such a punk back then."

"Basically," I said, feeling brave thanks to all of the alcohol. "I took it pretty hard when you left, and Nan had to deal with the brunt of it. It's not every day you go to see your cool senior boyfriend graduate and then get dumped on the campus lawn instead."

Adam ran a hand through his hair and stared at the ceiling for a second. "You still had three years left, and I was starting a different life. I feel bad about blowing you off like that, but I guess at the time it seemed like the easiest thing to do. Clean break, graduate, and move on to the real world."

I rolled my eyes. "The only problem with that theory is your idea of the quote-unquote real world consisted of babysitting your nephews since you couldn't get a job with a political science degree. No offense."

"None taken. Obviously that's why I went back to school for design. I must've been drunk when I chose that major."

We both laughed. "Seriously, though, I kind of get the college thing. But I screwed up when you moved to Chicago, and I need to apologize." If someone had told me I'd be fessing up to ruining my relationship with Adam tonight, I'd never have believed them in a million years, but for some reason the words had spilled out. "And I should've told you then, but I'm so sorry for bailing on—"

A skinny guy in a faded red Phillies tee pushed in between us, and it felt almost physically jarring to realize there were other people in the room. "Adam, my man! There you are."

Adam smiled and slapped his buddy's hand, but the grin didn't reach his eyes. "You remember Eric, right?" he said. I realized it was one of Adam's fraternity brothers; I hadn't seen him since I was a freshman.

"Oh, wow. Blast from the past, huh?" he said, turning to shake my hand. Adam mouthed "Sorry."

I wanted to tell him there was nothing to be sorry

for; in fact, I wanted to buy Eric a drink for stopping me from pouring the rest of my heart out over the sounds of "Pour Some Sugar on Me." Adam deserved an apology, but even in my buzzed state, I knew it wasn't the time and certainly not the place.

Adam said a few words in Eric's ear, and he trailed off across the room.

"He's going upstairs to see the band. But anyway—"

"Anyway," I said, "I was going to friend you on Facebook, but I didn't know if it would be weird since we haven't talked in so long."

I thought I saw disappointment cross Adam's features about the change the conversation was taking, but maybe I was imagining it. Luckily, he said he'd almost requested me as a friend too, but hadn't known what to say.

"Well," I said, whipping my phone out of my pocket, "I'll just take care of this now."

I opened my Facebook application and searched for him. Clearly, it could've waited, but my pal Miller Lite thought it was imperative to do RIGHT NOW.

Adam wasn't exactly winning any sobriety contests himself, so at least he thought it was funny. Leaning over my shoulder, he watched as I clicked the "friend request" button. Then he grabbed his phone and clicked a few buttons, nearly dropping it on the floor in the process.

"You, my friend, are accepted," he said. "I never post stuff on here, though; my profile is pretty bare. I don't like people tagging me and all that stuff."

He wasn't kidding. Besides a cover photo of some weird graphic design thing and a profile picture of him playing soccer, his birthday and our school were the only things listed on the page. He hadn't even enabled the setting allowing people to write on his timeline.

I was about to ask Adam why he was being so top secret when he excused himself to the bathroom. "I'll meet you upstairs," he said. "The band is about to start."

As I made my way through the throng of people, someone tapped me on the shoulder. I spun around to see a cute blond guy wearing a neon-green polo shirt and an awkward smile. He kind of looked like Leonardo DiCaprio, only less smug and a bit more boyish.

"Hey. You don't know me, but I just moved into your apartment building. I've seen you in the hallway but never got a chance to introduce myself." He extended a tanned hand. "I'm Justin."

It's raining freaking men here tonight. Luckily, I said something more appropriate.

"Liz," I said. "Nice to meet you. So are you new to Philly?"

His cheeks turned a shade darker. "I'm from Miami. And is it that obvious?"

I laughed. "You're way too tan and upbeat-looking to be from the Northeast."

Why did I always get verbal diarrhea around hot guys?

"I think I'll take that as a compliment," he said. "So are you enjoying the craziness?"

I shrugged. "Sorta. I came here with some friends and ended up running into someone I went to college with. The crowd is definitely annoying, though."

"I'd have to agree with you there," he said, putting his hand on the small of my back and guiding me out of the way of a girl who'd just dropped her bottle of Amstel. The touch caught me by surprise, but in a good way.

"Yikes, thanks," I said, turning to face him. We locked eyes, and I felt the temperature in the room shoot up by a few degrees. "Guess I need to get out more. Or not."

He laughed. "Yeah, it's not quite my type of atmosphere either. My family is in town from Florida so I dragged my brothers out tonight to see what the local bar scene is like."

He gestured toward two Justin clones chatting up some girls in the corner, all sun-bleached hair and brightly colored tee shirts.

"I'm sure you'll get used to Philly in no time." Over Justin's shoulder, I spotted Adam as he left the men's room and squeezed his way up the steps.

I hoped Justin didn't notice me staring across the room and think I was rude, because he seemed to take this as a cue to end the conversation. "I'm sure your friend is waiting, so I won't hold you up. But if you ever want to hang out, I'm in 6H."

Who knew potential date material was living just steps down the hall? "No way! I'm on the same floor. In 6B, if you ever want to pop by."

"Oh, nice," he said, lifting his beer bottle in my direction. "Well, have fun tonight."

"You, too," I said, and snuck one last glance over my shoulder as I walked away. His grin flashed almost as bright as his shirt. *Wow.*

I pushed my way up the steps, feeling slightly less eager than I had been to find Adam among the crowd upstairs. Of course the one night someone new and interesting—and possibly interested in me—showed up, I had my mind on the past and Adam. Justin seemed cool, and in any other circumstance I probably would've talked to him the rest of the night, but it would definitely be weird to be hanging out with him and Adam at the same time. I stood on my toes, dodging more of the same annoying bar-goers, and finally spotted Adam near the stage in the back of the narrow room.

"There you are," he said, handing me a rum and Coke. "You still drink these, right?"

"I think the last time I had one was in college, but thanks," I said, half-pleased he remembered my old favorite drink, yet half-annoyed he didn't know me well enough anymore to just order a glass of wine.

The band started playing "American Girl," and suddenly I was back at Adam's fraternity house, dancing to Pledge Paddle, the terrible band his friends played in at parties. It was one of those bands you didn't realize was crappy at the time, mostly because the guys were all really, really good-looking and you were probably drunk.

"Reminds me of Pledge Paddle!" I shouted, struggling to be heard above the music. Adam turned, shrugged, and shook his head, mouthing "I can't hear you," then grabbed my arm and pulled me closer to the stage. He twirled me around wildly and then put his arms around my waist as we danced closer. I was certain he was going to kiss me.

As the crowd spun around us, I stopped and gave him my best "I'm not drunk and I didn't just hysterically cry about my dead grandmother in a bar" smile and put my arms around his neck. Despite Adam's beer bottle whacking against my back when he danced, it was as close to a perfect moment as you could get at a jam-packed bar. Happy memories came whirling back, and it felt like old times again, when all we had to worry about was what color toga we were wearing to the mixer on Friday night.

I took a deep breath and led him away from the stage, cupping my hand around his ear.

"We should hang out more often," I said. "Like more than every four years. You could come over to my apartment tonight if you want."

Unfortunately, this was where it got awkward.

"Um, yeah. We should definitely hang out sometime. Not tonight, though," he said, removing my arms from his person and taking a small step back.

My smile faded instantly. "Hey, if you don't want to hang out, then just say so."

Adam squirmed, picking at the label on his beer. "Look, I'm sort of dating someone. It's complicated, though. And we kinda live together."

Let's just say my "What!" was probably heard clear across the Delaware. I handed him my stupid rum and Coke and walked away so he couldn't see the tears building. Kind of living with someone? Was he serious? On the other hand, I was the one who'd screwed him over the last time, so maybe it was some sort of cosmic payback.

Before I could reach the top of the stairs, he grabbed my hand.

"Liz, I'm sorry. I've had a lot to drink, and I saw you, and we have great memories . . . Wow, I'm an ass. And then, I don't know, I just wanted to be your friend. I miss you. And you look great. You should just smack me. I'm an ass."

Well, that we'd established.

"Whatever, it's fine," I said, shaking my head in disbelief. "Forget this happened. I need to go."

I pushed Adam away as he reached out for me again, and stormed down the steps in what I hoped was a dramatic fashion. I was rather pleased with my exit until I hit that pesky third step. And down I went.

Fortunately (or unfortunately), a certain green-eyed jerk raced to the bottom to help me up from the sticky floor. At least he sounded concerned.

"Lizzie, are you okay? You didn't hit your head, did you?"

I released my hands from his grip and glared at him. "I'm fine. Just leave me alone. And call Addie."

"What? Why do you want me to call Addie? Why don't you call Addie?"

"Adam, I'm wasted. I can't even maneuver down a flight of stairs. Obviously I need a ride home, and your drunk ass isn't driving me anywhere. I don't feel like spending money on a cab. And my arm hurts, so dial my damn phone."

Miraculously, he listened and scrolled through my contacts to dial Addie.

"Um, Addie? This is Adam. No, I didn't do anything to her. You don't have to call me a douche. Listen, Liz is drunk. She needs a ride and asked me to call you. Can you come get her at O'Connell's? Okay. Whatever. Bye."

Adam handed me my phone. "Addie says she'll meet you outside in five minutes."

I stared at the ground. "Thanks."

"Hey," he said, his voice sounding gentler. "Let me put my number in there. Can you text me so I know you got home safe?"

"I don't know why you care, but here," I said, shoving my cell back into his palm. He typed in the digits and slipped the phone into my purse.

"The offer still stands for the logo, by the way. I wasn't lying when I said I wanted to be your friend, but it's up to you."

I crossed my arms, rubbing the sore one, and leaned against the dark wood-paneled wall. "I don't know. I can't even talk about that right now."

"Well, you can get back to me. I'll see you later, Lizzie."

And with that he walked away, leaving me with a bruised arm and an even more bruised ego.

~ ~ ~

I WOKE UP on Thanksgiving morning with a pounding headache, a dry mouth, and a sinking feeling in my stomach that what had happened the night before wasn't a dream. I turned to my nightstand to find the ultimate proof—my phone.

Hoping not to find any interesting texts, I flipped it open and sure enough, Adam's number was in there, and the email confirmation that he'd accepted my friend request. At least I hadn't messaged him when I got home.

I fell back on the bed and stared at the ceiling, wallowing in my misery and relentless hangover. What the hell was I thinking, trying to come on to him? I'd never in a million years have complained about how he dumped me if I'd been sober, let alone invited him back to my place. Humiliation central.

As I reached for my neck to twirl the cameo while I thought about my mess of a life, my heart leapt. It wasn't there.

I leapt out of bed and ran to the dresser. No cameo. I shook my hair out, tore the covers off, and basically turned the entire apartment upside down. It was nowhere to be found.

The image of Nan's cameo lying on the floor of a bar and being stepped on, or, worse, stolen, crossed my mind. My throat started to burn, my stomach churned, and suddenly the contents of my night out threatened to come back up. I covered my mouth and ran to the bathroom, barely making it in time to rid myself of all the cheap booze and bad karma.

CHAPTER 4

LIZ

GETTING ADAM'S NUMBER had probably not been the best idea, I realized, after I finally stopped puking and got up from the cool tile of the bathroom floor. I knew it was just the result of too many beers (and that ill-fated rum and Coke), but deep down I wondered if getting sick was, in some twisted way, payback for being so careless with Nan's cameo.

I swished some Listerine around to get rid of the gross taste in my mouth, making a mental note to pick up the non-burning kind. As I spit the yellow liquid into the sink, I heard a loud buzz against its granite countertop. A text from Adam. I hadn't even noticed him typing my number into his phone, and part of me wondered if it had still been saved in his contacts all this time.

How r u this am? Sorry for being a jerk. Things kinda complicated, don't expect u to understand.

Despite what had happened at O'Connell's, I got a little thrill when I saw the message. Seeing Adam had definitely brought back a lot of memories. Everything had been so easy back in college; partying every night, sleeping until noon, tailgates and mixers, hanging out at the dive bar in our tiny middle-of-nowhere town. Adam reminded me of those days, and seeing him made me feel eighteen and invincible again.

But college was over, and so was our relationship, especially since he was living with some girl. Talking to him was only going to open that wound again. Although I had dated a few guys after Adam, he was my first real love and maybe I wasn't quite over him or that feeling yet.

But then I remembered the cameo, and he had been the only one with me after my friends left. I frantically texted the girls and waited for their responses; maybe it had even fallen into one of their bags when we hugged goodbye. A few minutes later I had my answers, and none of them remembered seeing it. Addie said she'd go through her car ASAP, so that gave me some hope, at least.

Against my better judgment, I texted Adam. *random q: did u see me wearing that cameo when u left? it's lost.*

His response was almost immediate: *sorry dont remember if u had it on then. did u call the bar?*

I replied: *T-giving. not open. going to cry or puke, or both.*

After scouring the hallway, elevator, lobby, and every other surface in and around my apartment building, I found myself anxiously awaiting Adam's response. This was not good. The doorman hadn't seen the cameo, either, so I hopped in my car and searched the sidewalk outside O'Connell's. Nothing. Finally, while I was half paying attention to the Macy's Thanksgiving Day Parade, I heard two loud buzzes from my phone. *o man. u were pretty gone. i'm going there tmrw for brunch, can look for ya. least I can do.*

Then he wrote: *really sorry about last nite btw.*

I reworded my message at least three times before sending something short and simple.

Appreciate u looking. Let me know tmrw.

I shot Addie a quick message, filling her in on the search, and flopped back onto the couch.

Did Adam feel bad about leaving me in the bar and this was his version of a peace offering? Or did he want something more? Who knew what his motives were. All I cared about at that moment, besides sticking my head in a toilet, was finding the cameo, and if Adam was going to help me, even better.

Addie's text flashed on my screen. *Basically tore the car apart. Not there.*

And: *u asked Adam to help?? You've GOT to be kidding me!*

Knowing what she did about my past with Adam, of course Addie wasn't going to be my biggest supporter in opening that can of worms. I'd have flipped out if she'd tried to get back with her ex, Pat, so I did see where she was coming from.

"Stop going back" was always Addie's sage advice, but I definitely didn't listen to her the last time Adam came back into my life. As my favorite *Golden Girls* character, Sophia, liked to say: "Picture it. Central Pennsylvania, 2007."

A freak thunderstorm had rolled through just in time for the end of my college graduation ceremony, and Addie and I held hands, screeching as we ran to the campus center for the reception afterward. Guys wearing dress shirts stained with red dye from the cheap graduation gowns and girls with hair plastered to their heads searched around for their families in the jam-packed lounge, stopping to take photos and exchange drippy hugs.

It was there that I saw him, high-fiving one of his fraternity brothers. His baby-blue polo shirt was soaked through, his damp hair messy and a bit too long.

I grabbed Addie's arm. "Shit. Adam's here!"

"Seriously? Where?" She whipped her head around

as I gestured in the general direction of his friends.

"He *would* be here," she said. "Isn't he, like, thirty by now? Time to get over the frat-boy days."

I glared at her. "No, he's twenty-five. And I'm sure he's just here because his cousin's graduating. But whatever. I'm avoiding him unless he approaches me first."

"Yeah, good plan. There's no need to make this day any worse."

Of course, Adam chose that moment to make eye contact. He gave me a hesitant wave and walked toward us as I fiddled with my stringy hair.

"Here we go again," Addie said.

Adam closed the distance between us in three long strides. "Congrats, college grad. Look at you. All grown up."

I stood there for a moment, arms crossed, not sure what to say. I settled for, "Thanks."

"Can I get a hug?" he asked, making me feel even more awkward. It reminded me of when a girl gets kicked off a dating show and the guy has the nerve to ask for a hug before she gets into the limo and bawls her eyes out.

I leaned in for a squeeze; he smelled like a mix of wet dog and Polo cologne. Addie cleared her throat loudly and we stepped apart.

"I'm going to look for my parents," she said. "Are you coming? If you want me to stay, I will."

"No, I'm fine. Really, go." Addie didn't look convinced, but she slipped into the crowd anyway.

"So . . . " I said. "What have you been up to? It's been, what? Three years?"

"I know; I suck. I've been crazy busy, actually. I went back to school for graphic design and I'm starting a little freelance business."

I gave Adam a polite "good for you" smile as he

continued to chat about his job, looking over his shoulder to see if my parents had showed up yet.

"I'm sorry, I'm probably boring the hell out of you," he said. "I forget that everyone doesn't get as excited about design stuff as I do."

"It's okay. I've just had a strange day," I said with a sigh. "I can't believe it's all over. I mean, moving back in with my parents and having no job and no idea what I'm gonna do just doesn't sound as appealing as hanging out with my friends twenty-four-seven. And no offense, but seeing you again is a little weird, too."

He laughed and reached out to pat my arm. "Don't I know it. But you'll be fine, Lizzie. You've got a good head on your shoulders, and anyone who doesn't want you is an idiot. Work or otherwise."

My smile, although weak, reached my eyes this time, at least. "Thanks. I probably should go find my family. It was good to see you, though."

"Of course," Adam said, reaching into his pocket and pulling out a phone. "Don't let me keep you; I'm sure they want to celebrate your big day and everything. Is your number still the same?"

"Yup," I said, surprised he wanted my info, not to mention the fact he'd never deleted my number. "Yours?"

He nodded. While I'd erased his number from my phone, unfortunately I hadn't gotten as far as my memory.

"Well, let's try and hang out sometime now you'll be back in the area. I don't get out much lately since half of my friends moved to Manhattan," he said, reaching out for a hug that lasted a few beats too long.

Maybe it was boredom. Addie went off to Europe for the summer, and besides job hunting and trash television, I didn't have much to occupy my time. But after a week of watching re-runs on the couch with my sisters, I gave in and called Adam. We met at the kitschy diner around the corner from Nan's house and sat there until two in the morning drinking coffee and catching up, and when he walked me back to my car, we kissed.

As the summer nights turned into chillier days, our relationship grew more serious, and by Christmas I was drinking eggnog with Adam's family and talking about a future together.

Of course, that future never happened.

Back in my apartment, I was mulling over all of the things I wished I could've changed when "Like A Virgin" blared from my phone.

"Are you decent?" Addie asked. I could hear she was in the car.

"Um, not your definition of decent, but yes, I am wearing clothing."

"I'm coming over. I know you're sitting there running through every detail of last night in your head and reading his texts and I'm sorry, but I'm not going to deal with his shit again."

There was no use in telling her to go home, so I agreed to hang out for a bit. I didn't have to be at my parents' house for a few hours, and she was right about me sitting there brooding.

About ten minutes later, she came barreling into my apartment with her gigantic Chanel sunglasses slipping down her nose and her short red hair blown in every direction imaginable. She juggled two cups from Starbucks, a box of pastries from my favorite bakery, and at least four gossip magazines. Addie didn't take two steps inside before the magazines fell on the floor and the pastries came close to it. I lunged for the box just before there was an unfortunate custard incident involving the hardwood floors.

"Oh my God, it's a freaking nightmare out there. By the way, nice job losing the cameo. Are you going to tell your mom?"

I stopped chewing for a moment and rolled my eyes. "What do you think?"

"So you're holding out hope that Adam is going to find it? Please tell me you don't think he's doing this because he wants you back."

I shrugged, feeling my cheeks turn pink.

"O-M-G, you actually think that, don't you?" Addie said, swatting my arm with a copy of *Us Weekly*.

"Stranger things have happened. And why would he offer to help look for the cameo if he didn't care?"

I reached for another croissant and the *Us Weekly*, studying Angelina's latest drama with the intensity of a Rhodes Scholar.

"He has a girlfriend," said Addie. "They're living together!"

"I know. But it sounded like they were on the rocks. I'm just saying he wouldn't go out of his way to search for my necklace for no reason."

"You, my friend, are officially delusional. I love you, but you've lost it this time." She paused for dramatic effect, and I knew her official life motto was coming next. "What would Madonna say?"

"Respect yourself? Wear a cone bra? I don't know, Ad. Do you want to call her and ask?"

She rolled her eyes. "I'm just saying you could learn a lot from her. Second best is never good enough."

"Yeah, yeah. I'd be much better on my own. I know the song. Can't you just let me have my little daydream?"

"That's it. I'm putting this on your mirror."

She pulled a Mont Blanc pen and a pad of Post-its out of her gargantuan red Marc Jacobs bag and stomped into my bedroom. I sighed and followed behind, watching her write "STOP GOING BACK!!!" before slapping the neon-pink piece of paper against my vanity mirror.

I raised an eyebrow. "Seriously?"

"This is the best piece of advice I've ever given you. Remember that."

I promptly told Addie to shut up, and we spent the rest of the morning reading the gossip mags and catching up on the latest about the animal rights organization where she worked as an in-house attorney. If Addie's behavior shopping at a sample sale was a little bit scary, I'm fairly sure witnessing her courtroom antics in person would be flat-out terrifying.

I relaxed on the couch with a DVR'd episode of *The Bachelor* after Addie left and was just getting to the good part (she was definitely *not* getting the rose!) when my mom called, asking if I could pick up a few bottles of soda on the way to her house.

"Oh, and I forgot to ask you about the desk," she said. "Did you find anything important or was it mostly just old stuff?"

Shit.

"Yeah, a lot of old stuff. I saved the greeting cards if you want them." It wasn't a lie, technically. I knew I should tell them about the cameo, but something was holding me back.

"Perhaps," Mom said. "Your aunts and uncles are going to help us go through some more things this week so we can get the house on the market soon. I hate to sell it, but none of us want to move. Not like we could afford the taxes on that big old place, anyway."

I wanted to point out my parents could certainly afford it with the inheritance money, but Mom was always too stubborn to accept handouts from Nan. She had probably already donated all of the cash to the school where she and my dad taught, or given it to Cate for her law school fund.

"Speaking of going through stuff—"

"Oh, Cate and Jesse just got here," Mom said. "The new haircut is so cute! Let me see the back. Angela always does such a nice job."

"Huh?" I said, and then realized she wasn't even talking to me anymore. *The moment Cate walks into a room, I'm a second thought.*

"Mom, why don't you take care of your guests," I said. I got a distracted-sounding "See you later," and I hugged a throw pillow against my chest and sighed. My parents had dinner with Cate and her boyfriend every week, but my mom couldn't even give me two minutes on the phone.

They'd only been going out since the summer, but Cate and Jesse spent every spare minute together, at least when they weren't studying, and my dad was even invited to golf at Jesse's parents' posh country club. He was a nice enough kid, but the gossip about Jesse's prominent family made it hard for me to take him completely seriously.

I tried to push the jealousy out of my mind and looked for something to calm me down until it was time to get ready. TV had suddenly lost its appeal, but then I remembered the diary was still in my bag. I managed to grab it without getting up from the couch, a maneuver involving using the throw pillow as a sort of fishing rod.

I was anxious to find out more about Nan's life, and the diary would definitely prevent me from thinking about Adam, too.

It was going to be an interesting Thanksgiving.

CHAPTER 5

ELLA

September 14, 1957

The house is a mess, so I should make this short. I wish I could say Lily's birthday went off without a hitch, but the day was a bit of a disaster. The party rental company was late and we were still setting up when our guests started arriving, but that wasn't the worst of it. About a half hour into the party, it started to pour out of nowhere and we had to move the whole crowd inside.

Lily was inconsolable for at least twenty minutes. Once that girl gets something in her mind, you'd better hope it happens the way she expects. I'll have to thank her grandmother for that trait. Luckily, we were able to stop the tears by letting her open gifts early. You'd think spending the afternoon stuck indoors with fifteen screaming children was bad enough, but Mom was in rare form. She even rigged pin the tail on the donkey so Lily would win. She was enjoying herself, at least, but I could tell she wasn't feeling so hot and was just doing a good job of faking it . . .

Ella swept up the last of the crumbs from the kitchen's floral-patterned tiles and propped the broom against the wall, surveying the afternoon's damage. A large pile of presents sat in the corner, but she didn't have the energy to put them away just yet. Pink streamers hung limply from the ceiling and the few balloons that remained un-popped floated haphazardly across the room as a warm September breeze blew in through the screen door.

Her once-spotless house had been taken over by everyone from her nieces and nephews to Lily's classmates to the neighbors. Ella played the role of hostess effortlessly as usual, making polite conversation with the adults and walking the children through the requisite party games, but she couldn't quite shake the feeling something was off.

"Now that the guests are gone, I hope my mother can relax. Don't you feel like something's not quite right with her today?" she asked Harry, who was sitting at the kitchen table, hunched over some paperwork for the restaurant.

"Seemed like her usual self to me, bossing around the tent guys and such. They definitely got an earful."

"Yes, Dear, but even so, I felt like her steps were slower today. Her comebacks were witty, but not quite as quick."

Harry rolled up the sleeve of his dress shirt and fanned himself with the papers. "Why don't you ask her? Maybe she just needs a cool drink and a good television program."

Ella hung her floral apron on a hook in the kitchen and peered into the living room, where the kids were playing some sort of made-up game that looked like a cross between hopscotch and a wrestling match. Lily's dress would definitely need mending after this.

"Are you feeling okay?" she asked. Gabriella leaned forward with one hand on the television set, her face pale.

"I'm fine. Who wouldn't be out of breath after chasing these hellions around?" Gabriella said, turning her head in the direction of her grandchildren. "I just need to take a second to collect myself."

Ella didn't buy it. "Let me help you over to the chair," she said, crossing the room.

"I said I'm fine!" Gabriella snapped. "Go back to the kitchen. The Lord knows it could use some cleaning after today. I'm not so much of an invalid that I can't walk over to my own damn chair."

Ella reached out to put her hand on her mother's shoulder, but snapped it back. If Gabriella didn't want pity, Ella wouldn't give her any.

"Okay, then. Let me know if you need anything."

Just as Ella dipped her hands into the soapy water to tackle some cake-covered dishes, a loud thud shook the house. A blue ceramic platter slipped out of her wet fingers and smashed on the floor as she raced into the living room, heart pounding, expecting to see one of the kids with a broken leg or worse. Why had she let them play that silly game?

Instead, Ella saw her mother lying facedown in front of the recliner with the children crying hysterically around her. Ella crossed the room in what felt like a single step, with Harry not far behind her.

"Oh my goodness! What happened?" She got down on her hands and knees, checking to see if her mother was conscious. Gabriella's head was bleeding, leaving scattered drops on the wood floor.

"I'll call for an ambulance," Harry said. "Kids, come with me."

Ella shooed a sobbing Lily and the twins into the kitchen. "Mother, say something, please! Are you all right?"

Silence.

Seconds felt like minutes before Gabriella moaned and began to roll onto her side. Ella felt her own blood pressure drop about a hundred points.

"What happened?" Gabriella mumbled.

"Don't get up," Ella said. "An ambulance is on the way."

"I don't need an ambulance, and I don't want to go to the hospital."

Ella sighed; why couldn't her mother just listen for once? She could hear Harry talking to the operator and felt a wave of relief knowing help would be there soon.

"Please don't make this difficult, Mom. You need medical attention; you were out cold."

Harry rushed into the living room and knelt next to them.

"They'll be here in a few minutes. The operator told me not to let her move until then."

Ella shot her mother a look that all but said, "Told you so." Gabriella muttered something in Italian containing swear words that Ella was glad her kids weren't in the room to hear. She didn't try to get up, though, which was a small miracle.

Harry tried his best to make conversation, talking about the party and even asking Gabriella questions about Florence.

"Can you just let an old lady take a nap?" she said, staring up at the crown molding. "You need to dust, by the way."

Ella and Harry exchanged an amused look. "I'm just trying to make sure you stay awake, since head wounds can be serious," Harry said. "Doctor's orders. They told me to ask you a few questions, too."

"Like what?"

"What's today's date?" Harry asked.

"September 14, 1957. Maybe I'm clumsy, but I certainly don't forget my grandchild's birthday."

"All right, then. Who's the current President of the United States?"

Gabriella frowned. "Mr. Eisenhower. Even though I voted for the other fellow."

Ella sighed, satisfied that her mother probably wasn't seriously hurt, but still uneasy from the afternoon's turn of events. She tapped her fingers on the floor. "Shouldn't the ambulance be here by now?"

Finally, there was a loud knock on the door and Harry greeted Officer Richard Brown, their neighbor across the street, along with two ambulance attendants, showing them into the room where Gabriella was lying on the floor. One of the attendants looked as if it might have been his first day on the job; he was twenty at most, and so slim Ella wondered if he could even lift a heavy child. The other was in his forties and certainly fell into the "burly" category. In any other situation Ella might have laughed at the absurdity of the pair.

"Looks like you've had a nasty fall," Officer Brown said, pulling out a notepad.

"They must have hired you for your keen perception," Gabriella said as the paramedics crouched next to her, checking her vital signs. Ella choked back a laugh.

The officer ignored her comment and looked at Ella and Harry. "Did anyone see her fall?"

Ella nodded. "My children did. I was in the kitchen and heard a crash. They were right next to her when it happened, though."

"Can you bring one of them in so we can get a better idea of what happened?"

While they waited, the younger paramedic applied

pressure to Gabriella's wound to stop the bleeding.

"Are you even old enough to be doing this?" she asked, swatting him away.

"She's being rude again. That's a good sign!" Harry called down as he took the steps two at a time. Gabriella scowled, but Ella was amazed her mother kept her mouth shut and let the men do what they had to do.

A minute later, Harry reappeared, carrying the distraught birthday girl. "Tell the nice men what happened to your grandma."

"Um, she was sitting in that chair," Lily said. "We were playing and Harry kicked me and it hurt. I was going to tell Nonni to yell at him and then I saw her stand up. She fell and it made a bang and she was bleeding. She's not going to die, is she?"

The burly paramedic patted Lily on the head. "It's okay, sweetheart. We're going to take good care of your grandma. I promise."

After asking a few more questions and putting her neck in a brace "just in case," the men lifted Gabriella onto a stretcher and Officer Brown headed out to his car.

Ella gave her husband a long hug. "I'll go with her. Calm down the children and I'll call you with any news."

"Are you sure? I can call my sister and have her stay with them. I don't want you to be waiting at the hospital alone all night."

"No, please stay. They need their father."

To Ella's relief, Harry didn't push the subject. He just nodded, giving her a quick kiss on the cheek before she grabbed her purse and joined the paramedics outside. Although she'd told the twins to stay in the playroom, Ella saw their little faces in the window as the ambulance drove away, sirens blaring.

CHAPTER 6

LIZ

"ARE YOU GOING to eat that?" Gracie asked, wrinkling her nose at the waxy-looking pumpkin pie Mom placed in front of us. I picked at the corner of the aluminum plate and mouthed, "No freaking way," sending my sister into a fit of giggles.

Mom snatched the dessert back and passed it to Cate. "Sorry, I'm not a world-class baker like your Nan."

I'd spent every Thanksgiving since I was born at Nan's house, and it felt very wrong not to be in her massive dining room, being guilt-tripped into having pieces of her homemade pumpkin, pecan, *and* apple pies. Instead, twelve of us were crammed into my parents' house, where I was relegated to the "kid's table" and treated to a $5.99 dessert special and dry turkey on paper plates.

As those who were brave enough to try the pie chewed away, Cate stood up, smoothing out her khaki skirt. Jesse stood next to her and they exchanged nervous, giddy glances. What was going on here?

"So," Cate said. "We thought since Thanksgiving is a day to celebrate family, we'd share some news with you." She paused dramatically as she took a ring out of her skirt pocket and slipped it on her finger. "We're getting married!"

My jaw dropped, Gracie let a choice expletive fly, and my mom leapt up to hug them. "Oh, isn't this wonderful?"

Wonderful? That definitely wasn't the word Mom had used when she found out Adam planned to propose.

I would never embarrass Cate in front of everyone, but I wanted to point out that she probably knew more about our dentist, Dr. Goldblatt, than she did about this guy. They'd only been dating five months, and Cate was still in college, for God's sake. Was I the only one who felt like this was the worst idea ever?

I watched in awe as congratulations were doled out and the happy couple made their way into the living room to exchange hugs with everyone. Cate thrust her hand out to show off her ring, which I could tell was Hollywood-sized even from way across the room. I wondered what Adam had done with mine. Maybe it wasn't as flashy, but the small solitaire surrounded by pink sapphires he'd picked out was perfect. Or at least it'd looked perfect from a distance, since the ring never actually made it onto my finger.

Gracie and I stayed in our seats, along with our Aunt Carol, Mom's sister. She had ended up at the kids' table somehow, too . . . maybe because she was the only other singleton.

"Are you kidding me?" I whispered.

Gracie shrugged, then pulled her phone out, most likely to tell all of her friends the news. "The guy's got money, at least."

I rolled my eyes and turned to Aunt Carol on my left. "I feel like twenty-one is so young to be getting married, especially to someone you barely know," I said. "I mean, Jesse seems like a good guy, but we don't know much about him other than he's in law school and his parents are loaded."

"In my day, twenty-one wasn't so young, but things have changed. I just hope your sister knows what she's getting herself into. Marriage isn't all pretty dresses and presents, you know."

I cringed at this comment; Aunt Carol's husband had walked out on her when I was a little kid. Even though it was more than twenty years ago, you could tell she had never gotten over it.

"I know it isn't, that's why I'm worried about her," I said. "Of course she was drawn in by a smart, older guy and the idea of some fairytale wedding. But I think she's making a mistake. Five months isn't long enough for me to commit to a skincare regimen, let alone a life partner."

Gracie looked up from her phone. "I think that was fairly evident after what happened with your old boyfriend."

Ouch.

"But anyway," Aunt Carol said, "I'm staying out of it. Our Cate is going to have to find her own way, and maybe this is the right decision for her."

"I doubt it."

"Lizzie, my dear, if you say something against the engagement, you'll just sound jealous."

"I'm *not* jealous! Why would I be jealous of her? I'm just saying, she could—"

Aunt Carol cut me off. "There's no way to sugar coat it: having your younger sister get married before you is a slap in the face. I understand, honey."

With that, she got up and joined everyone else in the

living room, pulling a reluctant Gracie along by the arm.

Sure, it did bother me that my sister, who was barely of legal drinking age, was engaged when I didn't even have a boyfriend. But I didn't need to be told it was a slap in the face. Trust me, I felt the sting.

In an alternate universe, I would've been coming up on three or so years of marriage. It's not like I could even convince myself I'd made the right decision . . . I never was truly sure I *had* done the right thing. And after her reaction to Cate's engagement, Mom's insistence on me not running off to get married right out of school felt hypocritical times a hundred. My future seemed so uncertain, and without Nan to confide in, the evening's turn of events sucked even more.

I glanced over at Jesse, who was looking proud as he talked to my younger cousins; I overheard a few snippets about him taking a special trip to New York City to buy the ring. *Ugh.* I studied him for a minute, taking in his slicked-back blond hair (way too much gel), broad shoulders, and wide smile. His pressed khakis and navy Burberry polo coordinated perfectly with Cate's navy sweater set and pencil skirt. There was nothing concrete I disliked about him, and I knew he was good to Cate. If Jesse acted like a complete ass, it would've made life a lot easier for me; at least I'd have had a reason to be pissed.

My parents passed the table on their way into the kitchen, big smiles plastered on both of their faces.

"Did you tell your sister congratulations yet?" Mom asked, handing my dad a bottle of champagne to open.

"Nope," I said, twirling my hair around my finger. "They seem busy talking to everyone. I'll go over in a minute."

Her lips twisted into a scowl. "I know this happened

faster than any of us expected, myself included. But she's genuinely happy. Play nice, okay?"

"Of course," I said. "Not like anyone else in this family ever had a chance at being happy and had it ruined."

Dad paused, cork in hand. "Liz, I know you're upset. But this isn't the night to bring up old wounds."

I took a second to collect myself and stood up. "I'm going to give them my best and head home, actually. It's been a long night and I have to get up at the crack of dawn for Black Friday shopping with Addie. Luckily, I'm not on the schedule at Plaid tomorrow."

Dad put the bottle down and patted my arm. "All right, then. Happy Thanksgiving." Mom just continued taking glasses out of the cabinet, shaking her head.

I felt a hollowness in my stomach as I heard the cork pop, and crossed the room to greet Cate and Jesse. It felt like the time I walked into Nan's house right after she'd died, only different. As if something was missing, and fizzy bubbles would never mask it.

"Hey," I said, giving Cate a hug and Jesse an awkward handshake. "Wow, I had no idea you guys were planning on getting married already."

Cate beamed. "Me, neither. It all happened so fast . . . Jesse took me to see *Phantom of the Opera* on Broadway and out to this swanky restaurant, and we're in front of the ice skating rink, and he just got down on one knee."

Jesse kissed her on the cheek. "Best day of my life!"

"That's great," I said, fake grin pasted on as well as I could muster. "*Congratulazioni* and all that jazz, as Nan would say."

Cate smiled tightly, and a long, loaded silence ensued.

"Well then," I said, clearing my throat. "I'm actually going to say bye to everyone and hit the road. Addie's picking me up at two to hit the sales, so I should probably rest up to deal with the crazies at the mall."

"You're not staying for some bubbly?" Jesse asked.

"Champagne's not really my thing, plus I have to drive and all. But congrats again," I said, my feet already pointed toward the door.

As I walked away, I heard Cate mumble, "You'd have to actually say congratulations in the first place to say it again."

I knew Cate was probably pissed off at my reaction, and I couldn't blame her. But I wanted my happy ending, too. Instead all I'd gotten was left behind again, and it made it hard for me to pretend to be excited about the engagement. Golden child Cate always coasted through life, collecting awards and popular boyfriends and top grades along the way. Of course she would find the perfect husband before she even graduated from college. Yes, I was being a Bitter Betty and needed to get over it, but that knowledge didn't change the dark cloud I felt hanging over the holiday.

I got home around ten and resisted the urge to tell Addie the news since I'd be seeing her in a few hours. Instead, I pulled the diary out of my dresser drawer, curling up with my favorite fleece blanket on the bed. It was weird to learn about this side of Nan. She had been about ten years older than I was when she wrote the diary, but had three kids on top of having to take care of a sick parent and help run a busy restaurant. I couldn't even take care of myself, let alone a child, and my jewelry business wasn't exactly thriving. I hoped Nan might have some good pointers for me.

I propped my head up on a pile of pillows and started to read. Next thing I knew, the sound of Madonna blared from my phone. The clock read 2:27. *Whoops.*

"Where the hell are you?" was Addie's greeting once I managed to figure out how to answer the phone in my sleepy daze. "I texted you twice."

"Bed. Sorry. I'll throw my coat on and be outside in five."

I padded into the living room, still bleary-eyed, slipped on the old blue Sketchers I wore to the gym, grabbed my coat and purse, and headed out the door without even checking my reflection. No one looked good at two in the morning, and judging from previous years, the other shoppers weren't going to be winning any fashion contests, either.

As soon as I stepped out of the elevator, I could see Addie's silver Audi SUV waiting outside, its headlights highlighting the steady rain that must've started falling while I was asleep.

I rushed to the car, my sneakers splashing through a growing puddle in the street. Inside, the air was vanilla-scented and stiflingly warm. Addie always had a tendency to be cold even when no one else was (probably because she was the size of a twig), and she cranked the heat up to uncomfortable levels as soon as the temperature dropped below sixty degrees. Her current obsession, some random British band, blasted from speakers that probably cost more than my entire car.

She turned the volume down as I slipped into the passenger seat. "Awake now?" Addie asked as she pulled away from my building, driving a little faster than was necessary or safe considering the weather. "You do realize we're never going to find a parking space."

I shrugged. "Sorry, but I had a rough night. You're never going to believe this . . . Cate got engaged and decided to tell everyone at Thanksgiving dinner."

"Whaaaat? Are you serious? She's known him for like two seconds!" Addie barely managed to keep her eyes on the road as we flew around Logan Circle, and I held on to the handle above my door for dear life.

"I know! It was the most awkward situation ever. And not like I could say anything to her in front of all of our family."

"So what *did* you say to her?"

"Nothing, really. They told everyone when we were in the dining room and she was way at the other end, so I just kind of sat there in shock," I said. "I gave her a hug goodbye, said congrats, and kind of ran out."

"Well, I'm sure she knew you were pissed off. No offense, but you're pretty shitty at hiding your feelings, and you do tend to be a little jealous of Cate."

"Okay, maybe I *am* jealous, but that's only because she always gets everything so easily. Why can't she have to struggle just a little bit for once? Now she's going to be marrying into the freaking Crenshaw family. I mean, come on!"

"Well, good for her, I guess. It's a shame he's, like, four years younger than us, or I would've thought to bag myself a Crenshaw." She frowned, clearly disappointed in her lack of foresight.

"Anyway, not that I'm saying I think it's great she's engaged or anything," she added. "I just think it was probably pretty damn obvious to everyone in the room that you were upset and embarrassed to find out your little sister is getting married when you can't even hold a steady relationship."

Leave it to Addie to lay things out on the table. "I'll deal with it," I said. "And thanks for reminding me about my crappy love life."

"I'm just trying to help. And you're not the only one with a messed-up family, contrary to popular belief," she said, reaching over to turn the lever for her windshield wipers up a notch. The rain pounded down increasingly hard as we drove, and the lights of Boathouse Row looked like a fuzzy blur as we whizzed past the river.

"Maybe we should just turn around," I said. "It's probably not a good idea to be on the roads."

"Hell, no. We both need some retail therapy, and you can't back out of Black Friday. It's tradition."

"Fine, whatever. Just slow down a little, will you?"

The miles passed in silence as we listened to the fat raindrops pelting against the car. "Vogue" came on the radio, but neither of us bothered to sing along. Finally we arrived at the outlet mall, and after driving around for about ten minutes looking for a space, Addie got antsy.

"Screw this," she said, and suddenly we were driving over a curb, parking on the grassy strip at the end of a row of spaces. The car made a horrendous scratching sound and a loud thump as we landed on the grass.

"Um, that didn't sound good," I said, trying not to laugh. Eventually it was too much and I broke into hysterical giggles, Addie joining in with me.

"Whew," I said eventually, rubbing my stomach. I'd forgotten how good it felt to truly laugh like that. "You're crazy sometimes, my friend."

"Isn't that what an SUV is for? Off-roading?" she said with a shrug, reaching for a giant golf umbrella in the backseat. "And dude, it's Black Friday. I don't mess around."

~ ~ ~

THERE'S NOTHING like outlet shopping to make you forget about your troubles. As usual, most of the Black

Friday steals I bought were for myself, but I did manage to find my dad a pair of nice leather gloves, and after waiting in the rain in a line that wound around the store, scored twenty-five-dollar Coach wristlets for my sisters and a matching one for myself.

Addie was being unusually selective and left the outlets with only a pair of sunglasses for her sister and a sweater for her mom. I chalked it up to the weather and the crowds, but something did seem off. Normally, I'd have to help her carry all of her bags.

"Is everything okay?" I asked as we navigated through the nearby mall, avoiding screaming kids and frazzled-looking husbands.

She fiddled with her umbrella, avoiding my inquisitive gaze. "Thanksgiving was just really, really crappy and I think—"

My phone vibrated in my pocket. "Sorry, one sec," I said, my pulse quickening when I saw Adam's name on the screen. Addie gave me a dirty look as I stepped aside to talk to him, leaning against the wall by Lord & Taylor.

"Hey, I just wanted to let you know I'm at O'Connell's waiting to meet my friends for breakfast," he said. "I just looked for your necklace, but I didn't see it anywhere."

My heart sunk. "Did you ask anyone who worked there? Maybe someone turned it in."

"I did. No luck. The manager told me to feel free to look around. I did everything but get down on my hands and knees and crawl under people's tables."

Part of me thought, *Well, why didn't you?* Instead I asked if he'd looked by the stairs where we were standing after I fell.

"Yup. I'm sorry, I wanted it to be there for you."

"It's okay," I said, as the hope drained out of

me. "Thanks for trying, at least. I've looked all over my building and outside. It could be down a drain somewhere, for all I know. I'll take a look at O'Connell's myself, too, just in case."

"True. Well, keep me updated."

After a few seconds of silence, Adam spoke up. "If you want to have lunch sometime, as friends, or you want to talk about the design stuff for your jewelry site . . . "

"Sure. I'll let you know. I'm actually with Addie at the mall, so I should get going. Thanks again."

I tried not to make eye contact with Addie as I slipped the phone back into my coat pocket. "So much for finding Nan's cameo."

"I'm sorry. It could still turn up," she said, giving me the side-eye before adding, "He was talking pretty loudly, by the way. I overheard him mention lunch. Are you actually going to let him help you with your website?"

"I don't know. I doubt I'll go through with calling, so probably not."

Addie rolled her eyes. "Whatever. But PS, stop going back."

"I'll do my best. But do you want Starbucks or not?"

"If you're buying, sure."

We joined the line and I spotted Jessica, a girl I knew from high school, standing at the counter waiting for her drink. Her trademark waist-length hair had been cropped to just below her shoulders, but I'd have recognized that high-pitched, singsong voice anywhere.

I tried to move behind Addie and hoped Jessica didn't see me, but being all of a hundred pounds soaking wet, Addie didn't make a very good human shield.

Jessica turned around and spotted me right away.

"Liz Moretti? Oh my gosh, girlie! How are you?"

She turned to her friend and told her she'd be right back. *Great.*

Jessica gave me a tight hug and took a step back, looking me up and down. I tugged on my sweater and shifted from one foot to the other.

"Wow, you look exactly the same!" she said.

I smiled tightly. "So, what are you up to these days?" I asked, not that I cared. Jessica and I had taken a lot of classes together, and we knew each other from drama, but we'd been more like frenemies than actual friends. She was definitely one of the most annoying people I'd ever met, due to her being a) an over-sharer, b) too peppy for her own good, and c) a secret bitch. If you're going to be bitchy, at least be upfront about it.

Jessica waved her left hand in front of my face to show off a round diamond surrounded by tiny pink stones. "I'm engaged!"

A sick feeling gripped my insides, and my mouth dropped open. I must've looked like I'd seen a ghost. Of all the rings in the world, hers had to look like *that* ring?

"I know, right?" she said. "Isn't this the best ring ever?"

"Yeah, it's definitely . . . unique. Good for you. Congrats."

"Thanks. My fiancé and I have been on-again, off-again, so I'm kinda ready to get this done and over with, you know what I'm saying?"

I was fairly sure I knew what she was saying: she was trying to rush him to the altar before he changed his mind.

Addie coughed to cover up a laugh, while I just smiled and said "Mm-hmm," hoping Jessica would stop talking.

"Actually, I have a little bit of an ulterior motive for coming over to chat," Jessica said. "I heard through the grapevine you were designing your own jewelry."

"I am, actually. Mostly earrings and rings, a lot of funky, beaded stuff. A local store started carrying it, so I spend most of my time making pieces for them."

"What about something custom? I've been just *dying* to finalize my bridesmaids' gifts and I want to get them some nice necklace-and-earring sets. Plus, I need to pick something out for myself, of course."

My shoulders slumped. As much as I didn't like Jessica, if I had to be honest, my bank account was heading toward "Do I need another job?" territory. And turning down an order wasn't going to do my business any favors. I took a deep breath and said, "Sure. Depending on when you need everything done."

"No huge rush! We don't have a date set yet or anything, although I guess I need to get that situated, don't I?"

"Gotcha. Well, when you're ready, let me know. You can look at my website if you want ideas."

I pulled a business card out of my wallet, telling her to drop me an email with her info. Luckily, Jessica's drink was ready, so we said our goodbyes.

"That's the girl who tried to give everyone in the choir voice lessons even though she sucked, right?" Addie said in a voice she probably thought was a whisper, but was far from it.

I nodded and put a finger to my lips. "We'll discuss after she leaves."

After Jessica strolled past, sipping on her iced coffee, with a cheery "Bye, ladies!" I turned to Addie.

"Did you see her ring?"

She nodded. "Kind of hard to miss it when she practically shoved the setting in your face. Are you okay?"

"Yeah. I'm not the only person in the world who ever asked for a pink sapphire engagement ring. It's just weird timing, ya know?" I grabbed the only empty table and threw our bags on it. "I seriously can't believe I'm going to have to work with her as a client, though. Shoot me now."

"Yeah, she's not exactly the subtle type, is she? You know she's probably going to make ridiculous demands and request something totally hideous and 1985-looking," Addie said. "But no one put a gun to your head to make crap for her, so why did you bother?"

"I know, but if she likes the jewelry, she'll tell all her friends. Can't hurt to spread the word. Plus, I'm not exactly rolling in the dough, working retail. Christmas is coming up, and turning down extra money would be dumb."

Addie sighed as she watched a couple of girls stroll out of Starbucks carrying oversized Gucci carrier bags, then kicked the table with her boot. "Tell me about it."

I raised an eyebrow. Addie's "from money," as they say; her parents had subsidized her slightly ridiculous lifestyle throughout college, and still did, to a point. But she didn't elaborate, so I changed the subject.

"All I can think about when I see Jessica is our spring musical senior year, when we both went for the same part. She got it, which was fine. Can't win 'em all. But she came up to me giggling and said, 'You've got such an *interesting* stage presence, it's a real shame you're only housewife number three, isn't it?'"

Addie laughed as if it was the first time she had heard the story. "Ew. But whatever, when are you going to have to see her again after this?"

She was right. Or at least I hoped.

After a few more stores we headed home and I asked

Addie to drop me off at O'Connell's, hoping Adam and his friends were gone. Luckily, there was no sight of them as I stepped into the bar area, wondering how a place could feel so different during the daytime. I guess it's not hard when you remove a hundred sweaty twenty-somethings and replace them with a few tables of civilized brunch-eaters digging into full Irish breakfasts.

"I think I lost a necklace here Wednesday night," I said to the hostess. "Do you mind if I look around?"

She tucked a strand of curly brown hair behind her ear and smiled. "Was that your boyfriend who was here earlier? He's hot."

I laughed. "No. No, he's not. I mean, my boyfriend. But yeah, I guess you could say he's good-looking and all. If that's your type."

She looked at me like I wasn't quite the brightest crayon in the box, but gestured behind her. "Have a look if you want. He didn't find anything, but guys are so lazy, so who knows if it's here. He seemed in a hurry."

"Ugh, men!" I said, not very surprised at this admission, but still irked. "I'm just going to look myself, then, and double check."

I thanked her and began combing the bar area where we'd been hanging out most of the night, avoiding the "WTF" glances from the few hung-over girls eating next to me as I stuck my head under the high-topped table. I didn't know why I'd entrusted this task to Adam in the first place. I had placed my trust in him before, and look how far that got me.

After examining the bathroom and every other surface in the place, it was clear the cameo wasn't going to jump into my hand anytime soon. I slumped outside with a "Thanks, anyway" to the hostess, disappointment and exhaustion weighing on my body and mind.

When I woke up from a much-needed nap later that afternoon, I wondered what kind of guy had decided to marry Jessica. Had they met at work, or maybe in college? She definitely didn't have many dates at Kennedy High.

I turned to my trusted source of gossip, Facebook. I didn't want to request her as a friend, but we had a lot of mutual friends, so I was hoping I'd be able to see her profile anyway. No luck; it was private. But I could see her profile pictures, and a couple of other albums, which was good enough for me. I clicked on the photos section and my heart plummeted to the ground.

Hands shaking, I pored through the album titled "J'adore Paris!" The cover photo was a picture of her and the alleged fiancé. They were posed in front of the Eiffel Tower, both wearing scarves and heavy coats. The wind was whipping through her blonde hair, but instead of looking messy, it gave her the appearance of having one of those supermodel photo shoot fans behind her. She was holding out her hand in front of her, pointing to the ring and making an exaggerated "OMG" face.

But the guy standing next to her wasn't some random guy she'd met at work or at school . . . it was Adam.

CHAPTER 7

ELLA

September 15, 1957

I'm finally home after spending most of the night in the hospital. They're keeping Mom overnight to do some tests and keep an eye on her. What we all thought was a simple case of tripping and falling seems like it was actually a mild stroke.

She's suffered some memory loss and confusion, which is to be expected, but she's going to recover. The strangest part is she's been speaking in an interesting mix of English and Italian. It really isn't funny, but I did get a laugh when Mom called the doctor enough swear words to make a pirate blush (which of course he couldn't understand).

Needless to say, any hopes I had of her living independently again have been dashed. What if she doesn't get better? What happens if she eventually doesn't remember me, or worse, the kids?

Lily's continuing to test my patience and the twins keep asking, "Where's Nonni?" It's enough to break your heart, but I can't help but feel relieved to be home and get a little break from sitting in that hospital. If Mom's hard to deal with on a

normal day, she's a hundred times worse sick. I'm going back
today and hoping for the best . . .

Ella hurried through the sterile halls of the hospital
toward her mother's room, saying a silent prayer nothing
had changed for the worse. She normally didn't mind
hospitals; their whiteness and cleanliness almost felt
soothing to her, and she liked knowing people were being
taken care of, that maybe they would get better.

But today, Ella felt little of that hope, and wished
Harry could've come with her for support. He was at the
restaurant as usual. Ella knew he couldn't ignore their
livelihood, but as she went through this ordeal all by
herself, the burden on her shoulders grew heavier.

The kids were none too happy about staying with
Ella's friend Trudy, and Lily repeatedly cried, "It's not
fair," when they found out children weren't allowed in
hospitals. Ella was glad for this rule; it wouldn't be helpful
for them to see their grandma looking pale and confused.

At first Ella thought her mother was fine, given the
circumstances. Although she'd hit her head pretty hard,
in the moments after the fall Gabriella had responded to
their questions and seemed lucid. But on the way to the
hospital she'd started repeating herself, asking the same
questions over and over (and in Italian, nonetheless).

"*Dove è* Harry?"

"He's with the kids, remember?"

Confusion flickered briefly over Gabriella's face but
she said, "Of course I remember. *Sono stanca.*"

Ella knew her mother was tired, but that didn't
explain why she asked where Harry was again not even five
minutes later. This went on for the next hour, and Ella
kept a record of which questions her mother asked and

how many times. Where's Harry? Three. Where are the kids? Six. When am I going home? Four.

It's just temporary because of the stroke, Ella told herself as she passed the nurses' station. *I'm sure a good night's rest made a difference.*

No such luck. After greeting her daughter with, "What took you so long?" Gabriella proceeded to ramble on about the "loose-looking" nurses and asked twice why her grandchildren weren't there.

Finally, Ella sighed and grabbed her purse. "I'm going down to the cafeteria," she said. "I just realized I haven't eaten all day. Do you want anything?"

Gabriella shook her head no. "Any excuse to get out of here, huh?"

Ella ignored her on the way out the door, even though it was true. If she didn't get out of her mother's room, even for just a few minutes, Ella would probably say something nasty that she'd regret.

After slurping down a lukewarm bowl of soup and having a quick chat with a friend of the family she'd run into while buying a cup of coffee, Ella took the stairs back up to her mother's room. Gabriella seemed to be enjoying herself, reading a *Life* magazine one of the nurses must've given her.

"You'll never guess who I saw down in the cafeteria," Ella said, scooting a chair up to the bed. "Your friend Rose's daughter, Jean."

Gabriella placed a subscription card between the pages of the magazine and tossed it on the blanket. "Jean Marie? Why are you surprised about that? She's worked here for years. She's still married to that no-good husband of hers, I assume?"

"As far as I know," Ella said.

"From what I've heard, that man was always friendly with the bottle, even as a teenager," Gabriella said. "Reminds me of the time your cousin Vincent showed up to church out of his mind with drink. Your father certainly set him straight."

Ella raised an eyebrow but didn't comment. Her mother couldn't recall something that was told to her five minutes before, but she was remembering a random incident from decades ago?

"In any case," Ella continued, "she is going to come up and visit you. I gave her your room number."

"I don't need her telling Rose all of my business. You know the entire town will hear about this before I'm even out of the hospital. That woman can't keep her mouth shut."

"Calm down, Mom, I told her not to mention this to Rose. She gave me her word."

"Humph," Gabriella said, picking her magazine back up and turning the pages as loudly as she possibly could. After a few minutes of this routine, Ella gave up.

"I'm going to find your doctor and see what's going on. If we aren't going to hear anything until tomorrow, I'm going to head home. I've got to pick up the kids from Trudy's before it gets too late."

Gabriella continued pretending Ella wasn't there, so she threw her hands up in defeat and walked out into the corridor. Dr. Smithson was chatting with some colleagues by the nurses' station, looking down every so often to reference something on his clipboard.

"Hello, Mrs. DiAngelo. Is everything okay?" he said, glancing up from his notes for a second.

"Nothing's changed. I was just wondering when we might have some news about her condition."

"Not yet, I'm afraid. You'd be best going home to get some rest. Waiting around won't do you any good, and the nurses will probably tell you to scoot soon, anyway."

Ella wasn't a fan of his patronizing smile, but nodded and said to call her with any updates. She began walking away but then stopped and turned on her heel.

"Actually, I do have a question. As you know, my mother's having problems with her short-term memory," she said. "But then a minute ago she just told me a story about something that happened at least twenty years ago, and remembered every detail. Is this normal?"

Dr. Smithson rested his clipboard on top of the counter next to him, crossing his arms and leaning against it in a casual manner that Ella thought belied the seriousness of the situation.

"That's not unusual, Mrs. DiAngelo. Short-term memory is the first thing to go. We see this all the time. I've had patients tell me stories about the old country from when they were seven, but they can't even remember why they are in the hospital or what day of the week it is."

Ella twisted her wedding band around and around her finger, a nervous habit she'd had for years. "But will this keep happening? Will she get worse?"

"It's hard to say," the doctor said. "Once we have all of her test results, I can make a more comprehensive diagnosis. I don't want to guess."

In other words, you have no idea what you're talking about.

"I guess we'll just have to wait and see then," she said. "Good evening, doctor."

She fought back tears as she walked back into room 224. Mary had been there earlier in the day, and Ella had promised she'd call as soon as they knew anything. Dr. Smithson's "I don't know" hardly qualified as news, so she wasn't going to alarm her sister if nothing was certain.

"Nothing to report, Mom. I'm going to head home," she said, crossing the room to grab her things. "How are you feeling?"

"Fine, fine. By the way, that doctor is certainly a good-looking fellow."

Ella tried not to laugh. "I suppose so. I hadn't really noticed."

"I had a fiancé who looked just like him once," Gabriella mused. "He was a vain son of a bitch, but my, was he a sight for sore eyes."

"Mother!" Ella said. The swearing was bad enough, but what was this about another fiancé? Maybe it had something to do with the medicine.

"Oh, stop being so uptight, Ella. Like it or not, I had romances in my day."

"You never told me you were engaged before Dad! What happened? What was his name?"

If this story was a ploy to get her to stay, it was working.

"If you must know, then have a seat," Gabriella said, pointing toward the chair next to her bed. "This could take a while."

CHAPTER 8

GABRIELLA

1905

THE SUN BLAZED especially brightly in Florence that afternoon, bathing the ancient city in a golden blanket of light. It was the height of summer and hordes of tourists queued for the Uffizi Gallery, crowded the cafés, and generally basked in the romance only Florence could evoke.

But Gabriella Capetti, or Ella, as her family sometimes called her, rushed past the centuries-old statues and awe-inspiring churches so many others had traveled across oceans to see. Although Gabriella was a Florentine by birth and returned nearly every summer to visit family, she also was technically a visitor herself, having moved to Manhattan nearly a decade prior.

Tourist or not, she remained oblivious to the beauty of her hometown, trying to walk as fast as she possibly could through the Piazza della Signoria without drawing unnecessary attention to herself. This, unfortunately, proved to be highly difficult.

Temperatures had soared into the high nineties,

and although Gabriella wore a light linen walking suit (a beautiful powder-blue number with enormous puffed sleeves), sweat trickled down her arms and other places she didn't care to discuss. Her brother, Giancarlo, struggled to keep pace, but being a good four inches shorter than Gabriella and not nearly as fast, it was an exercise in futility.

"Ella, I must insist that you slow down," he said in a loud whisper. "Half the city already thinks you're mad."

They squeezed through a group admiring the Loggia dei Lanzi's sculptures and Gabriella turned on her heel, glaring at her brother. She knew she probably looked a sight; she could feel the sweat beading on her brow and a few errant curls drooping limply on her neck.

"Well, Carlo, then I must insist that you keep up with me. The faster we get home, the faster I'm out of your hair."

She continued to march along with purpose, trying to push the afternoon's most embarrassing incident out of her mind. Gabriella had planned to call on her cousin and best friend, Lessie, and since Carlo and their other cousin, Massimo, were frequent cohorts, he had gone along to escort her.

Unfortunately, the visit was ruined when they encountered Salvatore Esposito, the love of Gabriella's life (or at least she thought he was at the time). One look at Salvatore, and Gabriella insisted upon leaving before they even reached their relatives' home.

It didn't matter that she'd been waiting for a marriage proposal from him on a trip to Capri the previous summer; now Salvatore was married to a girl called Concetta and had a baby daughter who'd arrived suspiciously soon after the wedding. Hearing about it from her cousin's letters had been bad enough, but seeing the two in person felt like pure torture.

Even worse, her mother had been right about Salvatore all along. Either that, or her constant interference had driven Salvatore away.

She'd ignored all of her mother's warnings about being foolish to fall for Salvatore's compliments and handsome façade. In the end, he turned out to be nothing but a rake who liked to tell pretty girls what they wanted to hear before moving on to the next victim. Concetta had been clever (or stupid) enough to get him to marry her, at least.

Gabriella and Carlo had been just around the corner from Villa Serena, the home of their aunt and uncle, when she saw the new Mr. and Mrs. Esposito and their little one. The smug look on Concetta's face as the pair approached was enough to make Gabriella want to scream and jump into the fountain across from them.

Even Gabriella wouldn't go that far, but it would've been preferable to watching Salvatore stroll past with his wife. She pushed an ornate black pram, looking like a cat who'd just swallowed a fish. Carlo grabbed his sister's arm tighter while managing to both ignore and glare at Salvatore at the same time. It was quite a skill.

Even worse, Joseph Rossi, her cousin Massimo's pompous friend, was sitting right there to witness the whole thing. He looked up from his table outside Gabriella's favorite café and raised his cup in her direction, eyes dancing with mischief. *The nerve!*

Everyone in their circles knew what had happened in Capri the previous summer; her friends had even wagered money on whether Salvatore would propose before the holiday was over. But with Joseph it was a hundred times worse since he'd actually been on the trip. He saw the stolen kisses on balconies and the way Gabriella had looked at Salvatore. How momentarily she'd turned into a silly, love-struck girl like all of the others.

For some reason, Joseph hadn't been particularly kind to Gabriella in Capri or since, but when she rushed past his table and they locked eyes, his expression softened. A look of pity.

Gabriella wanted to crawl under a rock and die.

On second thought, the fountain idea could possibly come in handy if she ever crossed paths with Salvatore again. She'd splash about until the police came (she would plead insanity, of course) and be taken away to a nice, quiet asylum, far away from Concetta's smug grin, Joseph Rossi, and her busybody mother. She was imagining how lovely and calm it would be when her thoughts were interrupted by Carlo waving a hand in front of her face.

"Ella? Are you quite all right? I think you've had too much heat!" She snapped out of it and blinked slowly, as if waking from a dream.

"I'm fine, you buffoon. Let's just go."

The pair continued on their journey back to the house, crossing the Ponte Vecchio, which was bustling with late-afternoon shoppers. Normally Gabriella would at least stop to admire the window displays of shimmering gold jewelry, but the thought of Salvatore and his new family had left her in no mood for frivolity.

She should've known to just stay home when Carlo found out their father had taken the car. Whether or not she liked traveling by automobile, Gabriella had a reputation to uphold, and she refused to travel in an outdated carriage when everyone knew they could afford the best, most modern mode of transportation. Walking, however, had proved to be a mistake. It would take even longer than usual to prepare for dinner with her current frizzy hair situation, and if she hadn't been walking, she could've just blown past Salvatore looking glamorous in Father's shiny red Fiat.

Finally, they arrived at the Capetti home, a sprawling old Tuscan-style villa with imposing stone lions in front. The enormous property, made of warm orange stucco, looked down on the Arno River and featured a long wrought-iron balcony stretching across the second floor. A three-tiered, slightly crumbling fountain splashed quietly in the courtyard, which was overrun with fragrant roses and ivy covering the walls. There was nowhere in the world Gabriella would rather be most days, except maybe Central Park.

Her plan was to go to her room straightaway to freshen up before dinner, but much to Gabriella's dismay, their mother was waiting for them in front of the sweeping mahogany staircase.

Mrs. Capetti, like her daughter, towered over most other women. But it wasn't just her height that made her intimidating. Her hair was always pulled back in a severe bun and her sharp, pointy nose made her look a bit like a witch (or at least the local children thought so).

"Your father tells me he saw Joseph Rossi this morning," she said, looking pointedly at Gabriella. "You'd best get ready. We've invited Mr. Rossi to dinner tonight, and I want you looking your best."

"Mother! How could you?" Gabriella shouted, stomping her foot against her mother's favorite Oriental carpet for good measure. Joseph was home for the summer from Oxford, this much she knew from Lessie. Although the Rossis were a good family and Joseph was certainly attractive, she thought he was awfully full of himself. And who wanted to be courted by someone who gave her pitying looks at cafés? Academics weren't Gabriella's type, anyway.

Mrs. Capetti gave her a dangerous look. "I've been very patient with you, Ella, but your father and I cannot ignore that you've reached twenty-one years of age with no husband secured."

"It's a new century, in case you've forgotten, Mother dear," Gabriella said. "We're not living in your day when girls were hauled off to church at fifteen and promised to a stranger."

"In case *you*, daughter, have forgotten, Mr. Rossi is not a stranger. He's a fine man and he's been asking your cousins about you. Don't embarrass us." She took Gabriella's arm and guided her toward the stairs. "A new dress is hanging in your sitting room. I was saving it for your birthday, but this is more important. Loretta will draw you a bath. Go along!"

Mrs. Capetti hurried out of the room, no doubt ready to boss the staff around and make preparations for the evening's dinner party.

This is not happening, Gabriella thought as she climbed up to her room in slow motion. Surely her parents couldn't be so astonishingly dim. It was plain to anyone in the city of Florence that Gabriella not only didn't care for Joseph; she flat-out loathed him. Didn't her opinion count for anything? She'd known Joseph since they were children, before Gabriella's father had decided to take their fortunes to America. But all she could remember was him being a just-a-few-years-older boy who pulled her hair and complained about the food at parties. When she was sixteen, he must've kissed every one of her friends during a whirlwind summer of balls. But Gabriella had never given boys like that her time or attention, especially ones who tried to woo her with God-awful poetry and bragged about being admitted to the world's top universities.

Loretta, her longtime nursemaid and now lady's maid, was waiting at the top of the steps with a bathrobe and a sympathetic glance.

"I know, I know, Miss Ella. Let's just get you ready." Gabriella sighed and headed into her sitting room.

"Your mother is a smart woman," Loretta said as she brushed Gabriella's long brown hair. "Just give tonight a try. I know you better than most. Would I steer you wrong?"

"I suppose it could be worse," Gabriella said as she eyed the pale-green dress Loretta brought over, running her fingers over the beadwork along the empire waist. "It's just one dinner, as you said. I'll ignore him most of the evening anyway. What color earrings do you think I should wear with this?"

Loretta squeezed Gabriella's shoulder and laughed. "That's my Ella. And the emeralds your grandmother gave you would do nicely." She retrieved the jewels from a small porcelain box and set them on the vanity for Gabriella's inspection.

Gabriella ran a finger over the sparkly drop earrings surrounded by diamonds. "I couldn't have chosen better myself," she said. "Not that I have a choice in much of anything."

Loretta sighed. "Now you just go and relax. Your bath is prepared just as you like it. Mind your hair."

Gabriella let out a small huff, but left the room as instructed. Within a few minutes, she could feel all of the stress of the day begin to evaporate in the piping-hot, lavender-scented water. She sunk back until the water reached just the top of her shoulders, careful not to get her hair wet.

There was no time for washing and drying her thick mane, and she hated to think what her mother would say if she arrived at dinner with a frizzy mess of brown curls. Not that her mother would likely have anything complimentary to say in the first place.

It was true Gabriella felt closer to Loretta than she did to her own mother, but Loretta was the one who saw Gabriella through her formative years while her mother remained involved with going to the theater and calling on friends. That was just the way it was, and Gabriella hardly thought about it. Except when her mother meddled with her love life, which happened more often than Gabriella would've liked.

As for Gabriella's friends, most had similar relationships with their mothers, with the exception of Lessie. She and her mother, Gabriella's Aunt Gia, were practically like sisters. Then again, that could've been because Gia was only seventeen years Lessie's senior, instead of the three decades separating Gabriella and her own mother.

Gabriella was brought back to reality by a soft yet authoritative knock. "Miss Ella, it's time to get ready. The guests will be here at half past."

Gabriella's oldest brother and his wife were due to join them for dinner along with about twenty other guests, mostly family and her parents' friends. In addition to Joseph, Gabriella wasn't looking forward to seeing her sister-in-law, who'd just given birth to her third boy and was quite possibly even smugger than Concetta Esposito. The thought of facing everyone at dinner caused Ella to sink deeper into the water . . . until she remembered her hair.

The knocks grew less polite. "Miss Ella? Don't make me come in there!" Loretta called from the other side of the door. Even if her maid was all of five feet tall and had the face of a cherub, she was one of the few people Gabriella didn't want to cross.

"I'm coming, I'm coming," Gabriella said, taking a reluctant step out of the bath and wrapping herself in a silky pink robe. It was time to face the music, and if there was one thing Gabriella Capetti was good at doing, it was preparing for a battle.

CHAPTER 9

LIZ

*E*VEN NAN'S DIARY couldn't distract me from what I'd seen on Facebook, and I closed it with a sigh. Although I was definitely intrigued by Nonni Gabriella and this Joseph character (was he *the* Joseph?), the past would have to wait until I got my own crappy love life sorted. I pulled my high-school yearbook from a shelf and started to flip through. Usually this is a surefire self-esteem booster; every time I felt particularly down on myself, I would go back to this book and it put things in perspective. I was "sweet and smart" and "a great friend," not to mention being "the nicest person I've ever met."

However, this was not such a situation. I was looking through the yearbook to torture myself. How the hell did Jessica Miller end up with Adam?

At least I was alone when I found out. I can't imagine what my face must've looked like when I realized not only that Adam's girlfriend was one of the most annoying people on the planet, but that they were actually engaged.

I'd say being engaged was a pretty big jump from "kinda living together," but what did I know?

My first instinct was to call Adam and ream him out, but I just didn't have the energy. Obviously, the first call went to Addie. I demanded she round up as many people as possible; we were going drinking.

In the end, Caitlin and Renee, two of Addie's friends from high school, were the only ones to join us. While they'd been nice enough to me over the years, I thought of them as fair-weather friends to Addie. They always seemed to be wrapped up in some sort of petty argument with each other. But at that point, I didn't care where we went or who was with us, as long as it got my mind off Adam and his stupid engagement.

Two hours later, I finally chose an outfit (black off-the-shoulder sweater, dark jeans, and my patent-leather pumps) and threw some pajamas, toiletries, and a change of clothes into an old Vera Bradley tote to spend the night at Ad's place.

I dialed her number as I walked through the lobby and into my building's garage. "Hey, I'm on my way," I said. "I hope there's street parking because I'd rather not pay to park in a lot overnight."

"Eh, I'm sure there is. It's freezing, so I can't imagine the bars are packed. By the way, I didn't clean, so be warned." Addie sounded distant, but maybe it was the connection.

"When do you ever clean?"

"Touché," she said. "Anyway, I'll see you soon."

A few minutes later, after a tricky parallel parking situation, I was standing in front of Addie's gorgeous one-bedroom condo in Old City. Addie had chosen it for its prime location above an art gallery and within a stone's throw of tons of trendy shops, bars, and restaurants—not to mention the exposed brick walls, custom cabinets, and high ceilings. Basically, it was my dream place.

Even though my apartment was nice and the neighborhood's crime rate didn't freak my dad out, I'd have loved something to call my own. My inheritance from Nan would help toward that goal, but I wanted to wait a few years (and get settled career-wise) before committing to a mortgage. Luckily for Addie, she didn't have to worry about saving up, since her parents had given her a lump sum of cash for a graduation gift/condo down payment.

I pressed Addie's buzzer and waited for the door to unlock. For a second I remembered when the two of us had toured her unit, and I'd told Nan about the gleaming, modern kitchen and glass-tiled shower. Right there she'd offered to take out a mortgage for me, for which I'd give her a bit of money every month. Mom turned that idea down faster than you could say "down payment."

While money was never an issue for my mom growing up, she insisted on doing things her way once she got married. My parents' salaries as junior-high teachers paid the bills, but we certainly weren't rolling in dough. Addie's parents, meanwhile, had enough extra dough to bake enough pies to open a bakery for Nan, and all of her descendants for that matter.

Addie's mother's decorating influence was evident as I walked into the condo, noticing a couple of new, fancy-looking gold throw pillows tossed on the couch and matching mosaic-tile-covered candle holders on the coffee table. I took a seat next to Ad and picked a pillow up, noticing the $215 price tag hadn't been removed. Sadly, we'd been friends so long that it barely fazed me.

Renee and Caitlin were sitting on barstools in the kitchen, sipping glasses of wine and discussing their latest dating troubles. Renee, who was even smaller than Addie, pulled her dark hair up in a sparkly clip as they talked. It was obvious she was only half paying attention at best, and every time she leaned forward to console Caitlin, her boobs looked like they were about to pop out of her bright pink V-neck.

Caitlin wiped a stray tear from one of her round cheeks and smiled, playing with the long strand of jet-black beads she had roped around her neck. With her prim black turtleneck, messy ponytail, and smattering of freckles, she looked wholesome, almost boring. But the rest of us (and half of the male population of Philadelphia) knew Caitlin had an incredibly, shall we say, "loose" reputation.

"Remind me again why I asked them to come out with us?" Addie said. Even though they'd been friends for years, the three of them tended to go through phases where they were either BFFs or hated each other. I sensed Addie was leaning toward the latter at that moment.

We left around ten and walked over to one of my favorite places in Philadelphia, the Continental. The retro diner vibe reminded me of Nan's kitchen, and she'd always loved the lights that looked like giant olives on a toothpick (not to mention the Szechuan shoestring fries). It was always packed there on weekends, and despite Addie's theory about the cold, that night was no different. We could barely move, and people kept bumping into me, splashing martinis on my sleeve.

"Maybe this was a bad choice," I said. "Should we put our names in for a table?"

Since no one seemed to be paying attention to me, I marched through the crowd as best I could toward the hostess stand. I made it about five steps until someone stepped on my heel, making me lose my shoe.

"Excuse me! Can you watch where you're going?" I

said, turning around to look up at one of the hottest guys I'd ever seen.

"Sorry about that." He kneeled down to grab my shoe and held it still so I could step into it. "It's crazy here, huh?"

"I'm starting to think I should've just stayed home with a bottle of wine," I said.

He laughed and extended a hand. "I'm Matt. Nice to meet you."

I shook his hand, taking in his perfectly styled and highlighted hair, baby-blue Lacoste polo with the collar popped, and extremely expensive-looking jeans. An alarm went off in my head, but I ignored it.

"I'm Liz," I said. "So do you live around here?"

"Sort of; I live over on Thirteenth and Spruce. How about you?"

"Art museum. I like my building a lot, but I'm thinking of moving closer to your area when my lease is up. Have you been to the new Cuban place? I love it there."

"That's one of my favorite restaurants!" he said. "I go there with my roommate all the time. He loves the mojitos."

The alarm rung a little louder, but I promptly put it on snooze.

"Me, too. The plantain chips are awesome. I haven't been in a while." I paused, gathering courage, and said, "If you ever feel like meeting up, maybe we could grab dinner there sometime."

At that moment, two equally attractive and well-dressed guys came back from the bar and joined Matt, both sipping on Buzz Aldrins, the Continental's signature Tang-filled martini. Suddenly, it was a five-alarm fire in my head.

"This is my boyfriend, Darren, and my roommate Jake," Matt said, turning to the others. My cheeks flamed, and I wanted to slap myself for ignoring my instincts.

"Oh, nice to meet you," I said, staring at my drink and feeling like the biggest dumbass on the planet. Addie, who must've been standing behind me the whole time, jumped in and said she was sorry to have to steal me, but she wasn't feeling well and needed to leave. I said a quick goodbye to the trio, Addie grabbed the girls, and we hightailed it the hell out of there.

"Are you freaking serious?" I shouted into the biting night air, loud enough for everyone on Second Street to hear me. I walked as fast as I could, considering the heels, weaving in and out of the bar-goers filling the narrow sidewalk.

Addie tried to pull me back, and finally I slowed down so we were walking arm in arm. "It happens to the best of us, I'm afraid. We're all bound to accidentally hit on a gay guy at some point. At least you didn't sleep with him, which is more than I can say for Caitlin here."

"Oh, whatever. How was I supposed to know he was just experimenting with women?" Caitlin said. Her romantic escapades never ceased to surprise me, but I was too upset to comment.

"I'm sure you'll never see him again, so I wouldn't be too embarrassed," Renee said. "On to the next bar. Bigger and better things ahead."

"I don't care if I'll never see him again or not, I just feel like I can't get a break. First my grandma dies, then Adam is engaged, then I start to talk to a hot guy, and I think maybe, just maybe something will go right for me. All I want is a nice, normal relationship. I'm sorry to keep bitching about it, but I'm just going through a really rough time right now."

Addie squeezed my arm. "It'll be okay. Really. We've all had our heartaches, so no judgment here. At least we have Christmas to look forward to, right?"

I stopped in my tracks, leading Addie to almost trip in her stilettos. "I bought Nan's Christmas gift already. It's in my closet. And now I can't even give it to her."

Then out of nowhere, I started to cry until my entire body was shaking. I tried to calm myself down with some deep breaths, but it was no use. The tears came fast and hard while people waiting in line at the bar across the street stared at me like I was certifiably insane (or really drunk). Addie swiftly guided us into a pizza parlor and the girls had to physically sit me down at a table.

I was crying like a preschooler so mad at her parents she couldn't form an intelligible sentence, screeching "I ha-ha-aaate YOUUUUUUUUU." Therefore, I got blank looks when I told my friends that "Aah-aah-dum does-huh-huh-huh-ent LOVE muh-huh-meeeeeeeeeeeeeeeeeeee and muh-muh-my Nan is di-di-deaaad and her necklace is GOOOOOOONE and I hit on a ga-ga-gayyy guyyyy!"

Caitlin and Renee gave each other, "Are you kidding me?" looks, and I couldn't say I blamed them. We'd never been close friends, and I didn't expect them to have to cut their nights short because I was acting like a nutcase. Addie, reading my mind, told them to head over to the Plough and the Stars, an Irish bar across the street, and that we'd meet them there soon. They did a shitty job at trying to hide their relief, and all but ran out of the pizza shop after they'd hugged me goodbye.

Addie bought me a Sprite and shoved it in my face. "Drink."

I obeyed her orders and slurped some soda down quickly, hiccupping every so often in between sips.

"I am going to hook you up with someone if it's the last thing I do." Addie looked uncharacteristically determined, even for her, which was a little scary to witness. I could see her eyeing the guys in the shop, most of them of the drunk, tight-shirt-wearing, frat-guy variety.

"I don't want a random hookup, Ad. My whole life, I've had my Nan's marriage and my parents' marriage drilled into me as examples of what my future's supposed to be like. The kids, the picket fence and all that jazz. Maybe I wasn't ready for that with Adam, but I am now . . . and it definitely won't be with Mr. Jersey Shore over there."

"What about speed dating or something?" she asked. "I'd go with you."

I wrinkled my nose. "I feel like that would be awkward. I did meet the new guy who lives down the hall from me. He seemed pretty cool, but who knows."

Addie twirled the paper wrapping from my straw around her finger. "Hmm. You should call him. And you also could try online dating. Wait, I know—apply for the next season of *The Bachelor!*"

We both burst out laughing as Addie plucked a fake plastic rose out of the vase on the table and asked in a dramatic voice if I'd accept it. At least I hadn't been publicly humiliated by Adam on TV, so there was that.

Two pieces of pizza and a half-hour later, we headed across the street to meet the rest of our group. It was another shoulder-to-shoulder crowd of early-twenties wannabes, and I had to shout over the music to attempt a conversation with Addie.

"CAN WE JUST LEAVE?" I finally said, motioning toward the door. Fortunately, she nodded and said something in Caitlin's ear, who frowned and mouthed, "Whatever." After all, it was just one fifteen, and we still had forty-five minutes left of bar time to go. God forbid.

The walk home was a short one, and soon enough, I was in my warm cupcake-print flannel pajamas, curled up in the guestroom with Addie's blue plaid comforter from college. She climbed into bed next to me after popping in a DVD of *The Golden Girls*. Just as I was laughing along with Sophia, Rose, and the girls, a text flashed on my phone.

I'll be in the city on Monday for a mtg. Meet for lunch? I already have some ideas for your site if that's okay . . . —A

The next thing that popped up was an image of the letters "L" and "M" with a blue heart entwined between them. "Designs" was written in a funky script font underneath.

It was perfect. Addie grabbed the phone from me, studying the logo. "Guy's got talent, I'll give him that."

I stared at the picture for a moment and hit reply.

Thanks. And congrats on your engagement.

Adam's response was almost instant.

What?? Who said I was engaged?

I saw your fiancée at the mall and her profile pic on FB. Nice ring, btw.

The next response didn't come back for about five minutes.

Oh boy. Long story, but Jess and I r not engaged anymore.

They broke up over the course of a week? I found this to be strange, but replied:

Ok then . . .

Ok then you'll have lunch with me?

I showed my phone to Addie. "This might be the cosmos talking, and you're probably going to die of shock, but dude, you need to go. Even *I* want to hear this explanation."

I raised my eyebrows but didn't question her logic.

Fine. Soho at one?

See you then. And sorry for the late-night text. Sweet dreams.

Yeah, like I would really do much sleeping.

CHAPTER 10

ELLA

September 16, 1957

I'm still trying to take in the info that Mom had another fiancé before she was married to Dad. Once she started to talk about her summers in Italy, it made me realize how little I knew about her. Granted, our personalities aren't exactly the same, but I never thought she would keep a secret like this for all these years. Part of me actually wonders if she's making it up. I wouldn't put it past her, but it seemed like an awfully elaborate story for someone who just suffered a stroke.

If all of this is true, I wonder if Mary knows. I don't want to betray Mom's confidence, though . . . it's a miracle she even told me to begin with.

She was starting to drift off just as she was telling me about her parents inviting this man Joseph Rossi to their house for dinner. I didn't want to tire her out, and visiting hours were nearly over, so I went home. Hopefully she'll tell me more when I come back today with Harry.

We should also know more about her tests, so the kids have been putting their nightly prayers to good use. All we can do is hope for the best . . .

"I see you brought a visitor today," Gabriella said as Ella and Harry walked into the room, carrying a small floral arrangement and a stack of magazines.

"How are you feeling?" Harry asked.

"Not too shabby, Carlo."

Ella exchanged a worried glance with Harry, then sighed and took a seat in the chair by her mother's bedside. "I told you, Har," she said.

"If you could please stop talking about me like I'm not here, that would be fabulous," Gabriella said, barely looking up from her new reading material.

"Why don't you tell us all about the new developments at the restaurant, Harry?" Ella said, trying to change the subject.

Harry took a seat and crossed one leg over the other. "The new menu seems like a success. All of the regulars were telling me how much they enjoyed that chicken marsala recipe you suggested."

"Of course they did," Gabriella said with a satisfied grin. "It's Loretta's recipe, after all."

"Anyway," Harry continued, "I think there are still some small changes to be made, so I'll be working some more late shifts and going over everything in the kitchen. It's a good start, though."

"I thought you said the worst of it was over?" Ella said. She hoped Harry didn't notice the disappointment in her tone. "If the kids ask one more time why you aren't home, I think I'll go insane." The thought of late nights with the kids and no help for another week or more caused her to sink further into the chair. She'd have to do some serious thinking about schedules and time management if a business were to become a reality. Why even bother bringing it up until things calmed down a bit at home?

"This won't last forever. But you knew how the restaurant business could be when you married me, right, Ellie?" He gave her a playful pat on the knee, but Ella turned her body toward her mother instead.

She leaned forward, taking the magazine from Gabriella and placing it on the windowsill. "I'm sure you'll have plenty of time to read later. Why don't you finish that story you were telling me yesterday? You were getting ready for some big dinner with Joseph Rossi."

"See the way my daughter treats me? I hope you don't act like this with your mother, or you deserve a good slap."

Harry just smiled, pulling his chair closer to the bed. "I'd love to hear about growing up in Italy, if you don't mind. You always tell great stories."

Flattery usually worked with Gabriella. Even though she was annoyed, Ella could tell it did the trick.

"Fine. I might as well tell you in case something happens to me. Lord only knows what the idiots in this hospital know about medicine."

"As long as you feel up to it, Mother," Ella said, trying to hide that she was actually dying to hear more.

Gabriella propped herself up with a few pillows, took an unnecessarily long time to rearrange her blankets, and finally, looked out the door to make sure no one was listening before starting her story.

"Very well, then. This dinner was a turning point for me. You don't always know the whole story about people. Remember that, Ella."

CHAPTER 11

~

GABRIELLA

1905

SOFT STRAINS OF MUSIC and the low chatter of guests filled the air as Gabriella burst out of her room to head downstairs. Promptness was not one of her strong suits, and since tonight was especially important, she spent even more time than usual getting ready. After two more warnings, a particularly frazzled Loretta nearly dragged Gabriella away from the mirror.

She could have spent a few more minutes fine-tuning the position of the flowers in her hair, but the final result was pleasing enough. She knew Joseph would be pining for her long after the evening was over, and that was the important part. She wanted to inflict as much damage as possible, and for Gabriella, beauty was one of her deadliest weapons.

There were few in Florence (or New York) who could match her when it came to looks, which was why it came as a surprise to many that she still was unmarried. However, if you asked around, many a suitor complained of her stubborn streak and tendency to be . . . well, rude.

Rudeness aside, heads turned as she entered the room, but Gabriella made sure to locate Joseph first so as to better avoid him. It wasn't hard, considering he stood almost a head above most of the guests. His back was turned to Gabriella, and he seemed to be engaged in an animated conversation with Carlo and Massimo.

He certainly wasn't an unattractive man, Gabriella mused as she watched Joseph from across the room. Besides being tall, which was one of Gabriella's musts in a man (she hated towering over her suitors), Joseph had sparkling green eyes and a head of thick, dark brown hair. His facial features were delicate for a man, but in an aristocratic way, offset by a strong, sharp jaw.

It was a shame Joseph had to be so horrible to her in Capri, Gabriella mused. If he hadn't, maybe things would've been different . . .

Her thoughts were interrupted by a firm hand on her shoulder and a familiar, booming voice.

"Ella, my dear. How kind of you to grace us with your presence."

She pasted on her best fake smile and turned around to greet her father.

"I just wanted to make sure I looked my absolute best for this evening's dinner. I hear we have an unexpected guest?"

Mr. Capetti raised an eyebrow. "Ella, I know you're aware that Mr. Rossi is joining us tonight. As he's a guest in our home, I expect you'll show him an enjoyable evening, yes?"

Gabriella simply nodded and excused herself to greet their guests. She was in no mood to hear about her parents' disappointment.

"Lessie! There you are," Gabriella exclaimed as she spotted her cousin, resplendent in a creamy yellow satin gown with dramatic pleats in the skirt. Pearls were twined through her black hair, creating a beautiful contrast of dark against light.

Lessie kissed both of Gabriella's cheeks and took a step back to admire her cousin's new ensemble.

"I didn't know you were having a new dress made for tonight! That color certainly suits you."

Gabriella sighed, smoothing an imaginary wrinkle from her gown. "It's my mother's doing. They've invited Joseph Rossi, and apparently I'm supposed to make nice with him in case he wants to propose."

Lessie tried to hold back her laughter. "Massimo and I thought we were seeing things when Joseph walked in. I thought he'd never speak to you again after last summer."

"I don't know what you're talking about," Gabriella said.

"Everyone in Florence knows what I'm talking about!" Lessie exclaimed. "You can't just push someone into a gigantic statue of David in the middle of broad daylight and expect it not to be discussed."

Gabriella rolled her eyes. "He was putting your brother down for not attending Oxford. I set him in his place."

Although Lessie was Gabriella's best friend, she was also keen to follow proper decorum, and therefore prone to being scandalized by her more brazen cousin's behavior. Noticing her discomfort at the topic, Gabriella changed the subject.

"I saw Mr. Rossi today, actually. We crossed paths in the piazza right as Salvatore and his ridiculous wife strolled by with their pram. It was humiliating how he looked at me, Lessie!"

"I swear Salvatore thinks every woman in Florence should be throwing herself at his feet, even now that he's married and has a child."

Gabriella threw her head back and laughed. "Too bad his wife monitors his every move. I heard he isn't allowed to leave the house without receiving approval."

Gossiping about Salvatore felt good; at least now she could bring up his name without feeling like someone had kicked her in the stomach.

"What are you going to do about Mr. Rossi?" Lessie asked, her eyes scanning the room for him.

"Ignore him at all costs."

As if he could sense the girls talking about him, Joseph chose that exact moment to turn around and meet their gazes. Gabriella looked at the ground, but it was no use. They were caught.

A slow smile spread across Joseph's face as he made his away across the room to the pair.

"Act natural. He's coming this way!" Lessie whispered.

Her version of "acting natural" entailed furiously fluffing her skirts and smoothing errant curls while having a pretend conversation with her cousin about the weather. Gabriella often wondered if her cousin had some sort of affliction that rendered her useless in social situations.

"I gather I'm the last person you wanted to be here tonight," Joseph said as he greeted them. Gabriella returned this remark with a stony stare.

"Well, since you took every opportunity to criticize me in Capri, no. You wouldn't have been at the top of the guest list if I had a choice in the matter."

Joseph's expression remained pleasantly neutral. "I didn't imagine you would be happy to see me. I tried to tell you this afternoon, but you looked like you weren't in the mood for long chats after the Esposito incident and all."

She wanted to look at the ground, but forced herself to stare Joseph in the eyes. "I don't care a bit about what he does or doesn't do. Not anymore."

"Salvatore's no friend of mine," Joseph said. "He shouldn't have led you to believe he had honest intentions. I just wanted to let you know I don't find that type of behavior acceptable."

"Yet you found interrupting Salvatore and me every chance you got acceptable? What about hiding my purse so I missed the boat trip?"

Joseph sighed. "Perhaps I didn't want—"

Gabriella had heard enough. "If you'll excuse me, there are other guests I haven't said hello to just yet, and I can't seem to locate a proper statue or a fountain into which to push you."

She grabbed her cousin by the elbow, barely managing a "Good evening, Mr. Rossi" before she pulled Lessie across the room to get a glass of champagne.

"The nerve of that man!" Gabriella said, slugging the entire flute of champagne in one quick gulp and slamming it down on a tray while Lessie and a waiter looked on in astonishment.

"Honestly, Ella, your guests are going to think you're loose."

That was the least of Gabriella's problems, considering her mother was crossing the room with a deadly look in her eyes. The girls quickly gathered their composure, flashing bright smiles.

"Hello, Aunt Rosa," Lessie said. "The party is lovely."

"Thank you, dear. May I have a word with my daughter in private?"

Lessie exchanged a pitying look with her cousin as she slipped into the crowd of partygoers.

"Please humor me and at least *attempt* to make conversation with Mr. Rossi, will you?"

Gabriella sighed deeply. "I've engaged Mr. Rossi in conversation already. There wasn't much to say."

"Then find something. Now."

A gentle shove sent Gabriella stumbling across the room, straight in Joseph's direction.

"Hello again, Miss Capetti," Joseph said, the corner of his mouth turning up just slightly as she nearly crashed into him.

"You seem to be enjoying yourself."

"I am. Your family has been quite welcoming," he said. "In fact, your mother just suggested that I escort you out to the gardens for some air before we sit down to dinner. Shall we?"

He took Gabriella's arm before she even had a chance to protest, so she just sighed in resignation and pointed him in the right direction. She'd do her duty as a good daughter and humor Mr. Rossi for a walk outside, feign a headache, and return indoors to gossip with Lessie.

As they made their way through the crowd, Gabriella caught a glimpse of their reflection in a large, gilded mirror and smiled despite herself. If nothing else, they made an attractive pair. However, this was no matter because Gabriella hated Joseph Rossi, and that was that.

Gabriella made no attempt at small talk as they made their way down the hall toward the back of the house. Their home was a large one, though, and eventually the silence became too awkward.

"So how are you faring at Oxford? I'd imagine it's terribly dull. All those academics fussing about."

"I find it rather exhilarating, actually," Joseph said. "There's always more to learn about the world, don't you think?"

"Of course there is. But I don't see any reason to associate with a bunch of bores. Snobbish ones, at that," Gabriella added.

Joseph let out a booming laugh. "You're full of opinions now, aren't you, Miss Capetti?"

She just sniffed and pointed to the left. "Just out these doors, over here." Joseph opened the French doors and Gabriella rushed past him out into the warm night air.

"It's a beautiful evening, don't you agree?" Joseph said, once again taking her arm.

She ignored the buzzing feeling in her chest and used words as her armor. "It would be, if I didn't have to suffer through it with present company."

"We've never really gotten on; I realize this. But I do apologize for my past behavior, and hope you know I truly regret it," Joseph said, sounding for once truly earnest.

Gabriella said nothing in reply, hoping her silence would inspire Joseph to stop talking so she could go back inside and make fun of him with Lessie.

"What I was saying was I hope we can move forward on . . . better terms. I think you'll find it would be easiest on all of us in the future. You see—"

Gabriella sighed loudly and cut him off before he could continue. "So do you make it a habit to go about throwing heartfelt apologies at every beautiful woman in Florence you've wronged? If so, I'm afraid it would take you months. Perhaps even years."

Joseph smirked. "But none of them are quite like you, are they?"

"What do you mean by that?" Gabriella said,

reaching down to pluck a petal off a rose.

"You're truly one of a kind. And that's a good thing." He gave the rose petal an inquisitive glance.

"Oh. This is the exact color I wanted for my new dress," Gabriella said, pulling a pin out of her hair and sliding it through the petal. She bent down and fastened it to the top of her shoe.

He laughed. "You never fail to surprise me. That's what I meant by one of a kind."

"What other type of person is there?" she asked.

"So your family's place in New York is quite lovely, I've heard," he said, ignoring her question. "You must be very proud to live in such a stately home."

Gabriella was thrown off by this remark, and all she could say was, "Oh . . . thank you. Yes, I am."

"One can tell your mother takes great pride in running her household. I'm sure you would take the same care someday as lady of your own house."

"I'm not sure what you're getting at, but yes, of course I would. Who wouldn't be proud to have a beautiful home?"

A few moments of awkward silence passed before Joseph suggested they go indoors as not to forget about the other guests. This was just fine with Gabriella, but for some reason she had a feeling their conversation wasn't over by a long shot.

CHAPTER 12

LIZ

AS THE HOURS PASSED Thanksgiving weekend, I couldn't stop thinking about Adam's engagement (or according to him, former engagement). I knew it happened in Paris; that much was clear from Facebook. But did he propose at the top of the Eiffel Tower? Was there a crowd of cheering onlookers while he was down on one knee? How did they meet? And more importantly, what did he see in Jessica?

The nitty-gritty details were irrelevant, because the ring that had been meant for me now belonged to Jessica—or used to at least—and it was my own fault. Anything could set me off. Greeting-card commercials: check. Christmas carols: check. Hell, if *Supermarket Sweep* had been on TV, I probably would've cried, too.

I tried to distract myself by reading some more of Nan's diary. Everything was spelled out in painstaking detail, from my mom's potty habits to Nonni Gabriella's doctor visits to what new recipes Nan made for dinner, so it was hard to plow through the book quickly. I didn't want to miss any details, so skipping a page or two seemed criminal. But reading about what I assumed to be a budding love story wasn't exactly helping, either.

Sunday morning, I drove to my parents' house. Mom had guilt-tripped me into going dress shopping for Cate's wedding. She had a full day of appointments planned for us and Gracie, despite the fact Jesse and Cate's engagement had only just been announced.

They hadn't even set a wedding date, but that was no matter; my mother had become a wedding planning machine the second she heard the news. When I'd called her the night before, she had been scouring the Internet for Jordan almonds and telling me I had to "start picking up the slack" since I was maid of honor. *What slack?* I knew throwing herself into the wedding was her way of dealing with Nan's passing, so even though she was going a little overboard, I kept my mouth shut.

"Oh good, Liz is finally here!" Mom called out from the kitchen as I walked through the door. "We should leave in five minutes."

"I thought our first appointment wasn't until eleven."

"Yeah, but it will take us at least a half hour to get there," Mom said, looking down at her watch. "You look tired. What's wrong?"

I almost told her about the necklace, but Gracie came barreling down the steps in a fluffy blue bathrobe with pink skulls on it.

"Seriously, Mom? The shopping center with Bedazzled is like fifteen minutes away, tops. It only takes half an hour to get somewhere when *you're* the one driving."

"Keep talking back and you won't be coming at all," Mom said. "Now scoot. Get dressed!"

Gracie padded back up the steps as slowly as humanly possible, drips from her hair making tiny wet spots on the cream carpet.

Mom rushed back into the kitchen, opening and closing drawers and generally acting like she'd just drunk an entire pot of coffee. "Can you please make sure your sisters are ready? I need to grab my camera battery off the charger and get all of the magazine clippings to bring with us."

My eyes widened. "Magazine clippings? Didn't you find out about the wedding, like, two seconds ago?"

Mom continued her search, shaking out a large manila envelope. "There's a lot to be done, you know. No time for dilly-dallying. Go get your sisters, would you?"

I rolled my eyes and whispered, "Okay, crazy lady," as I headed up to find the girls. "What the hell happened in here?" I asked, reaching the top of the steps. Gracie had spread makeup and hair products of every conceivable variety on the counter, toilet seat, and floor of the hall bath.

"Um, I'm doing my hair. What does it look like I'm doing?"

The white porcelain sink was covered in a film of deep tan bronzer and the air smelled of a mix between nail polish remover and Bath & Body Works sweet pea lotion. I wrinkled my nose and decided against wiping the counter down. Not my house, not my problem.

"Listen, just hurry up and get dressed," I said. "We're not seeing any boys today. No need to spend hours primping."

Gracie looked at me like I had two heads. "I'm sorry, but I don't go out in public looking gross, unlike some people."

"What's that supposed to mean?"

I took a look in the mirror. Granted, there hadn't been much time to get beautified that morning, but I didn't see a problem with my appearance. I'd pulled my hair back with a thin braided leather headband, and my brown cardigan and ribbed tank combo was fairly cute. Faded jeans, my favorite suede boots, and a pair of dangly earrings with brown beads I had made the night before finished off the outfit.

"First of all, you've had that sweater for like five years. It's faded and has a peanut butter stain on it, and you're not even wearing any makeup."

"I *am* wearing makeup! Mascara and some powder."

"Whoop de doo."

"I'm not trying to impress anyone," I said, dabbing at my sweater with a wet washcloth. "You know, since there will be so many available men at a bridal store."

Gracie replied with her trademark, "Whatever," and I went into Cate's room, partly to drag her out of there so Mom wouldn't kill us, but also because I didn't feel the need to be criticized by a teenager any longer.

Cate sat cross-legged on the bed with a magazine on her lap, surrounded by stacks of other wedding books and a large pink binder. She ripped out a page and looked startled when I cleared my throat.

"Oh, hey. Are we leaving?"

"Yeah, you know how Mom gets when we have to be somewhere. So annoying."

She gathered the papers around her and slipped them into a turquoise pocket folder with a label on the front. "WEDDING" was written in all capital letters in my mother's handwriting with a heart over the "I." A pang of jealousy shot through me. I could picture Mom running out to buy supplies and wedding magazines for Cate, taking ages to pick just the right ones and then saying "screw it" and getting all of them. If the tables had been turned, I wasn't so sure she'd buy me anything. At least, she wouldn't have with Adam.

"Can you grab Gracie before you come down? I'm going to talk to Mom," I said, turning to leave her pink-and-purple mess of a room.

"Liz?" she said, sounding slightly hesitant. "I know you're probably upset about me getting married, and it's okay. I'm sure I'd feel the same in your situation."

"And what situation is that, exactly?" I said, folding my arms.

"I didn't mean . . . I just meant, you know, since you're older and I'm still in school and all. And since you almost got engaged to Adam and it didn't work out . . . "

My nostrils flared. "There's no need for a pity party. Maybe I'm not getting married, but I happen to enjoy my life, so please don't think I'm some sort of charity case. And you're acting like I'm thirty-five or something. I'm freaking twenty-seven. It's *normal* for me to be single."

Cate slammed her binder shut and stood up. "Well, excuse me for trying to clear the air. No one's forcing you to come today, you know. Or be in the wedding at all, for that matter."

It was bad enough when I was stewing silently about the engagement, but being told to my face I was jealous and bitter sucked. Knowing it was true felt even worse. It was time to put my big-girl shoes on.

I sighed. "I know. Just forget about it. I'm fine. And I'm sorry if I've been acting weird. I just wish you would wait until you're out of school. People change a lot, even from college to my age. Trust me on that."

She tucked a lock of hair behind her ear. "Yeah. Well, I know what I'm doing. And I actually asked Jesse's mom if she could call a favor in for you and talk to her buyer friend at Nordstrom. But if you're so against this wedding, maybe I should just tell her not to bother."

My mouth dropped open. "Are you serious? Oh my God, that would be amazing. Do you think she would actually help me out?"

Cate shrugged. "She said she would see what her friend could do."

I would've hugged her, but Cate remained across the room, hand on her hip, so I just smiled weakly. "Anything would be great. And thank you. I mean that, Beep."

She walked back to the bed to toss the binder and a few other things into a green monogrammed canvas tote. "You're welcome. This whole thing is overwhelming and ridiculous enough. I could use some support, you know."

I wasn't quite sure what she meant by that, but I nodded. "You got it. I'm going to go grab Mom before she goes and tries on dresses without us."

I walked down the steps in slow motion, thinking about what a big department store could do for my line. I couldn't believe Mrs. Crenshaw had agreed to help me, and suddenly I felt like a first-class bitch for having been such a downer about the wedding. It was going to happen whether I liked it or not, after all, and in the words of Nan, "No one likes a party pooper." I didn't want Cate to think I was only acting excited because of the news about her future mother-in-law, though.

Fifteen minutes later, we were finally corralled in Cate's car and headed over to the bridal shop. The atmosphere inside the shop could best be described as complete wedding chaos. There must've been at least twenty-five people crammed into the small space in the front of the store waiting for a consultant, and in the back, women were rushing around in various states of undress, some carrying heavy-looking plastic bags with white gowns inside.

"Remind me why we're here again?" Cate asked, wrinkling her nose. My sister's taste was definitely more Madison Avenue, and I knew Jesse's stuck-up parents wouldn't be thrilled about dresses that came from a strip mall. But Mom had insisted we go to this cheesy local shop called Bedazzled to check out their bridesmaid dresses and that Cate at least, "try on a few gowns for fun."

So there I was in bridal hell, while Cate went to check in and Mom grabbed Gracie to start perusing the racks of gowns. With nothing else to do, I headed over to the bridesmaids' section. Cate hadn't mentioned whether she wanted us to wear short or long dresses, but I saw a few styles that weren't hideous and began looking to see if they had any in my size. I was throwing a few of them over my arm when Cate came over with a dark-suited bridal consultant in tow. I could smell her perfume from at least six feet away.

"You must be the maid of honor. I'm Nancy," she said, shaking my hand. Her hair was pulled up into a teased French twist accented with a rhinestone-and-pearl comb, and she wore dime-sized pearl earrings along with a fuchsia silk scarf tied around her neck like a 1960s flight attendant.

"We're going to go pull some gowns for this beautiful bride-to-be," Nancy said. "Would you like to help?"

"You go ahead. I'll just pick out some choices for the bridesmaids."

Cate shrugged. "That's fine. Just make sure they're available in my colors."

"And what would those be?" It was probably bad I didn't know my own sister's wedding colors, which the look on Nancy's face confirmed.

"Pale blue and silver. Just find something that can be worn with a sash because I want white sashes, okay?"

I nodded and walked deeper into the racks, feeling shame wash over me. *Stay positive. Be helpful.* I grabbed a few more dresses that looked like they'd fit Gracie and me and sat with her in front of the two dressing rooms we'd been allotted.

To the right of us, a group of about eight women was oohing and ahhing as a bride stepped out in a form-fitting ivory gown. She appeared to be about forty and one of the women, who I assumed was her mother, wiped away tears as the consultant came over with a lace-trimmed veil and secured it in the bride's hair.

"My baby's finally getting married," she sobbed.

"That's probably what they'll say when you get hitched!" Gracie said, patting me on the back.

I pretended to whack her with my wristlet. "Remind me not to ask you to be a bridesmaid then, brat."

Finally, Cate, Nancy, and my mom returned, each carrying several large plastic garment bags. Cate disappeared into the fitting room with Mom and came out a few minutes later in a huge princess-style gown with a silver sash around the waist.

"I hate it," said Cate. Before anyone else could comment, she retreated into the dressing room.

Gracie rolled her eyes. "What a drama queen."

It went pretty much like that for the next half hour: Cate coming out, taking a look in the mirror and storming back into the room. Halters, ball gowns, trumpets, mermaids, we saw them all.

I decided on the spot that working in a bridal shop must be cruel and unusual punishment. Even Mom was starting to lose her optimism. After deeming three new choices from Nancy "unwearable," Cate decided maybe it was too early to look for a dress after all, and I all but ran out the door after her.

"I thought you were excited to look for a dress," Mom said as she slid into the passenger seat. "You've never been this picky before."

Cate threw her arms up in the air. "*You* were excited to shop for dresses. When did I ever bring up looking for gowns? We haven't even set a date! You're totally obsessed with this wedding. Just lay off, okay?"

Maybe I wasn't the only one who was a little uncomfortable about this engagement.

✺ ✺ ✺

MONDAY WELCOMED a steady stream of shoppers, which made it easier to keep my mind off lunch with Adam. Almost.

Luckily, I hadn't heard from Jessica since the awkward encounter we'd had on Black Friday. I hoped she would change her mind about the jewelry, but I already planned to be busy for the next year if she asked. The whole engagement thing was so bizarre, and I wondered if he'd confronted her about our run-in.

The next thing I knew, it was 12:45. Although the restaurant was only a few blocks away, I made sure to leave early because I wanted to get there first. Maybe it was weird, but I always felt getting somewhere before the person I was meeting put me in control. Like they were the one entering my space. I hate having to walk into a place to look around for someone, and feeling awkward when I realize they aren't there yet.

The air felt clean and crisp, and the sun shone brightly, but it was still a little too cold for my liking. I pulled my blue knit hat down a little further over my ears and shivered, walking as fast as possible down Market Street. When I arrived at Soho, my favorite pizza place, the line stretched to the back, as usual, with the lunchtime crowd.

The brick ovens definitely upped the temperature, and eventually it got so warm I took my hat and scarf off, folding them in my bag. A quick time check revealed that it was 1:06.

The longer I waited, the more my stomach fluttered. I had no idea what was taking Adam so long, considering he worked from home and was his own boss, but I figured he must've been tied up in traffic.

Finally he blew into the restaurant, just as I paid for my pizza. His hair was messed up from the wind, but unlike his ridiculous fiancée's profile photo, Adam's hair looked like he had just woken up. He spotted me right away and gave me a quick hug. His cheeks felt freezing cold as I pressed against his stubble.

"Wow, it's jumping. I'm gonna get my food. Save us a table?"

I nodded and grabbed the only empty table in the place, which unfortunately put us right up next to the humongous line of customers. I wasn't going to back down from my agenda, even if we had an audience. I'd nearly finished my barbecue chicken slice when he finally sat down across from me.

"So . . . " he said, taking a deep breath. "I talked to Jessica. I'm really sorry about what happened. Believe me, I am not pleased with her about the situation."

"I just don't get it," I said. "Why would she say you were engaged if you weren't?"

"We *were* engaged, that's true. Emphasis on the word 'were.'"

"Judging by the picture on Facebook, I kind of figured that out."

Adam ignored this comment and continued. "I broke it off with her six months ago. We just got back together, but the engagement is by no means back on. We're trying to work things out, kind of on a trial basis."

"Then why was she wearing my ring and asking me to make bridal jewelry for her?"

Adam picked at the edge of his paper plate. "It's complicated. And I'm sorry you had to see her wearing the ring. That probably sucked for you. Although, to be fair, you didn't want it."

Ouch. "I know. I probably have no right to be pissed, but it *is* kind of weird to give someone else the ring you bought for me."

"No, you're right. Honestly, I was holding on to it because I always thought we'd work things out. But, then I met Jess at a party back home and, well, you know the rest."

I grimaced. "No need to elaborate."

Adam sighed. "So, first of all, I took the ring back as soon as we broke up. She cheated on me. It was a one-time thing, or so she said, and we tried to work things out in counseling, but the relationship kind of imploded after that. I couldn't trust her."

"Like Nan always said, 'once a cheater, always a cheater,' right?" I said in my best lecturing tone. "Sorry. Continue."

He shrugged. "No need to apologize. But anyway, we had to see each other every so often because I was still doing design projects for the theater where she works. We had coffee one day and she said her 'transgression' was the worst mistake of her life. She really was trying to change, and despite everything, I missed her. It's not always so black and white, ya know?"

I couldn't tell if that was a sign he loved her more than he'd loved me, or vice versa. I'd never even accepted the ring, let alone cheated on him, but he wouldn't speak to me, answer my emails . . . Chicago might as well have been Timbuktu.

"Well, you've gotta do what you think is best," I said, even though I thought he was seriously lacking judgment on this one. "So, the ring?"

"Ah, yeah. When Jess moved back in, she automatically assumed the engagement was on again. I walked in one day and she was wearing the damn ring."

I raised my eyebrows, but said nothing and nodded for him to continue.

"Trust me, we've had that fight," he said. "I need some time to make sure this is going to work before making a commitment to her again. And right now it's looking like that might not ever happen. She's never home, and when she is, she's chatting online with theater people till two in the morning. We barely even interact."

I was officially confused. "So her way of coping is just continuing to plan the wedding?"

Adam let out a bitter laugh. "I think her reasoning was that if she started making concrete plans for a wedding, it would somehow happen and I'd just go along with it."

While it did sound like typical Jessica behavior, I still remained skeptical. "Why didn't you just tell me this up front the other day? I had no idea you were even with anyone. The way you were acting, I thought—"

"I know," Adam interrupted. "That's why all of this is so confusing. I wish I had run into you months ago, I really do."

I tried not to choke on my pizza. Did he mean he'd rather be with me?

"The thing is, although it's not going so great with Jessica right now, I do need to give our relationship a real shot. Who knows what will happen, but I don't want to lose touch with you again . . . at least as a friend."

I had no idea what to say. On one hand, I didn't realize how much I missed Adam until I saw him again. On the other hand, I was headed down a dangerous road. I knew that being "just friends" might be impossible. Then again, maybe being platonic was a better option for us, after all.

"I'd like to be friends," I said. "But I can't get in the middle of your relationship. You need to figure that out first."

"Oh, I know. I'm not asking you to go on a date or anything, of course. I just want you to be in my life," he said. "We can hang out in a group. I don't care."

"Well, Addie's birthday is this weekend. We're all going out for drinks. If you want to come, let me know."

Adam scrunched up his nose. "I'd love to get together, but do you think she's going to want me there? Addie's not exactly my number-one fan."

"I know, but she is my best friend, and she's who I hang out with most of the time. If you want to be friends, you guys are going to have to deal with each other, like it or not."

Adam hesitated for a moment, and then nodded. "Okay. Just text me and let me know where you'll be."

He cleared his throat and pulled a sleek laptop out of his bag, pushing our empty plates to the side of the table. "Not to change the subject, but I looked at your website and Etsy shop and came up with a couple of ideas. The logo I texted you was just part of it. What do you think?"

He turned the screen toward me to reveal a mockup

of a website. A bright turquoise, pink, and gray design featured the logo and scrolling images of my jewelry in the middle. At the bottom, inside a sketch of a frame, was a picture of me holding up a pair of earrings. My mouth dropped open. "Oh my God. I love it. But how did you . . . ?"

"Facebook," he said with a grin. "I grabbed a couple of images of you from an old album with jewelry stuff." He turned the screen back around and clicked a few keys. "This is the second one."

I felt my smile widen as I looked at a simpler design with my name in big pink swirly letters at the top and a heart-shaped collage of jewelry in the center. A different pink-and-gray logo with a chevron border jumped off the page.

It must've taken him the entire weekend to do this for me, and my mind started racing. Was it a gesture of forgiveness, or what?

"Adam, this is too much. Really. Thank you."

His face lit up, warming me like an electric blanket. "This is just the homepage, but I figured I could build the rest if you liked it. We can totally set it up for e-commerce or just link to Etsy if you'd rather do that."

"Wow. Yeah, we can talk about that later, I guess. This is amazing, seriously. Makes my old site look like crap."

He laughed. "Nah, it's just a little face-lift. You're an awesome artist yourself. I'm glad you like it, though."

We both slurped on our sodas and chatted about some ideas for the website and his meeting at one of the big advertising agencies. I looked at my phone and realized it was almost 1:45.

"Oh crap, I need to get back to the store," I said, gathering up my trash.

Adam winced. "Whoops. Sorry to keep you for so long. I guess I'll see you on Saturday?"

"Yup," I said, although I already regretted the invitation. Addie was not going to be pleased and it *was* her birthday . . . what was I thinking?

He followed me out onto the sidewalk. "Actually, I'll walk you back. I could use the exercise, and I have some time to kill before my meeting."

"Sure, if you want. But don't blame me if you get frostbite."

Adam raised an eyebrow. "Frostbite? It's beautiful today."

"Beautiful is seventy-five degrees."

He shook his head. "You're just as bad as Addie sometimes. Remember how she brought a giant space heater to my house because she couldn't stand sleeping over in Kevin's room?"

We walked along Market Street, laughing about old memories, when someone nearly knocked me over.

"Ow!" I turned around and saw a tour group taking pictures outside the old Ben Franklin post office. One of the teenagers wasn't paying attention and had backed right into me, trying to get a shot.

The kids kept pushing in front of me and I couldn't get around. Before I knew what was happening, Adam grabbed my hand and pulled me over to the side, sending me crashing into him. We stayed like that for a moment, pressed up against the brick building. I held his gaze for just a second too long, and felt my heart pound.

I backed away before anything could happen. "Sorry about that," I said, brushing off my coat and trying desperately to act casual. "You know how clumsy I am."

Adam smiled, but I could see the sadness in his

face. "Hey, I actually remembered I have a few things to do before my meeting. I should probably set up shop in Starbucks or something."

My face fell. "Oh. All right then."

"I'll probably see you Saturday," he said and hugged me, then patted the top of my head. "Be good."

He turned and walked away, leaving me wondering what the hell had just happened.

CHAPTER 13

LIZ

I DIDN'T HEAR from Adam again that week, but I replayed our lunch in my head a million times. Instead of crinkling tissue paper into balls for a display, I was thinking about the way his eyes crinkled when he laughed, and his look of pride when I told him how much I loved the designs. One lunch and suddenly I was a freshman back at the Alpha House, staring at Adam as if he were the sun and I needed a good tan.

Maybe it was his giving nature, or his ability to make friends with anyone, but I hadn't been the only girl who had basked in Adam's glow at our school. One of the downsides of such a small university was everyone knew your business, and it felt like being dumped all over again having to face Adam's unofficial fan club sophomore year. The gossip mill ensured that practically the entire student population had heard he'd broken up with me after his graduation. Silly freshman, thinking she could hold onto the golden boy. Ironically, when I finally got him back, I was the one who let go.

Before I knew it Friday arrived, the day before Addie's party. I'd told her about Adam after our lunch, and although she wasn't thrilled, she didn't ask me to disinvite him. I took that as a good sign.

Addie took the day off, and I wasn't working, either, so we agreed to meet at the mall to look for party outfits and have lunch. One vehicle fire and close to an hour later, I found Addie waiting for me in Nordstrom. She stood in front of a rack of quilted Burberry coats, and I saw her look at a price tag and sigh.

"What on earth took you so long?" she asked, jumping a little as I came up behind her.

"Traffic was a fiasco. And we need to step away from the expensive stuff because I have the urge to do some serious power shopping after that drive."

"That's fine. I don't need anything here," she said, gesturing to the mall entrance.

"Really?" I said, my tone laced with surprise. "Do you have a fever or something?"

Addie walked briskly past a row of sequin-clad mannequins dressed in a New Year's Eve theme, her eyes facing forward. "I'm just tired of this store."

"Okay, then," I said, unconvinced, but dropping the subject. We caught up on Addie's latest case at work and her sister's new Ivy League boyfriend as we headed from store to store, Addie whirling through like a tornado and deeming everything to be unacceptable.

"This is why I like to shop at the outlets," she whined. "I want to wear ridiculously expensive clothing but pay a normal-person amount of money."

"Since when do you care about how much anything costs?" I asked, pulling out a floral-print silk top and holding it up for her approval. We were browsing at BCBG, one of Ad's favorite stores, but for once she didn't like anything.

"I'm just trying to be more responsible," she said, dismissing the top with a disgusted wave. "Maybe we should try Dragonfly."

"*Dragonfly*? I didn't know you liked that store." It's not like there was anything wrong with Dragonfly; I thought their clothes were pretty cute, and best of all, cheap. But Addie rarely bought anything the typical high schooler could afford.

She shrugged. "We're just going to the brew pub, I don't need anything fancy."

"Fine with me," I said, shaking my head. Usually it was a "you really shouldn't buy all five of those dresses" situation when shopping with Addie.

Finally, we left the store with a belted cobalt-blue sweater dress for me and a winter-white blazer and sequined tank for Addie. Satisfied with our new looks, we headed upstairs to the food court to take a break.

"So A. A. is still on board for Saturday?" she said as we waited in line for our salads.

"Yes, as far as I know, he's coming. And I'd appreciate it if you didn't refer to him as 'asshole Adam,' if you don't mind. We're not in college anymore. People change."

Addie sniffed and gave me an eye roll as she took her salad from the friendly middle-aged woman we always saw when we got lunch there.

"Tell her she needs to stop going back," Addie said to the woman. "Going nuts over her ex. I've got my hands full with this one, I'm telling you!"

The server smiled at me in a motherly sort of way. "Guy troubles, hon?"

What was I supposed to tell her? *Yes, I think I'm still in love with my ex boyfriend, who may or may not be engaged?*

I settled for "You don't know the half of it!" and after

the requisite "You'll be fine, you're better off" remarks from my apparent new love life consultant, I joined Addie at a booth in the back.

Stabbing my lettuce with a little more zeal than necessary, I dug into my salad, stopping every so often to take a sip of iced tea, and refusing to make eye contact with Addie.

We continued to sit in uncomfortable silence until she finally gave my ankle a soft nudge with her pointy black flats. "Cheer up. You know I was just kidding."

"I know, Ad, but that was embarrassing. I don't need to divulge the details of my personal life to the lady in the food court and all of her customers."

"I highly doubt any of them were paying attention," she said. "And I might joke around about Adam, but I don't want you to make another mistake, that's all. He sucks, and you're sitting there obsessing about him twenty-four seven like it's freshman year all over again. News flash: it's time to come back down to earth and get over him."

I was so not in the mood to deal with Addie, and for once I snapped. "Oh, since you make such great choices in men? At least I didn't date someone who hid that he was married and had a kid for a year!"

Addie looked genuinely shocked at my comment, and on top of that, hurt. But I kept going. "Don't look at me like that. Who was there to talk you off the ledge every time you'd drive past Pat's house and see him doing yard work with his wife? Who told you that you weren't a slut when you slept with half of the town to make yourself feel better afterward? Oh yeah, me. But I go to lunch with my ex once, and according to you, *I'm* a nut job?"

"Is this really the time or place for this discussion?"

Addie asked, tears glistening in her eyes.

"I'm sorry, but I'm tired of you telling me how to live my life like you're some sort of expert. Maybe things didn't work out the first time with Adam, or the second time for that matter. Maybe we'll just be friends and nothing more ever again. Who knows? But I need to figure this out for myself."

With that, I stomped over to the trashcan, dumped my tray and left. I hadn't taken two steps out of the food court before the tears began to flow.

What the hell was wrong with me? I never snapped at people like that. Granted, Addie had been working on my last nerve, but bringing up her ex was cruel. Somewhere around Forever 21, I stopped in my tracks and rushed back to the salad joint, hoping to catch up with her and apologize. As I suspected, Addie was gone. I dialed her cell but it went directly to voicemail.

As I retraced my steps back to where I had parked, I caught a glimpse of a big-screen TV in the window of an electronics store. Oh, fantastic. It was Adam's dad with one of his ridiculous commercials. Adam's family owned a car dealership and was infamous for their totally over-the-top (and low-budget) TV spots.

A dancing panda bear entered the picture, and the words, "It's PANDA-MONIUM at Bill Shipman Ford" flashed across the screen. Oh. My. God.

I was willing to bet good money that the person in the panda suit was Adam. This at least cheered me up. I bust out laughing, imagining his face when he found out he was the one who'd have to do "the panda shuffle." At least Mr. Shipman wasn't rapping like he had been in the last commercial. The thought of the Shipman Ford rap made me laugh even harder.

People were looking at me strangely as I stood there in front of the store, laughing so hard tears were streaming down my cheeks, but I didn't even care. I was still chuckling long after the commercial was over, which was an improvement over acting like a psycho bitch.

As soon as I got home I called Addie again and it rang twice then went to voicemail. *Crap, she pressed the ignore button*, I thought. Her birthday was a few hours away and I didn't want us to be on bad terms. Plus I felt truly bad for the comment about Pat. Over the course of a few hours I called three more times with no luck, and finally decided I would just show up at her apartment.

Normally, I wouldn't turn up unannounced at someone's apartment at eleven o'clock on a Friday night, but desperate times called for desperate measures. In the eight-plus years we'd been friends, Addie and I had never had a real fight, so I felt the need to make things right with her.

I called a cab, cursing myself for wasting money. I just wasn't in the mood to search for a parking spot. A group of teenagers were running up the art museum steps as we drove past, and I could almost hear them humming the *Rocky* theme song. I sunk back in my seat and said a quick prayer that Addie would be home.

She'd always been the bossy one, which had never been a big deal; at least we balanced each other out. But I had been getting a little tired of her looking down on me for still having feelings for Adam when everyone knew she'd made terrible decisions herself.

Take Pat, for example. Addie had met him at Whole Foods, perusing the organic cereals. They'd started talking about the merits of one brand over another (don't ask me, because I've never bought organic anything), and suddenly he had her number. Pat was a few years older than we were, and although he wasn't my type, he was cute in a "rough around the edges" sort of way.

But after a couple of months, things had gotten weird. She never went to his place, because he was "in the process of moving," and he frequently disappeared without explanation for days at a time. Ad was insistent he was just busy, or her place was nicer, or it took nine months to move somewhere. I didn't have proof, and my constant suspicions had started to drive a rift between us, so I gave up. About a year into their relationship, Addie and Pat were in Atlantic City for a weekend and ran into a coworker of his, who asked how Pat's wife and daughter were doing. And that was the end of that.

We don't talk about Pat. Ever. Which was why I was rushing out of a cab, hoping she'd be home and would forgive me. "Can you wait here for a second, in case my friend's not home?" I asked the driver, winding my scarf a few more times around my neck. The sky looked like it was going to start snowing any second.

I pressed her buzzer and waited. No answer. Buzzed again. Maybe she was in the bathroom. I tried her cell but it rang and rang, eventually going to voicemail. Finally I gave up.

"She's not home; you can just drive me back," I said, feeling defeated.

As we got closer to my building, I got that sinking feeling, the one you get when you're fishing for something important in your purse and realize it's not there. I frantically felt around the lining of the bag, turned out my pockets, and checked around the cab. No keys anywhere.

"Excuse me, sir? Have you seen a set of keys lying around?"

"No, miss. Are they on the floor?" he said, not seeming overly concerned.

"Nope. They aren't anywhere back here. I'm sorry, can you take me back? I need to make sure I didn't drop them outside."

I felt officially sick to my stomach now. Even worse, the cab ride was going to be double the cost, and as if on cue, fat white flakes began to fall from the sky. After combing the street and sidewalk, there was nothing, so one twenty-dollar cab ride later, I was in the lobby of my building, shaking snowflakes out of my hair and praying that Lucy was home. A quick call confirmed she was there, the first thing that had gone right all night.

I couldn't picture Lucy ever saying something so cruel to a friend. She was one of those people who are so together it almost makes you sick, but she was also so genuine that you couldn't be anything but happy for her. Hopefully my surrogate big sister could share some words of wisdom, and my spare key.

At some point on the elevator ride upstairs, the tears started flowing. Thinking about Lucy and her charmed life made me feel even worse. Addie wasn't speaking to me, I had no idea what was up with Adam, and I missed Nan like crazy. Nothing had gone right since I lost the cameo, and everything was my own fault.

I rang her bell, and Lucy opened the door with a laugh. "I told you this would come in handy one day," she said, dropping the key into my hand. Her smile faded when she saw my tearstained face. "Liz, are you okay? What happened? Besides losing your keys, I mean."

"It's a very long story. Can I come in?"

I stepped inside Lucy's warm, bright apartment, amazed as usual at how her place had the same exact layout as mine but managed to feel like another world. Granted, two artists lived there, but from the rainbow-hued artwork covering the walls to the giant, hand-painted vase of yellow roses on the kitchen table, everything was vivid, cheerful, and loud.

Lucy walked over to the dining room table and pulled a chair out, instructing me to "sit and spill."

"Addie and I aren't speaking right now. More like she won't speak to me. I snapped at her today at lunch and told her she had horrible taste in men and to stop telling me how to live my life. I brought up her ex, the married guy. Now she won't take my calls, and so I went to her apartment tonight. That's when I realized I didn't have my key."

"Wait, so you're telling me you haven't spoken in a few hours? That's why you're so upset?"

Leave it to Lucy to put things in perspective.

"It's just we've never been mad at each other for this long. Which sounds crazy, but it's true. And her birthday is tomorrow. Today, actually, considering it's after midnight. And I made her feel like shit and now I feel like shit."

Lucy put a hand on my shoulder. "We all make people feel like shit sometimes. What counts is how you handle things afterward."

"I called, I texted, I even went over there. I don't know what else I can do to let her know that I'm sorry."

"Give her some time. If she still hasn't called by tomorrow afternoon, I'd go over again. You know she'll be home getting ready for the party, right?"

I nodded. "I just can't believe I was so cruel. It wasn't her fault that Pat was married. She had no idea. I'm the one who's knowingly pining after someone in a relationship."

Lucy didn't say anything but got up and dropped a coffee pod into her Keurig machine. "Green tea for you, right?" she said, pulling out a mug with "Number-one friend" scrawled under a picture of two little stick figure girls. The irony of that one wasn't lost on me.

She leaned against the counter and folded her arms. "So what's going on with Adam, anyway? Did you ever ask him about the whole engagement?"

"Yeah, we had lunch yesterday, actually. He said they broke things off but she refuses to accept it and keeps planning the wedding like everything's fine."

Lucy wrinkled her nose. "Do you believe him?"

"I do, actually. Jessica was always kind of nutty and she's been planning her wedding since high school. I'm pretty sure she wouldn't let a little thing like a broken engagement get in her way."

"Wow," Lucy said. "Good luck with that one."

I rolled my eyes. "Yeah, basically. And now he's coming to Addie's party, which makes things even more complicated. I'm wondering if I should just ask him to stay home."

"Hmm. Yeah, that seems like a good idea," Lucy said, taking a sip of her coffee before popping my K-cup in the machine. "If Addie's already angry with you, she's probably not going to want to have a reminder of the whole argument there at the party."

I took my phone out and started typing before I changed my mind.

"What did you say?" she asked, placing my mug on the table.

I handed her my phone and she read the text aloud. "'Long story, but Addie and I are in a fight. Sorry to bail on our plans for her party. Can we meet up next week instead and talk more about the web stuff?'"

She slid the phone back across the table. "Perfect. And it's not a lie. If she's pissed off, you might not be going to that shindig anyway."

I bit my lip and stared down into my tea, wishing I could read tea leaves or something like that professor in *Harry Potter*. Then again, I might not want to know the unpleasant truth.

"You just need to find a nice, normal, *single* guy," Lucy said. "What happened to joining a dating site? I said I'd help with your profile."

I frowned. "Believe me, I've heard the stories of people who met online and got married and all. I just don't know that it's for me. I would feel weird meeting up with randoms from the Internet."

"And how is that any different from going out with someone you meet at a bar? You'd probably know more about a guy from his online profile than you'd find out from an hour of yelling in each other's ear over a cover band."

I shrugged, finishing the last few sips of tea in a big gulp and putting my mug in the dishwasher. "Yeah, my dating life is kind of a sore subject right now."

Lucy bit her lip. "I'm sorry. It will get better, though, I promise."

"I think I'm going to head home, I'm pretty tired, but thank you so much for the key," I said, giving Lucy a hug goodbye.

"Don't worry, we all have our bitchy moments. She'll forgive you."

"I'll let you know how it goes!" I called from the hallway, eager to just lie down and relax.

I unlocked the door and sure enough, my keys were hanging on the hook in the entryway. Figures. At least they weren't in a gutter or something, but the whole night felt like a wakeup call: stop and pay attention to what's going on. What else had I missed out on while I was wallowing in my own misery, worried about Adam and our nonexistent relationship?

CHAPTER 14

ELLA

September 17, 1957

This morning, Mom asked me where Dad was, and I didn't exactly know how to tell her he passed away seven years ago. On the bright side, the details about her past are still pretty clear, so maybe the short-term loss is a temporary thing.

It's so interesting to hear about Italy, although she gets very tired and at times it's difficult to convince her to talk about it. Somehow I get the feeling that she never really got over this fiancé. She still hasn't told me who he is, although I can only assume he was this Joseph Rossi character.

It's a little hard to hear my mother talk about this other life so fondly, even if she did have a love/hate relationship with Joseph. If she'd married him, I wouldn't exist. Deep down, I wonder if she thinks it would've been better that way, but Harry thinks I'm being dramatic.

If I don't find out now, the story will be gone forever. Hopefully she'll be more inclined to relax and talk when we get her back home . . .

"Make sure you don't forget my books," Gabriella said. "Mary brought those. And don't put that on top of the blouse!"

Although she'd only been in the hospital for a few days, Gabriella's belongings had somehow piled up, and she felt it necessary to oversee Ella's packing from her hospital bed. Although it was great her mother was feeling well enough to go home, Ella also felt reluctant to leave behind the twenty-four-hour care that the hospital provided. Harry said they would pay a nurse to come in and help, but Ella had a feeling that having a stranger in the house wouldn't go over smoothly with her mother.

Gabriella had spent most of the morning doling out orders and generally being unpleasant. Ella's patience was wearing out.

"I've got it, Mom. Packing a small overnight bag isn't rocket science."

"Where's your sister?" Gabriella asked for the second time that morning. "I'd like to go stay with her. Her husband is a millionaire, you know."

Ella looked up from the quilted blue duffel bag and threw her hands in the air. "I'm sorry, but unfortunately you're stuck with me. And Mary doesn't even want her own children to live in their house, so what makes you think she'd want to take in a sick mother?"

She regretted the words as soon as they came out of her mouth, but it was too late.

Gabriella didn't even bother to respond, and instead folded her arms and went back to flipping through one of her magazines. *Great, the silent treatment.*

"I'm going to go see if they have your discharge papers ready," Ella said, grateful for an excuse to leave the room.

She came back a few minutes later with a nurse in tow, who rattled off a list of instructions as Gabriella made a show of laying out her clothing. Ella listened carefully and asked as many questions as she could. Even if they had a nurse coming, Ella had a feeling much of the day-to-day care would be up to her, and since Gabriella refused even to pretend to listen, who else would know what to do?

Once they were alone, she helped her mother dress in a bright pink floral-print sheath and a strand of pearls. Hospital or not, Gabriella had to dress her best, and she spent longer than was probably necessary arranging her hair in the cramped hospital bathroom.

"So," Ella said, after the silence had become too stifling, "you didn't get to tell me what happened after that dinner party in Italy. Did Joseph Rossi ever come to see you again?"

"Of course he did. Your mother was the most beautiful girl in Florence, you know."

"And the humblest, I bet," Ella said.

Gabriella smiled. "Something like that. Anyway, do you want to criticize or do you want to hear what happened?"

CHAPTER 15

GABRIELLA

1905

GABRIELLA WOULD NEVER have admitted it to anyone, but she dreamed about Joseph Rossi almost every night after the dinner party. In one dream, they were strolling together in Central Park, and another was a bit hazy, but she knew it involved a wedding (although for some reason her piano teacher served as maid of honor).

But the storyline was very different the morning Loretta decided it was imperative to wake her up at the ungodly hour of eleven o'clock. The maid mumbled something about Mrs. Capetti needing Gabriella downstairs to discuss something, but Gabriella felt so shaken up that she wasn't paying a bit of attention.

She couldn't remember all of the details, except for loads of noise and someone flying toward the ground, but the dream left Gabriella with such an uneasy feeling that Loretta's repeated attempts to drag her out of bed didn't even faze her.

"Sorry, Miss Ella, but I have strict orders from your

mother to bring you downstairs at once." Loretta pulled on Gabriella's arm, forcing her to sit up.

She blinked back sleep before yanking her arm away from Loretta with a humph. "Fine. Do what you will," Gabriella said, walking in slow motion toward her dressing area as Loretta frantically pulled dresses out of the closet for consideration. Gabriella stared into space as she stepped into a simple pink dress with a high neck and sat down for Loretta to fix her hair.

"You're awfully quiet this morning," Loretta said.

"The past week . . . it was confusing." Gabriella thought she saw Loretta stop for a split second, pin in hand, and smile into the mirror, but when she looked up Loretta was pinning curls as usual. She must've imagined it.

"Now why is that? My Gabriella is the most self-assured girl in New York or Florence. You've never been one to be confused about anything you want in life, now have you?"

Gabriella sighed and spritzed her favorite perfume on her wrists. "Joseph Rossi wasn't *entirely* terrible at the party. It confused me. I've always disliked him, but it made me wonder if I just don't know him very well."

"Everyone deserves a second chance," Loretta said. "I take it you haven't responded to his letters?"

Gabriella squirmed in her chair and let out a deep sigh. "Not exactly."

Joseph, in fact, had sent two letters over the past week and a half since the party. The first was thanking Gabriella for a lovely evening and offering his apologies for their differences in the past. Although it seemed sincere, the note read as overly polite and bland. She could feel the lack of emotion behind the words and felt he was just doing his duty as a gentleman, and nothing more.

The second was an invitation to meet him in the Boboli Gardens for a stroll. The letter had been passed to Loretta by a member of the Rossis' staff while she was at the market. Gabriella disliked the secretive nature of it—if he wanted to spend time together, why not invite her family to dinner, like a normal person? And, for that matter, she refused to go on secret assignations with someone she didn't even like.

Gabriella knew how far in life secret meetings got you: ruined. Lucky for her, things had never gotten to that level during her time in Capri, but it could easily have happened. She shuddered to think of how much worse the Salvatore situation would seem if she'd made that one mistake.

"What are you going to say when you see him at the ball tonight?" Loretta asked.

Gabriella shrugged. "Don't worry. I'll think of something." Joseph's parents were hosting a late-summer ball that evening, and the thought of an awkward encounter after the unanswered letters filled her with dread.

Loretta arranged one last curl and patted Gabriella's head. "Your mother's waiting, dear."

Now that she actually felt awake, Gabriella *was* a bit curious about all of this fuss so early on a Saturday. She rarely got out of bed before noon, so being fully dressed by eleven-thirty in the morning was certainly unusual. It was most likely something silly about the ball or reminding her not to ignore Joseph, she decided.

As she reached the bottom of the staircase, Gabriella felt a strange energy in the house. Doors slammed, furniture squeaked across the floors, and two maids rushed past, clutching baskets of linens. It seemed like everyone was preparing for something . . . but what? A third member of the household staff breezed past Gabriella, but not before she could grab the young woman's arm.

"What on earth is the fuss about?" Gabriella demanded.

The maid, who was about seventeen years old, turned bright red and began to stutter.

"M-m-miss, I was told not to say anything to anyone. Not even y-y-you." She slipped out of Gabriella's grasp before she dropped the stack of dishes in her hands.

"This is ridiculous," Gabriella said under her breath, gathering up her skirts and marching through the house. After an initial sweep, her mother was nowhere to be found, so Gabriella went the one place she always went when she was looking for answers: the kitchen.

Caterina, the cook, would certainly tell her what was going on. Gabriella was her favorite, and the plump, chatty woman was also the world's biggest gossip.

"Caterina! Where are you?" Gabriella stormed in and took a step back, not expecting her mother to be there. Various containers of sugar and flour, bowls filled with eggs, and fresh spices covered almost every surface of the long, simple wood table where Mrs. Capetti stood consulting with the cook over what appeared to be a list of menu items.

"Hello, Mother, I was just looking for you. Loretta told me I'm needed?"

Mrs. Capetti ignored her daughter and continued to dole out orders to the cook. Finally, she gave one last direction and turned toward Gabriella.

Expecting her mother to tell her what on earth was going on, Gabriella opened her mouth to speak, but Mrs. Capetti pushed past her. She walked with purpose into the hall, and Gabriella tried to keep pace as her mother flew upstairs and through the house. Only one person could walk faster than Gabriella, and unfortunately that was Rosa Capetti.

"Mother, please! Loretta woke me up at the crack of dawn, telling me you had to see me at once, and now you're ignoring me? Can you please just tell me what all of this nonsense is about? You'd think we were having a ball at our home and not the Rossis'."

Mrs. Capetti turned on her heel and narrowed her eyes. "Do you think that I don't know about the letters, Ella? You're not doing yourself any favors by ignoring Mr. Rossi, and you won't embarrass us at their ball tonight."

"And when have I ever embarrassed you?" Gabriella said, hand on hip. "Honestly, you treat me like such a child. I couldn't care less about Mr. Rossi, but I won't be rude to him in his own home, for God's sake."

"Enough!" Mrs. Capetti said, holding out her hand in warning. "All I wanted to tell you was please don't be surprised if Mr. Rossi proposes. Or act surprised, if you wish. Frankly, I don't care what you do, as long as you say yes. Now if you'll excuse me, I have preparations to make for your engagement dinner. Pray that it happens."

CHAPTER 16

~

GABRIELLA

ALTHOUGH GABRIELLA could've thought of a hundred places she would rather visit, she had to admit that the ambience of the Rossi home certainly felt inviting. Dozens of candles gave the room a soft glow, freshly cut pink roses in stunning crystal vases filled almost every surface, and the tinkling of a piano could be heard in the distance as the Capettis were welcomed in the foyer.

Conversation buzzed and champagne flowed in the ballroom, and Mrs. Rossi gave Gabriella a tight smile as she made her entrance. She could tell the older woman was immediately giving her the once over, taking in everything from the cut of her dress to the authenticity of her jewels.

Luckily, there was nothing about Gabriella's appearance that Mrs. Rossi could possibly criticize. If Gabriella were another girl, it might have been a different story, but if the Capetti family was known for anything, it was taste.

Gabriella's dark hair was twisted up, her grandmother's antique diamond brooch pinned in her curls. Mrs. Capetti had chosen a gown of pale-gold mousseline for her that dipped into as deep of a v as propriety would allow. The city's finest dressmaker had slaved over this creation night and day upon receiving the order, and even Mrs. Capetti was pleased with the outcome.

Gabriella smiled with her eyes, not wanting to relay her true emotions by opening her mouth and saying something unladylike.

Mrs. Rossi and Mrs. Capetti had traveled in the same circles growing up, but weren't confidantes, especially now that the Capettis resided in New York. However, that night you would've thought they were best friends.

They walked arm in arm, conspiring about something or another, most likely the marriage of their children and impending wedding plans. *Wonderful*, Gabriella thought. *A gown has probably already been commissioned.*

Fortunately, she spotted her cousins, and after a quick trip to freshen up in the dressing room, she headed over in their direction. They had been roped into a conversation with Antonio and Chiara Marino, a brother/sister duo who were distant cousins of the Rossis. They were tolerated only because of the family connection, but anyone of importance tried to avoid them at all costs. At the age of twenty-five, Chiara had yet to find a husband and instead spent most of her time nosing into others' affairs, dragging her mousy eighteen-year-old brother along as a companion.

Gabriella and Lessie had often mused that Chiara wouldn't be so bad if she made an effort to pretty herself up. But alas, the girl chose to wear her auburn hair pulled back in a severe, matronly bun (which only emphasized her large forehead) and chose skin-tight gowns that did little to flatter her round figure.

It was clear Lessie and Massimo wanted to escape, and relief was visible on their faces when Gabriella arrived.

"Cousin! You look lovely," Massimo said, kissing both of Gabriella's cheeks.

"Miss Capetti, how do you do? Now what is this I hear about you and Rossi?" Antonio asked with a raise of an un-groomed eyebrow.

"I don't know what you're talking about."

"No need to be coy, Gabriella," Chiara said, giving her a smug grin. "It's all over town. Just admit it, you've been promised to Joseph Rossi."

"With your keen eye for, erm, fashion, it's a wonder you have time to keep up with gossip at all," she said, her eyes traveling down to Chiara's outdated shoes and back up to the mounds of flesh spilling over the top and sides of her extremely low-cut navy dress.

Lessie had to turn around to disguise her giggles, and Massimo coughed loudly behind his hand.

"It would behoove you to learn the meaning of class, Miss Capetti," Chiara said, flicking her fan in Gabriella's direction and grabbing her brother's arm. Gabriella had no doubt the older girl would relish in telling the story to anyone who would listen, not that she cared. In addition to the fact that no one liked Chiara, everyone already thought Gabriella was a bit uncouth anyway, so what did it matter?

"As if anyone would take lessons in etiquette from Chiara Marino," she said, looking around to make sure no one important had witnessed her talking to Joseph's long-lost cousins. She had a reputation to uphold, after all.

"She's horrible, and her brother isn't much better," Lessie agreed. "The two of them cornered us and wanted to know all of the details about your alleged affair with Joseph Rossi. If I didn't know better, I'd think they were providing the gossip columns with their tidbits."

They were interrupted by a deep voice over Gabriella's shoulder. "Shall I have the honor of dancing with you, Miss Capetti?"

It was Joseph, wearing a slightly bemused expression and an expensive, new-looking tuxedo.

"You look as if you've just overheard something fantastically interesting," Gabriella said.

"I have, in fact," Joseph said, and turned to greet Lessie and Massimo, who made a show of excusing themselves to refresh their drinks. *Traitors*, Gabriella thought.

She held out a gloved hand and let Joseph lead her across the pale marble floors to the center of the room, making a point to shoot Chiara a look of death as they fell into step with the rest of the dancers.

The polite ladies in attendance held hushed conversations behind their fans, while the more brazen, like Chiara, stared blatantly at the pair.

"You love to be the center of attention, don't you?" she asked as they twirled around the room.

Joseph simply smiled and continued to follow the steps.

"It's perfectly understandable if you do," Gabriella said. "I'm just trying to make conversation."

They swayed back and forth in silence, and Gabriella couldn't help but feel slighted. She wasn't fond of the silent type and certainly was not used to being ignored.

Finally, sensing his companion's discontent, Joseph met her gaze. "Who wouldn't want everyone to know that the most beautiful woman in the room was on his arm? Together, no one can match us."

"You certainly have a high opinion of yourself," Gabriella said, but she couldn't help but smile.

He didn't need to say anything else; Gabriella was

enjoying listening to the bright sounds of the waltz and the satisfying swish of her skirts as they spun through the ballroom.

Joseph was an accomplished dancer, this she knew from years of balls and parties. But the last time she'd danced with Joseph she had been a young girl; it felt different now with his hand holding hers.

They floated past Mr. and Mrs. Capetti, whose stiff waltz left little to desire. As they whirled around, Gabriella noticed a small smile cross her mother's lips.

"Do you remember that Christmas before you left for New York?" Joseph asked. "I tried to get you to dance with me on Christmas Eve."

Gabriella laughed, remembering how she'd stepped on his foot so hard that they thought his toes might've been broken. "I was a lovely child, wasn't I?"

"A lovely child, and an even lovelier woman," he said, briefly removing his hand from her shoulder blade to spin her in a graceful walk-around turn.

Normally, Gabriella would have rolled her eyes, but she couldn't force herself do it. The moment was too nice to ruin things.

"So, I take it you didn't receive my letters?" Joseph said, his smile suddenly fading.

Gabriella bit her lip. "I'm terribly sorry, but I didn't find it appropriate to meet with you in secret. Regardless of what you think of me, I do have a reputation to consider."

Joseph raised an eyebrow. "You didn't seem to have a problem going off with Salvatore in Capri."

Gabriella would have stormed off at that very moment, but causing a scene probably wasn't the best of ideas. Instead she gritted her teeth and continued to dance.

"Let's not discuss Capri," she said. "I'm simply

making a point that you could have called on me in a proper, gentlemanly fashion to arrange a meeting."

"I realize this, but it was imperative for me to speak to you before tonight. Alone."

"And why is that?" Gabriella asked, tilting her head to the side and pursing her lips.

Before she could get an answer, the song came to an end. Gabriella curtsied toward her partner, and Joseph took a step away from her, bowing slightly.

"If you'll excuse me," he said, "my mother is beckoning me to come say hello to our dear neighbors. Thank you for the dance."

Gabriella walked away with her head held high, even though she felt as if she'd been slapped in the face. *If he thinks I'm that lovely and memorable, why is he running off as if someone had lit a match under his trousers?* As she crossed the room to locate Lessie, Gabriella spotted her mother watching with interest from a nearby corner, no doubt blaming her for whatever had caused Joseph to leave. *Wonderful.*

She turned her head and hurried over toward Lessie, who was engaged in an animated conversation with the beautiful, shiny-haired daughter of one of her father's friends.

Gabriella held her fan up to her face and mouthed "over here, now" while giving it a half-hearted flick or two. Fans were terribly useful in this sort of situation; she didn't want anyone to see her distress, and especially not Miss Blonde Locks.

Lessie said her goodbyes and joined Gabriella behind a large column trimmed in gold leaf.

"Why are we hiding back here?" she asked, looking around for clues.

Gabriella sighed and leaned in closer. "Since you

weren't paying attention, I'll fill you in on Mr. Rossi's intentions. He flattered me left and right and then left me standing there on the dance floor while he went to talk to his elderly neighbors."

"Why on earth would he do that? I thought he was keen on proposing to you."

"His behavior is puzzling. First he hates me, then he wants to go on a moonlight stroll and talk about being cordial. . . The next thing I know, my mother is warning about a proposal but he disappears?" Gabriella said. "He also mentioned Salvatore in quite a negative manner. Again."

"But Gabriella, I thought you hated Joseph, too?"

Gabriella's stomach fluttered, and she fanned herself a few times, hoping to distract Lessie from seeing her flushed cheeks. "Of course I do. I'm just pointing out that his behavior is terribly rude."

"Well, yes. It is a bit confusing. But maybe he doesn't want to seem outwardly eager in front of everyone?"

"I suppose. Or perhaps my mother is just mad?"

The pair watched as Joseph excused himself from the conversation with his family across the room and headed in their direction.

"Maybe you were overreacting, as usual," Lessie said with a smirk as he approached.

"Miss Giardano, would you mind terribly if I escorted your cousin for a walk in the garden?"

Lessie told him she didn't mind in the slightest, and all eyes were on the couple as they left the room, which for some reason Gabriella found to be hilarious. A small chuckle escaped despite her best efforts to hold her composure, and to Gabriella's surprise, Joseph started laughing, too.

"It won't be long before they take out their telescopes, I'm afraid," Gabriella said, rolling her eyes.

"Don't worry, my mother probably has spies in the garden taking notes."

"Only in the garden? What about on the rooftops?"

"Remind me not to let our mothers chat too often," Joseph said, guiding her over to a bench off to their right once they were outside. It was far enough away from the house to seem secluded, but close enough that prying eyes could watch them through the back windows. Gabriella thought as much as Joseph joked about their lack of privacy, he truly must enjoy the spotlight.

Gabriella took a deep breath of the muggy, lavender-scented night air and sat down with her hands folded in her lap, waiting for the inevitable.

Joseph cleared his throat and took her gloved hand. "Gabriella, I know you don't care much for me, but I think, in time, maybe your feelings could change."

He took a small box out of his pocket and procured a dainty cameo pendant on a gold chain. For a second, Gabriella's heart sunk, which was ridiculous, because she didn't even want to be married to him.

"I bought this for you last summer," Joseph said. "It was before . . . I didn't know you cared for Salvatore then. The night I was going to give this to you, I saw you on the balcony with him." He paused and looked down; it was obvious the memory was still painful. It was also the first time she'd seen him display any sort of vulnerability.

Gabriella's mouth dropped open. "I don't understand," she said. "You were horrible to me that summer. You purposely smeared gelato on my new dress, for God's sake! You're trying to tell me you've always had romantic feelings for me?"

"Now calm down, Ella. Do you want the entire city to hear?"

"Would it make a difference? It seems I'm the last one in Florence to find out. Even your horrible cousins knew." She could almost feel the blood boiling through her veins. Why hadn't he told her before? She didn't know why, but him pursuing her as some sort of unrequited love interest felt entirely different than the idea of their parents arranging a sensible marriage. The latter almost made more sense. Love? That raised the stakes.

"Please don't be upset," he said, taking her other hand and squeezing them both tightly. Gabriella immediately dropped both from his grasp.

"I'm sorry, but this is far too much information to digest at once," she said, standing up and turning toward the house.

Joseph stood too and reached out for her arm. "I always thought you were the most beautiful girl I'd ever seen. Forgive me; this is probably a surprise for you. I'm sorry."

Images of Capri raced through Gabriella's head. It did make sense, once she thought about it. Hiding her purse so she'd miss the boat trip, for example. She'd been forced to spend the entire day in the hotel with Joseph (and he'd made a show of telling her parents he'd look after her) while Salvatore went off with the rest of the party. Joseph had always flirted with her before, and although she thought he was boring and a bit too pretty for her taste, he was never exactly rude until after she developed feelings for Salvatore.

"I've never been able to figure out what I could have possibly done for you to dislike me so much. I suppose this explains it."

Joseph clicked open the latch on the cameo and held it out to show her that it was actually a locket.

"I've been saving this since then, hoping I could give it to you one day. Or that you'd talk to me without pushing me into a fountain."

She took the necklace and examined it, noting there wasn't an inscription or a photo in the locket, which in her mind defeated the purpose.

"It's quite lovely," she said, pressing it back into his palm.

"Please, take the necklace. When you're ready, there's something I'd like to have engraved inside of it. Can I put it on for you?"

Being in a state of shock, Gabriella was for once, speechless. Finally she nodded and tipped her head down so he could fasten the gold clasp around her slim neck.

"There's something else I need to say to you," Joseph said, his eyes darting back to the house, where Gabriella was certain she saw faces in the window. "Our parents have spoken about an engagement."

She laughed. "Of course they have. What do you think I expected tonight? A song-and-dance routine?"

Joseph cracked a smile. "But what I want to tell you is that I'm not proposing. Not now. It doesn't feel right."

Her shoulders relaxed, but just barely. "For once I agree with you, Mr. Rossi. But what are we supposed to tell our parents? My family wasted no time in setting up their expectations, and I'm sure yours didn't, either."

Joseph's closed his eyes for a moment and sighed. "I'm going to tell them you fainted from the heat right after I gave you the cameo and insist they take you home at once. That will buy us some time, at least."

"You think that's going to work? My mother is going to call me an actress and probably drag me back to your house by my hair. And while I appreciate this," she said, gesturing to the cameo, "please do not take my acceptance of the necklace as a sign I'll accept a proposal from you now, or ever."

"All I'm asking is for you to try to get to know me. I don't want your hand to be forced, and I won't be doing myself any favors by having an unhappy bride. But our parents aren't going to stop until this happens. So you might as well get used to the idea."

"Then I'll just leave town early. We're going back to New York in a month anyway," Gabriella said. She grabbed her skirts and marched up to the house, fighting back tears as her heels clacked against the stone walkway. No one told her whom she had to marry, especially not Joseph Rossi. Even if he was starting to grow on her for reasons she couldn't explain to herself.

Unlike her short-legged brother, Joseph caught up to her quickly. He grabbed Gabriella's arm and she whirled around, shooting him an exasperated, slightly tearstained look. His features softened, and he tucked one of her frizzed curls behind her ear.

Gabriella's heart raced, and she took a deep breath. "What do you think you could possibly say to change my mind, Mr. Rossi?" And with that, Joseph pulled her in and kissed her until her head was spinning, any thoughts of running away slipping from her brain.

CHAPTER 17

LIZ

ADDIE'S BIRTHDAY started out quite the opposite of a steamy night in Florence—bright and cold, the night's snowfall shimmering blindingly as I walked to Buzz, my favorite neighborhood coffee shop. Luckily, I'd remembered my red D&G sunglasses, a birthday gift from Addie. It made me sad knowing we weren't even speaking on her special day, but I fully intended on tracking her down and making things better before the party. Either that, or I'd show up to the shindig anyway.

She wouldn't be able to ignore me, and I doubted that she'd make a scene in front of her friends and family. I was also counting on her downing a few drinks before I got there, which would make Happy Drunk Addie more inclined to forgive and forget.

A rush of warm air, cheery piped-in music, and the inviting smell of roasting beans welcomed me as I walked into the coffee shop, stomping my bright-pink rubber boots on the mat. A hot cup of coffee and a good book were just what I needed to start the day on a high note. I had an appointment after lunch with a hot new boutique on the Main Line that I'd been dying to get my jewelry into, and needed all the good karma I could get.

As I stood in line, humming along to the Mariah

Carey Christmas album, I thought I heard someone say my name. I figured they must've been talking to someone else and kept bopping my head to the music until I felt a tap on the shoulder.

I turned around and saw Justin, the guy I'd run into at O'Connell's, standing in front of the door. I hadn't really thought much about the encounter after losing Nan's cameo and the drama with Adam (other than hoping I might run into Justin on the elevator), but suddenly I felt my mood lift. "Oh, it's you!" I said, and instantly wished time had a rewind button.

"Is that a bad thing?" he asked, joining me in line. His cheeks were flushed from the cold and he looked dorky-cute in a snowflake-patterned knit hat and a bright-yellow puffer vest.

"No, no," I said with a laugh, holding out my mittened hand to shake his. "Sorry, I'm not quite awake yet."

Relief visible on his face, he smiled. "No prob. I'm not a morning person, either. Is this place any good? Joe in 6A told me about it."

I told him I went there almost every day, and we chatted about the building and how he was adjusting to the move. Justin had been transferred by his company, a large pharmaceutical firm, after living in Miami for most of his life, and was slowly getting used to life in the Northeast.

"My mom knitted me this hat because she was worried about the cold," he said with a lopsided grin, "just so you don't think I'm into Christmas sweaters or something like the dude in *Bridget Jones's Diary*."

I reached out and gave the hat a little tug so it fell over his eyes. "Actually, I dig the hat. Not many men can pull off the whole Nordic look. And I appreciate a guy who can reference *Bridget Jones*, by the way."

"I have two sisters. Comes with the territory."

I laughed. "It's okay if you like Bridget; I won't tell."

Wait a minute, was I flirting? Maybe Lucy was right, and all I needed was to meet someone new. And single. Like Justin. He was definitely cute and funny, and hopefully not just making friendly small talk with a new neighbor. *I'd like to do more than make small talk with him, that's for sure.*

The next thing I knew, Justin was tapping my shoulder again. "You're up," he said, and I could tell he was holding back a laugh. Who knows how long I had been standing there, staring into space.

"Thanks," I said, feeling my cheeks turn pink. Perhaps inappropriately daydreaming about your new neighbor while you were supposed to be placing an order wasn't the greatest way to make a first impression.

I stood off to the side and waited for my drink as Justin paid for a cappuccino, handing the barista a Miami Hurricanes travel mug.

"Environmentally conscious, or showing your school spirit?" I asked once he joined me.

"Hmm. How about sixty percent A and forty percent B?"

"That's a very precise answer," I said, taking my warm paper cup and slipping a cardboard sleeve over it.

"My brother goes to Miami, so I follow their team, but to be honest, I'm not a huge sports person. The mug was a gift."

I took a tentative first sip of my drink. "Fair enough. I should probably get one of those so I stop spilling coffee on myself when I walk down the street."

He laughed. "Hey, I don't know if you're in a rush, but I was going to hang out for a little while if you want to join me. I mean, if you're not busy or anything."

"Sure, I'd love to," I said. "I was planning to hang out for a while, too."

We spotted an empty couch and before I knew it, almost an hour had passed. Justin and I talked about everything from our jobs to our building's weirdo superintendent to our shared dislike of candy canes. I was surprised how disappointed I felt when he looked at his watch.

"Hey, I'm really sorry but I have to get going. The cable guy is supposed to be over between noon and four, and I already missed him once. You can only watch so many *Lost* DVDs before you go nuts."

"No problem. I should be going myself. It's my best friend's birthday and I was planning on heading over to surprise her."

"Well, tell her some guy she doesn't know said happy birthday," Justin said, standing up to stretch. I definitely took notice of the biceps hidden under his fleece as he offered me a hand and pulled me up from the couch with zero effort.

Maybe I was blinded by the hot arms, but suddenly I blurted out, "Will you be around tonight? A bunch of us are going out for birthday drinks in Manayunk around ten o'clock. You should come."

"Yeah, for sure, if your friend wouldn't mind," Justin said. "I wouldn't want to butt in on your party."

"No, no, it's totally fine. She told me to bring anyone I wanted. And you did say you wanted to learn more about the city, right?"

He smiled. "That I did. So do you want to ride over together? I totally got lost the last time I drove out there."

We exchanged numbers and gave each other a semi-awkward hug goodbye, but at least it was awkward in the "we just met and obviously like each other, but aren't sure what to do yet" kind of way.

I braced myself for the cold as I headed outside, but this time it felt refreshing. I *really* must've had a good time with Justin, or else there was something seriously wrong. Snow and I were not friends.

On the way back to my building, I thought about how it had worked out for the best that I'd texted Adam not to come. He'd said it was fine and suggested meeting on Tuesday after work to go through the website. Part of me wondered how the night would've played out if I'd gone through with bringing Adam instead, or (yikes) both guys.

Even Caitlin never showed up to a party with two dates, or sort-of dates, or whatever Adam and Justin were to me.

Comparing the two of them, it was clear Justin was exactly what I'd asked for. No live-in-girlfriend-slash-ex-fiancée. No complicated history. Attractive. Decent job. He definitely ticked all the boxes, at least on paper. But even if our history was complicated and sometimes messy, I couldn't completely shake those feelings for Adam. I hoped Addie's party would give me some answers. Maybe I just needed a new reason to "stop going back."

I hurried back to the apartment to grab my car, head to Addie's, and stop by Target before my boutique meeting. Miraculously, I found a metered spot just down the street from Ad's apartment that I pulled right into without having to cause a parallel parking scene by backing in and out five times. I took this as another sign that it was going to be a good day.

My pulse quickened as I pressed Ad's buzzer. I knew she wasn't going to be happy to see me. I sighed with relief when her voice came across the intercom.

"Yeah? Who is it?"

"It's me," I said. "Please let me up. I'm so sorry about what happened at the mall."

She didn't respond, but I heard the soft click of the door, granting me access to the building. I picked away at my cuticles as I took the elevator up to her floor, hoping there wouldn't be a scene. After I knocked three times, she finally opened her front door, dressed in yoga pants and a pink hoodie. She narrowed her eyes, but stepped back and let me in.

"I'll start," I said. "I didn't mean to say those things to you, I was just upset and mixed up about Adam and everything just kind of erupted."

She nodded, and sat down on one of the barstools at her kitchen island, patting the one next to her. I took a seat and tossed my purse on the concrete countertop, not bothering to remove my coat. I figured I wouldn't be there long.

"Your little outburst was pretty messed up," she finally said. "You know what I went through with Pat, and comparing that to going back to Adam is totally different."

"I know, and again, I'm sorry," I said. "It was wrong and I shouldn't have brought him up."

I hesitated for a moment, not wanting to make things worse, but realized that I needed to get something off my chest, and I might not have another opportunity to clear the air.

"To be honest, though, I feel like you sometimes try to rule my love life, telling me who I can and can't go out with . . . it's like you're my mom. You aren't always going to like the decisions I make, but as my best friend I need you to try and be there for me even when you don't agree."

"I don't try to rule your life, Liz," she said. "I just try to get you to stop being an idiot about Adam. The guy is engaged, or used to be. Whatever. The point is, he has a girlfriend and you're working pretty closely with him on your business and almost kissing on the street. Don't you see anything wrong with this?"

I put my head in my hands. "Yes. And no. It's complicated. I don't expect you to understand, but I do want to be his friend, if nothing else."

"Fine," she said. "But he'd better not cause drama tonight."

"Don't worry. He won't be there."

She raised her eyebrows and I could tell she was fighting back a smile. "Interesting. Why?"

"I didn't want to cause problems and figured this is your day to celebrate, so I told him not to come," I said, which triggered my memory. "Oh crap, speaking of, I didn't even say happy birthday. I'm the worst friend ever." I reached over and gave her a quick hug.

"I guess I'll forgive you this time," she said, patting my back. "After all, who else is going to put up with me?"

I pulled away and laughed, wiping a stray tear away before she could see it.

"And for what it's worth, I guess I shouldn't have called you crazy in front of everyone in the food court."

Apologies were rare from Addie, so I figured I'd take what I could get.

"Thanks," I said. "Oh, and by the way, I invited someone else to come tonight. That new neighbor I told you about, Justin."

"Wait a minute, stop the presses," she said, hopping off her stool. "This is just what I wanted to hear. But please tell me he's not engaged, too."

"No, he is not engaged. I mean, as far as I know," I said. "He definitely flirted with me at Buzz this morning, though. He just moved here from Miami and doesn't know anyone in the city."

Addie nodded with approval. I was sure the wheels were already spinning in her head, trying to come up with ways to make sure this worked. "So what's this guy like?"

"He's pretty cute, kind of laid back. Seems like more of a jeans-and-sneakers type. Super easy to talk to, but we'll see what happens."

Addie grabbed a rhinestone tiara with the words "Birthday Girl," and plopped it on her head, doing a little spin. "Well, looks like we have something else to celebrate."

AS I GOT READY for the party, I thought of Nonni Gabriella and how she'd been hurt by that guy Salvatore. If she could get over him, I felt like maybe I could get over Adam eventually, too. I'd always thought love was so cut-and-dried: boy meets girl, they date, boy proposes to girl, big white dress, they live happily ever after. No one threw in "boy dumps girl, girl dumps boy, then boy proposes to someone else, boy dumps other girl, then tries to 'just be friends' with girl number one while still dating girl number two."

I took a look in the mirror and examined the results of my handiwork. The dress, thanks to its handy cinching belt, made my waist look smaller, and my usually haphazard hair was tamed into a stylishly messy side fishtail braid. I'd even used liquid eyeliner, which Lucy had taught me how to do after I'd gotten home from Addie's place earlier that day. The overall impression was very me, just slightly sleeker.

In fact, I'd have to credit my mini makeover in part to the success of my meeting at Dressed, the newest store that would be carrying LM Designs. The owner had said she "loved my whole look," and thought designers should be reflective of their brands, just like I was. I'd made a mental note to step my fashion game up a notch moving forward, and bought a cute new chevron-print blouse before I left the store with my order in hand. All I needed was a few more hot stores like that—especially ones the Main Line momarazzi frequented—and I'd be set.

I took a deep breath, grabbed my clutch, and walked the short distance to Justin's apartment, just six units down from mine. I heard the clicking sound of paws against hardwood and a deep bark that sounded like it came from a dog weighing more than Addie. *Great,* I thought. I loved animals, but dogs kind of freaked me out, especially big ones. I could thank Nan for that fear. My hands shook a bit as I pressed his buzzer.

The door opened to reveal a freshly shaved Justin and a tiny pug that looked as if it was about fifteen pounds soaking wet. I laughed, the tension leaving my shoulders, and stepped inside.

"I thought you had some sort of attack dog hidden in here."

"Nah," he said, giving me a quick hug. "Bo just likes to think he's a big dog." Bo put his front paws on my leg and wagged his tail, tongue hanging out the side of his mouth. Despite my anti-dog platform, I had to admit he was kind of cute.

That was until his claws ripped a hole in my new black tights.

"Bo! Bad boy! Get down," Justin yelled, picking up the squirming dog and carrying him into the kitchen. He closed a baby gate and Bo sat behind it, gazing at us pitifully from behind the bars.

"I'm so sorry, I'll replace them. He was just trying to be friendly, but unfortunately he gets a little too excited sometimes."

I looked down at my ruined tights, trying to remember if I even had another black pair.

"It's not a big deal," I said. "Don't worry about it. I'll just run home and change."

"Why don't I just come with you? We can leave from there."

I agreed, and we headed back to my place, but at that point I had a bad feeling about the whole night.

"So how was the rest of your afternoon?" he asked, leaning against the wall as I unlocked the door. He looked very J. Crew-catalog in a navy wool pea coat over his striped button-up.

"It was good. Addie, the birthday girl, and I sort of got in a fight yesterday, so I went to her place to talk it out. I was a little nervous that she'd still be mad and not want me to come tonight, but we made up."

"Yikes," he said. "What happened?"

I went with a vague, "It's a long story."

"Aren't they all?"

I grinned. "Especially when it comes to Addie. I'll be right back. Have a seat."

Justin had no problem making himself at home, plopping down on the couch and picking up the copy of *Entertainment Weekly* I had laying on the coffee table.

"Wow, Britney is still around?" he called out. Someone needed a celebrity news intervention.

After realizing my only other options were an old pair of red fishnets from Halloween or 1980s-style shiny, dark tan stockings my mom had given me, I threw on a pair of black leggings under the dress, switched from heels to boots, and decided to call it a day.

"Sorry," I said, peeking my head into the living room. "Wardrobe malfunction."

"I'm the one who should be apologizing. Damn dog, trying to mess up my date."

Date? My heart skipped a beat, and I tried to keep the glee out of my voice as I sat on the couch next to him. "No big deal about the tights. So anyway, this is my place. I'd give you a tour, but it wouldn't be very exciting since we have exactly the same floor plan."

Justin laughed. "Yeah, I thought it looked kind of familiar. Anyway, we should probably get going, right?"

He extended his hand and we headed out the door, arm in arm. Maybe Addie was right and the night wouldn't be so bad, after all.

CHAPTER 18

LIZ

JUSTIN TOOK MY ARM as we walked into the dimly lit bar. In the summer months, the crowd would gather outside on the deck, overlooking the not-exactly-scenic canal while tipsy girls danced to the latest and greatest cover bands. But tonight, couples clustered at tables near a roaring fire in the back, and an acoustic guitar player was set up in the corner, singing Oasis's "Wonderwall."

Justin sung along quietly to himself, and I looked up at him and smiled. He actually wasn't a bad singer, which caught me by surprise.

"I love this song," he said, cheeks turning pink after being caught.

"Oh, there's my friend," I said, pointing toward Addie, who held court at the far end of the bar.

She was sitting atop a barstool and her brother, his wife, a few cousins, coworkers, and assorted friends were standing around her. I spotted Renee and Caitlin, for once happy to see them. Addie has always had a very eclectic assortment of friends who come in and out of her life in cycles, and I didn't know most of the people who had showed up for her party.

Addie wore her tiara and new outfit from our disastrous shopping trip, along with some sort of flashing button pinned to her lapel. She sipped a Cosmopolitan and seemed to be telling a good story, making exaggerated hand gestures and waving her arms around so intensely she almost fell off the stool. I checked the time: 10:22 p.m. It was going to be a long night if she was already on her way to Drunkville.

I saw Addie look Justin up and down as soon as we approached.

"Happy birthday, Ad!" I said, cutting my way through the group to say hello. She remained perched on her stool, but leaned down to give me a hug, revealing some serious cleavage.

"And this must be Justin," she said, reaching across me to shake his hand.

"It's nice to meet you. Are you having a good birthday so far?"

She paused for a moment, taking in the scene around her. "I am, actually. It got off to a bad start, but I think it's definitely improved."

Addie doled out introductions to the rest of the group, and Justin started talking about the upcoming Eagles game with Addie's brother. I found this funny, considering Justin was neither a local nor an NFL fan, but I took this as my opportunity to grab a beer and pull my best friend aside for a debrief.

"So, what do you think?"

"Very cute," Addie said, throwing subtlety out the window and turning around to give him another good once over. "He seems normal, at least."

This was a compliment coming from her, so I smiled. "Yeah, I feel super comfortable around him even though we barely know each other."

Addie raised her drink, exposing the red string

she'd started wearing on her wrist years ago during the whole kabbalah craze. "Cheers to you."

We clinked glasses just as Caitlin and Renee came over to join us.

"So, what are we toasting?" Renee asked.

"My birthday, obviously," Addie said, smiling at me.

Caitlin took a sip of beer and turned to look at Justin. "So where'd you meet? He's hot."

Considering Caitlin's reputation, I wasn't exactly thrilled about her comment. Even though I could tell Justin probably wasn't the type of guy to show up with one girl and leave with another, I didn't know him *that* well yet, and Caitlin definitely was the type to go home with whomever she felt like.

"He lives in my building," I said, not caring to add in any more details.

"Oh, cool. Good luck. I know the whole Adam thing has been pretty hard on you," she said.

Behind me, I could hear Addie's brother intensely discussing football, and I excused myself to save Justin from being stuck into an hour-long convo about the Eagles . . . and also to save myself from being pitied about Adam.

"So what's the verdict? Are we going to win?" I asked, pulling him aside.

"Nah, don't think so. Not that I really care, though," he said. "But sports are always a good icebreaker."

"Hey now, don't knock my team," I said.

Justin cocked his head to the side. "Hmm, I didn't peg you for a big football fan."

"I grew up going to Eagles games," I said. "My grandpa had season tickets for years, and when he passed away, my Nan kept paying for them so her grandkids could go. I know you aren't from Philly, but it's a big deal to have Eagles season tickets. There's a waiting list of like fifty thousand people, and people almost never give up their seats, so do the math."

"So you're saying if I sign up now, I might get tickets when I'm a grandpa?"

I laughed. "Basically."

"You must have a pretty cool grandma, then." Justin said. "But why aren't you going tomorrow?"

"My sister and her fiancé have the tickets for this game. They're taking my parents with them," I said, trying to keep the annoyance out of my voice. I'd been dying to go to this game since it was against the Cowboys, our ultimate rivals.

"Bummer. So I guess your grandma is a hardcore fan? It's got to be expensive to shell out for four seats."

"Nan hated football, actually. She just took us because it was something her grandkids liked to do. I think it made her feel close to my grandpa." I paused. "She passed away a few weeks ago."

"Oh, wow. I'm *so* sorry. Now I feel like an ass," he said. "Are you okay?"

I reassured him it was fine; there was no way he could've known. Justin seemed to relax a little after that.

"Were you close?" he asked.

"Yeah, we talked every single day and went on trips and stuff together all the time. It's really hard not having her around, especially since my mom and I don't always see eye-to-eye. I always went to Nan for advice."

Justin reached over and gave me a hug. "I'm sorry, I know what you mean. I lost my grandpa last year and it was rough."

"Thanks," I said, not wanting to pull away. He was warm and smelled nice and had good hair. *Please let this work.*

We chatted for a bit about our families, and I told him about the cameo.

"Have you tried any pawnshops?" he said. "I mean if someone was at a bar and found something that looked like it was worth money, maybe they sold it."

"I haven't, actually, but you're right," I said. "There are tons of stores around here that buy gold and stuff." The idea gave me a glimmer of hope that maybe the necklace was still out there, but also made me feel like an idiot that I hadn't thought of it myself.

"Exactly," he said. "Don't give up on looking if it's that important to you. You never know what could happen."

I nodded; he was right. I couldn't believe I'd just sat back and wallowed in my own pity, figuring it was gone and there was nothing I could do about it. Sending Adam to look at the bar hardly counted as trying.

Renee came over and started passing around shots; apparently they were called "little beers." I had no idea what was in mine, but the shot did look like a tiny beer, complete with a foamy top.

"To Addie," she said, raising her shot glass in the air. "Happy birthday, chica!"

We clinked our shots together and downed the strong, butterscotch-flavored liquor.

"Not bad, although that tasted *nothing* like beer," Justin said, taking my shot glass and putting it on the bar along with his. "I'm gonna get another drink, want anything?"

I told him I was good and turned to watch the performer, who Caitlin informed me was named Chase McCoy (apparently she had slept with him a few years ago). I got excited when I heard the first few chords of "Crash," one of my favorite Dave Matthews Band songs, and was soaking up the moment, singing along to myself, when I felt a hand on my shoulder. Thinking it was Justin, I turned to my right with a big smile, but I was oh so wrong. It was Adam.

I stood there for a moment in shock, not quite believing what was happening.

"Fancy seeing you here," he said, while I continued to stare at him blankly. "How about hello?"

I scrunched up my face. "Sorry. Just didn't expect to see you tonight. Addie and I were fighting earlier, which is why I sent you that text. I figured she'd still be pissed and not want me to show up."

"No big deal. I figured I could use a guys' night and my boys wanted to come here," he said.

Lie. I knew Adam had always hated this particular bar. *Did he think I was trying to get out of seeing him and figured he'd show up anyway?*

"Who's your friend?" Justin asked, touching the small of my back. I tried not to panic. There was no time to ask Addie What Would Madonna Do, but I knew what Bridget Jones would do. *Introduce people with thoughtful details.*

"This is my ex-boyfriend, Adam," I said. "We went to college together and he's a freelance graphic designer. Adam, this is Justin. He recently moved into my building from Miami and works in pharmaceutical marketing."

"Nice to meet you," Justin said, giving Adam a just-a-little-too-vigorous handshake.

"Miami, huh? I guess you're into the party scene," Adam said, trying to subtly flex his fingers behind his back. I assumed the handshake was worse than I thought.

"Nah. I never liked any of those clubs. I'm not big on paying thirty-dollar cover charges and trying to impress a bunch of wannabes."

"I guess you're fitting right in here in Philly already. How long have you guys known each other?" Adam looked back and forth between the two of us as if to decipher the seriousness of our relationship.

"We just met last week," I said. "I thought I'd show Justin around the city and introduce him to some people."

"Interesting. Well, I'm going to get back to my friends. Call me about Tuesday." Adam reached in for a long hug and kissed my cheek, leaving the faint scent of his aftershave behind. I watched him walk away, feeling like I'd been dropped into the *Sex and the City* scene where Carrie's on a date with a Yankees player and runs into Mr. Big at the bar. Why was it so hard to let go?

"Sorry about that," I said to Justin with a sheepish smile. There was no way Adam could've known I was coming to the party with a date, but it felt like he had some sort of ESP anyway, just when I was trying to move on.

He shrugged. "I take it there are some unresolved feelings there?"

I looked down at my glass. "Not really. It's . . . complicated. We recently got back in touch and we're trying to be friends again, but it's easier said than done, I guess. He's creating all of the design materials for my jewelry business, though, which is a huge help."

"Gotcha."

"Adam lives with his girlfriend," I added for good measure, just in case he thought there was any funny business going on.

"Believe me, I get it. I'm friends with a couple of exes from back home. Mostly just on Facebook, but it can be a little weird reading about their fiancés and stuff."

"Yeah, Adam was engaged to a girl I knew from high school and they broke it off, but just got back together again. I was never a big fan of hers, so it's not like I plan on going on double dates with them," I said. "I don't know, maybe it's one of those things where you run into someone so you feel obligated to talk again, but eventually you just go back to being strangers."

Justin nodded. "That makes sense. Sometimes people just grow apart, and when you try to force things, it's unnatural."

"Anyway, enough about him," I said, eager to change the subject. "What do you think about the bar?"

"Not bad," Justin said, taking a sip of his beer. "Totally different scene than Miami, obviously, but it's more my style. I'd rather go somewhere kind of laid back where you can actually have a conversation."

"Philly is glad to have you." *And so am I*, I thought. Despite Adam showing up, and the minor incident with the dog, it was one of the best dates I'd been on in ages. Hanging out with Justin made me feel relaxed but excited at the same time, a hard combination to find.

Justin clinked glasses with me, and we stood there, chatting with Addie and enjoying our drinks for a while. Out of the corner of my eye I spotted Adam and his two friends at a nearby table facing the stage. If he'd stared at us any longer, I think his eyes might have popped out of his damn head. *You're doing nothing wrong. He's the one with the girlfriend.*

The infamous Chase McCoy announced he was taking a break before his next set, and one of my favorite '80s songs, "Let the Music Play," blared over the bar's speakers. Justin took my hand and twirled me around.

"Care to dance?"

We joined Addie and a few others in front of the stage to create a makeshift dance floor. Justin wasn't a great dancer, but what he lacked in moves he made up for in sheer effort. No one ever said I was a candidate for *Dancing with the Stars*, anyway.

Addie shimmied her way over to us and gave Justin a high five.

"I love me a man who can dance!" He laughed and joined her in demonstrating various ridiculous moves, including "the lawn mower" and my personal favorite, "the shopping cart."

We were having so much fun pushing invisible shopping carts that I nearly forgot about our audience . . . until Justin spun me around so fast that I nearly crashed into Adam's friend. Luckily, I regained my composure and managed not to make eye contact as I rushed back over to my date.

"Thanks for inviting me tonight," he said, pulling me closer. We were inches away from Adam's table, but I didn't care anymore.

"I'm glad you're here," I said. I leaned in, and he pressed his lips to mine. The room seemed to disappear for a moment. We eventually pulled away and I noticed two things: Addie giving me a thumbs-up over Justin's shoulder, and Adam's back as he walked toward the door.

CHAPTER 19

ELLA

September 21, 1957

Now that she's home with us, Mom seems to be in much better spirits, but I wouldn't say she's improved much, memory-wise. Harry keeps telling me she might only get worse, but I guess I keep hoping that having her out of the hospital will spark some sort of recovery.

The kids were thrilled when they found out their grandma was coming home, but I don't think we prepared them enough for her condition. Lily asked me why Nonni was acting funny and it just about broke my heart. I feel so unprepared to deal with all of this, and the silly pamphlet they gave me at the hospital was of no use. As if a pamphlet could tell me how to explain to my children why their grandma doesn't always know what's going on.

Selfishly, I wish Mom could have gone to live with Mary or one of the boys, but we all know that would never happen. I probably shouldn't have pointed that out to Mom, but I guess it just got to me. They're too busy living it up to deal with an ailing parent. Mary came down to the hospital from New York twice and acted as if she deserved a medal for it. Meanwhile, I'm the one who's had to deal with everything.

As soon as the time comes for a will to be read, I'm sure they'll have plenty of time to visit.

Mom and I have never been close. How am I the one who wound up being with her through this? Harry thinks I should take the opportunity to try to bond with Mom before it's too late . . .

Ella poured herself a cup of tea and breathed a sigh of relief. It was nice to not have to worry about going to the hospital, but the stress of having her mother at home weighed on her even more. Harry was outside entertaining the kids for a few hours before he had to go to La Bella, and Gabriella was napping again. This meant precious alone time, and Ella wasn't about to give up the opportunity.

She'd just finished baking two apple pies for the "to-go" pastry case at La Bella, and took a moment to admire how perfect the latticework looked, shining with sugar crystals. Ella loved the precision that baking required; there wasn't much room for happy accidents like in cooking. The quiet sound of flour pouring into a measuring cup, or the satisfaction she got from the perfect consistency of batter—those were the things that calmed her down after a hectic day. A bit too much salt could ruin the recipe . . . and lately Ella felt like her house was full of Morton's.

She longed for those honeymoon days, choosing just the right curtains for her new office or curling up with Harry on the sofa and listening to their favorite records after a long night together at La Bella. They still shared the same love and companionship, but now Ella was long asleep by the time he got home from the restaurant, and she missed that sense of camaraderie from working to build the restaurant together. Mary had once told her marriage was like a lemon pastry: sweet and tart at the same time. Now she understood.

As she put away the kids' tiny cups in the cupboard, she reminded herself how badly she'd ached for a family and how long it had taken for that dream to happen. *Be grateful*, she told herself. Maybe all she needed was more quiet time like this to recharge.

Ella lined the spices up on their rack, brushed a few stray crumbs from the counter, and headed into the office. Even if she couldn't be at La Bella in the flesh, she could contribute in another way, and that day it translated into pie making and sewing the new aprons for the kitchen staff. They'd turned out lovely so far, a burgundy-and-cream toile pattern with deep pockets in the front. Embroidery wasn't her forte, so she planned to take them to a local shop to have "La Bella" emblazoned across the front. An hour passed before she knew it, and Ella only had a few more aprons to finish when Harry knocked.

"Sorry, El, but I have to get to the restaurant. I gave the kids an early lunch." He kissed her on the cheek before heading out the door. "Love the aprons, by the way."

"Thanks, dear. I wish you didn't have to leave, though. If I had a few more hours, I could finish them."

Harry leaned against the doorframe and sighed. "You know I can't take another day off."

Story of my life. He'd been able to finagle some time away from La Bella while Gabriella adjusted at home, but two days off from the restaurant caused more problems than it was probably worth, and now Harry would have to work even more hours.

"I know, I know. I was just looking forward to finishing these today and ticking that off my to-do list so I could work on some new cake recipes," she said. "Have a good day at work." Ella gave Harry a sad wave goodbye, knowing the aprons, baking, and anything else she wanted to do would have to be put on hold.

Once Harry left, the children's volume level went up a few decibels. Fearing they'd wake their grandmother, Ella set her work aside and closed up the office.

"We want Nonni to read to us!" Lily said, sticking out her bottom lip.

"Nonni read," Carol said solemnly, pointing to a picture book about cats.

Ella sat on the floor, tucking her gray skirt under her knees. "I'll read to you." She didn't want her mother to struggle over the words like she'd done a few days prior. Watching Lily correct her grandmother, and seeing the look of defeat on her mom's face, just about broke Ella's heart.

Lily stomped her foot. "No! We want Nonni Gabriella."

Ella sighed, knowing her daughter wouldn't give up so easily. "She's taking a nap. But if you wait here, I'll check and see if she's awake yet. You have to promise not to bother her if she's still sleeping, though. Pinky swear?"

Lily linked pinkies with her and smiled. "Okay."

As Ella approached her mother's room, she heard a hoarse, "Just send them in!" All three children went tearing in seconds later, immediately crawling onto the bed and showing their books to Gabriella.

"Story!" Harry Jr. said, pressing a pudgy cheek against his grandma's hand.

Ella took a seat on the edge of the bed. "Your grandma was just telling Mommy a story the other day, actually. Maybe you'd like to hear it instead of a book."

"What kind of story?" Lily asked. "Is it about princesses?"

"No princesses, I'm afraid. I don't think you'd be very interested in this story," Gabriella said.

"Oh, I'm sure they'd love to hear about Italy. Wouldn't you, kids?" Ella was sure that Lily, Harry Jr., and Carol couldn't care less about the story's topic; she just wanted to find out more about Joseph Rossi. That, and avoid another storybook incident.

"Yes, tell us about Italy, Nonni," Lily said, much to Ella's relief.

"Ittie! Ittie!" Carol and Harry Jr. shouted.

Gabriella smiled. "I suppose it's unanimous, then. So Nonni was visiting Florence one summer, that's where I grew up. And my mother wanted very badly for me to fall in love . . . "

CHAPTER 20

GABRIELLA

1905

*T*WO DAYS AFTER the Rossis' party, Gabriella searched through her wardrobe until nearly every surface in her room was covered in clothes. She wondered what would be suitable for confessing to a secret kiss with someone she hated.

Nothing too frilly, she decided. No soft colors, no lace.

She didn't want to appear wistful or romantic, lest it seem that the kiss was her idea. Finally she settled on one of her favorite day dresses and called for Loretta to come help her get ready.

The blue-and-white dress had three-quarter sleeves and small buttons trimming the high neckline. She had been wearing it the last time she saw Salvatore, but that didn't make her sad. Gabriella wasn't the type of person who connected events to clothing, unlike Lessie, who once destroyed an extremely expensive evening gown because her favorite dog had passed away the night she wore it to the Capettis' annual Christmas Eve ball. Gabriella had nearly cried, and it wasn't even her dress. But then again, she wasn't a dog lover, either.

The cameo didn't quite match her ensemble, so she slipped it under the gown's neckline and tried to focus on getting ready. The whole situation with Joseph was confusing to begin with, and after the Rossis' ball, her head was an utter mess. She didn't necessarily want to be engaged to him, but if he hadn't gone and kissed her like that, it would've been a hell of a lot easier to hate him.

After said kiss, Gabriella hurried inside and feigned sickness, with Joseph heartily backing her up. ("Next thing I knew, her head hit the bench and I thought she was out cold!") Mr. and Mrs. Rossi's driver had Gabriella and her family taken home straight away, and she rested in bed for the next day, with Loretta checking in on her constantly.

Although Mrs. Capetti was less than pleased, it seemed like everyone had fallen for their scheme, which gave her an excuse to lie low for a bit. But Gabriella knew she couldn't hide from Joseph forever.

That morning, she decided to visit Lessie and get her advice. Her cousin always knew the right things to say, and it would be helpful to have a second opinion on the matter. Deep down, though, Gabriella knew she didn't have much of a choice. It seemed as if their parents (and Joseph) had been plotting this for ages, probably even before the Capettis left New York.

With no other prospects, Gabriella knew her chances at marriage were dwindling with each passing day. She'd been too depressed about Salvatore to even entertain the thought of a suitor in New York, not that she cared for any of the lookalike, act-alike American boys who ran in her social set. She had a feeling her mother felt the same way and preferred an Italian husband for her . . . a husband like Joseph.

But while she certainly had a mind of her own, Gabriella also was practical. A life of luxury often came at a cost. Gabriella knew what it meant to be a spinster, and that was no existence for her. Also, as much as she hated to admit it, she'd been imagining what her life would be like as Joseph's wife ... and it would be a nice enough life indeed. What if she *did* grow to love him in time? The possibility didn't seem so absurd after their kiss. Gabriella just wished she had more time to make a decision, since their return to New York was getting closer each day.

Carlo was going along with her to their aunt and uncle's house, as he had plans to play cards with Massimo anyway. Gabriella glanced at the ornate clock in the corner of her room. *Damn.* She was supposed to meet Carlo downstairs at quarter past. She rushed down the steps to join him, nearly barreling into one of the maids on the way down.

"Ah, on time as ever," Carlo said, turning on his heel and heading out the door. The pair barely acknowledged each other's presence along the way, which suited Gabriella just fine. When they spoke, they mostly quarreled, and she knew a jab about Joseph would be coming eventually.

But no such remark came. Instead Carlo walked in silence, whistling a jaunty tune every so often. *Something has him in good spirits,* Gabriella thought.

As they approached their aunt and uncle's home, Carlo turned to his sister. "That cameo suits you," he said with a smug grin.

"I'm not even wearing it, Carlo. And honestly, I'm shocked it took you this long to say something. You must have been simply bursting at the seams on the way here."

"Calm down, old girl. It was a compliment, actually. Rossi is a fine man. I say go for it."

He strolled off to the drawing room to greet Massimo, whistling the whole way. Gabriella simply rolled her eyes and waited while the maid went to fetch Lessie. A moment later, Lessie rushed into the room, exclaiming, "Oh, Cousin, you must tell me everything!"

"Well, hello to you too," Gabriella said. Lessie gave her a quick hug and kiss, and immediately asked to see the cameo.

"Your mother was beside herself when you had to leave early, you know. The rest of the party was absolutely dreadful without you, and Chiara was telling everyone you were faking it."

"I'm sure she did. But can we please go somewhere more private? I don't need the help gossiping about this, too."

Lessie nodded and led her into the library, a cozy, dark-paneled room with wall-to-wall bookcases, a frescoed ceiling, and boring artwork of people riding horses and such.

Gabriella sat in an overstuffed leather chair in the corner and reached under her collar to pull the cameo out, arranging it on the deep-blue fabric for her cousin to see.

Lessie, sitting in the chair next to her, leaned as close to Gabriella as possible to examine the locket, squinting and staring at it until her cousin asked if she'd care for a magnifying glass.

"Don't be so cross, Ella. Last I knew, you couldn't stand Joseph Rossi, and now you're practically engaged and accepting tokens from him?"

Gabriella's eyes grew wide at the "practically engaged" part. "We are not and, if I have my way, will never be engaged. I accepted the cameo because, honestly,

I was in shock. He told me he was in love with me and that he bought this in Capri. Can you imagine? The night he was going to give it to me, he found Salvatore and me on the balcony together."

Lessie, always fond of a scandal, jumped out of her chair and let out a loud squeak. "Sorry," she whispered, sinking back down into the soft leather after Gabriella shot her an exasperated look.

"I never would've guessed our Mr. Rossi was in love with you, although it does explain why he was so cruel toward the end of the trip. My goodness, he must have been broken-hearted!"

"You know what they say. Nothing cures a broken heart like a good insult," Gabriella said. "When I think back to Capri, everything makes perfect sense. There was no other reason for him to behave like such a boor."

"You have to admit, Ella, it is a bit romantic," Lessie said with a dreamy sigh.

"I suppose it is, if you like those sorts of stories," Gabriella said, holding back a smile. A long pause followed before she added, "He kissed me in the garden."

"He *kissed* you?" Lessie squealed, forcing Gabriella to leap up and cover her cousin's mouth.

"Do you want the entire city to hear?" she said, finally removing her hand only when she was sure Lessie had calmed down.

"I promise I won't carry on if you just tell me the rest. Please?"

Gabriella sat back in her chair. "Very well, then. Joseph told me he didn't want to force my hand, but our parents wouldn't stop until the match was made. I got upset and tried to run off, but then he kissed me." Her heart did a tiny flip at the very mention of the word, and she gripped the seat's armrests. *Calm down. It was just a silly kiss.*

"And?" Lessie said. "How was it?"

She never would've admitted to Lessie in a million years how many times she'd replayed the scene in her head, and settled for, "It was nice. Very nice, in terms of kisses. Not like I have much experience in that realm, of course."

"Of course," Lessie agreed, even though Gabriella knew her cousin didn't believe her for a second. "So then what happened? What did he say?"

"Nothing," Gabriella said. "That's when I rushed inside and feigned sickness. I left and haven't heard from him since, but I'm certain something will happen soon. Besides running away to Paris, I don't know how else to get out of this engagement."

Lessie pursed her lips. "Have you ever considered that you might be happy with Joseph?"

Even though she was usually up for a good scheme, Lessie was certainly the more traditional of the pair, and in the same situation, Gabriella knew her cousin would have happily accepted a proposal from Joseph Rossi. Lessie had at least two suitors waiting in New York, and although none of the boys were exactly thrilling, they came from good families and were kind and respectable. That was enough for her, but not quite for Gabriella.

"While I don't know if I want to marry Joseph, I'm not getting any younger, and we both know I have no other marriage prospects. What am I supposed to do? Wait around and hope someone else wants me? If I turn him down, my parents will probably disown me, and I don't think a life on the streets would be very romantic."

Lessie appeared as if a wave of relief washed over her. "Maybe you'll surprise us all and be sensible for once. It seems as if you can be swayed, at the very least."

Gabriella sunk back down into one of the chairs, resting her chin on her hands. "Just what I always wanted to be. Sensible."

CHAPTER 21

LIZ

USTIN AND I were walking down our hallway, happy, tipsy, and tired, when my phone vibrated inside my bag. We'd just returned from Addie's party, and I was trying to decide whether or not to extend the evening. I chose to ignore my phone as we stopped outside my door, assuming it was a drunk-dial from Addie.

"So, I had a great time," he said.

I shifted my weight from one leg to the other, wondering if I should invite him inside, and then deciding against it. No need to rush things. "Me too," I said, standing on my toes to kiss him.

"Do you want to maybe go out to dinner this week? You'll have to make a suggestion, of course, but I'll treat," he said, his arms still around my waist.

"Definitely. How about Thursday?"

"Thursday it is. Um, do you want to . . ?" Justin's mouth turned up at the corner, adorably nervous.

"I'm actually kind of wiped out right now and have to work tomorrow, so I'm going to pass out, if you don't mind. But I can't wait for Thursday," I said, running my fingers through his hair for a few seconds before leaning in for another long kiss. I hoped that would take the edge off turning him down. Rushing into something physical didn't seem like a great idea with everything going on in my life. Even if I really, really wanted to invite him in.

"No prob. Sleep tight," Justin said after we'd pulled away, squeezing my hand before I watched him walk down the hall. Hopefully he didn't think I blew him off.

I stepped inside my apartment, sinking down against the door after locking it. I wasn't drunk, but I was on the verge, and the room felt a little shaky. I sat there for a few minutes, replaying the evening's events, when my phone vibrated again. I had one missed call (Addie) and one new text. Of course it was from Adam.

What was up with you tonight? Didn't realize you were dating someone . . .

I sighed and tossed my phone across the hardwood floor, letting it slide all the way into the living room. What happened to "just friends?"

Eventually I got up and stumbled into the kitchen, poured myself a glass of water from the Brita pitcher, and pulled my stash of M&M'S out of the cabinet. I shoved a handful of chocolaty goodness in my mouth and walked past my phone, deciding whether or not to acknowledge Adam's text. I knew I hadn't done anything wrong. He was dating someone else, for God's sake.

I bent down, typed "I'll talk to you on Tues," and flopped onto the couch. Friends or not, it still bothered me to know he was upset about Justin. Did he actually want to be with me, or did he just want what he couldn't have?

Meanwhile, in the diary, Nonni Gabriella was on her way to getting married to Joseph at twenty-one years old, and here I was, a few years from thirty and still playing stupid head games. It was getting ridiculous, and I knew there were more important things to think about. Namely, making a list of pawnshops and antique stores to visit so I could search for Nan's cameo.

Although I barely knew him, I kind of wanted to invite Justin along on the hunt. It was, after all, his idea. But since we already had plans Thursday and I didn't want to seem pushy, I decided to set out on the task alone. I created a list of twenty places around the city and figured I would try to visit at least three or four a week.

By lunchtime on Monday, I was itching to get started, so I headed over to Jewelers' Row and popped into a few of the stores on my list. Although some of the shops did have antique cameos, none of them were Nan's. I trudged back to the office feeling cold, hungry, and defeated. The only thing that cheered me up were the cute, jokey texts Justin sent me throughout the day, talking about our sweet dance moves and sharing some stories about the annoying new intern at work. Even Kaycee asked why I had a stupid grin on my face every time my phone buzzed.

The next day I made trips to three more stores, including the extremely classy Joe's Pawn and Check Cashing. But I still ended up minus one cameo and plus two extremely painful blisters from hoofing it around the city in high-heeled boots.

On the bright side, the owner of two small accessories boutiques in the suburbs finally called me back. I'd been trying to get her stores to carry LM Designs for at least a year, and after seeing my jewelry at Dressed, she agreed to stock some of my earrings and rings for the holiday season. Finally, it seemed like my business was starting to take off.

I smiled out the window on my bus ride home, oblivious even to the toddler crying next to me. Maybe my life was about to turn a new page. The only thing nagging in my gut was that Adam was coming over to talk about my website. The confusing feeling I got from his text hadn't left, but I vowed to make our meeting more about work than my dating life. Frankly, it wasn't his business who I chose to date.

Once I got home, I did a quick sweep of the apartment, throwing empty glasses into the sink and stacking a pile of books and magazines under the coffee table. I took off the boots and my trendy animal-print wrap dress (I didn't want to look like I was trying too hard) and changed into jeans and a casual off-the-shoulder tunic. Finally, I opened Spotify on my computer and chose my favorite playlist. The sounds of Dashboard Confessional were drifting through the living room when Adam rang my doorbell.

"Cool building," was his greeting, along with a kiss on the cheek. Despite the freezing weather, he wasn't wearing a coat, just a black North Face fleece and the same fraternity baseball cap he'd always worn. Old habits die hard, I guess.

"You can put your stuff on the coffee table," I said. "Just let me call the pizza place. One sec." I took a seat on one of the barstools in the kitchen and dialed, watching as he walked around the living room and examined the picture frames arranged on the windowsill. I hung up just as he lifted a silver frame that held a picture of me with Nan on the beach a few years ago. It was the summer I graduated . . . the summer Adam and I got back together.

"This is a really good shot of you guys," he said with a sad smile.

I leaned in and studied the picture, and how my face seemed so much happier and more carefree. "Thanks. You know how she loved the shore."

"Remember when we went to Atlantic City right

after you'd turned twenty-one and you were so annoyed that everyone kept carding you?" he said, eyes crinkling with amusement.

I laughed. "I almost forgot about that. And then you won $112 on video poker and we blew it on ice cream, wings, and stupid boardwalk souvenirs." I could almost taste the salt air and feel the wind on my face, picturing myself walking hand-in-hand with him down the boards, cracking up about the hideous tie-dyed T-shirts we had made with "AC is for Lovers" on the front.

Desperate for a subject change, I took the frame and placed it back on the window, brushing his hand in the process. A zing traveled up my arm, and as I turned to face him I realized I was fooling myself thinking we could be casual friends. The broody emo music wasn't helping the situation, either. It felt like I was in an episode of *The Hills* or something as "Hands Down" blared from the computer behind us.

"Lizzie . . . " he started, but I hightailed it to the couch. Now I had to sit here with him and pretend like it was fine talking about my website and his girlfriend and who knows what else. What had I gotten myself into?

"So, do you want to look at this binder? It has tons of pictures of things I've made, and some sketches and stuff." I tried to act casual, and plopped the massive binder down on the cushion next to me, intending for it to be a makeshift divider of sorts. Instead he picked it up, sat down close enough that our knees were touching, and spread the binder out across his lap.

For a minute the only sound, besides the music, was the swish of the plastic sleeves as he flipped through the book. "These are really good. You've always had an eye for drawing."

I shrugged. "It helps for me to sketch something out before I make it. Like Nan did with her cakes."

The song changed to an up-tempo tune from one of our shared favorite bands, Saturdays in London, and he started tapping his fingers on the binder. "I can't believe what happened to Ellie B.," I said, referring to the group's singer, who'd committed suicide a few years earlier. "She was our age."

Adam frowned. "You know, when I found out, the first person I thought of was you. It was weird not to talk to you about it."

I'd felt the same way, but I didn't want to tell him. "It's weird they have a guy singer now," I said instead.

He looked down at a picture of purple hoop earrings and then back at me. "Speaking of new people . . . what's the deal with that guy Jason?"

"Justin. And I don't know. Last night was the first time we hung out."

"Ah," he said, flipping the page. "He seemed really into you."

"You think?"

"I think."

A few seconds of awkward silence passed, and I looked at the time on my phone. "Want to go down to Giuseppe's with me to get the food? It's just in the lobby."

He closed the binder, stood up, and stretched, offering me a hand. It was like a crazy déjà vu of the coffee shop with Justin, and I had to stop myself from laughing at the absurdity of the situation.

"I see you still have the coffee table, by the way," he said. My shoulders slumped. It was the same one we'd picked out for our apartment . . . well, Adam's apartment, in Chicago. I was supposed to bring it with me, but since I bailed on our moving date, it stayed in Philly. I should've just returned the damn table, but maybe it was my way of punishing myself, a constant reminder of the promise I broke.

"I wasn't ready then. You know that." I tried to hold the tears back as I grabbed my keys and left the apartment. Adam was right, love wasn't always such a black-and-white situation.

He followed behind me to the elevator. "Slow down. Will you just talk to me for a second?"

I didn't stop until I reached the elevator doors, whirling around to face him. "Talk about what? How my mother gave me a guilt trip about chasing you across the country for a relationship that 'probably wouldn't work out?' That I was terrified to leave my friends and family and everything I knew after being back together for less than a year? How I second-guessed my decision every single day for God knows how long afterward?"

The doors slid open before he could answer, and we took the longest elevator ride of all time to the lobby. Adam stood, hands in his pockets, looking at the ground, while I bit my lip until I was certain it was bleeding.

"It's okay, Lizzie," he finally said as the doors opened. I stepped out ahead of him, walking briskly toward the pizza shop, and his presence behind me felt like a cloak.

"What's okay?"

"I'm not allowed to be pissed off that you're dating other people. What happened with us was a long time ago. Ignore me, I'm acting like a jerk."

He opened the door to Giuseppe's, holding it for me, and I joined the line without comment. We stood in silence while I studied a boot-shaped menu.

"Oookay then," he said.

"You said to ignore you." I said. "That was me. Ignoring you." Despite the hurt, I managed to crack a smile.

He laughed and threw an arm around my shoulder. "I'm sorry. This is harder than I thought."

I leaned against him for a second and sighed. "I know. I'm sorry, too. About everything."

I wanted to stay in the moment a bit longer, but the door jingled and smacked me in the butt—the only downside of my favorite pizza joint being the size of a postage stamp.

I turned around, scooting to the side to give the person room to walk into the tiny shop. And then I realized the person was Justin.

Shit. Shit. Shit.

"Liz! Agh, sorry about the door." He sported some serious dark circles under his eyes and looked like his polo shirt could use a good ironing.

His expression, and his tone, turned colder when he saw Adam next to me. "Must be a popular night for pizza."

"Jason, right?" Adam said, and I knew this time he was doing it to be a jerk. His competitiveness on the soccer field had always translated into the rest of his life, too. Especially when it came to other guys.

"It's Justin. So, what are you two up to tonight?" I could feel the annoyance brewing, and couldn't blame him. Why couldn't I have met Justin a year ago? Or even a month ago, before Adam showed up and sent me on a trip back to Regretsville.

"Remember how Adam was helping me with my website?" I said. "We're working on that. Figured it was easy to run down and grab some food here while we looked over stuff." I tried to make it sound like Adam hanging out in my apartment was no big deal, and not a huge jumbling mess of emotions sprawled across my stupid Ikea coffee table.

While Adam paid for our pie, I turned to Justin, hoping to salvage the situation. "So are we still on for Thursday? I thought we could try this BYO called Carla's. They have awesome Italian food."

"Sounds good to me," he said, brightening a bit at the change in topic. "I could use a break from the office."

Adam turned around, carrying the pizza. "You could join us if you want," he said, even though I guessed he was only offering because he knew damn well Justin wouldn't accept the invitation.

"I was just going to grab a slice real quick," he said. "Unfortunately, I have some work to do from home. Liz, I'll see you on Thursday for our date, though?" He said the word *date* a bit louder than necessary. Guess Adam wasn't the only competitive one.

"Sure, no prob," I said, touching him lightly on the arm as I turned to leave. "See you Thursday."

"I guess we're heading back up. Good seeing you, buddy," Adam said, giving him the classic hand-slap guy handshake.

"Right," Justin said, returning the slap, then stopping to squeeze my hand as I walked out.

Disappointment washed over me as we waited for the elevator, and I was afraid to turn around for fear Justin might walk out of the pizza shop. The elevator doors remained firmly shut as I chanted to myself, *Open, please freaking open.*

We stepped inside the elevator just as I saw Justin starting to walk into the lobby, so I hit the "close door" button about five times in a row.

"Soooo . . . fancy running into Justin again!" I said with forced cheer.

Adam clutched the pizza box, but I had a feeling if his arms were free he would've slapped his forehead. "Talk about awkward. Eh, I wouldn't freak too much, though. He seemed stressed out from work or something."

I looked at him like he was nuts. "You do realize he must think we're doing more than working on a website together."

"Sorry. I'm screwing everything up for you, aren't I?"

I just shook my head as the doors opened. I was afraid even to talk on our floor for fear Justin would somehow pop out of the woodwork again.

"So can we look at the updated idea for the homepage?" I asked once we were back in the apartment. I figured getting him talking about business was an easy way to change the direction of the conversation.

"Yup. Let me bring up the files," he said, sitting in the same spot on the couch and opening his laptop. I carried the pizza box over and two bottles of beer, taking a seat on the floor next to the coffee table and digging into a slice. He turned the screen toward me.

The design hadn't been changed much, other than the colors and a couple of other tweaks, but it gave off a totally different vibe. "Perfect! This is it," I said. "If you want to pick some of the images from the binder, I'll send you the files and you can just replace the ones we talked about in the heart graphic."

"Definitely. What do you think about this one?" He minimized the file and brought up another page design, this one an "About the Designer" section. The picture was different from the one he'd originally grabbed from Facebook. It was me in Atlantic City, taken the exact day we'd just talked about. I was sitting in one of the

Adirondack chairs inside an upscale shopping complex called The Pier Shops at Caesars, feet in the "sand" and a pile of shopping bags next to me. I gave the camera a thumbs-up and a huge smile.

I got up from the floor and took a seat next to him, leaning closer to see the photo. "I can't believe you still have this."

"You were still in a folder on my computer. Even if you weren't with me." Our eyes locked, and this time I didn't look away.

The opening notes of "Say Goodbye" from Dave Matthews Band played in the background. How many times had we made out to this song in college? The irony of the lyrics about getting together with a friend wasn't lost on me, and maybe it was the music, or the nostalgia, or who knows. But this time he really was going to kiss me, and I knew I was going to let him.

The kiss felt soft and familiar, yet passionate and full of longing . . . but bittersweet, too. I didn't want it to stop, but still found myself knowing it had to. I pulled away before things went any further, my voice shaking. "I can't do this."

Adam stroked the side of my face and then reached for his phone. "I'll end it with Jessica. Now, even," he said matter-of-factly, as if he were cancelling a doctor's appointment. Even if Jessica didn't deserve him, I didn't like the idea of her being dumped on the freaking phone.

"Are you crazy?" I said, confiscating the phone before he could grab it. "Let's take a step back." *Next thing I know, he'll be whipping a ring out of his pocket*, I thought, but then remembered someone else already had it.

"I was already heading in that direction, and after spending tonight with you, why wait? My mind's made up." He leaned in again.

"Just like that?" I said, pushing back against his chest. I couldn't let another kiss distract me.

"You sound like I'm being flippant. This breakup has been a long time coming."

I threw my head back against the couch and stared at the ceiling. The only realization that came to mind was my crown molding, like Nan's, could've used some dusting.

"Tell me what you're thinking," Adam said.

I sat up and turned to him. "I think . . . I need to think about this. About us. And you need to decide if you're ending your relationship because it's not working or because you're chasing after me out of jealousy."

"You're the love of my life, Lizzie. I should've fought harder for you. I should've given up the job in Chicago and stayed with you. I don't know what else to say."

He leaned in and touched his forehead to mine, and I sat there frozen, drawn to him yet holding back. The music rose to a crescendo around us. I knew eventually I'd have to say good-bye.

"Why don't we just wrap things up for now, and I'll call you tomorrow, okay?" he said. I nodded, and he kissed me lightly on the lips. My heart raced like I'd just run five miles on the treadmill as he gathered his stuff and let himself out. Before I knew it, tears were sliding down my cheeks, and I couldn't stop them.

At some point I must've cried myself to sleep, and I woke up with a start around one o'clock as my phone buzzed insistently against the cursed coffee table. Adam's name flashed on the screen along with a picture that appeared to be a screenshot of his Facebook page. Confused, I tapped the image. My mouth, and my phone, dropped to the floor.

Adam Shipman is single.

CHAPTER 22

LIZ

*T*HE CLERK SHOOK his head. "Sorry, haven't seen any new cameos come in."

I sighed and told him thanks anyway as I walked out of the cluttered pawnshop, disappointment and a bitter cold wind smacking me in the face. I wanted to be optimistic, but after checking the bar again and going to eight different jewelry and pawn stores, the thought I would actually be able to find the necklace seemed ridiculous.

The added stress of Adam confessing his feelings (and breaking up with Jessica) only made things worse. I hadn't responded to his text message. What was I supposed to say? "Thanks for breaking it off with your girlfriend when I don't even know for sure if I want to be with you?" Sure, the feelings were there, but I couldn't tell if I was just wrapped up in a memory or actually wanting to love Adam in the present. And to complicate things even more, I was really starting to like Justin.

The only thing keeping me from feeling totally down in the dumps was my date with Justin, a.k.a. Jason (*sigh*). We had emailed earlier in the day about dinner, and he kept saying how much he was looking forward to it, so the anticipation of the night ahead got me through my shift at Plaid. The only problem was Adam, and I knew Justin was going to bring up our run-in at Giuseppe's. I definitely had some 'splainin' to do, like Nan's favorite, Lucy Ricardo.

With the miserable weather (a "wintry mix"—my favorite), we hadn't been too busy at Plaid, and the rest of the afternoon seemed to drag on endlessly. The only bright spot of the day was when a woman came in and bought all three of my remaining earring designs as gifts for her daughters. Finally, it was six o'clock, and I made a beeline to the restroom to freshen up for dinner.

Addie had helped me choose a new date-night look from Plaid: slim black pants and a gray blazer with a ruffled black chiffon polka-dot top underneath. It wasn't my usual style, but I had to admit the outfit was perfect. The only thing that would've completed the look was Nan's cameo, but instead I wore one of my own designs, a beaded sterling silver heart.

It seemed crazy to me how Nan didn't know anything about the cameo until her mother got sick, but on the other hand, it wasn't entirely surprising. The stories I'd heard about Nonni Gabriella made it seem like she and Nan weren't close, so I guess it made sense she had never shared that part of her past with her daughter.

That Nan had never told me, however, was beyond weird. We had a closer relationship than any grandmother/granddaughter combination I've ever known, and it almost felt like a slap in the face that she hadn't trusted me with our family's secret.

I frowned and dug through my purse for some lip gloss, resigning myself to the idea that I probably wasn't going to find the cameo and would have to keep the story behind it under wraps for good.

After a quick touch-up of powder, I headed out to meet Justin at the restaurant. The sky was already pitch-black, which brought my mood down a few notches as I trudged along the sidewalk past the Liberty Bell and Independence Hall, completely devoid of tourists for once. I splashed through puddles in my pink rain boots and wondered why I'd thought it was a good idea to wear my relatively thin red trench coat. It was the cutest item of outerwear I owned, and the only one with a hood, but it did little to protect me from the freezing rain. A slight buzz came from within its pockets and I fumbled around until I found my phone. It was a number I didn't recognize.

"Elizabeth? This is Lori Masters, from Nordstrom."

My heart just about jumped out of my chest and across the street, but I tried to play it cool. "Oh, hello. My sister mentioned you were a friend of her fiancé's mother, Jacqueline Crenshaw?"

"Yes, don't you love her? Anyway, she told me all about your designs, and after looking at your pieces online, I have to say I'm impressed. Now you're currently in some local boutiques, correct?"

It took me a moment to regain my composure, but somehow I answered calmly. "Yes, in a high-end shop called Plaid here in Philadelphia, and three other small boutiques in the Main Line area. I'm actually working on more designs this weekend because everything has sold out at Plaid."

"Wonderful," Lori said. "Listen, we'd love to schedule a conference call with you after the holidays. Just an initial discussion to see if we might want to work together. Learn about you, what sales have been like, and so forth, and tell you about how we operate. We're going to be spotlighting some up-and-coming local designers next year at each of our stores, and I think your line would be a perfect fit. Does that sound good?"

I stopped in my tracks, mouth dropping to the ground, feeling the urgent need to pinch myself.

"Thank you! Yes, I would love that. I mean, that would be great. January definitely works for me," I said, still unable to believe the conversation was actually happening. "Sorry, I'm a bit overwhelmed right now. Nordstrom is one of my favorite stores and I really admire the company."

"Awesome," Lori said. "I'm glad to hear it. I have your info, so I'll get my assistant to shoot you an email with some dates. We'll talk soon. Happy holidays!"

I slipped the phone back in my pocket before jumping up and down in the middle of Chestnut Street like a crazy person, splashing water everywhere. *Yesss!* If I'd smiled any harder, my mouth would've fallen off. Even the rain couldn't wipe the excitement from my face.

Despite my happy dance, I arrived at the restaurant ten minutes early, thankful to thaw out in the heat for a while and call Cate with the good news before Justin got there. The hostess seated me at a tiny table in a nook by the window and I settled in, watching the rain pound down and enjoying a peaceful moment before calling my sister. While the restaurant's décor wasn't exactly cutting-edge with its columns and typical murals of Italy that reminded me of Nan's house, the food more than made up for it, and it was usually quiet enough to have a decent conversation.

The adrenaline still rushed through me after I hung up with Cate (after promising her various favors for the rest of her life), and I flipped through emails and Facebook for a few minutes, stopping to check my reflection in the phone. I must've been very intently studying myself, because when I looked up Justin was pressed against the glass, making a ridiculous face at me. I turned about three different shades of red and tossed the phone in my bag, managing a halfhearted wave.

The door opened, bringing a rush of cold air around the corner, and he appeared a moment later, folding up a large black umbrella and still laughing.

"Do you know how long I was standing there?" he asked as I stood up to hug him.

"How about don't tell me?"

"I thought it was cute. You were so serious about fixing your hair. I guess I should take it as a compliment that you want to look nice, right?"

I laughed. "When you put it that way, it sounds much better." We both sat down and made attempts to scan the menu, but neither of us paid much attention to the food.

"So how was your day?" he asked, leaning across the red-and-white checkered tablecloth. "I can't imagine there are too many people out and about with this weather lately."

I shrugged. "Yeah, not exactly. But there will always be holiday shoppers, and I'm swamped trying to finish up last-minute orders. I got a call with some good news today, though. I'm going to have a meeting with Nordstrom after the holidays!"

"Seriously? That's awesome," he said, sounding genuinely excited and giving me a high-five.

"Yeah, I'm psyched but it still hasn't sunk in yet. This is actually happening because of my sister. Her fiancé's mother has a lot of contacts."

"I find that hard to believe," he said. "I mean, it's nice to know people, but if you weren't a talented designer, I'm sure this lady wouldn't want to meet with you, contacts or not."

I smiled and squeezed his hand. "I guess. But in any

case, it's the biggest thing that's happened to me in ages, so I'm kind of freaking out."

He asked me more about my line, and seemed to legitimately care about what I told him, asking intelligent questions and listening to everything from the crazy customer stories to my aspirations of owning my own store. We were so caught up in the conversation that neither of us realized the waitress, an older Italian woman, had been standing there, trying to get our attention.

She cleared her throat lightly and we both jumped. "Hello there, I'm Antonia. You two look so smitten that I didn't want to interrupt, but I am guessing you do want to eat, yes?"

I laughed. "Sorry. Could we have a few more minutes to look over the menu?"

Antonia nodded and pulled out a corkscrew, opening the bottle of Pinot Grigio Justin had brought along.

"I hope you like it," he said, examining the label. "I'm not a big wine person so I asked the guy at the liquor store. It's so weird how you can't buy booze in a grocery store here like in a normal state."

"Hey there, no Philly bashing! And you chose a good one. My friend Adam used to always buy this brand. It's actually one of my favorites."

Justin made a face, but in a second it was gone, so I thought maybe I was imagining things.

"Speaking of," he said, "Adam didn't seem thrilled to run into me at Giuseppe's."

"You know how guys can be. Well, you are one," I said with a nervous laugh. "Sorry. He can be kind of jealous even though we aren't together anymore."

"Well, I'd be jealous if I had let you get away, too," he said.

Nice save, I thought.

We clinked glasses and the rest of the dinner went by in a blur of pasta, wine, and general giddiness. We talked about some serious things too, though. Justin told me more about his family and the older brother who died when he was a teenager, and I shared my fears of Cate getting married so young. I usually don't confide in people I don't know well, but for some reason I felt like I could tell Justin anything.

By the time we finished eating, we had polished off the bottle and were both feeling pretty good. Antonia came over to give us the check, and stood there for a moment just looking at us with a satisfied grin.

"I never give unsolicited advice, but I know a good couple when I see one. Trust me, I see a lot of kids come in here, and they come back with different dates all of the time. You two are the real thing. Now don't screw it up."

She patted my arm and left the folio on the table as I started searching in my bag for my wallet, trying to avoid making eye contact with Justin. Hopefully he wasn't a commitment-phobe or something. Most guys would feel pressured, or at the very least, weirded out by a comment like that on a second date.

"Somehow I'm gathering 'I don't give out advice' means our friend Antonia gives out advice to everyone she waits on," Justin said with a laugh, reaching across to take the bill from me.

I felt a huge sense of relief wash over me; it didn't seem like he was turned off by our nosy waitress.

"I know, right? She reminds me of my Nan in a way. Maybe it's just the Italian grandmother thing."

I started to pull some cash out and Justin shook his head.

"Don't even think about it. My treat." He slipped some bills into the folder and stood up. "I'm going to give this to the waitress and hit the men's room before we leave."

I took the opportunity to call Addie and share my news about the Nordstrom meeting. "So besides your big business accomplishment, are you okay?" she said. "Please tell me your date isn't already over. Is he pissed about Adam?"

"No, no, everything's fine. He's in the bathroom. It's going better than I expected. The waitress even told us she thought we were meant to be together and he didn't flinch."

"Wow, that's kind of intense for a second date. And here I thought Adam was the one who moved fast."

"I know, but we also finished a bottle of wine, so maybe that's why he didn't seem bothered by it."

"So are you going to invite him back to your place? Or go to his? I mean it's kind of impossible not to, considering you live on the same floor."

"I guess," I said. "I'll see how it goes. I still don't even know what's going on with Adam. And last time Justin and I went out I didn't invite him in, so I don't think it's expected."

"Please. You're totally sleeping with him."

"Addie, seriously! Wait, I gotta go, he's coming back to the table. Bye."

I tucked my phone away just as Justin rounded the corner to the table. "Ready to go?" he asked. I turned to get my coat when I realized he'd already grabbed it and was standing there holding it out for me. Major points in the chivalry department.

Justin had also called for a cab before he went to the bathroom, so we didn't have to wait long. We were laughing at anything and everything and holding hands as we entered the building, a fact our doorman no doubt would tease me about later. As we stepped out of the elevator and faced our floor, it suddenly became a little awkward. One of us was going to have to make the move.

"So do you want to come over for a while? If not, that's totally cool. I know you're probably tired and it's a work night," he said.

"Definitely," I said, the words coming out of my mouth almost before he finished the sentence. "I'll stop by for a bit."

Justin grinned and took my arm as we walked down the hall. "Just don't mind the mess. Maybe I should've thought ahead and cleaned up a bit."

"Wouldn't that have been a little presumptuous?"

"Nah," Justin said, opening his front door as Bo came running up to greet us. "Who wouldn't want to come hang out with me and my dog?"

I knelt down to pet Bo, thankful I wasn't wearing stockings this time. "Do you want a drink?" he called from the kitchen.

"Sure, actually, water is fine since I have to get up early for work and all."

He came over with a glass of water for me and a beer for him, and we sat on the couch. "I just got that new Steve Carell movie if you want to watch."

In my experience, when a guy invites you over to watch a movie, it's code for "let's make out on my couch and totally not watch the movie at all." However, I was absolutely fine with that turn of events, so I agreed.

Justin popped in the DVD and sat back on the couch, stretching his left arm around me with an exaggerated yawn.

"Oh, pulling out the yawn-and-stretch, I see?" I said, snuggling up against his chest.

He laughed. "Yup, I'm full of smooth moves."

The menu for the DVD came up on the screen, and I realized which movie it was. "Oh, I've been meaning to see this one! Adam's cousin actually has a small part in it. He was excited about a speaking role, even though I think he has maybe two or three lines. I haven't had a chance to see it yet."

"Oh, really?" Justin asked, a tinge of annoyance in his forced casual tone.

"Yeah. His cousin is a couple of years younger than us and we went to the same school. He's been an extra in a few TV shows and movies but this is his first time actually having a line. I used to tease him all the time about it."

Justin tensed up a bit. "Oh, that's cool. So about Adam . . . is this a friends-with-benefits situation or something?"

I sat up straight, dreading the way our conversation was headed. "Nothing is going on with us, but in the spirit of full disclosure, we did kiss once the other day. I'm not saying it was a good idea, but it happened. To be honest, I think he was mostly jealous after we ran into you."

"Oookay," he said. "I don't know how I'm supposed to respond to that."

I ran my fingers through my hair with a sigh. "I know. I'm sorry. I think it's hard for him to see me dating other people, which is ridiculous because he lives with his girlfriend. Well, ex-girlfriend, I guess. They broke up the other day."

Stop running your mouth, Liz. You're making things worse.

"How long did you guys go out?" he asked, hitting play on the remote.

"We dated all of my freshman year of college. We broke up once he graduated, and then we started to see each other again a few years later. He moved for a job, and wanted me to come with him. I wasn't ready, so we broke things off. We didn't talk again until the night before Thanksgiving, when I ran into him at O'Connell's."

Justin raised his eyebrows. "Oh, *he* was the friend you were looking for that night? I thought you guys had been back in touch for much longer."

"Why's that?"

"I don't know, it's just you talk about him a lot."

"Do I? When have I ever mentioned him except just now about the movie?"

"At dinner," Justin said. "You said he drinks that wine I brought."

I felt my shoulders tensing up, annoyance flowing through my veins. Who cared if I made a passing remark about the wine? It wasn't like I said I used to pour it all over Adam's naked body. Which I didn't, just for the record.

"I didn't mean anything by it," I said. "Does it bother you that I talk about him?" The movie still played in the background, but neither of us was watching.

He shrugged. "I'm not trying to make a big deal about it. But from meeting Adam, it just seemed like there was something there that maybe you aren't telling me about. You kind of changed when you were around him. I didn't say anything the other night, but it sounded like you invited him to the bar and then lied and said you weren't going and asked me instead."

I had no idea Justin had overheard that part of my conversation with Adam, and I stared at him, wide-eyed, feeling our dream date slipping away by the second.

"Adam said you texted him saying you were staying home. He seemed pissed that you went after all."

"Oh, that. I originally invited him to the party, but

just in attempt to be friendly. Addie hates him, though, and since we were fighting I figured it wasn't a good idea to add any fuel to the fire, ya know?"

"So you said you weren't going? Why didn't you just tell him the truth? He must not have believed you weren't going to be there because he showed up anyway."

I leaned forward and rested a hand on his knee, trying to be reassuring but probably failing at it. "I didn't think I was going. It wasn't a lie. I'm sure this all sounds bad, but it was a serious, complicated relationship. We almost got engaged. I don't think anyone really gets over something like that, even when you both move on. And I do like you. A lot."

"Okay, then," Justin said. "I know we haven't known each other for very long, but I like you and want to see where this goes, so I just want to know if there's competition or not. That's all."

I looked at him and sighed. "I can understand why you'd think he was after me or something. And maybe I should've sorted everything out before dragging you into this weird triangle. I'm sorry for causing drama."

Justin grabbed my hand. "Don't worry about it. It's probably just the wine talking and me being stupid. This is our second date . . . it's not like we're exclusive."

I leaned back into him and we stared at the TV in uncomfortable silence for five minutes or so, but I couldn't concentrate. It bothered me that Justin had accused me of lying about my feelings toward Adam. Then again, I sort of had. Why did I keep slipping back into old patterns? I made a mental note to look at Addie's Post-it message more often. For what it was worth, I truly did want things to work out with Justin . . . at least I did until that moment.

I looked up at Justin, who was now tapping his fingers against his beer bottle, not even pretending to watch the movie.

"Sorry if I ruined the mood," he said. "I think you're really cool and honestly, Adam seems like kind of a jerk. I don't want you to get hurt."

"I understand. And I like you a lot, too. It's getting kind of late, though," I said, standing up and walking toward the front door with Bo on my heels. He started barking and pawing at my leg as if he knew something was up.

"Are you mad?" Justin asked, following his dog.

"No, I'm just tired and kind of buzzed. I can't drink like I used to."

He smiled at my lame excuse, but tension still hung in the air. We hugged and he said something about maybe hanging out on the weekend. I had a feeling that wasn't going to happen.

My head felt fuzzy and my stomach uneasy from all of the food and wine; I probably should've just gone home in the first place. Then I wouldn't have been on the verge of tears and making an emergency phone call to Addie the moment I stepped into my apartment. Even though it was fairly late to be calling someone on a weeknight, I knew she'd answer.

"So yeah, just kidding about the date going well," I said, bypassing the normal greetings.

"Figures. What happened?"

"He said I talk about Adam all the time, which isn't true! I mentioned him twice, and it was just in passing."

"What do you mean by 'in passing,' though? Not to play bad cop, but was it necessary to bring up your ex twice on a date? Especially when he just saw the two of you together getting pizza and probably making googly eyes at each other?"

Of course Addie had to be snotty about it.

"He asked if I liked the wine and I said yes, my friend Adam used to buy that kind a lot and it was one of my favorites."

"All right, what else did you say?"

"I told him how Adam's cousin had a part in the movie we were watching. I mean, it's a valid point of conversation if you actually *know* someone who is in the movie."

"True. I don't see the big deal. I could see if you were going on and on about how funny Adam thinks Steve Carell is or that you have issues trusting men because of him, but you were just making small talk."

"Thank you! And then he got all weird and said he just had a feeling something was going on between me and Adam and he wanted to know about it, because he likes me a lot and wanted to continue seeing me."

"Well, that's a valid point. You just had this dramatic make-out-slash-confessing-your-feelings session with Adam the other day, and if you hadn't been the one to pull back, who knows what would've happened."

When she put it that way, it did sound kind of bad. "Yeah, I know. I did tell Justin we kissed, but it was probably a mistake. I felt like we just kept talking in circles so I told him I was tired and left."

"So what *are* you going to do about Adam?" Addie asked. "And PS, stop going back."

I hugged a throw pillow to my chest, replaying the scene that had happened on the sofa right next to me in my head. "Not one hundred percent sure, but I'm thinking you're right and I need to move on. I was starting to like Justin a lot, so it figures Adam had to show up and complicate everything. You thought Justin was nice, right?"

"Yes, but talking to someone at a bar is one thing. We all know I've been wrong about guys in the past."

I didn't like where the conversation was heading, and decided to call it a night.

I couldn't blame Justin for wondering what was going on between Adam and me. It's not exactly normal for your ex to be accosting your date in a bar and storming out after he sees you kissing. And it was true Adam crossed my mind more than once a day, but so did Justin. More importantly, I wondered if Adam had potentially ruined my new sort-of-relationship, and if he was worth it.

I tried to think of what Nan would say about this situation. My mother had never been the type to get into lengthy discussions about guys, so I'd never felt comfortable talking to her about my love life. Nan, on the other hand, always knew exactly what to say when I was upset, and had expertly counseled me on dramatic breakups and boy troubles ranging from Mickey Pearson in the third grade right through Adam (the second time).

Most of the comforting involved chocolate chip cookies, but still, it would've been nice to talk to someone with a little more life experience than my twenty-something friends. I missed her more than ever that night.

CHAPTER 23

LIZ

*A*S SUSPECTED, Justin didn't call or text the next day, or that weekend (no matter how many times I checked), and my computer remained conspicuously free of his funny, flirty emails. I didn't realize how much I had counted on his messages to brighten up my workday until they were gone, and all that remained of our budding relationship was a sick, empty feeling. I could have contacted him, but what was I going to say? He was clearly annoyed about Adam, and I needed to make a serious decision before talking things through with Justin.

The absence of Justin, in addition to the horrific weather, put me in a foul mood at work. I went out at lunchtime on Monday to check a few more jewelry and antique shops, and left again with nothing, which only added fuel to the fire.

The tears fell fast and hard as I slipped along the icy sidewalk back to Third Street. Thankfully, my sunglasses did a good job at hiding my distress, although sadly, they wouldn't help once I was back in the store. Wearing giant shades indoors kind of screamed "I just went out to smoke pot on my lunch break," and getting fired was the last thing I needed.

Back inside the boutique, there weren't any customers, and Kaycee was chatting with a friend of hers on the phone, so I took a minute to sit down at the computer and check my email. One from a jewelry client, a promotional code for free shipping at Asos . . . I was reading some chain email about a recipe swap Aunt Carol had sent when the door opened. I looked up and it was Adam.

"Hey," he said with a hesitant smile, holding out a single red rose. *Oh. My. God.*

He walked up to the sleek wood counter I was standing behind and placed the rose next to the store's computer.

"I'm sorry about the other night. And I don't want you to feel pressured into anything. Can you meet me after your shift for a drink so we can talk?"

"I . . . " my mouth opened, but the rest of the sentence couldn't come out.

"Things aren't so good right now. I could use a friend. Please, Lizzie."

An apology was about the last thing I expected from him, and I wondered if he felt lousy from the breakup, or me, or if something else was going on. Since things were pretty much on the rocks with Justin, I figured it wouldn't hurt to show up for a drink and find out.

"Okay. Let's talk then," I said. "And thanks for the flower."

I told him what time my shift was over, and he suggested meeting at El Vez, a Mexican restaurant we had gone to a few times back in the day. The significance behind his choice wasn't lost on me, but I decided not to jump to conclusions.

"I'm heading back home but I'll see you around six-fifteen, then." He walked around the counter and kissed my forehead. "You look great today, by the way."

"Thanks," I said, breathing in his signature Adam scent of musky aftershave and coffee. Kaycee's eyes widened as she walked to the front of the boutique, and I waved Adam off.

"That wasn't your ex, was it?"

"Indeed," I said, my cheeks probably still flushed.

She laughed. "Ah, the stuck-in-the-college-days boyfriend. We all have one."

I lifted the rose off the counter and sniffed it, then laid my head down on the counter. "I think I might have to break up with someone I'm not even dating."

∼ ∼ ∼

ADAM WAS SITTING at the bar when I got to the restaurant, a loud, trendy place packed with the happy hour crowd. He absentmindedly played with his phone in the way people do when they're waiting for someone and don't want to seem like a loser for being there alone.

I'd expected he was going to change when he went home, but his outfit consisted of the same zip-up hoodie, cords, TOMS shoes and tweed newsboy-style hat he'd sported when he showed up at Plaid. It wasn't what I would've chosen, given the location; everyone else was dressed in "just from the office" attire or some combination of jeans and a blazer.

"How's everything going?" I said, hopping up on the stool next to him.

He kissed me on the cheek. "I've been better. You probably think I'm an ass, but I do appreciate you coming."

I didn't respond, but nodded and grabbed the drink menu, studying it intently even though I knew exactly what I wanted. After a minute or two, I ordered a blood orange margarita and turned to Adam.

"Do you remember the first time we came here?" I said.

He laughed, reaching over to pat my knee. "You were so worried they were going to throw you out for having some of my beer."

"Hey, I was only eighteen! I'd never tried to drink at a restaurant before."

"Can you believe we were ever that young?"

I turned around and saw a group of girlfriends laughing and clinking glasses in a booth near the back. I remembered us huddled in the same booth, stealing kisses every two seconds and making promises that were never kept.

"No," I said, feeling sadness wash over me.

We sipped our drinks, knees touching. "How did we end up like this?" he finally asked.

"Hmmm. You rented a U-Haul to Chicago and I didn't show up? I moved on . . . you proposed to Jessica? Pick one."

"Life's never easy, is it, Lizzie?" Adam said after a few beats of uncomfortable silence. "But for what it's worth, I'm glad you're here now."

He reached out and grabbed my hand. I didn't let go, but it didn't feel quite right, either. A few weeks earlier, I would've been thrilled to be back at El Vez holding hands with him. At that moment, I felt nothing except confusion.

"How's work going?" he asked. "I actually just emailed you all of the updated files for the site. Everything's set up so it's ready to go."

"Oh, cool. Thank you. You really didn't have to do all of that for me. And it's great, actually. I just got into three new boutiques, and I have a call the first week of January with a buyer at Nordstrom."

Adam squeezed my hand. "No shit! Congrats. I always knew you'd make it big."

Although it was good to share the news with someone who'd known me back when I was just starting out, something still felt way off with him.

"By the way, did you ever find that necklace?" he asked.

"No. I'm pretty sure it's gone for good. It was nice of you to look, though."

"I'm sorry. I know how much your grandma meant to you."

I smiled, holding the tears back. "Anyway, enough about me. What happened with Jessica? I'm sorry I didn't respond to that text or your voicemail . . . I just felt responsible, and it didn't sit right."

"It's okay. Kind of a messed up story, actually. I got home from your apartment, ready to end things, and all of her stuff was gone. Left a 'Dear John' note on the table. Apparently, she was cheating on me with some weirdo she met performing in a regional production of *Cats*. Typical Jess, right?"

My eyes grew wide. Talk about a blow to the ego. I thought he had dumped her because he was in love with me. Granted, he was planning on breaking it off, but she conveniently gave him an out instead. Would he have gone through with it anyway?

Having no idea what to say except "Wow," I fiddled with the oversized pink cocktail ring I'd made the night before.

"I just don't get it," he continued. "Jessica was the one pushing the wedding. I thought this was what she wanted. But the past couple of weeks, she'd been acting so weird. I should've seen it coming."

I finally let go of his hand. "I thought this was what you wanted. You told me on Tuesday you were going to call her and dump her. Am I supposed to feel bad that she did it first?"

"I'm just telling you what happened, if you'd give me a second."

I took a long sip of margarita and stared up at the giant bicycle hanging above the bar. I didn't know what had come over me, but for once, Adam wasn't winning me over.

"I don't know," he said. "I guess I was just mixed up about her, and seeing you made me start to question my relationship with Jess even more, so I tried harder to fix things with her to take my mind off my doubts. That is, until we hung out the other day, and then everything became crystal clear. You're the one. You always have been. And I was stupid to second guess it."

I rested my chin on my elbow. Everything I thought I wanted was in front of me, but something had changed. Suddenly I realized the difference between Justin and Adam: it was feeling like myself versus having no idea how I was supposed to feel. Every time I was with Adam, he left me off balance. Despite the short amount of time we'd spent together, Justin was a steadfast presence. No years of hurt and regrets, just someone who was full of fun and energy (when he wasn't second-guessing my relationship with Adam).

"Whether you want to admit it or not, you know there's still something between us," he said. "Third time's the charm, right?"

I took a deep breath. "It kills me to say this, but I really don't know that we'd work out. And I can't go through losing you three times. I think we're hanging on to old feelings and our original plan to just be friends is for the best."

Adam just kind of stared into space for a minute, and then turned to me with puppy dog eyes. "I'm not confused, Liz. I want to be with you."

I stared at my chipped manicure, picking away at a few stray pieces of bright-green polish and flicking them onto the bar. Finally I looked up at Adam. "I don't think we should go there."

The middle-aged guy sitting next to me leaned over. "Jeez, give the guy a chance. He's pouring his heart out!"

"Oh shut up, George," a woman in a tweed blazer said from behind him. She turned to me. "Don't take him back, hon, stick to your guns."

Adam and I exchanged uncomfortable glances. "Do you want to get out of here?" he said. "Somehow I think this might not be the best place to have a serious conversation."

Although he was right, there was no way I'd invite Adam back to my apartment. Maybe all it took was for me to see the drastic difference between him and Justin to realize I had something pretty great already. I wasn't about to further jeopardize my already questionable relationship by risking another potential run-in.

I lowered my voice a notch and leaned in toward him. "That's probably not a good idea. We should just clear this up right now. Yes, I had feelings for you for a long time, and maybe I still do. But I'm seeing someone else now, and I want to give it a real shot. I owe that to myself."

Adam let out an exasperated sigh. "You barely know that kid. Just come back to my place, then. We can talk things through."

"I'm not driving all the way back with you to your

apartment to have a simple conversation we can have right now."

"Then I'll come to yours. Please, just hear me out. I'll stay over; we can talk all night if you want."

"You'll stay over, i.e., you think I'm going to sleep with you?"

"That's not what I meant, but correct me if I'm wrong, you've been sending out a lot of signals over the past few weeks. What about that kiss?"

My cheeks flamed. "I'm not the only one who sent signals. And correct me if *I'm* wrong; you kissed me."

"Okay. So what if we end up spending the night together? It would be amazing, and you know it."

I grabbed my things, realizing instantly I'd made the right decision. "If you think I'm just going to jump in bed because you got dumped by someone you didn't even want, I feel sorry for you."

Adam wrinkled his nose and tugged on his Justin-Timberlake-wannabe hat. "Is that what you really think?"

I frowned and nodded.

"Well, then," he said. "We should probably just end this conversation now."

"What does it look like I'm doing?" I pulled my coat off the stool so hard it toppled backward, whacking me in the knee and nearly knocking me to the ground with pain in the process.

The nosy older couple asked if I was all right, and I made it a point not to cry as I put my coat on, back turned to Adam.

"Good luck with Mr. Miami. Did you tell him you were coming here tonight?" he asked, his tone laced with jealousy.

I whirled around to face him. "That's none of your business."

He laughed. "Thought so. Tell me, why would you have to hide that you were coming here?"

"I'm not hiding anything. Justin and I have only been out a few times. There's no need for me to check in with him as to my daily whereabouts."

Whether or not Justin would've been pissed was another story entirely, and not one I felt like sharing with Adam.

I threw a ten-dollar bill on the counter and grabbed my purse, giving him a flick of the wrist that barely qualified as a wave.

"I'll talk to you later, Lizzie."

"Right," I said, turning on my heel, knowing I was one hundred percent *never* going back.

CHAPTER 24

ELLA

October 5, 1957

I'm going to make this short today. The kids are at a birthday party so I have at least three glorious hours of solitude! Harry's at work, of course, and Mom is taking a nap. I think I'll read for a bit and listen to the new Elvis Presley record Trudy let me borrow. Today I just feel like celebrating. The new menu has been a hit, and we even got a nice review in the paper. La Bella has been packed all week. We've always been busy, but the new menu seems to be taking off.

As for Mom, she is making improvements each day. The memory-loss issues are still apparent from time to time, and she complains about her face feeling numb, but the headaches and other symptoms are not nearly as bad as the week she went to the hospital. The doctor says she's incredibly lucky her stroke was so mild, and that she's progressing so nicely, especially at her age.

I think being in the house is getting to her, though. Some days she talks my ear off and others she clams up, refusing to tell me more about Joseph. The kids loved hearing about Italy, so I bet if I plant a bug in their ears, they'll convince her to tell us more . . .

Ella felt the dark clouds were finally starting to lift. Maybe her mother would never be back to one hundred percent, and she definitely still needed some physical therapy, but her condition wasn't getting worse, and they no longer needed a nurse to come to the house. That felt good enough for Ella, who'd been sick with worry about what to do if her mom's health declined further. Despite their differences, she would've felt awful about putting her headstrong mother in a nursing home.

Since Gabriella was resting and the kids were away, Ella tried out a new cheesecake recipe and then retreated to the office, listening to music, reading, and generally enjoying her own company. But the afternoon passed by far too quickly, and the grandfather clock eventually struck four. "Quiet time" was officially over.

Ella wrapped a light shawl around her shoulders as she walked over to Trudy's house to pick up the children. Although the sun shone brightly, she could feel the promise of cooler days ahead in the late afternoon breeze. It seemed hard to believe her mother had been living with them for nearly two months. Soon enough it would be Thanksgiving, then Christmas. She hadn't spent the holidays with her mother in years and wondered what it would be like now that she was in charge.

Gabriella had always made a big deal out of Christmas, hiring professional decorators to come into their old brownstone and deck every hall until the house was covered from floor to ceiling in Christmas finery. Ella possessed a more laid-back approach to decorating: a small tree in the living room, a wreath on the door, and homemade decorations from the kids here and there. Harry always put Christmas lights outside, fumbling with the ladder and making a spectacle for the neighbors.

She didn't know what Gabriella would think about their toned-down festivities, but for once it was time for Ella to do things her way.

She hummed "Jailhouse Rock" as a few kids came running down the driveway, riled up by sugar and the excitement of the party. Ella headed inside and spotted Trudy, dressed in a pale-pink dress covered by a cherry-print apron. Her brown locks were falling out of what had likely started as a neat bun, as she handed treats to the remaining children, all while keeping an eye on her four sons, who were quite literally bouncing off the walls.

"Need some help?" Ella asked, taking in the scene.

Trudy gave her a grateful smile. "That would be wonderful. Could you give these to the rest of the kids while I handle the boys?"

Ella stepped into action, giving quick hugs to her three before doling out the candy. Lily tugged at the bottom of her mother's dress as she was finishing up her task. "Mommy, I told Ruby Nonni was a princess and went to a real ball and she didn't believe me. Can you tell her I'm not lying?"

Ella tried not to laugh, but also wondered if it was a good idea for her to let Lily listen to her grandmother's memories after all. Then again, storytelling seemed to put Gabriella in a good mood, so it couldn't have hurt much. She'd just have to be sure to set the record straight.

"Lily, you know your Nonni wasn't a real princess. But she did go to a ball and dress in a beautiful gown, and that's just like something a princess would do."

Little Ruby turned to Lily with a smug look. "Told you she wasn't a princess."

For an instant Ella felt bad for telling the truth when she saw the dejected look on Lily's face, but she didn't believe in lying to children, even when it made life a little more difficult.

"Ruby, how about you come over to our house to play soon? Lily's grandmother can tell you all about her life in Italy and the handsome men she danced with at the balls. Would you like that?" Ella said.

Ruby nodded and this seemed to appease Lily, so Ella continued helping with cleanup and chatting with the other kids' mothers. After the rest of the party guests cleared out, Ella sat down at the kitchen table with Trudy, grateful for a few minutes with her friend and a cup of coffee.

"So, congratulations on that review. Harry must be over the moon," Trudy said.

"Thanks. We're all pretty excited, but it's been a double-edged sword. We might actually have to hire some more servers because it's been so crowded, and people are complaining they can't get a table."

"That's a great problem to have, isn't it? Plus, now your mother is feeling a little better, maybe you can finally talk to Harry about the cake idea."

Ella took a long sip from her mug, trying to choose the right words. She'd had a feeling Trudy was going to ask her about the bakery again. They'd spoken about the idea once more since that initial phone call, and the more they talked about it, the more Trudy seemed to support the dream. She'd even suggested helping to run the shop.

"I just don't know if it's a good idea," Ella said, pursing her lips. "Yes, business is doing well right now. But it means Harry's busier than ever. How could we possibly open a cake shop, even if we had help? He'd think I was loony for even suggesting it. And that would mean more work for him to research all of the money aspects and whatnot."

Trudy leaned back in her chair, touching a finger to her lip. "You just need a plan. I could have my Stan help us come up with a whole business proposal. We can even type it on fancy paper. How can Harry say no if you've thought through every detail? We'll lay out the financials and everything."

She has a point, Ella thought. "I suppose we could do that, but I'm still nervous Harry won't think it's a good idea with how busy we are lately. You're sure Stan wouldn't mind helping us?"

"If it's one thing my husband is good at, it's business. Plus, he owes me for missing the party. Damn work trips."

Ella grabbed her friend's hand. "Thanks, Trudy. I really appreciate this. I still don't think it's going to work, but I appreciate your confidence all the same."

About an hour later Ella was back home, clearing the dinner table, when she heard Lily's screeching laugh come from the living room.

"What does 'pompous' mean, Nonni? That's a funny word."

"It means someone who thinks they are the bee's knees," Gabriella said. "And that's exactly what Nonni's friend Joseph thought he was."

Ella shook her head. Her mother seemed to forget every so often Lily was, in fact, five years old. Whether she grasped the concept of pompousness or not, at least she seemed to be entertained. Ella strained to hear the rest of the story as she did the dishes, listening with a smile as Lily asked all about her Nonni's special friend and whether or not she'd worn a tiara.

CHAPTER 25

GABRIELLA

1905

WORD ABOUT GABRIELLA and Joseph's encounter at the ball spread like the plague throughout the city, and soon enough even Gabriella's grandmother in Lucca knew about the cameo. She had written to inquire about their wedding plans, which forced Gabriella to address the topic, as much as she wanted to avoid it.

Several days after receiving the letter, she took to the drawing room to finally start on a reply. An hour later, there were three sheets of crumpled paper at her feet, but nothing even resembling a proper letter on the table.

She started out with the blunt ("Despite the rumors from my mother, Mr. Rossi and I are not to be engaged"), moved on to the disingenuous ("I am unaware of the engagement of which you speak") and then tried pleading ("Nonni, I beg you to talk some sense into my parents!").

Unhappy with all of her attempts, Gabriella bit her lip and tried to think of something vague enough to not promise an engagement, but detailed enough to satisfy her nosy grandmother's expectations. Finally she wrote:

Dearest Nonni,

I hope this letter finds you well. It has been a lovely summer here, although I do hope the hot weather doesn't continue as it has been. I suffered from a fainting spell at the Rossis' ball due to the heat, as I'm sure you have heard.

Other than the unfortunate fainting incident, we all had a wonderful time. I wouldn't be surprised if my mother tried to steal their chef away, as the food was some of the best we've tasted. The Rossis are gracious hosts and I am sure we will be enjoying their company again in the near future. Mr. Rossi was kind enough to give me a cameo necklace, which I am wearing at the present moment. Lessie complimented it greatly when I saw her this afternoon.

Everyone is in fine spirits and looking forward to seeing you again before we return to New York next month. Until then, you are in my thoughts and prayers.

Your affectionate granddaughter,
Gabriella

Satisfied with the letter, she placed it in a thick cream-colored envelope and wrote out her grandmother's address in careful script.

Gabriella didn't dare tell her Nonni (or anyone except Loretta, for that matter) she was actually going to see Joseph that very night. She had received a note requesting her presence in the Capettis' garden at midnight. Joseph had some matters he wanted to discuss.

There was no use in ignoring him. If she didn't meet with Joseph in private, she'd just be forced into another dinner, and a formal proposal would be made in front of everyone. But despite everything, a small part of her was looking forward to seeing him again. Perhaps it was the waltz, or the kiss in the Rossis' garden, that had been the turning point, but her heartbeat quickened at the thought of what could happen next. Confusion seemed to be the emotion of the summer.

The rest of the evening passed painfully slowly, and Gabriella found herself pacing back and forth in her room, reading Joseph's letter over and over again. She didn't know what to say to him, but one thing Gabriella did know was, like it or not, it seemed she had little choice in the matter of their engagement. Luckily, she didn't hate him as much as before, and that was a step.

Loretta was under strict instructions to come up to her room at eleven on the dot so she could properly get ready. The choice of outfit for the occasion had been painstakingly made. She didn't want to appear too formally dressed, but she couldn't exactly go out in her nightgown, either. After much deliberation, Gabriella chose a deep-purple dress of heavy cotton with a ribbon belt that showed off her narrow waist.

At last Loretta slipped into the room. "Part of me is happy you're finally taking Mr. Rossi's proposal seriously," she said. "But another part worries you'll be caught doing who knows what in my mistress's gardens at such an hour. Please humor me and behave appropriately, Miss Ella."

Gabriella rolled her eyes. "Now what would I do to dishonor my name, other than a secret meeting, of course?"

Loretta just shook her head and directed Gabriella to sit at the vanity. The pair finally decided on a high bun with loose curls framing her face.

"What time is it?" Gabriella asked, fidgeting in her seat. She felt sweat beading under her arms, and the curling tongs weren't helping the situation.

"Miss Ella, you asked me the time about ten minutes ago. You must be patient."

Gabriella pulled on a curl and sighed. "I don't even know why I've agreed to meet him. He's not the man I expected when I dreamt of my future husband. Even if he is handsome, and maybe not such a terrible person."

"Because deep down, you're a good, sensible girl. That's why you're meeting him. And perhaps your feelings will change when you get to know him a little better."

"What if my feelings don't change, Loretta? Do I simply marry him and live in a loveless marriage like the rest of the world? Yours was a love marriage and it worked out just fine. Why can't I wait for my true match as well?"

Loretta stared in the mirror for a moment, and Gabriella noticed the sadness in her eyes. "My marriage was for love, this is true," she said. "But familial expectations aren't exactly the same when you're a poor girl marrying the coachman."

"Maybe I'll find myself a nice coachman, then," Gabriella said, letting out a small "humph."

"Oh, Miss Ella," Loretta started, putting one final pin in the mess of curls, "you know many of the best marriages weren't initially love matches. You could grow to become very fond of Mr. Rossi over time. He's already becoming less irksome, am I right?"

Gabriella got up from the plump cushion in front of the vanity and marched into her dressing room, ignoring the comment. Her head was spinning as she examined her choice of dress, wondering if there was perhaps a better option. She didn't even know why she cared. It was going to be dark, after all.

"Do you truly think I'm doing the right thing?"

"Yes, I do, Miss Ella. Although sneaking out at midnight wouldn't ordinarily be something I'd condone, and your mother will have my hide if she finds out."

Gabriella laughed. "Oh, don't fret. I've been slipping out of the house at midnight or worse for years. I won't be caught."

Loretta raised her eyebrows, although she shouldn't have been surprised at this revelation.

"I didn't hear anything," she said, leaving Gabriella to the business of meeting Joseph Rossi.

Slipping outside was simple. Mr. and Mrs. Capetti were asleep, and their rooms were located far enough from Gabriella's that she didn't need to walk past them, anyway. All she had to do was remove her shoes so the stairs wouldn't creak, tiptoe through the main hall back to the servants' entrance, and creep out the side, around to the garden.

Gabriella's skin tingled, and she could feel anticipation in the air as she walked along the stone path and sat on a bench behind a large cypress tree. This way, she could keep an eye on the garden's entrance but still remain somewhat hidden in case someone found her out of bed.

This, unsurprisingly, had happened before, when she was fourteen and tried to meet Lessie for a covert operation in the wee hours of the morning. They had a theory that the Capettis' cook was having an affair with their gardener, and set out to prove it. To their dismay, they were spotted by Loretta's husband and sent inside at once.

Hoping there wouldn't be a repeat performance, Gabriella shifted a little further back behind the tree. It had been three minutes past midnight when she'd slipped out of her room, so she figured it must have been at least seven or eight past at that point. Where was he?

She decided to wait ten more minutes and if he didn't turn up, it would be his loss. Although Gabriella had a habit of tardiness, she did not take kindly to others who shared the trait.

She tapped her foot, paced back and forth, and then finally decided to take advantage of the extra time by smoothing out her dress and rearranging her curls as best she could without a mirror.

Finally a shadow moved across the villa's stone façade, and Joseph stepped tentatively into the clearing, looking around for her. She sat back and let him wonder for a minute. *That should teach him to turn up late.* Gabriella took her time getting up from the bench and hid behind the cypress until he walked past.

"Over here," she whispered, grabbing his arm. Joseph jumped at the sound of her voice.

"Could you please try not to scare the wits out of me?" he said, brushing a stray leaf from his gray waistcoat.

Gabriella shot him a dirty look. "You're the one who wanted to meet me out here."

"Yes, I'm sorry. I just have a lot on my mind right now. Please, sit down and let's talk."

He motioned toward the bench and Gabriella shook her head. "I'd rather venture further back, if you don't mind. Just in case we're spotted."

She led him past a stone urn overflowing with ivy and across a small bridge that stretched over the water-lily-covered pond, finally slipping behind another cypress.

"This should do," she said, placing one hand against the tree trunk and the other on her hip.

"I apologize for asking you to come out here at this hour, but I didn't know how else I could speak with you alone."

"I'm here, Mr. Rossi. What did you want to discuss that couldn't be done in a public forum?"

Joseph hesitated for a moment. "I'm going to call on you tomorrow. To propose. I know you're concerned about the match, and honestly, I don't want to risk humiliation."

Gabriella burst into high-pitched giggles; a terrible nervous habit of hers. She never thought such uncertainty would come out of Joseph Rossi's mouth, and it was actually somewhat endearing. "I'm sorry, let me get things straight. So you're trying to test the waters and make sure I'll accept?"

"Well, yes. And you don't have to laugh at me, thank you very much." Joseph narrowed his eyes, clearly not used to women reacting in such a way to him.

"I apologize. Do continue."

He took a step closer. "I told you we could get to know each other better. So I want you to ask me anything. Anything at all."

"And you think I'll make a decision based on a few hasty questions in a moonlit garden?"

Joseph looked a little embarrassed at this remark, and looked at the ground. "Erm, I suppose so."

"I know just as well as you do that it matters very little what I think about the arrangement."

"But it matters to me."

"Only because you don't want a miserable bride." Gabriella smirked, actually enjoying their banter. Maybe it was because she knew the proposal was coming, but her nerves about the whole situation felt more at ease, the tension in her neck beginning to loosen.

"Who wants an unhappy spouse around them all day? But that's not the only reason. I like how you speak your mind. You're not afraid to tell everyone when you don't agree."

"Yes, and look how far it's got me in life," Gabriella said, releasing her grip from the tree. "Twenty-one and unmarried."

"And I'm thankful for that," he said, taking her hand. Gabriella dropped it and turned her back to him. While she appreciated his modern views on women, she thought it couldn't hurt to let the cat chase the mouse a bit. If he wanted her heart, he'd have to work to earn it.

"Fine, I'll ask your questions if you're so insistent on playing this little 'getting to know you' game," she said.

"Can you at least turn around and look me in the eye when you speak?"

Gabriella remained rooted in her position, arms crossed, so Joseph shook his head and walked over to face her.

"Where would we live? If we were to be married, I mean," she asked.

"We could live in England until I finish my studies at Oxford. Then we could come back to Florence, if you like."

"I'm not leaving New York." Florence was lovely for a summer visit, but the thought of moving away from her beloved Manhattan made Gabriella's chest tighten.

"I suppose location is something that certainly could be discussed," he said. Gabriella thought she could see the wheels turning in his head, thinking maybe he'd underestimated her independent streak.

"What is your position on dogs?" she asked next.

"Dogs?" Joseph asked, raising an eyebrow.

"Yes, dogs. I hate dogs. There will be no dogs in any home of mine."

"Fine with me," he said, trying to conceal his

laughter with a well-timed cough. "Is that all you want to know? Whether I like dogs?"

Gabriella sighed. "What is your favorite color?"

"I happen to be rather fond of navy blue," he said with a twinkle in his eye. Gabriella hated that he was enjoying this stupid game. She just wanted to get on with her life, which reminded her of another question.

"And there would be a ring involved, I trust? The cameo is lovely, but it's not exactly an appropriate engagement gift for a girl of my stature."

"I have a beautiful and suitably ostentatious ruby-and-diamond ring that belonged to my grandmother. I'm sure you'll find it to your liking."

Gabriella pondered this for a second, imagining a bright, flashy stone, and then reached around her neck to unclasp her locket. She knew the engagement would have to happen, and a part of her even wanted it to happen. At least it could somewhat be on her terms.

"Here you go," she said, dropping the cameo in his hand. "Feel free to go off and do with it what you like. You said you'd want it back to engrave it, correct? I assume with a proposal?"

"Yes. But—" Joseph started.

Gabriella cut him off. "I'll expect you tomorrow afternoon, then. Goodnight, Mr. Rossi."

Joseph opened his mouth but nothing came out as Gabriella ran toward the house, leaving the necklace still curled up inside his open palm. When she made a decision, Gabriella didn't look back.

CHAPTER 26

LIZ

THE SUNDAY AFTER the incident at El Vez, I was sitting at my kitchen table surrounded by jewelry supplies, humming along to the '90s playlist on my iPod (I'd at least temporarily banned Dave Matthews Band from my life), when I realized something: for the first time since Thanksgiving, I hadn't woken up crying about Nan or pining over Adam. I actually felt something close to content, which was a nice change.

Of course I would never forget about Nan, and knew the healing process was far from over. But all it took was that fight with Adam to realize it wasn't worth wasting my life on someone I wasn't sure about, especially knowing how things can change in an instant. Now all I had to do was make things right with Justin.

Other than the handsome Mr. J., the only other unresolved issue was Adam's email with the design files. I did love the site, but I knew it would be weird for me to use it and have that constant reminder of him. I decided to give myself some time to cool off and think about it later. I had more important things to worry about. Like Justin.

Suddenly I found myself overwhelmed by how much I wanted to see him. Before I knew it, my tweezers and beads were tossed on the table and my feet headed out the door. *You can do this*, I told myself as I stood outside Justin's apartment.

My two sharp knocks sounded way more confident than I felt, and I bit my lip as I waited for an answer. None came, not even a bark from Bo, so I sighed and walked back down the hall. *He must be taking the dog for a walk*, I thought, trying to console myself. I had a ton of work to do, anyway, so I vowed to come back in a few hours before I was supposed to head out and meet Addie. This was definitely not the time for a text message. I needed to see his face and tell him I wanted to make things work.

As I passed the elevator, the doors opened, and Lucy walked out in a neon-pink ruffled coat, arms weighed down with grocery bags. "Need some help?" I asked, trying not to laugh as she juggled three bags in one hand, two in the other, and a reusable grocery tote on each shoulder.

"That would be a huge 'yes,'" she said, as I took three of the bags off her hands. "And where have you been lately?"

"Ugh, you don't know the half of it," I said. "But I basically had to tell Adam I didn't want to be with him."

Her eyes widened. "Hold up. I thought you were just friends? This is what happens when I go away for a few days. I miss all the gossip!"

I filled her in on the night at El Vez and the current situation with Justin as we put her groceries away, and eventually her fiancé, Thomas, spoke up.

"If you want a guy's perspective about all of this, I think Justin really is busy with work . . . but if he wanted to contact you, he would. I'm sure he's seriously questioning whether you're over Adam and wants to play it safe. Especially when he saw you with Adam at Giuseppe's. You can't blame him for feeling weird about you hanging out with, and making out with, your ex."

"You're right," I said. "But I don't know how to fix things with him. I miss him, and I think I really screwed up."

Thomas tossed some apples in a ceramic bowl on the table and sat down. "All you can do is tell him you're sorry. Maybe invite him over? Too bad he's not a girl, or you could make him some jewelry as an 'I'm sorry' gift."

"Yeah, somehow I don't think he wants to wear some statement hoops."

Lucy put a hand on my shoulder. "Well, hopefully you'll be able to stop by when he's home. And if he doesn't want you, then it's his loss. But it is Christmas . . . the season of miracles, right?"

↔ ↔ ↔

BACK AT MY APARTMENT, I finished up a pair of turquoise studs, made another cup of coffee, and sat back to admire my latest pieces. A few customers at Plaid were looking to buy more of my earrings, so Kaycee asked me to make a new batch since holiday shopping was at its peak.

Even better, one of my designs showed up in *Philadelphia Style* magazine's blog as a great holiday gift, and listed the store's contact information. Kaycee was thrilled and I even got an email from her best friend, who works for a PR firm in New York. She'd seen the blog, and mentioned a few contacts she had at fashion magazines who might be interested in my pieces for spring. I planned to devote my afternoon to working on a pitch letter and choosing some pieces to feature (with help from Addie, who'd done a brief stint at a PR firm before going to law school), until I received a frantic call from Cate.

"Are you home?" she asked, her voice low and shaky.

My blood pressure shot up about a thousand points. "Yeah, I'm here. What's wrong? Is everyone okay?" I prayed this wasn't going to be a call like the one about Nan.

"I'm sorry. Yes, everyone's fine. It's nothing like that. It's, um, personal."

"Way to scare me to death," I said, taking a few slow breaths to get my heart to stop racing. "But you do realize you're going to have to tell me what it is for me to help, right?"

Cate sighed. "It's about me and Jesse. I'm kind of having second thoughts about getting married."

"Oh," I said, unsure about the appropriate response other than, "I told you so." I had to admit I'd seen it coming, but I wasn't going to rub salt in her wound.

"Can I come over? I don't want to talk to Mom. You know how she is, and especially because she's like, obsessed with this whole wedding. I'm not going to worry her unless I've made a concrete decision."

I took a look at my table full of jewelry. Work would have to wait. "Sure, let me just clean up. I have beads and stuff everywhere."

Cate seemed relieved and told me she would be there in an hour. I sent Addie a text to reschedule our little business meeting and began organizing my beads, hoops, and other pieces into their containers. I'd have to put off seeing Justin, too, but family was more important.

Despite initially having felt jealous of her engagement and relationship in general, I sympathized with Cate. It had to be hard to break up with someone like Jesse, and his well-connected family was nothing short of intimidating. Accepting his proposal probably seemed like the right thing to do, but maybe she'd finally realized that marrying someone so young and so quickly wasn't a good idea.

Cate arrived almost exactly half an hour later, and while the casual observer would think she was slightly overdressed for a rainy December Saturday (especially in contrast to my leggings and "Ocean City, New Jersey" hoodie), I could instantly tell something was very, very wrong. She might have fooled someone else with her combination of bright-pink Lacoste sweater, striped button-down, and dark jeans tucked into Hunter wellies, but the truth was her outfit did a decent job at covering up how she was actually a hot mess.

Cate's usually-sleek brown hair was pulled back with a wide pink ribbon, likely to disguise how it was frizzy and in need of a good washing. She wasn't wearing any makeup, and had made no attempt at covering up the small pimple sprouting on her chin or the dark circles under her eyes. Her signature scent (Chanel No. 5, like Nan) was noticeably absent, and her perpetually French-manicured nails were polish-free and bitten down to stubs. This meant serious business.

"Are you okay?" I asked, eyeing up her left hand. The ring was still there, but that didn't mean anything.

"I don't know. Can you fix me a cup of tea?"

I always thought Cate should've been English; she was incapable of having a proper conversation without it being over a cuppa. I went into the kitchen to put the kettle on, attempting to get her to spill in the process.

"So, does Mom know you're here?" I asked.

Cate shook her head no. "Like I said, I don't want her to know about any of this. I told her I was going out with Jesse."

"Ah. So what's going on with you two? I see you're still wearing the ring at least."

"Yeah," she said, absentmindedly turning it around her finger a few times. "It's not that bad yet."

"How bad *are* things, then?"

Cate sat at the kitchen table and sighed. "I told him I wanted to postpone the wedding to give us a little more time to just be engaged and get to know each other better. Let's just say that didn't go over very well."

"What did he say?"

"He didn't understand why I needed more time if I'd already said yes to him. He said we have our whole lives to get to know everything about each other."

"Interesting," I said, pulling out two mugs. "How did you react?"

"I just told him I thought things were moving along too fast and that I wanted a longer engagement. It doesn't mean I have doubts about him, personally." She fiddled with the vase of fake flowers in the center of the table before continuing. "Did you know his parents are talking about booking The Union League for this June?"

"June? I thought you were set on a winter wedding. That was always your dream, right?"

"Yeah, you know that. I thought we could do it next New Year's Eve, which would at least give us a year. But his parents want a summer wedding because it fits their work schedule better, plus his mother 'doesn't like winter.' And they're paying, obviously."

Of course Jesse's parents were paying. The Crenshaws were the type who often showed up in photos on the society pages (when they weren't traveling the world helping those less fortunate, of course) and seemed to have many, many acquaintances but few real friends. His mother was a semi-famous author of self-help books for women and spent most of her time doing public speaking gigs, and his dad was the retired CEO of a big regional bank, with a big attitude to match.

Although they certainly gave a sizable amount of

money to charities each year, I wondered if they did it mostly for the globetrotting, posing for photo ops with impoverished kids because it meant good press. Mrs. Crenshaw, despite her talk of women's empowerment and sisterhood, had a reputation around Philadelphia for being a royal B-word, and the Mister was no better. Mrs. C. agreeing to help with my line was a little surprising, although very kind, but I figured they were the types to help out "their own." Maybe it was a goodwill gesture toward Cate, now that she and Jesse were engaged and all.

"Just tell them that Mom and Dad will pay. I'm sure the fire hall and some crepe paper wedding bells will do just fine for the big photo spread in the paper, right?"

Cate rolled her eyes. "Can you imagine? They're such fucking snobs."

"Whoa, using the big guns?" I asked, my mouth dropping open. Cate had always been one of those people who never, ever cursed; typically she'd chastise me for letting even a minor swear word fly. She had to be pretty pissed to let the f-bomb out.

"Whatever. I mean, I'm only twenty-one years old, and his parents expect me to act and dress like a senior citizen. Going to these events with them is torture. Like last week, you know how we went to that benefit?"

I nodded. The Crenshaws had invited her to a big black-tie event at The Four Seasons, and Cate had posted a few pictures on Facebook of herself and Jesse in their swanky new outfits. I'd spent that night on the couch with Nan's diary and a bag of Cheetos, so feeling sorry for her didn't cross my mind.

"So I got that new pink dress, and all night I had to hear from Jesse's mom about how it was quote-unquote 'a shame' I hadn't chosen a red dress to match the theme, and how she wasn't sure that a one-shoulder gown was appropriate. She wouldn't give it up! The woman even said something to the random people at our table about it."

"Ew," I said, pouring tea in Cate's mug and trying to seem compassionate. It sounded pretty rude, but if fashion criticisms were Cate's biggest problem, I didn't want to hear it.

"Anyway," she continued. "Then, when a photographer from some snobby magazine wanted to get our picture, she totally pushed us out of the way and had the guy take it of her and Jesse's dad instead. She said something like 'leave this to the pros.' Meanwhile the photographer just stood there like he couldn't believe this lady was for real."

"Whaaat?" I said. "That's pretty attention whore-ish, even for her."

"I know. And when I said something to Jesse about it, he just kind of rolled his eyes and said not to worry about it. If it had been the first time she'd done something like that, it would be one thing. But she tries to embarrass me in public constantly. Remember when she introduced me to the mayor as Jesse's 'flavor of the month?'"

"It's hard to forget," I said, cringing. Cate had come home in tears that night and they'd almost broken up.

"Have you ever had a serious conversation with Jesse about this? I mean besides after the mayor incident?" I asked.

"Yeah. He just brushes it off and says something lame like 'Oh that's her way.' I'm sorry, but just because she's always acted like a bitch doesn't make it acceptable."

I nodded in agreement, not sure what else to say. My only real "in-law" type experience had been with Adam's mom, and she was always warm and friendly. She'd even sent a special care package to me during finals, which I actually think weirded Adam out a bit.

"I just don't know what to do. I can't stand there and smile on Jesse's arm in these pictures like everything is perfect. I'm tired of trying to be such a goody two-shoes. And now that I'm engaged to a Crenshaw, there are all of these expectations. God forbid I have too much to drink one night and end up in one of the gossip blogs."

"You're like a regular Kate Middleton," I said, meaning to lighten the mood, but realizing I probably sounded bitter.

"I'm not trying to be all 'poor little rich girl,' but can you just sympathize with me for a minute?" she said, staring down at her mug with a dejected look. Cate had always been great at making me feel guilty.

"Look, I'm sure it's hard to deal with a monster-in-law, but if you really love Jesse, shouldn't that trump everything?"

Cate looked up, her eyes now filled with tears. "I don't know. That's the problem. What if I'm making a huge mistake?"

"What makes you think that?" I wanted to assure her it wasn't a mistake, but considering I was ninety-nine-percent sure it was, I stuck with asking tactful questions instead. Until she forced me into it, I was going to steer clear of any wedding bashing.

"I always had a serious boyfriend so, you know, I didn't do the whole frat party thing. Which was fine, but I feel like I never got to experience college and now it's over. What if I end up being, like, thirty-five with two kids and then I realize I've never even slept with anyone else?"

I made a face at this admission. I had no interest in hearing about my sister's sexual exploits, or lack thereof. "First: TMI. Second: I do kind of think it's important to at least have fun while you're young and unattached. So many couples break up when they get married too young. You know that's why I panicked about getting engaged to Adam right after college."

Cate made a face. "I know. That's what makes me nervous about this. Who wants to be a divorcée in her twenties?"

"So what are you going to do?" I asked.

Cate twirled her ring a few times, finally letting out a deep sigh. "Mom is probably going to kill me, but I don't think I can go through with this wedding."

"Hey, at least I can be the golden child for once," I said with a sad smile. "Seriously, though, I think you're making the right decision. If you were going to have a long engagement, it would be one thing . . . but getting married after a few months at your age is definitely pushing it."

"You're right. And I've felt like this for a long time, even the night he proposed. I just never said anything."

"I'm sure it's hard to say no when someone's waving a three-carat Asscher cut in your face," I said, allowing myself the first extended glance I'd ever had at her huge platinum ring. It must have set him (or his parents) back an easy forty grand.

"You're telling me," she said, waving her hand around a bit as we both admired how the stones caught the light. "I shouldn't have accepted it, though."

"Probably not, but that doesn't mean you have to break up. Maybe you could just agree to a longer engagement. I'm sure he'll come around."

Cate shook her head. "I don't think so. He was pretty pissed last night. He actually told me to get out of his apartment."

Although cursing him out probably wasn't helping

the situation, I couldn't help myself. After a few choices expletives (Cate gave me a sideways glance, which must've meant she was feeling a little better), I snapped back into responsible advice-giving mode.

"I'm sure he was probably just hurt and caught off guard by everything. Did you say anything before that about not agreeing to the June timeline?"

"Considering yesterday was the first I'd heard of it, no."

"What? So he just sprung it on you like PS, we're getting married in June, deal with it?" I said, suddenly thankful I was still single.

"Pretty much. Can you imagine your fiancé's parents actually choosing your wedding date and acting like that's normal?" Cate said, shaking her head in disbelief. "We've had literally no input at this point. They think because they're paying for everything we should just be grateful, but personally, I would rather elope than deal with their BS."

"If I can interrupt, it sounds like most of this drama is about the wedding, not about whether or not you actually want to marry Jesse. Am I right?"

"Well," she said, staring into her now empty cup of tea. "There's something else."

"Something as in . . . someone?" I guessed.

Cate was silent and finally gave a tiny nod. "Nothing's *happened*. It's not like that. I don't even want to be with him, I want to be with Jesse. But this guy from one of my classes, we were in the same group on a project and spent a lot of time together. He asked me out."

I gave her the hairy eyeball but she threw her arms up in the air. "I said no, of course! But there was a part of me that wanted to say yes. He made me realize there are other people out there and other experiences. Why am I tying myself down now? What if I'm too young to even know if Jesse's the one?"

"I'm not going to argue with you, Cate. Yes, I think you're too young to be getting married. Hell, sometimes I think *I'm* too young to be getting married, and I'm five years older than you. But if Jesse seriously is the one, why do you need to be running around seeing other people?"

She shrugged. "Life experience?"

"All I'm trying to say is you can make it work with him and still be able to do things on your own and experience being young. No one said you have to act like you're fifty because you're married. Believe me, you don't want to end up like—"

I thought about Nonni Gabriella and her forced engagement. I didn't want to tell Cate about the cameo and the diary. It felt like a secret between Nan and me. As dumb as it sounded, it was almost like she was still there when I read it, and I didn't want to share that feeling with anyone just yet.

Cate looked at me expectantly, and I realized I'd almost said too much. "Like who?"

"No one. I just mean, like those people who end up divorced at twenty-four. Anyway, why don't you take some friends and backpack around Europe? Dance on some tables. Do something crazy while you still can."

Cate rolled her eyes. "I'm sure Mrs. Crenshaw would love that."

"But do you get what I'm saying? Just because you don't want to be married now doesn't mean Jesse is wrong for you. It means you need to take a little more time, that's all. And if he doesn't understand, then I guess that's his loss."

"I know, but what about Nordstrom? I wouldn't put it

past her to make that woman cancel the meeting with you."

"Are you serious? I'll be fine, trust me. If it's meant to be, it will happen, with or without Jesse's mom."

Cate was silent for a while and finally stood up to put on her coat. "Don't worry. I'll make sure it happens. I owe you one for today."

I smiled. "No prob, Beep."

She turned away but I still caught her wiping away a tear. "Anyway, I'm starving," Cate said. "Do you want to grab some Chinese food? My treat."

I never could resist Chinese, or free food in general, so I just smiled and grabbed my coat. "We'll need to create a game plan for breaking the news to Mom," I said, wrapping my woolly scarf a few times around my neck. "But that's what sisters are for, right?"

CHAPTER 27

ELLA

October 15, 1957

Haven't written in a while since I've been so busy. Trudy and I have been spending every spare minute working on the business plan for our cake shop. Lord only knows if this is going to work, but I have to try. Harry doesn't suspect a thing since he's been at La Bella so much lately. Trudy was definitely right about creating a plan instead of just surprising Harry with the notion of a bakery. I don't want to toss out an idea into the clear blue sky without having the information he needs to make a decision. And once he sees all of the work we've done, he'll know I mean business . . . literally.

Other than that, I've been busy taking Mom to doctor's appointments and to visit her friend Rose. Sometimes I feel more like a chauffeur than a daughter, but it's nice for her to get out of the house and spend time with someone her own age.

Halloween will be here soon enough, and the kids are excited about their costumes. Well, Harry Jr. and Carol don't understand it yet, but they seem interested in dressing up like a skeleton and a witch. Lily has decided to be a nurse, "like the ones who helped Nonni."

*Speaking of Nonni, she still won't show us the cameo,
even though the kids have begged her about it for days. I wonder
if it's because she doesn't have the locket anymore and doesn't
want to admit it, or if there's another reason . . .*

No one knew about Ella's secret bakery dream, except
for Trudy, of course. That was, until Gabriella walked into
the kitchen one day and overheard them arguing about the
potential business's name.

"La Bella Cakery just makes sense," Ella said. "We
already have an established name, and I'd like to feed off
that reputation as much as possible."

Trudy shook her head. "I think it needs to be
different. Something young and exciting! We want to
catch a bride's attention, right?"

Ella was pondering the nicest way to tell her friend to
shut up. It was *her* business, after all. But then she noticed
Gabriella standing in the doorway, decked out in a cobalt-
blue ruffled blouse, a rather large diamond pendant, and
a skirt with a busy print involving what appeared to be
birds. "Do you need something, Mom?"

"No. But I agree with you, Ella. If you're opening a
bakery, it should be attached to the restaurant, shouldn't it?"

"Who said we were opening a bakery?" Ella asked.

Gabriella shuffled over to the chair opposite Trudy,
propping her cane against it. "Don't play dumb. Fill me in
on the plan! I could use some excitement after being stuck
in this house all day."

Ella and Trudy exchanged nervous glances. They
hadn't told anyone besides Trudy's husband about their
plan, and Gabriella's ability to keep quiet was doubtful.
Ella did feel bad for her mom, though, and she could tell
Trudy did as well.

"Fine. Trudy, we'll tell her."

Ella turned to her mother. "The cake shop is just a dream at this point. Harry doesn't even know about it yet, so please don't mention it."

"And you think I can't keep a secret?"

"It's not that, Mom—" Ella pressed her lips together. Yes, she was nervous that the news of La Bella Cakery would spread to the senior center crowd (and then the entire town), but the biggest reason she hadn't mentioned the bakery to her mother was because she didn't want the idea to be shot down. Gabriella Capetti had never worked a day in her life, let alone operated a business, and Ella couldn't imagine she'd understand the drive to create something from scratch.

"Trust me, dear. I can keep my own counsel when necessary," Gabriella said. "How long was it before you knew anything about Joseph Rossi?"

"Oooh, who is this?" Trudy asked. "He sounds handsome just by the name. Where'd you meet? The senior center?"

Ella laughed. "No, nothing like that. He's a mysterious someone from Mom's past. But she hasn't been in the mood to talk about him lately."

"Why not?" Trudy asked.

"The best stories are revealed over time, don't you think? I need to create some element of suspense. Keeps 'em interested."

Ella looked down at her chapped hands, twirling her ring. Harry's words about getting to know Mom better while they still had the time echoed in her brain. If her mother was going to reveal this story, which was getting more interesting by the day, it was only fair for Ella to offer something of her own in return.

"Fine. We'll let you help us with the plan for the bakery if you promise to tell us more about Joseph. Anything that's said at this table stays here. *Capisce*?"

"Deal," Gabriella said. "But only because there's nothing better to do in this godforsaken town. Now what do you want to know?"

CHAPTER 28

GABRIELLA

1905

*T*HE REALIZATION THAT she was about to become engaged didn't hit Gabriella until the next day as she sat in the drawing room, sipping espresso with her mother, Lessie, and Aunt Gia. They had just returned from mass at Santa Maria del Fiore, where the usually stoic Mrs. Rossi had spent a good five minutes complimenting Gabriella on her dress, complexion, and just about anything else there was to comment upon. Her excitement, combined with Joseph's notable absence, pointed toward Joseph moving forward with his plan as promised.

She knew that telling her family about the midnight assignation wasn't an option, but how else was she going to explain the missing cameo? She wore it every day, and hoped its absence wouldn't be too noticeable. These thoughts were going through her mind as Mrs. Capetti brought up the subject of Joseph Rossi.

"I was speaking to Mrs. Carlino after mass and she told me an interesting story," she said, looking pointedly at her daughter. "Her son Anthony, as you know, is good friends with your Joseph, and it seems that he was in their shop yesterday. She said he brought in a cameo, although Anthony wouldn't tell her the reason. I can't help but notice you aren't wearing yours today."

Gabriella's stomach churned and she silently cursed that busybody Mrs. Carlino for owning a jewelry shop and making her life even more complicated.

"Is there something you'd like to tell us?" her mother asked, taking a small sip of her espresso, her face a perfect mask of calmness. Gabriella knew her mother was just as boiling as the contents of her dainty floral-trimmed cup, though.

Gabriella remained silent, trying to think of an excuse. Lessie turned to her cousin. "Did something happen with Mr. Rossi? You can tell us."

"He took the cameo back."

"What?" Mrs. Capetti said, nearly flying out of her seat. "Why would he do that? Please tell me you weren't foolish enough to turn down a proposal!"

"Calm down, mother," Gabriella said. This time it was her turn to lift her cup and take a leisurely sip. Getting her mother riled up was one of Gabriella's greatest pleasures in life, and she was enjoying herself.

After swallowing as slowly as possible, she finally spoke. "One of their maids came over last night with a letter. He wanted it back from me." Even if she wasn't fighting this engagement anymore, Gabriella would never give her mother the satisfaction of knowing she'd given the necklace back, exactly as Mr. Rossi wanted, before he'd even asked. Her mother had ruled over her for long enough.

Mrs. Capetti's face turned the color of a ripe tomato. "Let me see this letter. Get it immediately."

"Sorry, but I've gone and burnt it. I had no interest in keeping tokens from Mr. Rossi."

Lessie's eyes were growing wider by the minute, and Aunt Gia simply sat watching her sister and niece in battle, her head turning back and forth like she was watching a tennis match.

"You burnt it?" Mrs. Capetti asked. "What kind of fool are you?"

Gabriella shrugged. "It didn't say why he wanted it back. The letter simply said to please give the cameo to his maid, and that he had something he needed to do with it."

"Now that doesn't mean he's lost interest in our Ella," Aunt Gia chimed in. "Perhaps he took it to the jeweler to have it updated, or engraved with a personal message?"

Lessie nodded. "You're right, Mama. I'm sure that's it. He's probably planning a surprise. Don't you think so, Aunt Rosa?"

Mrs. Capetti finally let out a sigh. "Perhaps. But if you've done something to ruin your chances with him, I swear, Gabriella . . ."

They were interrupted by a maid stepping in and clearing her throat. "I'm sorry to intrude, but Mr. Rossi is here to see Miss Gabriella. He would like to know if you are accepting visitors."

Everyone turned to stare at Gabriella. "Don't just stand there! Bring him in," Mrs. Capetti said, causing the young maid to practically run into the foyer to fetch Joseph.

Although she was already expecting Joseph's arrival, Gabriella still felt a little flutter of nervousness as he appeared in the doorway.

"Good afternoon, ladies," he said, smiling at

his potential bride. "It's lovely to see you all, but I was hoping to have a word in private with Miss Gabriella, if you don't mind."

"Of course," Mrs. Capetti said with a warm (for her) smile. "Gia, why don't you escort them to the garden."

Gabriella rolled her eyes. She always felt the whole escort nonsense was a little ridiculous, especially for a woman in her twenties, but she didn't dare contradict her mother in front of their present company. Everyone in the room knew that for Mrs. Capetti, the matter of an escort had little to do with propriety and everything to do with having a spy.

Gabriella took her hat, a large navy-style with a thick cream ribbon that trailed down the back, and took Joseph's arm as they followed behind her aunt through the house.

"It's so nice of you to call on us this afternoon, Mr. Rossi," Aunt Gia said. "How is your sister? I hear congratulations are in order."

"Yes, thank you. She's doing well. They've named their daughter Annamaria, after my grandmother."

Gabriella tuned out their boring baby conversation and tried to think of some clever things to say to her mother later. She didn't want anyone to think that she'd accepted Joseph's proposal just because her parents expected it.

She remained silent as they stepped out into the stifling late-afternoon heat and started their stroll, Joseph making polite small talk with Aunt Gia about the approaching autumn season and their expectations for a milder winter than the last.

He said all of the right things to impress Aunt Gia, complimenting her new gloves, and even sharing a tidbit of local gossip that he was sure would be of interest (it turned out that Aunt Gia's former best friend, who was married to one of Joseph's father's business associates, had been caught in a compromising position with her tailor).

Gabriella perked up at this news. Not only was gossiping one of her favorite pastimes, but she was impressed at his ability to dig up a story. Even she hadn't heard of that indiscretion, and there wasn't much that got past her when it came to salacious news.

"I'm afraid I can't top your story, Mr. Rossi," Gabriella said, looking at him with genuine admiration and wishing her aunt would disappear so they could have at least a modicum of privacy. Being talked into a marriage was bad enough, but having an audience for the proposal would make it even worse.

"I have to agree," Aunt Gia chimed in. "You must keep us informed if you hear anything else about that little situation. But if you'll excuse me for a moment, I'm going to have a word with the gardener about these shrubs."

And off she went, turning to give Gabriella a quick wink over her shoulder as she headed toward the greenhouse.

Gabriella smiled, grateful for this small gesture. Under the circumstances, any other chaperone wouldn't have given them the opportunity to be alone. However, she wished her aunt could have been a little less obvious, considering it wasn't her home and she had no reason to be speaking with her sister's staff.

"That was kind of her," Joseph said with a bemused smile. "It's refreshing to see family who truly care about each other."

Gabriella looked at him, confused. "I thought your family was close. They've always given off that impression, at least."

He shook his head. "They just put on airs. My mother and father hardly speak, and with me living in another country, it hasn't exactly helped us grow closer."

"I understand. My parents and I don't quite get on most of the time, but I suppose that's not a shock. If I didn't have my Aunt Gia and Lessie, I don't know what I would do." She smirked as she caught a glimpse of her aunt's head peeking out from behind the greenhouse.

"I'm quite close with my aunt and uncle as well," Joseph said. "They're probably more like parents to me than my real mother and father, which is a bit sad, I suppose."

"I don't think it's sad," Gabriella said. "As long as you have someone in the world who understands you, it doesn't matter how horrible your parents are."

Realizing she'd just called her potential in-laws horrible, Gabriella put a gloved hand up to her mouth. "I'm sorry, I didn't mean to insinuate—"

"It's fine," he laughed. "I didn't take offense. Like you said, even though my parents and I don't always see eye-to-eye, I've managed to do just fine. An Oxford education will take you places with or without a loving mum, right? I'm going to be successful no matter what."

Gabriella nodded, thinking he was a bit full of himself, but trying to give him the benefit of the doubt. While her mother was bossy and controlling, at least she wasn't nearly as stuck up as Mrs. Rossi. She chose her words carefully, as not to stick her foot in her mouth again.

"I believe family is whom you choose."

Joseph turned and smiled. "I wholeheartedly agree. My friends from Oxford have become much like family. In fact, my good chum Matthew is staying with me for a few weeks."

"That's nice," Gabriella said, getting antsy. *Just give me the ring, for goodness' sake.*

"It's hard being away from people you care about," Joseph continued. "Living in another country teaches you that, as I'm sure you know."

Gabriella shrugged. "I miss places more than people."

"Isn't there anyone in Italy you'd wish to see more often?"

Gabriella knew he was fishing at something, but she refused to bite. "Not particularly. I've lived in New York just as long as I lived here, and everyone I care to associate with is back in the States. But yes, I do miss Italy sometimes. Florence has a different energy to it. Not as hectic as New York, at least."

"Indeed. But now you're a New York girl through and through. I can tell."

Gabriella smiled. "It suits me. I know you didn't come here to chat about travel plans, though. So to what do I owe this visit?"

Joseph guided her back toward the cypress where they had met the night before. "I wanted to give this to you," he said, pulling a small box out of his trouser pocket.

After prying open the box, Gabriella felt her face fall a bit. Inside the light-blue lining sat the cameo.

"Oh . . . thank you. It looks the same."

Joseph, who must've noted her clear displeasure, grinned and took the box out of Gabriella's hand. "You have to look inside."

She pried the latch open to reveal an inscription. Gabriella, having somewhat poor eyesight, squinted to read the words, and then gasped.

Although it was very romantic, it wasn't the "will you marry me" message in the cameo that surprised her; she was expecting a proposal, after all. It was the enormous ruby ring Joseph had procured from his other pocket while she was busy looking at the necklace.

"Gabriella Capetti, will you do me the honor of becoming my wife?"

CHAPTER 29

GABRIELLA

"*I* THINK BLUE SUITS my complexion better than pale pink, but you are the bride, after all," Lessie said, lifting up a swatch of fabric and holding it up to her round face.

Gabriella shrugged. "It makes no matter to me. Choose whichever fabric you like."

In just a matter of days after she said yes, plans for a whirlwind wedding unfolded. Mrs. Capetti insisted that the union be made before their return to New York, dashing Gabriella's hopes for an elegant Manhattan-style affair in a few months' time. None of her friends were in Italy anymore, and now they wouldn't even be able to see her get married. Many of her parents' friends, however, were still in Florence, and impressing them was more important.

Now they were picking out fabric and planning dresses, and Gabriella felt a bit queasy and overwhelmed.

"We'll take the pink," Mrs. Capetti said, ignoring her niece and doling out orders to the seamstress.

The selection for Gabriella's gown had already been made, and despite her distaste at the accelerated timeline of the wedding, she couldn't wait to see how it would turn out. The sketch featured a lace bodice with tiny beads scattered along the high neckline and long lace sleeves ending with large satin poufs at the shoulders. Her favorite part was the full satin skirt with an enormous train. It looked rather heavy, even in a pencil drawing, but Gabriella didn't think she would mind. When it came to eveningwear she often favored the dramatic, and she wanted her wedding dress to command attention.

Gabriella had only seen Joseph once since the proposal, at their engagement dinner. Mr. and Mrs. Capetti spared no expense, and although the party consisted of their close friends and family, talk of the event had spread all over town. With champagne flowing freely and all eyes on her, Gabriella had started to feel relieved about her choice in Joseph. She might have had a gentle push in his direction, but that was no matter. Being the future Mrs. Rossi suddenly became an exciting prospect, and Gabriella was sure she'd grow to love him in time. She even found herself thinking about him during quiet moments alone and replaying their ridiculous conversations in her head.

Once the initial exhilaration wore off and actual wedding planning began, it sunk in that Gabriella would (finally) be a bride. This meant endless fittings, choosing fabrics, menus, flowers, ambience . . . thank the Lord she only had to do this once.

They were planning to meet that evening at the Teatro della Pergola; Mr. and Mrs. Rossi had invited Gabriella and her family to join them in the family's box for a performance of *Tannhäuser*. Gabriella wasn't exactly an opera connoisseur, but no one paid attention to the show anyway. She knew the sole purpose in attending was to see and be seen, and in this case, it was the very public coming out of her and Joseph.

Gabriella forced herself back to the present moment after Lessie started asking her silly questions about dresses again. She ignored her cousin and adjusted her hat in the mirror at least three times before pacing back and forth through the shop, opening and closing her fan repeatedly and giving it a little toss in the air every so often. The shop girls must've thought she was crazy (if they hadn't already), but her family paying a very rich sum for bridal attire was probably enough to squelch any desire on the staff's part to comment.

"You're anxious about tonight, yes?" Lessie said. "Even for you, this behavior is a bit extreme."

"Of course not. What do I have to be nervous about? I'm just overheated and bored over this dress nonsense."

Lessie made a sour face but didn't argue with her cousin. "I'm looking forward to the performance tonight, at least. It was so very kind of the Rossis to include us. Just imagine, we're going to see *Tannhäuser* in person!"

Gabriella rolled her eyes. "Oh yes, the joy is so great I don't know how I'll be able to stand it."

Lessie, an accomplished pianist, more than made up for her cousin's lack of interest in the opera. Gabriella didn't understand the fascination, but Lessie had grown quite enamored with Wagner over the years and could hold her own in conversation with even the most uppity of opera buffs.

"At least one of us will enjoy the opera and not be fussing with her gown the entire night and hoping people will notice her ring," Lessie said, her cheeks turning red.

"Don't be such a cow. I'm trying to—"

"Girls, that's enough," Mrs. Capetti interrupted.

"It's time to move on. We have a lot to accomplish today."

The three women stepped out in the bright afternoon sun on the bustling Via Tornabuoni, dodging the flower girls along the Palazzo Strozzi and walking briskly toward Mrs. Capetti's favorite perfume shop. They spotted Carlo entering a café with a pretty young blonde woman trailing behind him.

"I wonder what he's doing here," Lessie said. "My brother said the two of them were going for a motor car ride with a friend of Mr. Rossi's from university."

"That's interesting, now, isn't it? He told me he'd be spending the afternoon with his father," Mrs. Capetti said, narrowing her eyes. "Excuse me for a moment while I see what my son has up his sleeve. Stay here, girls."

Lessie and Gabriella exchanged confused glances as Mrs. Capetti marched across the busy street. "Don't just stand there!" Gabriella said, grabbing her cousin's hand.

Once Mrs. Capetti was out of sight, they raced across to the café, peering through the windows to see a bewildered Carlo greeting his mother. The girl, who upon closer inspection, was more plain than pretty, cowered next to him.

"Do you think your brother is having a secret romance?" Lessie whispered, ducking when she thought her aunt saw them spying.

"It certainly appears that way. And with an English girl, nonetheless."

"How do you know she's from England?" Lessie asked, taking the girl in.

"First off, only foreigners come to this café," Gabriella said. "And in any case, you can just tell."

The girl was a tiny thing with terribly skinny arms and an elfish face. Her youthful appearance, combined with a slightly-too-large and out-of-fashion hat, gave her the appearance of a child playing dress-up in her mother's clothes.

Gabriella looked back through the window, watching Mrs. Capetti grill the washed-out, possibly English girl. She seemed to be responding politely, but it was clear that it wasn't a friendly chitchat.

"We're foreigners, too," Lessie said, sounding defensive for the girl. She always had to be the nice one, to Gabriella's annoyance.

"No, we're not. We were *born* here."

"But we've lived in New York longer than we lived in Italy. Summering here hardly counts as being a local."

"Lessie, why are you being so argumentative today?"

Her cousin stared at the shoppers rushing past them, avoiding Gabriella's gaze. "I'm just trying to say that you're not always right, Ella."

Gabriella ignored this comment and watched her brother through the glass. He wore a rather pained look on his face, and if she wasn't mistaken, his hands were shaking. What on earth was going on with him?

"I don't know about you, but I'm famished. Let's go in and have a bite, shall we?" Gabriella said, strolling toward the entrance.

"Are you mad? Your mother told us to stay here. And 'here' is across the street, in fact."

"And?" Gabriella asked, flinging the door open and stepping inside. Lessie threw her hands up and followed her cousin. They found Carlo, Mrs. Capetti, and the mystery girl standing off to the side in the entryway.

"I'm so sorry, Aunt," Lessie said as Mrs. Capetti whirled around to look at the girls. "I'm coming down with one of my headaches, and Ella wanted to let you know that I need to go and—"

"How do you do?" Gabriella said, extending a hand to Carlo's young friend and internally cringing at her cousin's horrible lying skills. "Since my brother doesn't have enough manners to give a proper introduction, I suppose I'll have to do it myself. I'm Gabriella Capetti and this is our cousin Alessandra, but we call her Lessie. And you are?"

"Edith Carbury. How do you do, Miss Capetti?" she said, barely looking up from the ground.

"Miss Carbury and I were just about to enjoy some tea with her brother, Matthew. He's Mr. Rossi's friend from Oxford," Carlo jumped in, giving Lessie a pleading look.

"Oh yes, my brother mentioned that this morning," Lessie said. "I'm afraid I wasn't paying attention and got the details all wrong. I thought you were going out in an automobile."

"Why yes, we went out with my brother earlier through the countryside," Edith said, brightening up at the mention of their excursion. "Tuscany is quite lovely, isn't it?"

Gabriella smiled. "We're proud to be from such a beautiful country. Being a tourist, everything must seem very exciting, I imagine!"

Mrs. Capetti finally lost her patience and took her daughter and niece by the arms. "I'm afraid we must get going. More errands to run before the opera tonight. Carlo, I trust you'll be joining us in the Rossis' box?"

"Of course, Mother. Miss Carbury will be there as well, along with her brother."

Mrs. Capetti didn't respond to this, but simply nodded and turned toward the door. "Carlo, I'll see you at home. Good day, Miss Carbury."

Gabriella remained behind to wait for Lessie. "Good to meet you, Miss Carbury," Lessie said, taking Edith's hand and giving her a kind smile. "Perhaps we can get to know each other a little better this evening."

"I'd like that," Edith replied, looking relieved.

"Girls!" Mrs. Capetti called from the street, and Lessie and Gabriella rushed off, leaving Carlo and his new friend to enjoy their solitary tea.

CHAPTER 30

LIZ

*I*T SEEMED crazy to me that my great-grandmother was essentially being forced into a marriage with someone she didn't love. Sure, she might've been starting to feel a little something for Joseph, but her parents and even her best friend schemed to get them together so she wouldn't be a spinster. Meanwhile, I was trying to talk my sister *out of* getting married at the same age.

I was still thinking about my relatives' doomed weddings and digesting tons of Kung Pao shrimp when the phone rang.

"Do you know what your sister just said to me?" Mom yelled. I held the phone away from my ear and winced.

"Way to almost blow out my eardrums. And hello, by the way."

"Yeah, hi, Liz. Did you know about this?"

"Know about what?" I said, feigning innocence. There was no way I was going to admit to having my little meeting with Cate.

"That she's calling off the wedding? Can you please talk some sense into her? I'm sick over this."

I paused a moment and, drawing upon my extensive high-school acting skills, pretended to be shocked and scandalized by Cate's news. I was actually enjoying myself for a minute until I realized Mom was sobbing into the phone.

"All of this work . . . for nothing," she wailed, crying so hard I couldn't even get a word in. I let her go on for a minute or two, and once she finally quieted down, I tried my best to talk her off the ledge.

"I'm sure Cate had good reasons for wanting to call things off. What did she say?"

"That she was too young and she needed to explore the world and find herself or some mumbo jumbo. What am I going to do with four hundred wedding-ring-shaped napkin holders?"

I ignored the tackiness of this statement and kept the focus on Cate. "I can understand that. She *is* awfully young to be getting married, you know."

"Your father and I were married at her age," she said with a sniff. "What's wrong with that?"

I sighed. "It's not the eighties, Mom. Things are different. And Cate hasn't had a lot of experience when it comes to being young and having fun. She's been in one serious relationship after the next and always with older guys. You don't want her to regret getting married, do you?"

After a long pause, she finally mumbled a miserable, "No."

We talked for a few more minutes, and I only hung up once I was sure she wasn't going to do something irrational with a yard of tulle. At least Dad was there to keep her sane.

Mom took the news even worse than I'd expected. Still, I was proud that Cate had stuck to her guns. It must've been incredibly hard to tell my parents the news, knowing how excited they (and by "they," I meant Mom) were about the wedding.

I had my own issues to worry about, so I hurried down the hall to Justin's apartment. Once again, no answer, but Bo barked like a maniac this time. I sighed and pulled a crumbled-up receipt out of my purse, and scrawled: *Stopped by, hoped you'd be here. I'll call you later — Liz.* I left the paper on his snowflake-print doormat (another gift from his mom?) and hoped he'd see it.

Since Justin was still MIA, I picked up the phone to let Addie know I was coming earlier than planned. Going out to dinner and working on a PR plan for LM Designs would be a nice break from my family and love life drama, at least. As I walked through the lobby, I heard a familiar voice call out my name.

So there he was.

I turned to see Justin dressed in a faded University of Miami tee, jeans, and another dorky knit hat, this one with flaps on it.

"Glad I finally found you."

"Huh?" he said, and I could tell he hadn't thought I'd be seeking him out.

"I stopped by earlier but you weren't home. I actually just knocked on your door a second ago, too."

"Oh yeah, I was probably walking the dog. And I just came down to grab some food at Giuseppe's," he said, gesturing toward the takeout bag in his hand.

We stood in awkward silence for a minute until he finally broke the tension. "So, what have you been up to? I'm sorry I went MIA. Work sucks."

I shrugged. "Not too much. Busy working on jewelry and stuff. How about you?"

"Same old, same old. Listen, I know you're probably still pissed about the other night," he said, folding his arms across his worn gray shirt. "I'm sorry if I was a dick."

"I understand why you thought something was up with Adam. And you weren't a dick. But you don't have to worry about him, because we aren't talking anymore. We got in an argument and let's just say I was very stupid about him."

"So wait, there *was* something going on with you guys?" he said, loud enough that the pizza guy coming in the door did a full turn to see what was going on.

"No. Well, not really. It's complicated. I just meant I've decided not to be friends with him. It wasn't a good idea in the first place and I should've realized that."

"Oh," he said, looking at the ground and kicking at an invisible piece of dirt. "What happened?"

I took a deep breath, and was about to tell him the whole story when a horn honked. I looked back and forth between Justin and Addie's car waiting outside. "Ugh, I'm sorry, but I have to go. My ride's here. Addie was supposed to help me out with some PR stuff for my line and then my sister came over with a wedding-related crisis . . . Long story, but I was supposed to meet up with Ad hours ago."

Justin shrugged and gave me a "do what you gotta do" look. "Okay then. I'll talk to you later, I guess."

"Bye," I whispered, feeling worse than I had in days. Of course I had to run into him when I was on my way out the door. The way I'd imagined things in my head (instant reconciliation, romantic movie night continued) didn't quite play out in real life. Instead he looked tired and annoyed, and worse, didn't seem like he even cared if he "talked to me later."

The entire car ride was spent reliving the encounter over and over in my head. I must have been staring out the window for a while, because Addie started waving her arms in front of my face.

"Dude, snap out of it! We're here."

I slumped out of the car and followed her up to the condo, not realizing until she took her hat and coat off that Addie looked like hell. Mascara was streaked on both red, puffy cheeks and under her jacket she wore an old Juicy Couture tracksuit from college.

"Wait, have you been crying?" I asked. "What happened?"

"I just got off the phone with my dad before I picked you up, so I was too upset to get ready. Do you mind staying in tonight?"

I nodded. "That's fine, we don't need to go anywhere for dinner. It's too cold, anyway."

"Soho?" Addie said, and I called our pizza order in without bothering to ask what she wanted; it was one of the comforts of being friends with someone for so long.

I de-bundled myself and plopped down on the couch. "So what happened? Is everything all right with your family?"

Addie rolled her eyes and sat down next to me, tucking her knees up to her chin. There was a chocolate stain on her left knee, which she picked at with her thumb. "I'm not going to the Bahamas this year."

"What? But you always go to the Bahamas for Christmas! Why did they call it off this year?"

Addie's family had gone to the Atlantis resort in the Bahamas for as long as I'd known her, a family tradition going back to the late nineties when none of their relatives could make it for Christmas.

"They didn't. I said I wasn't going."

She might as well have told me that she was shaving off all her hair and joining a punk band.

"I don't get it. Why the hell would you skip

Christmas? It's your favorite week of the entire year. What about the dolphins? And the craps tournament with your dad? You swore you'd win this year!"

"It's complicated. There's been a lot of stuff going on with my parents and it's not good. I think they might split up."

"Whaaaat?" I said. "Why didn't you tell me this before?"

"You've been just a little preoccupied lately."

Her comment stung, but I couldn't deny it was true. Between Nan's death, Cate's wedding, and my relationship drama, I hadn't even asked about anything going on in Addie's life.

"I'm sorry. I've probably been a shitty friend. But you know you can tell me anything."

Addie took a deep breath and looked at me. "Okay, but you have to promise not to tell anyone." I nodded and she launched into the story.

It turned out her dad had been hiding a sizable amount of debt from the family. He lost a lot of money in the stock market during the recession, but hadn't told anyone because he thought he could easily get it back. Addie's mother had no way of finding out; she'd never been interested in the nitty-gritty details of their finances, and left those decisions up to him. She didn't even know how to access most of their accounts, anyway.

Apparently, her father had been running up the credit cards so the rest of them didn't suspect anything was wrong. Basically, they were living the same lifestyle but without the money to back it up.

"So how did you find all of this out?" I asked, biting my lip. I was still in shock over Addie's father betraying his family like that. A few things started to make sense, though, like Addie's refusal to shop much on Black Friday.

"I overheard a conversation on Thanksgiving. My dad was on the phone with his broker. I confronted him and he told me what happened, but made me promise not to tell my mother."

"So did you?"

"Not yet," Addie said. "He made me swear. Plus, it's not my secret to tell."

"So that's why you don't want to go to the Bahamas," I said, the story finally clicking.

Addie nodded. "I said it wasn't a good idea to go on vacation this year, but Dad said it was already paid for, so we should just go."

"That makes no sense," I said. "I'm sure he could cancel the hotel rooms without a penalty, even if the flights were nonrefundable."

"Yeah," Addie said with a sigh. "I just don't want to be around him. I can't believe he lied to us. And now I'm freaking out about my condo, too."

"What about it?" I asked, giving her a strange look. I often suspected her parents had bought the condo outright, although she always claimed that they just gave her the down payment and "helped a little with the mortgage." Addie's position didn't pay much as far as legal jobs go, but with no other bills, it didn't seem unlikely that she could afford the payments on her own.

"Well," she said, squirming a bit, "you know how they help me with my mortgage and all? They actually pay for it every month. Like, the whole thing."

"Oh," I said, after a long pause. "Interesting."

"What's that supposed to mean?"

"I don't know. What else do you say when you find out your best friend has been lying to you for years? You could've just told me."

"I know it's not exactly normal for your parents to pay for your place, but they have the money, or they used to, at least. I guess I just didn't want to make you feel awkward . . . I know your parents aren't in the same financial situation. And I didn't want to rub it in after your mom refused to let Nan help you with buying a place in the building. That's all."

"Well, you don't have student loans or a car payment or anything, so it's not like you can't afford to pay for it. Why don't you just take over the mortgage?"

She went back to picking at the stain on her velour pants, and I realized the condo probably cost a lot more than I thought it did. "Oh," I said. "I'm taking it you can't afford the payments?"

She shook her head no. "Not if I want to pay for gas or eat, too."

I sighed. "If worst came to worst and they had to sell it, you could always move in with me. I know it's not exactly what you're used to, but it's better than having to move back home."

Addie laughed. "While that sounds awesome and I appreciate the offer, I don't think it's the best idea. Have you completely blocked out junior year?"

"What was so bad about junior year? We had a lot of fun in that house." While yes, our roommate situation hadn't always been ideal, I didn't think it had been *that* awful. Or maybe I was just romanticizing college as usual.

Addie looked at me like I was nuts. "It was a nightmare! You threw your shit all over the room and I was always cleaning up after you. And you got pissed at me for always having guys over. Remember the time you slept in Meredith's room for a week because I locked you out after the spring formal? You wouldn't even speak to me."

"Oh yeah, that," I said. "You know I have a selective memory. But in any case, I'd rather have you live with me and drive me crazy than not have a place to stay."

Addie reached out and patted my knee. "Thanks, but I think I'll be okay. Maybe I can just move into a smaller place. We'll figure it out."

Our food showed up a few minutes later, and Addie was mid-bite when I finally told her about my encounter with Justin in the lobby.

"Seriously, do you want me to choke?" she said, coughing a few times before continuing. "So let me get this right: you told him that you and Adam weren't talking any more, and he accused you of messing around with him again?"

"Sort of. But, to be fair, it's not like Justin was entirely wrong. I did kiss Adam that night at my apartment. Which was clearly the mistake of the year. "

"Clearly. But anyway, either this guy really likes you or he's a little bit crazy. Or both."

I laughed. "Justin's a good guy. I think he was just jealous."

"There's only one way to find out, right? Just give the kid a chance. If you don't like him, whatever. But you know you're going to kick yourself if you just give up. I have a good feeling about him, though. Trust me on this one."

"What about stop going back?" I said with a smirk.

"Screw you. How about a princess marathon while we work on your jewelry stuff? I think we both need to get our minds off real life for a few hours."

"You don't have to ask me twice," I said, jumping and grabbing her *Aladdin* and *The Little Mermaid* DVDs. We had discovered a shared obsession with Ariel during freshman year and since then had spent many nights singing "Part of Your World" at the top of our lungs.

She plopped down on the couch and we cuddled up with our blankets, her laptop, and my binder of jewelry photos.

"Everything will be fine, Ad. I promise," I said, handing her the printout of the blog piece with my earrings. She just smiled and put a finger over her lips, cranking up the volume to "Arabian Nights." Avoidance was her favorite coping mechanism, so I just shrugged and sang along, as usual.

CHAPTER 31

ELLA

October 24, 1957

I'm almost afraid to write this in case I jinx things, but La Bella Cakery feels like it might become a reality. Having Mom on board has been more helpful than I imagined. Last week, she was able to get her friend's architect son to sketch out a rendering of what the shop might look like, and I can't believe something so perfect could be mine one day! Pictures of gleaming black-and-white tile floors, modern mint-green appliances and matching counters keep floating through my head . . . we could even have a mannequin in the window with a different wedding dress each season.

Mom gets tired easily so I have to keep our little work sessions to a minimum, but when she's around, we've been able to get her to tell us a little more about Italy. Now that I've heard more about my grandma, it's easier for me to understand why my mother acts the way she does. I always knew Nonni was a little domineering, but it sounds terrible the way she tried to force Mom into marrying Joseph. Maybe she just wanted to get Mom out of her hair; I can relate to that, at least.

It's funny, though, because despite the occasional insult,

Mom has been on her best behavior. Trudy and I actually enjoy her company. Go figure.

"This is it," Trudy said, closing the thick, spiral-bound stack of papers and placing it on Ella's kitchen counter. It was their business plan for La Bella Cakery, ready to present to Harry.

Ella felt like her face turned a shade of green. "I think I'm going to throw up." She couldn't bear the thought of Harry turning down her idea. What if all of their work turned out to be for nothing? La Bella was thriving, and they weren't pressed for cash, but they certainly weren't rolling in dough, either.

"Oh, come on, now," Gabriella said, slapping her daughter on the back. "Buck up. It's a business plan, not a death sentence. If he doesn't want to invest in your idea, then just tell him you already have a secret financer."

"And where am I going to find one of those?"

"Right here. What else am I going to do with all of my money besides spoil my grandkids and buy clothes?"

"You'd do that for us?" Ella's mouth dropped open and her eyes nearly popped out of her head. Never in her wildest dreams did she think her mother would be interested even in helping with her plan, let alone financially backing it.

Gabriella shrugged. "It's nothing. Just make sure the business doesn't tank, and I'll be happy. You need something of your own, Ella."

"I know. But being a mother is a full-time job in itself. And I help out at La Bella when I can."

Trudy tugged on a strand of her dark hair, obviously trying to phrase her response carefully. "Ella, it's just that La Bella is Harry's restaurant. Whether or not you work there or help with cake recipes, it's always going to be his name that stands out. I think your mother is trying to say you deserve to shine. Your cakes are amazing!"

Ella plopped down on one of the kitchen chairs. "Thank you. But thinking and dreaming about opening a business is one thing. Actually doing it is another. How am I going to have time? I must have been crazy to go along with this plan."

"You have talent, and don't let anyone tell you otherwise," Gabriella said, an unusual warmth in her tone.

Ella stared at her mother in disbelief, the knot in her stomach loosening at the thought of her mother's support. It was probably the first time she'd ever given her a compliment. "I don't know what to say."

"How about thanks?" Gabriella asked, hobbling over to take a seat at the table. "Common courtesy, you know. Now get me a cup of coffee. I'm going to need some caffeine if you want to hear the rest of this story, and something tells me you need a distraction right now."

CHAPTER 32

GABRIELLA

1905

THE RICHLY DRESSED crowd gathering outside the *Teatro della Pergola* might have been abuzz about the upcoming performance, but the arrival of one Gabriella Capetti trumped the excitement of any opera. She stepped down from the car in a gown of deep sapphire blue, making sure to give her father her left hand so the crowd wouldn't miss a glimpse of her nearly four-carat ruby ring.

Although she found the whole scene a bit comical, Gabriella knew her engagement to Joseph had provided the city's elite with the kind of gossip that didn't come around every day. The Capettis were a well-respected family, but Gabriella was, by all accounts, a loose cannon. She'd heard the rumors: many wondered if Joseph would follow her to New York, while others had placed considerable bets on whether the wedding would take place at all.

Although the stares didn't bother her, Gabriella's heart still fluttered. Everything about the night should've been perfect. It was a balmy September evening, she was wearing a gorgeous new sapphire necklace, and she'd been invited to an opera in the box of her future family. But for some reason, Gabriella couldn't shake the feeling that something was off, and her stomach had been in knots for most of the day.

"It's just nerves," Lessie had said earlier. "You want to make a good impression on Joseph's parents, and all brides get a little anxious before the wedding, right?"

Gabriella told her she was fine, and blamed her brother's incident in the café for her mood. Something was certainly up with him and Miss Carbury, but she didn't have the time or energy to investigate much further.

She tried not to let her anxiousness show as her parents chatted with old friends outside the grand theater, turning every so often to glance down the street and see if Joseph had arrived. Carlo joined his sister in the nervous looks and general twitchiness.

"Looking for Miss Carbury, I imagine?" Gabriella said, turning to give her brother a look that had just the tiniest amount of compassion.

"I'm sure you think something is going on between us, but I assure you, it's not. I'm simply providing her with companionship while her brother attends to business," Carlo said. The look on his face, however, betrayed his words.

"Tell yourself whatever you like to make yourself feel better, but our mother is no idiot," Gabriella said, leaning in closer so she could be heard over the street noise. "Anyone can see you're fond of that girl, and you know Mother will do anything to stop a romance with someone she doesn't deem fit. Look at what happened with Salvatore."

Carlo folded his arms. "Maybe I don't care what she thinks anymore."

Gabriella raised an eyebrow. Now *this* was interesting.

"Edith isn't like the girls back in New York," he said, speaking more to himself than to Gabriella. "She doesn't place the same emphasis on status and material things. She even writes gorgeous poems. She wants to be the next Elizabeth Barrett Browning, you know."

Gabriella bit her lip. "Erm, that's . . . lovely."

"I suppose none of this matters since she returns to London in three weeks. Unless I plan on proposing, of course."

Gabriella's hand flew to her mouth in shock as yet another automobile not belonging to the Rossi family pulled up in front of them.

"I'm sorry, Carlo, but that is very—"

"Enough. I shouldn't have said anything." He stormed off and went inside the theater, leaving Gabriella to wait for the rest of the party.

If he'd given her the chance to actually finish her sentence, she would've told Carlo that it was very brave of him to forge his own path, even if his choice of partner was a girl with a crooked hat who gave Gabriella an uneasy feeling. She took a moment to compose herself as her aunt, uncle, and Lessie arrived.

"Cousin, you look simply lovely!" Lessie exclaimed, climbing down from the car with what could best be described as a thud. Luckily, their driver had quick reflexes.

Gabriella cringed, hoping there would be no such incidents at the wedding. "Lessie, that gown is gorgeous. I told you that pink suits you just fine."

Lessie, dressed in a rosy pink gown trimmed with pale green ribbons and delicate lace sleeves, smiled at the compliment. "I suppose I could get used to it. At the very least, tonight will be a good test for having to wear this color at the wedding."

They linked arms and followed their parents into the elegant marble lobby, spotting Carlo in conversation with a group of people across the room. Gabriella couldn't tell who they were from where she was standing; in addition to having poor eyesight, the throng of opera-goers and massive columns had obstructed her view, and all she could see was her sibling's back.

"Where is your brother?" Mrs. Capetti asked, her eyes darting back and forth across the room.

"He's just over there, talking to Miss Carbury," Lessie said, gesturing with her fan in his general direction.

Gabriella stood on her toes to try to get a better view over the many men's hats. "Miss Carbury? Are you quite certain?"

"I didn't realize you hadn't yet seen her," Lessie whispered. "She's right next to him, wearing a navy gown. I believe that must be her brother with them."

"I couldn't care less about Edith Carbury. If the Carburys are in the lobby, that must mean Joseph is already here, too. They're staying with the Rossis, remember? I was waiting for him but I suppose they've already arrived."

Lessie's eyes widened with recognition. "Oh. I forgot they were even coming tonight. I was so excited about the performance and fussing with this dress and such."

"Girls, this way," Mrs. Capetti interrupted. "We don't want to offend our hosts."

Gabriella forced herself to smile as she walked toward her brother, realizing that Joseph and his parents also had joined the group. She watched as Joseph said a brief hello to Carlo, feeling an uncomfortable flurry in her stomach. Lessie reached out and gripped her hand, and Gabriella squeezed back, grateful for this small comfort.

Matthew Carbury and his sister stepped forward to say hello, and for a moment Gabriella thought a look of panic flickered over Joseph's finely drawn features. In an instant it was gone, and he shook his burly friend's hand and greeted Edith rather coolly. Edith looked as if she were trying to tell him something, but Joseph walked away. Edith took a step back, looking rather unhinged, and excused herself to the ladies' room.

"Did you see that?" Gabriella whispered to someone she thought was Lessie, until she realized her cousin was no longer standing next to her.

"See what, my dear?" Joseph asked without even the hint of a smile.

Ugh, she thought. Humiliating herself in front of her new fiancé wasn't exactly top on Gabriella's list of goals for the evening.

"My apologies, I thought my cousin was standing next to me."

Joseph nodded. "I see. You look lovely this evening. That shade compliments your eyes."

"Thank you," Gabriella said. She chose not to mention she had selected the color because it was his favorite, and instead turned to her future in-laws. "It was very kind of you to invite us this evening, Mr. and Mrs. Rossi."

"We're very happy to have you join us. You'll make a fine wife for our Joseph," Mr. Rossi said, slapping his son on the shoulder.

Mrs. Rossi gave her a small smile but remained silent, her hands clasped in front of her silky gold skirt. Now that the match was finally made, it seemed like she didn't need to butter Gabriella up anymore.

Mr. Rossi turned to Gabriella's father. "I'll be at the bar. Care to join me for a scotch, old boy?"

With that, the two men disappeared into the crowd, and the rest of their party began to make their way up to the Rossis' box.

Joseph offered an arm to his fiancée, and they fell behind the rest of the group. "So how are you faring on our first public outing?" he asked.

"I'm doing fantastically. Why wouldn't I be?"

"You look on edge. I know my family can be intimidating, but this will be an enjoyable evening, I promise."

Gabriella tried to quell her irritation, but couldn't help herself. "I'm sure it will be lovely. But if anyone is on edge, I'm afraid it must be you."

"Excuse me?"

"You look as if you've seen a ghost."

"Oh, that," he said, sighing almost imperceptibly. "I was just a bit surprised at the arrival of Miss Carbury."

"Surprised? My brother said she was staying with your family."

Joseph's tone was calm, but Gabriella could hear him grinding his teeth. "Well, that's news I was quite unaware of until a few moments ago. Her brother is over for a visit, as I mentioned to you before. I have no idea why she's here."

Gabriella narrowed her eyes; she was officially befuddled. "But Carlo mentioned that Miss Carbury—"

As if on cue, Edith crossed their path on the way to the box. "Oh, I'm very sorry to interrupt, Mr. Rossi. I was just looking for my brother."

"I believe Matthew went to the bar," Joseph said, not even making eye contact.

Edith smiled at him (over-familiarly, Gabriella thought). "I see. Would you mind escorting me to the box, then?" Edith asked.

Gabriella had not missed the girl's slight; Edith made no attempt at acknowledging her presence. Even worse, now she was forced to share her fiancé's arm with a nobody.

"So much for our big entrance into society," she said, making sure it was loud enough for Edith to hear.

Joseph nudged her gently with his elbow, which just made her even more incensed. Gabriella sighed with relief when they finally reached the sumptuously upholstered burgundy-and-gold box and Edith took a seat next to Carlo.

"Exactly what is your brother at with Edith Carbury?" Joseph asked. He leaned in close enough that Gabriella could smell his spicy cologne, and it took her a moment to regain composure before answering.

"I just made her acquaintance this morning, but I do believe they've been spending a lot of time together. Which leads me back to my original question before we were so rudely interrupted. According to Carlo, Edith has been staying with you for a fortnight. So why is she lying?"

Joseph looked across at Edith and Carlo, who were deep in conversation. "That's ridiculous. I haven't seen Edith in over a year. You must have misheard him."

"Ask my brother yourself then."

"And what am I being asked, dear sister?" Carlo said with an ear-to-ear grin.

"Sorry, chap, I believe your sister misunderstood something, that's all," Joseph said.

Carlo gave them a strange look, but before he could say anything, the lights dimmed and the orchestra played its opening notes.

"She must be lying," Gabriella whispered, leaning closer to Joseph than was probably considered appropriate in public. "Why else would she tell my brother something that is clearly an untruth and then behave so oddly around you?"

Joseph just shook his head and put a finger to his lips, staring out at the stage, which didn't improve Gabriella's mood. In any other situation, she would've kicked him in the shin until he acknowledged her question, but in their present company she decided that would likely be an unwise decision.

Instead she sat silently, hands in her lap, and tried to enjoy the opera. She caught a glimpse of Lessie out of the corner of her eye and despite herself, cracked a smile. Her cousin was so thoroughly engrossed in the performance that she had leaned forward to the point where she was dangerously close to falling out of her seat. It wasn't long before Mrs. Capetti grabbed her niece's shoulders and yanked her back into a more ladylike sitting position.

The performance stretched on for ages. Gabriella felt her eyelids start to droop, so she took out her opera glasses and instead focused on watching the audience. She found people to be endlessly fascinating, and even more so when they were behaving badly. Her opera glasses scanned the room, passing over a sleeping husband (she didn't blame him) being scolded by his wife, and more than one girl fiddling with her skirts.

Gabriella settled her gaze on the young Miss Elizabeth Blakely and her spinster sister, Emma, both of them dressed in rather boring pink ensembles and talking to Mr. James Collingsworth, a notorious rake and controversial writer. The Blakely sisters were part of Florence's growing English expatriate community, as was Mr. Collingsworth, and they made no qualms about sharing their views on everything from politics to literature to women's rights.

Gabriella wondered if the Carburys were acquainted

with them. If anyone knew about the goings on of little Miss Edith, it would be the Blakelys.

She glanced at the stage; from the brief overview Lessie had given her before the show, it seemed as if the first act was nearly over. There were grown men parading about in tights and the main character was in love with Venus, which Gabriella found utterly ridiculous. Joseph, however, seemed to be engrossed in the show (or his own thoughts), and stared intensely at the stage.

Gabriella watched him like this for a few minutes until finally he turned to her and asked if there was something wrong.

"Not at all. You just seem very absorbed with the performance."

Joseph shrugged. "I usually don't pay attention to these things, but once you figure out the plot it's actually quite interesting."

"You don't say?" Gabriella looked back at the stage, thinking she couldn't disagree with her fiancé more. "I suppose the opera does have its merits. You never know what will happen here, even if the performance is absolutely yawn-inducing."

Joseph raised an eyebrow. "I assume you aren't talking about the action on stage?"

"Of course not. I find real life to be much more interesting."

Joseph cracked a smile and turned his attention back to the stage just as the first act came to a close.

Gabriella sighed with relief. *Finally*. The crowd filtered out into the lobby for refreshments, nose powdering and the like, and Gabriella was quick to grab Lessie and head to the ladies' room.

"Something is up with Edith Carbury," she said,

linking arms with her cousin as they walked through the crowd.

"Most definitely," Lessie agreed. "In the rush of saying hello to everyone and going to the box, I wasn't able to pull you aside, but I overheard her tell Joseph that she needed to speak with him urgently. He looked rather angry and then went to say hello to your parents. That's why she rushed off."

Gabriella took a moment for this to sink in, sitting on one of the overstuffed floral cushions in the ladies' salon.

"Do you think they were romantically involved?" she finally asked, looking around to make sure no one was listening. "Not that I can imagine him dallying with a girl like her. She's, what? Sixteen, perhaps?"

"I think a romance is unlikely, but then again, she's probably only eight or nine years younger than he is," Lessie said. "We know men who have taken far younger wives."

Gabriella tapped her fingers on the armrest, pursing her lips. "Thank you for the vote of confidence."

Lessie adjusted her bodice in the mirror and pinched her cheeks a few times. "There's only one way to find out. Ask him."

"Do you think he'd actually tell me if something illicit had been going on between them?"

"Joseph seems to be unusually open. Plus, you're going to be his wife, after all. Don't you deserve to know?"

"You're right," Gabriella said, gathering her skirts and marching out into the hallway. "This is ridiculous. I'm going to find him and ask what all of this nonsense is about."

"Just don't say anything you'll regret. Remember your parents are here, and your future family as well," Lessie said, huffing as she tried to keep up. It seemed as if the whole theater had decided to head back to their seats at once. Lessie "pardon me"-ed her way through the densely packed hall while Gabriella simply pushed through, looking back at her cousin with a wink as they approached the box.

"Shhh," she whispered, ducking behind a heavy velvet curtain and pulling Lessie next to her. A few seconds later, Lessie must have realized the reason for their ridiculous hiding place, because she covered her mouth before Gabriella even asked.

"I thought I made it quite clear when I left England that I wanted you to leave me alone." It was Joseph, speaking in a low, angry tone. "It's bad enough you snuck along with Matthew on his visit, but running around town with my fiancée's brother to try to get information on her? You've crossed the line, Edith."

Lessie and Gabriella exchanged shocked glances, and Gabriella was thankful her cousin was able to retain her composure for once.

"I hoped maybe you had said those things in haste," Edith said. "I know my family isn't as grand as the Capettis, but we're kind and loving, and that's more than I can say for your fiancée."

"Stop, Edith. Just stop. This is bloody ridiculous. I'll be having a word with your brother when he returns," Joseph said. "You can stay for the rest of the performance if you like; I don't want people to talk if you run out of here causing a scene. But I expect you not to cross my path again. Do you understand?"

"No. Honestly, I don't. What about that night?"

"I told you before, it was a mistake. It can't happen again."

"Even so, you had no right to give her that necklace,"

Edith said, so softly that the girls had to strain to hear.

"You sold it. What I did with it afterward is my business, and mine alone."

Gabriella squeezed Lessie's arm, her complexion turning nearly as white as Miss Carbury's.

"I never would've given it to you if I'd known you were going to use it as a romantic token and not sell it for me to your jeweler friend like you said," Edith continued, this time sounding more confident.

"Everything all right, old chap?" a deeper male voice asked before Joseph had a chance to respond. The girls heard some rustling and muffled conversation and then realized their spying would have to come to an end. The rest of their families were back in the box and would surely notice their absence. Gabriella, who felt quite sick to her stomach at that moment, peered around the corner.

"We have to wait until the coast is clear," she whispered. Lessie reached out to touch her shoulder, but Gabriella pulled back. "I'm fine. We're going to get to the bottom of this situation. Everything will be fine."

Gabriella tried talking herself into believing this as they made their way into the box. She sat down, folding her hands in her lap and taking care not to make eye contact with Joseph. Her hands shook, and her blood pressure rose to levels that could have required a doctor's visit, but there was nothing she could do given the circumstances. What could she possibly say with both of their parents seated right behind them? The cameo felt like it was burning against her skin and she wanted to take it off and throw it at the deceitful girl who was currently staring doe-eyed at Carlo.

Why would Joseph give her another girl's jewelry? All of the pretty words he'd told her suddenly felt false. Of course, just as she finally felt excited about her groom and her future, something had to ruin it. *And I'm sure Mother will somehow find a way blame it all on me*, she thought.

The second act went by rather quickly, as Gabriella spent most of it imagining dramatic confrontations. While Tannhäuser engaged in a singing contest, she pictured pushing Edith over the balcony. There seemed to be some sort of ruckus happening on stage with swords and such, but Gabriella was too busy dreaming up an elaborate speech in which she told Joseph he was a no-good rake before tossing his ring across the theater, hitting Tannhäuser in the head.

Her thoughts were interrupted when the act came to an end and the rest of their party left for the lobby, leaving Joseph, Gabriella, and Lessie in the box. Lessie took the opportunity to study her notes on the performance, giving her cousin the chance to be at least somewhat alone, but with backup close by.

Gabriella, however, refused to acknowledge her fiancé's presence. Finally, Joseph turned toward her, tilting his head and taking her in for a moment. "You're awfully quiet. Are you feeling out of sorts? I was expecting a few sarcastic remarks about the costumes, at least."

"I've found that I'm not in the mood to talk opera, and if you'd like to know why, perhaps you should ask Miss Carbury."

"Miss Carbury? What does she have to do with anything?" Joseph asked, crossing his legs in a casual manner. Gabriella wanted to slap him.

"I'm not a fool. I overheard what she said to you about a romance and the cameo. How do you think my parents will take this news? Because I have a mind to tell them as soon as the evening is over."

Joseph put his head in his hands. "The situation with Edith is . . . complicated. But I assure you that it's not what you think."

Gabriella laughed bitterly. "I'm afraid most things usually turn out to be *exactly* what I think. But go on."

"As you know, Matthew is an Oxford chum. Since my family is so far away, his parents took me in as almost a surrogate son, inviting me for dinners and such. So Edith and I spent a good deal of time together, and she developed feelings for me."

Gabriella rolled her eyes but let him continue.

"I spent Christmas with them last year, and after one too many glasses of brandy, Edith and I shared a few innocent kisses on a balcony. Nothing more happened, but she assumed the encounter meant more than it did. It's entirely my fault, and I shouldn't have put her in such a situation."

Gabriella felt her stomach begin to unclench, but not by much. "One can't blame the girl. You don't just go around kissing people for the fun of it. At least, not if you're respectable. But what about the cameo?"

Joseph looked at the ground. "Her parents were in a bit of a tough financial spot last year. Their business was failing, and Edith wanted to sell some personal effects in order to help them. I offered to take the cameo and a few other trinkets to a jeweler friend in Oxford, but the cameo stood out to me for some reason. So I kept it and gave her some money in return."

"But you didn't even know you were going to give it to me back then," Gabriella said, feeling rather confused. "We hadn't even been in contact."

"I suppose I thought I'd hold onto it for the future, for whomever happened to come along. I shouldn't have done it, and it was probably a mistake pretending that I had bought the cameo especially for you, but does it matter? The sentiment behind the necklace is the same as ever, Ella."

This was the wrong answer. Gabriella shot him a dirty look and stood up, gathering her skirts.

Joseph sighed. "Again, I'm sorry, but you have nothing to worry about. And Edith will be leaving soon enough."

"Are you so sure?" Gabriella asked. "She and my brother do seem quite cozy. He even mentioned the possibility of a proposal. Isn't that ridiculous?"

Gabriella posture stiffened when she saw the look of alarm on Joseph's face. "Well," he said. "That's certainly interesting information. If you'll excuse me for a moment . . . " Joseph got up and made a hasty departure to the bar, leaving Gabriella to wonder if her marriage was doomed before it even started.

⋘ ⋘ ⋘

"COULD THE OPERA have been more of a disaster?" Gabriella said, throwing herself into one of her aunt and uncle's parlor chairs with a dramatic sigh the next day.

Instead of dreaming about her perfect wedding, she'd spent a sleepless night agonizing about the strange encounter with Edith and why Joseph had given her a cameo he took from another woman.

"It was definitely an unusual situation," Lessie agreed, pulling out a deck of cards. She hesitated and then said, "Do you think he was being truthful?"

Gabriella shrugged. "I don't know. I believed him, but the whole evening just didn't make sense. Miss Carbury is up to no good, and we're going to find out why."

"We are?" Lessie said, nearly spitting out a piece of

cookie. She took a napkin and dabbed at her mouth. "What I meant to say is, don't you think we should do some more fact-finding before trying to bring her down in front of everyone in Florence? Maybe it's not what you think."

"That's exactly what I meant. We need to dig up some dirt about Little Miss Peaches and Cream. Don't you think it's a bit odd she showed up in Florence and suddenly took an interest in the brother of her ex-paramour's fiancée?"

"It doesn't sound like Joseph was ever a paramour," Lessie said. "He told you they'd only stolen a few kisses at a Christmas party, right? You know, mistletoe and all." She fanned herself a few times before passing Gabriella her hand of cards.

Gabriella threw her hands up in the air. "You aren't still mooning over Thomas Church, are you? That was nearly a year ago!"

Gabriella had accidentally walked in on Lessie sharing a kiss with Mr. Church under the mistletoe at her family's Christmas ball the year before. Unfortunately, their affair was short-lived, and after a few dances and passed love letters, Mr. Church had gone off to Paris.

"Of course not. I just meant it's quite easy to get caught up in the moment during the Christmas season. That's all."

"Whatever you say," Gabriella said. "In any case, we do need to find out something about Miss Carbury before it's too late."

"Too late?"

Gabriella didn't know how to convey the nagging sensation in the pit of her stomach, but it was certainly there, eating away at her insides as she tried to pretend everything was okay. It was something more than the conversation she had overheard at the opera; she'd just had a bad feeling about Edith from the moment that she'd laid eyes on the girl.

"I just don't like her, plain and simple. Are you with me or not?"

Lessie set her hand of cards down, staring at the ceiling and sighing deeply. Finally she looked at her cousin and nodded.

"Of course I'll help you, but I just want to make sure you know what you're getting yourself into. What if Joseph gets angry with you and calls off the engagement?"

"Nonsense. He already knows I'm concerned about the situation, so I can't imagine he'd be too cross with me for doing a little fact finding. It's my future, after all."

Gabriella had convinced herself that snooping on Edith was not only a good idea, but the responsible thing to do. Would Lessie want her to end up married to someone with unresolved love interests floating about? Surely not.

"If I didn't know better, I'd think you two were up to no good!" The girls jumped slightly as Aunt Gia entered the room.

"Oh, erm, good afternoon, Mother," Lessie said, fumbling with her plate of pastries and looking quite guilty.

Gabriella had to wonder why on earth she was asking the world's worst actress to help her on a spy mission, but instead smoothed her skirts and stood up to give her aunt a quick kiss.

"Oh, just some girlish talk and a little game of cards," she said with a smile, making sure to give Lessie an annoyed glance over her shoulder.

Aunt Gia obviously knew better, but just shook her head and helped herself to some cookies. "So, Ella, how did you enjoy the performance last night? I don't think

I've seen such an exuberant display of costume and song in quite some time."

Gabriella bit her lip, trying to think of a good response. It was clear her aunt knew that she hadn't been paying a lick of attention to the show and was just trying to torture her.

"Oh yes, I agree. It was quite good, wasn't it Lessie?"

Lessie leaned forward, eager to contribute to the discussion, but her mother cut her off before she could wax poetic about Tannhäuser's breeches or something equally ridiculous.

"What was your favorite part? I know mine, but I would love to compare."

Gabriella racked her brain trying to think of anything from the night before, but all she could remember was the snide look on Edith's face as Joseph had escorted them both to the box.

"Erm, I did rather enjoy the bits with the dueling."

"Really? Why is that?" Aunt Gia asked.

"I just thought their performances were quite . . . inspired. Very dramatic. Unrequited love and whatnot."

"Hmmm," Aunt Gia said, a crack of a smile almost breaking through. "What did your Mr. Rossi think of the show?"

"Oh, he seemed to like it, considering. You know how men can be."

"Your uncle saw him dash out into the lobby after the second act. Was everything all right? I hope he wasn't feeling ill."

Gabriella and Lessie locked eyes. "He's quite fine," Gabriella said, careful to choose her words appropriately. "He heard an old friend was visiting and went off to find him."

"Ah, that's good to hear. In any case, we're all looking forward to the wedding. I trust Mr. Rossi is, too."

Her aunt's voice sounded off, something in her tone suspicious. But Gabriella decided it was her mind playing tricks. The arrival of Miss Carbury had caused her to become so paranoid that just about anything could cause alarm.

"We're all very excited," Gabriella said, sounding as bland as she felt. She had to find out what was going on, and soon.

"You know that your uncle and I wish you all the happiness in the world. Now if you'll excuse me, I'm off to call on some friends. Be good, Lessie." She gave her daughter an affectionate pat on the head and left the parlor, the sound of her heels echoing throughout the room.

"Do you think she knows something?" Lessie asked as soon as her mother's footsteps had died away.

"Maybe. But if she heard anything, it would be from my mother, and I doubt she'd let any nonsense get past without accosting me."

The pair sat in silence for a while, both contemplating the wrath of Mrs. Capetti, until Lessie sprung out of her chair.

"Oh! I can't believe I forgot about this. Massimo said he was going to the pub with your brother, Joseph, and Matthew this afternoon. That means Miss Carbury will definitely be on her own, right?"

"I suppose. But how are we supposed to find her? She's not staying at the Rossis' home, so who knows where she's lodging."

"I do," Lessie said, looking quite proud of herself. "I asked the Blakely sisters after the second act. They said Edith wasn't very friendly, but they've definitely seen her dining at Doney et Neveux with her brother, and overheard she had rented a room at that new boarding house along Via Maggio."

Gabriella jumped up to hug her. "Good work. But we can't just barge in and demand to see her. Even if we did, she might not be there."

"No, I suppose that wouldn't do," Lessie said, as if she had considered the idea for a moment. "But we could find out when she's supposed to spend time with Carlo again and then trail behind them. Discreetly, of course."

Lessie's idea of discretion was certainly debatable, but that was no matter. They had work to do, and Gabriella had a plan.

"Come along; I think I suddenly have the urge to visit Miss Carbury after all. I've been pondering adding another bridesmaid, and I think she's just the candidate."

"Bridesmaid? Do I need to check you for a fever?"

"Yes, bridesmaid," Gabriella said, sounding more excited by the moment. "It's the perfect plan! You know what they say, keep your enemies close and whatnot. If Edith's a bridesmaid, we'll have all sorts of opportunities to get to know her better. And she'll be so busy with the wedding plans, it will be difficult for her to go running about after Joseph and stirring up trouble."

"What if she objects when the priest says the bit about 'Speak now or forever hold your peace?'" Lessie sat down, looking almost faint at the thought.

"Don't be ridiculous," Gabriella said, rolling her eyes. The truth was, she had already considered that scenario, but ultimately decided it was something that only happened in novels. She wrote her own story, and no one was going to change it.

Or at least, she hoped they wouldn't.

CHAPTER 33

～

GABRIELLA

"I F YOU'RE LOOKING for Miss Carbury, she's no longer lodging there," Emma Blakely said.

She rounded the corner, arms full of books, just as Gabriella and Lessie were about to get out of their car.

"Word is, Mr. and Mrs. Rossi invited her to be their guests for the duration of her visit, and she checked out this morning," Emma said. She tilted her head a bit, looking straight at Gabriella and clearly trying to gauge her reaction.

"You don't say," Gabriella said, resting back against the leather seat and forcing a smile. "That's very interesting information, indeed."

More like exasperating information, she thought. With Edith in the same house as her fiancé, who knew what she would try to do.

Emma smiled back, but hers was genuine. "Isn't it? But I should be going. These books aren't getting any lighter. Ta-ta!"

Gabriella gave Emma a halfhearted wave. "Of course. I wouldn't want you to strain yourself."

They said their goodbyes and Lessie instructed her

driver to take them to the Rossis' villa immediately.

"Don't worry, we'll figure this out," Lessie said, but her expression mirrored Gabriella's dread. The closer they got to the Rossis', the more nauseated Gabriella felt, and she nearly had to tell the driver to pull over so she could vomit.

Once inside, they were led to the Rossis' front parlor to wait for Edith. Mrs. Rossi was not at home, so luckily they would only have to deal with one unpleasant woman that afternoon.

"Their home is a lot grander than I remember," Lessie whispered to her cousin, eyeing their surroundings. "Everything looks different at night, especially after a few glasses of champagne."

Gabriella preened a bit at this comment. After all, the Rossis' house was practically hers now, too. "Their designer came straight from Paris. Joseph said his family accepts only the best when it comes to décor."

Lessie smiled politely, taking in the gilded columns and heavy brocades. Gabriella knew it would certainly qualify as "tacky" in New York, but then again, everything in Italy was different from Manhattan.

"What on earth is she doing up there?" Gabriella asked, glancing toward the door. "If we had announced my brother was here, I bet Edith would've made a run for the parlor."

Lessie stifled a giggle. "Maybe she's attending to . . . you know, personal business?"

"No, she just wants to be unkind and make us wait."

The pair sat in nervous silence until they heard the soft tap of footsteps. Gabriella sat up straighter while Lessie squirmed in her chair.

"Miss Capetti, Miss Giardano, to what do I owe

the pleasure of your visit?" Edith said, standing in the doorway. She wore a faded pink-and-white floral dress with little shape to it, and a sour expression that made it clear their presence was not, in fact, a pleasure.

"I wanted to ask you something rather important. Why don't you have a seat?" Gabriella suggested, gesturing to the third teacup on the small table in front of her.

Edith hesitated for a moment and then crossed the room to sit beside Lessie.

"Since you and your brother are such dear friends of Joseph's and you'll be in town for the wedding, I thought you might want to be a bridesmaid."

"A bridesmaid?" Edith said, her face draining of the small amount of color it had. "That's very kind of you, but we hardly know each other. Wouldn't you prefer another friend of yours?"

"I insist," Gabriella said. "All of my friends are in New York, anyway."

Lessie gulped her cup of tea louder than necessary and gave Edith a small smile to try to cover up her gaffe. "We would love to include you, Edith. The dresses are lovely! Wait until you see them. I'm sure you'd have a wonderful time."

Edith remained tight-lipped, then finally sighed. "Forgive me for being blunt, but I know you don't like me very much. Why on earth would you want me to stand for you as a bridesmaid? Is this some sort of trick?"

Gabriella wasn't counting on Edith to see right through her request, but she refused to show any signs of defeat.

"We just thought that it would be a kind gesture. I'm sorry if I upset you," Gabriella said with a sniff, taking a handkerchief out of her small beaded purse and dabbing her eyes with a dramatic flick. "If being a part of my wedding is so offensive to you, then I would prefer you not attend at all."

Lessie's eyes darted back and forth between Edith and her cousin, unsure as to what to do next. She settled for rushing over to Gabriella's side to console her. "Now, now. We'll just have to ask Chiara Marino, I suppose."

"I can't resort to begging Chiara to take part in my wedding," Gabriella said, wailing rather convincingly into the lace handkerchief. "I'll become the laughingstock of Florence!" Edith, who must have heard stories about Chiara from Joseph's family, looked on in horror.

"Calm down, Miss Capetti. I'll do it. No need for dramatics."

Gabriella lifted her head from her cousin's shoulder, wiping her eyes and smiling at Edith. "Wonderful. I'll send the dressmaker over to get your measurements."

Edith nodded and asked a few polite questions about the details, while Gabriella rattled off the pertinent information, heart racing. She couldn't believe it had worked.

"I'm afraid we must be going," Lessie said. "As I'm sure you can imagine, there are many things to do before the big day arrives, right, Ella?"

Gabriella reached out to clasp Edith's hand. "Oh yes, we should be getting on with our afternoon. I'm so glad you can be a part of the wedding, though."

"It was nice of you to ask," Edith said, her face stony. "Thank you."

Only once they were outside did Gabriella let out a huge sigh of relief. "I'm honestly shocked she went along with it," she said as they navigated the cobblestone walkway to the street, where their driver was waiting.

"She isn't as dim as you think, Ella," Lessie said with

a hint of warning in her tone. "Miss Carbury is on to you; I'd be very careful."

Gabriella laughed and climbed into the car. "And what's a stupid little girl like her going to do?"

⋄ ⋄ ⋄

A FEW MINUTES LATER, the imposing yellow villa was out of sight and they pulled onto the Via Tornabuoni, headed toward Gabriella's favorite shops. The only thing to get her mind off Edith was to immerse herself in distractions, perhaps a new book and a nice shiny pair of shoes.

As Lessie and Gabriella argued about where to start their outing, Lessie tugged on her cousin's arm with a wild look in her eyes.

"What on earth is wrong with you?" Gabriella asked, turning her body to see Edith strolling down the street, swinging her arms and looking around in general amusement at the busy Florentines passing her.

"Do you think she's gone out to find Joseph?" Lessie asked. "The pub is just around the corner from here."

Gabriella didn't respond, but leaned forward and told the driver to change directions and head to fetch their brothers instead. She sat back, twisting her gloves, until Lessie took them from her. "You're going to rip a hole in them," she said, "and for that matter, let's not cause ourselves undue stress."

"I'm ignoring you, dear cousin," Gabriella said, snatching her gloves back. "But thank you for the words of encouragement, in any case."

The pair sat in silence as they approached the pub, finally climbing out and asking the driver to wait as they entered the bookshop across the narrow cobbled street. "I wanted to visit this shop anyway," Gabriella said. "And we can watch out the front window to see if Miss Carbury shows up. Perfect."

After lingering around the display of poetry books in the front of the shop for several minutes, there was no sign of Edith. Lessie headed toward the back to peruse the music books, and a few moments later Gabriella came running.

"Edith's outside and most certainly waiting for the gentlemen to leave. She's standing across the street and fiddling with her hat, practically shaking. Honestly, we need to get this situation sorted sooner rather than later."

Lessie closed the heavy volume she was reading and tapped her fingers on one of the ancient-looking pine shelves. "Should we confront her?"

Gabriella sighed. "I don't know. But we should most likely decide—"

Just then, the door to the bookshop swung open and in walked Edith. The girls were out of sight, fortunately, and took quick steps behind the massive shelf next to them. Gabriella moved several books aside, tossing them on the floor so she could see through. "She's looking out the window. Exactly what we were doing. Maybe she realized it would be a bit awkward to stand outside waiting for them."

The girls remained hunched behind the shelf for a good ten minutes or so, long enough that Gabriella's back and shoulders began to ache and Lessie finally took a seat next to the pile of books on the dusty wood floor.

Finally they heard the tinkle of the front door as it opened, and Gabriella pulled Lessie to her feet with a rough "oomph."

"She's leaving. That must mean they're here," she said, pulling her cousin behind her. Sure enough, they spotted Joseph, Massimo, Carlo, and Matthew laughing as they exited the bar, along with Edith crossing over to greet them.

The look of annoyance on Joseph's face was clear, even from across the street.

"What are they saying?" Gabriella asked, straining to see what was happening. While lip reading wasn't one of her talents, fortunately, it was one of Lessie's.

"I think her brother just asked why she'd come alone and why one of us hadn't accompanied her to the bookshop? Why on earth would she ask us to come?"

"I don't know," Gabriella said. "I'm sure he has no idea that she's after Joseph. Men are much dimmer about these affairs than you think."

Lessie stood on her toes, nearly knocking over a stack of books. "Oh! Now Edith is saying something to Joseph. I believe she said 'Can I speak to you in private, if you don't mind?'" The pair watched as the other men climbed into a waiting automobile and Edith and Joseph began walking down the street together.

Gabriella's nostrils flared. "I'll show her private! Let's go." She rushed past Lessie on her way to the front door, but Lessie pulled on her cousin's arm.

"Perhaps we should wait until we can follow behind them without being noticed?"

Gabriella grabbed the doorknob and flung it open, her heart racing as fast as the traffic outside. "They won't see us. I've got to be able to hear what they're saying."

It was clear that Edith was engrossed in conversation with her schoolgirl fantasy, and once they were within a safe distance, Lessie and Gabriella fell in step behind them.

"So what kind of trouble are you planning on stirring up involving my fiancée and her cousin?" Joseph asked, cocking his head to the side.

Edith looked at him with sadness in her eyes. "Why do you always assume the worst about me?"

"Because it's usually true."

Gabriella had to stifle a giggle at Joseph's response. At least he wasn't encouraging her silly pursuit.

She watched as Edith threw her head back and laughed, her hat slipping to the side. "I suppose I deserve that. But anything I've done was only to be closer to you, so I can't say I have regrets. But back to your fiancée. She paid me a visit this afternoon."

The girls shared worried looks, linking arms as they tried to get just a bit closer to better hear the conversation.

"She came to the house to see you? Are you sure she wasn't looking for me?" Joseph asked.

"Yes, of course I'm sure. Miss Capetti was there with her cousin and they asked if I'd be a bridesmaid in the wedding."

Joseph, who suddenly had a coughing fit, turned toward the street to regain his composure. Gabriella and Lessie stopped in their tracks, stepping quickly in front of a flower shop so they wouldn't be seen. This meant they had to struggle to hear, but even with the bustling crowd around them and Joseph's back turned, his raised tone was blatantly audible.

"Gabriella asked you to be a bridesmaid in our wedding? Why on earth would she do that?" he asked.

"That's what I want to know," Edith said, frowning. "It doesn't add up. When I questioned her motives, she burst into tears and said she wanted me to feel included since Matthew would be taking part as well. Do you know anything about this?"

"No, I don't. Although I do agree it was an uncharacteristically kind gesture, it doesn't mean she was being malicious."

"Good," Edith said. "Because if she has some sort of

plan to ruin me, it's not going to work."

Joseph's message was clear, much to Gabriella's relief. "You and I will never be together, Edith. It's time to give up the fantasy. Either take my Ella up on her offer and be part of the wedding, or don't attend. It's your choice."

Edith appeared to be wiping tears away as she headed toward the street. "On second thought, just leave me alone. I don't want anything to do with you or your wedding, Joseph. I should have just ended it all like I planned that night back home. You had no right to stop me."

Lessie's eyes widened. "Ended it? Do you think she tried to . . . you know?"

"Off herself?" Gabriella asked, always queen of tact. "Sounds like it." She took a step away from the roses with a loud sneeze.

As Lessie shook her head, shushing her cousin, Joseph chased after Edith.

"For the love of God, Edith! Be reasonable and come back to the house. You can't go running off alone like this whenever you want. If you don't care to attend the wedding, that's fine. But I don't want you to hurt yourself."

Edith ran into the middle of the busy street, carriages, people and automobiles rushing past her. Joseph shook his head but followed behind, and Gabriella covered her mouth with her hand.

"What on earth does she think she's doing?" Lessie whispered, burying her head in her cousin's shoulder. Gabriella wrapped her arms around Lessie, trembling too much to even formulate a response.

"Just let me go," Edith shouted, giving Joseph the hardest shove her skinny arms likely could muster. Suddenly she locked eyes with Gabriella, her mouth dropping open while a look of pure hatred passed between the two. Joseph whirled around and what happened next was a blur to Gabriella. The screech of tires, the automobile's horn, Joseph . . .

The last thing she remembered before blacking out was a sickening thud and her fiancé lying in the middle of the street.

CHAPTER 34

ELLA

"SO THAT'S WHY you never went back to Florence," Ella said, reaching for a tissue. She'd assumed the wedding was called off, not that Joseph had died in his mid-twenties, for goodness' sake. No wonder her mother acted the way she did; who could imagine seeing their fiancé run over in front of their eyes?

Gabriella nodded, her face betraying no emotion. "I gave the ring back to Joseph's parents after his funeral, and I left Italy for good. My grandmother died a few months later, so there was no reason for me to go back. My parents visited their friends from time to time, but I never came along."

"But what happened to Edith?" Trudy asked. "She never married your brother, did she?"

"Unless she's going undercover as a busty Italian woman named Daniela, then no," Gabriella said with a laugh. "Edith ended up staying in Italy, actually. She became quite popular in the expat community. Published a few volumes of poetry. I never cared for it."

"Imagine that," Ella said. "But why didn't you ever tell me about Joseph?"

"It was a very confusing time for me, Ella," she said. "If I didn't talk about him, then it never happened."

Ella twirled a lock of hair, trying not to appear angry. Maybe they weren't that close, but it seemed like a huge bombshell for her mother to drop so late in life.

"You're always telling me not to be so reserved, to open up more. But you've kept something huge from your family for years? Talk about irony."

Trudy grabbed her friend's hand. "Calm down, hon. I'm sure it was hard for your mother to deal with the whole situation. I don't know if that story would be something I'd tell everyone, either."

Gabriella didn't look angry, just disappointed. "You're right, Trudy. It's not something I cared to relive. I suppose my life flashed before my eyes when I went to the hospital. You have plenty of time to muse about things when you're in a goddamn hospital bed, in case you're wondering."

Ella shrugged, feeling about five years old. "I guess that's understandable."

"I truly did start to have feelings for Joseph, even though I couldn't stand him at first. Imagine seeing your future disappear in front of your eyes."

"But what happened when you got back to New York? You always said you met Dad at a party and it was love at first sight."

Gabriella looked down. "It was just different once I got back to Manhattan. The parties, my friends . . . nothing was the same. Lessie got engaged not long after we returned from Florence, so she wasn't around as much. Your father's proposal came at a time when I wanted to erase that summer from my memory. So I accepted. I always blamed myself for the accident, you know. If I hadn't asked Edith to be in our wedding, she probably never would've confronted him, and

Joseph wouldn't have died."

A tear slid down Ella's cheek. She'd always suspected her mother wasn't happy or that she never really wanted her, but this felt a lot like a confirmation.

"Don't look so offended," Gabriella said. "I'm not saying I never loved your father or the rest of you. He gave me a very nice life. It just wasn't the life I planned for, that's all."

Ella nodded. She could judge her mother all she wanted, but if the tables were turned, Ella wasn't sure that she would've been able to move on at all.

"Mother, I'm sorry—" She paused. "What I mean to say is that I've had a lot of resentment toward you over the years. For not being the mother I wanted you to be. But now I realize that I've never tried, either. Instead of attempting to make our relationship better, I sat here wallowing in my own misery. I never knew what a hard time you had when you were young. I wish you'd told me."

Gabriella laughed. "I just did. And you're right. I'm an old fool. But it doesn't change how much I care about you. Now get me that magazine, will you? I've got to finish catching up on my Grace Kelly news before I forget what I read."

✧ ✧ ✧

MONDAY WAS HARRY'S DAY OFF. It was now or never, and Ella was pacing in her office, flipping through the proposal she had spent so many hours creating with her mother and Trudy.

"I guess this is it, huh?" Gabriella said. She entered the office without knocking and held out a small box. "Take it. Maybe it will give you better luck than it gave me."

Ella looked at her mother with confusion, then back at the box. "Just open the damn thing, will you?" Gabriella said, watching with a wry smile as her daughter pulled the cameo out of the box.

"Oh my. I can't accept this!" Ella said, clicking the locket open to examine the inscription.

"Why not? I was going to leave it to you in my will anyway, so you might as well take it now."

Ella managed a faint smile. "All right then. Maybe I should wear it today. For luck."

"It can't hurt. Just do me a favor and keep the story to yourself. I have a reputation to uphold, after all. Don't want everyone thinking that I got soft."

Ella adjusted the locket's clasp and admired herself in the mirror. "Whatever you say. And thanks for all of your help."

Maybe the cameo didn't give her mother the happiest ending, but Ella was determined not to let the past determine her future. She felt a tiny jolt of confidence with the weight of the locket against her chest, even though her heartbeat raced as Gabriella followed her into the living room. Harry was watching *Captain Kangaroo* with the kids, who were dancing around in front of the television with glee and singing a song that Lily had made up. "Kangie kangie time!" Carol shouted as she saw her mother and Nonni approach.

"Yes, kangie time, indeed. Come and sit with your old Nonni for a few minutes while your parents take care of some business."

"Business?" Harry asked, looking at Ella with concern. "Is everything okay?"

"Everything's great. Nothing to worry about," Ella said. "I just wanted to show you something. Can we go in the kitchen?"

"Sure. Now you've piqued my curiosity, Dear," he said, taking a seat at the kitchen table.

Ella took a deep breath and dropped the business plan on the table's checkerboard tablecloth. She had to admit it looked impressive, thanks to her mother's connections.

Harry's eyes grew wide, but he smiled nonetheless. "La Bella Cakery? What's this all about?"

"I've been thinking a lot lately about this idea, and I think it would work. You know the customers are always asking to special order cakes and things from us, but we just don't have the staff or the time. If we added a cake shop, just think of the extra business we could bring in. Wedding cakes cost a pretty penny and let's face it, our customers aren't hurting for cash. We could do birthdays and other events, too."

Harry flipped through the proposal as she spoke, scanning each page thoroughly. Finally, he looked up. "How much is this going to cost?"

"It's all there on page twelve. My mother already offered to give us the money to get started. I'm confident that once we get going, we'll be making a profit very quickly."

"Your mother? Wow. I can't say I was expecting that, but it was very kind to offer. Who would run the shop, though?"

Ella spun her wedding ring around a few times before regaining her confidence. "I would, with some help from Trudy. Since we'd be specializing in events, the shop would only be open a few days a week, and Saturdays. We've also figured out a babysitting schedule. That's in appendix C."

Harry chuckled, flipping to the back. "You weren't kidding. It looks like you've thought of everything. But why didn't you just tell me you wanted to open a cake shop? It's a sound idea. I would've heard you out."

"You were so busy with the new menu, and stressed

about my mother being sick and moving in. How could I add another burden?" she said. "I kept trying to talk myself out of the idea, but it wouldn't get out of my head. So Trudy and Mom helped me with a plan. I wanted you to know how serious I was about this."

"Ellie, even if I'm not always here for the day-to-day, we're a team. And so you know, I've just hired another manager to help ease the load on me at work. Hopefully that'll mean some extra time to help you out with your cakes."

Ella leaned forward in anticipation. "Wait, is that a yes?"

Harry closed the proposal and handed it back to Ella. "It's a lot to think about, and we need to sit down and really hash out all of the expenses, but yes. I actually think La Bella Cakery is a great idea."

Ella jumped up and threw her arms around Harry. "Thank you, thank you, thank you! You'll see; this is going to be wonderful."

"I'm sure it will be," Harry said, embracing his wife. "After all, you're the one with the baking skills here. I just cook Italian slop."

Ella laughed, punching him playfully on the arm. "Slop that's rated best in the area." After a quick kiss, she rushed to Gabriella's side in the living room. "Did you hear?"

Gabriella rolled her eyes. "Of course I did. You're talking to a professional eavesdropper. And congratulations."

"I couldn't have done it without you," Ella said, placing her hand on top of her mother's. For once, Gabriella didn't pull away. "Thank you again."

Gabriella simply nodded and patted Ella's arm before she headed back into the kitchen. Maybe it wasn't a hug, but it was another step forward.

CHAPTER 35

LIZ

A RAGING HEAD COLD greeted me the day after the princess marathon. Stuffy nose, sneezing, the works. It didn't help that I'd just finished reading Nan's diary and found out Joseph was actually dead. It all made sense now: Nonni Gabriella's inability to connect with her family, Nan leaving that note for me about the cameo. She knew I'd understand. There was no reason to keep it a secret anymore . . . and maybe it was time to finally mend fences with my mom, too.

I said a silent prayer for Joseph and Nonni Gabriella. Maybe they were even together again right now. The thought made me smile, but it also reminded me of Justin and I felt my stomach ache. What was I missing by not fighting harder for him?

I desperately wanted to see him, but based on our last encounter, he didn't seem to return the feeling. My hands started shaking just thinking about knocking on his door. Just in case he turned me down, I sent a feeler text out.

Hey, are you home? Can I stop by later?

Even if he didn't write back, at least I tried.

I gathered up my pile of crumpled tissues and headed

into the bathroom to get a start on the day when the phone rang. Cate.

"Is everything okay?" I asked. "Mom didn't find out you tossed that case of bell-shaped mints in the dumpster behind McDonald's, did she?"

"Not that I know of. I just wanted to tell you I talked to Jesse and we're going to try to work things out."

"Wow, that's awesome. I'm happy for you, Beep." And for once, I truly was.

"He showed up at the house today and begged me to forgive him. You should've seen it. It was like the part in *Father of the Bride* when Bryan comes over looking all ragged and depressed. Except he hadn't given me a blender for our anniversary, of course."

Father of the Bride was Cate's all-time favorite movie, so that scenario must have been a dream come true. Hell, she probably wished he *had* given her a blender.

"We're going to push the wedding out another two years or so, and he told his parents that they'd just have to deal with it." I could hear the smile in Cate's voice.

"I'm sure they were thrilled," I said between sneezes. "But I'm glad that you guys are working things out. By the way, are you going to be home today? I was actually thinking of coming over to hang out and maybe stay for dinner."

"I was going to run to the mall to do some last-minute Christmas shopping, but I can wait for you if it's not going to take too long," she said. I could hear Mom singing in the background, and the strains of the "Hallelujah" chorus from her favorite Christmas CD. *Oh brother.* I told Cate I'd be there ASAP. After hanging up, I checked my texts . . . one new message.

I'm here.

It might not have been the most welcoming of

invitations, but I'd take it. A minute later I was standing on Justin's silly doormat, about to lose the contents of my breakfast.

Deep breaths. Act natural.

He answered the door almost immediately, looking slightly less scruffy and annoyed than during our last encounter. "Hey, stranger," he said, stepping back and extending his arm. "Come on in."

I walked past him, bending down to pat Bo's head. "Wow. Somebody's excited to see you," Justin said with a laugh as Bo's tail twitched wildly and he lunged at my face to give me puppy kisses.

"It's reassuring to know *someone* wants me here." I said it with a smile, but from the expression on his face, I knew Justin could tell I was only half joking.

"Why would you think I don't want you here?"

I stood up, brushing the dog hair off my coat. "I don't know. The whole mess with Adam. You just didn't seem thrilled to see me in the lobby." I paused, looking down. "I never wanted to ruin my chances with you. I'm so sorry."

He took my hand and led me to the couch. "Have a seat." I plopped down next to him and Bo, who'd trailed behind us, unsure whether Justin wanted me to sit down so he could break some bad news, or what.

"So . . . " he said.

"So . . ."

"Listen, I—" we both said at exactly the same time, followed by nervous laughter.

He turned toward me and cracked his knuckles. "I'll go first. I'm not mad. But it just seemed like you were really into me, then I saw you with Adam that night . . . and after you told me you'd kissed him, I just figured I'd take a step back. If it was meant to be, it was meant to be."

"Well, you're right. I *was* really into you. Still am," I said. "I just got caught up in memories and I hadn't seen Adam in so long. Deep down, I think I felt like I owed him something for bailing on our plans, and turning down the ring and messing up his life. But then I realized he was just fine without me. And I'm sorry for—"

He held his hand up. "You really don't have to keep apologizing. It wasn't fair for me to hold it against you for pursuing whatever it was you felt like you had to pursue, or get closure, or whatever, from Adam. We'd just met; we weren't serious. And as long as it's over and done with between you guys, we can just move on."

It felt like Justin had lifted an entire jeweler's case of weight off my shoulders, and for the first time in weeks the knot in my stomach completely unraveled. "I'd like that. A fresh start for the new year."

"I think it'll be a good year. I have a feeling." He slid closer to me, and I felt my pulse race . . . until I broke into a sneezing fit, which simultaneously sent Bo into a barking fit.

"I'm so—A-CHOO, sorry. Can't—A-CHOO, stop sneezing." He rushed up and grabbed me a tissue as Bo spun in circles on the cushion, barking. "How's that for a romantic reconciliation?" I said.

I started laughing. Justin joined in, and soon tears were running our down our cheeks. I knew right then that everything was going to be all right.

"I'm surprised you aren't back in Florida for the holidays, by the way," I said, once I'd finally regained composure.

"I'm actually flying home Tuesday morning. I won't be back till New Year's Day." He stroked the top of my hand. "Maybe we can do something that night, though. Belated New Year's celebration?"

The idea of being so far from Justin once we'd finally gotten things back on track sent my mood spiraling downward, but at least we had a new start to look forward to now. "Sounds perfect."

I looked at the time with a sigh. "I hate to leave you, but actually, I do need to get going. I'm finally telling my family about the cameo and the diary and everything."

"Wow," he said. "Do you think they'll be upset?"

I pondered this for a second and frowned. "Yes. Almost definitely. But I need to fess up. It's so weird that I'm the only one that knows any of this, like how my great-grandmother gave the necklace back to her fiancé and he had it engraved with the proposal, and him being killed in an accident . . . the story is crazy. Nan trusted me with the secret, but it can't just be my burden alone anymore, ya know?"

He stood up and followed me to the door. "Whatever you do will be the right choice. And even if they're pissed off for a while, they'll get over it."

"You say this like you've had experience," I said with a smirk. "Just kidding."

Justin wrapped his arms around my waist and pulled me in close. "Do you want to come over after work tomorrow? You could help me pack. Exciting stuff."

I smiled into his soft fleece pullover. "Absolutely. I'm an excellent packer, in fact."

"It's a date then." He pulled back and tucked a lock of hair behind my ear. Even though there was no kiss, my day couldn't have gotten any better. "See you then, Liz."

∽ ∽ ∽

ASAP ENDED UP being quite a bit later than I expected, thanks to my visit to Justin's and all of the holiday traffic.

I stepped inside my parents' house to the sound of "All I Want for Christmas is You" and the living room twinkling with white lights, even though it was barely lunchtime. Mom was always a fan of keeping the Christmas lights on all day, a tradition of which my Dad (and the electric bill) was never fond.

Cate sat on the couch, arms folded and lips pursed, but looking a hundred times better than the last time I'd seen her. She checked her gold Cartier watch, a gift from Jesse, and frowned.

"You're like an hour late. Are you ready to go?"

I paused for a moment, and then pulled the diary out of my bag. "There's something I wanted to show you and Mom first. It's kind of important."

Cate took one look at the worn diary and back at me with understanding.

"Where did you find this?" she asked, running her hand over the faded leather cover.

"It was in Nan's desk. I found it in there that day we all cleaned up the house."

I could see Cate doing the math in her head. "That was weeks ago. Why didn't you tell us before?"

I sighed. "It's a long story. Can you get Mom? I want her to hear this, too."

She gave me a strange look but called up the steps just as Dad walked into the living room. "Hey, kiddo, I didn't know you were coming over. What's the occasion?"

I gestured toward the couch. "Sit down, Dad. I should probably tell everyone. And I guess get Gracie, too."

A minute later everyone sat on the couch, looking at me expectantly. "You're not pregnant, are you?" Gracie asked with a look of thinly veiled panic.

"Gracie! Seriously," Mom said, before turning to

me and adding, "You're not, are you?"

"What?" I said, giving Gracie a death stare. "Let's back this train up. No, I am not pregnant, unless there is going to be another divine birth this Christmas. The reason I came over was because I found out something about Nan. Well, more about Nonni Gabriella, actually."

Mom cocked her head to the side. "Oh? What's that?"

I sat down and dug my nails into the armrest of the old recliner, then remembered that Nonni Gabriella was brave enough to tell Nan the truth about Joseph. I took a deep breath and continued.

"So the desk Nan left me in the will . . . I found this old cameo locket inside one of the drawers, and a note from Nan telling me that I'd know what to do with it. Basically, it had an engraving inside that was a marriage proposal. From a man named Joseph."

Mom and Cate exchanged confused glances. "Joseph? Are you sure?" Mom said. "I never heard anything about someone before Pop."

"That's just it. The necklace wasn't Nan's to begin with. It was Nonni Gabriella's. Joseph was her fiancé before she married your grandfather, but he was killed in a terrible accident."

"Wow," Mom said. "I know she told us stories about Italy when I was a kid, but I was too young to remember any of them. I had no idea about another fiancé. How did you even find this out?"

Cate picked up the diary off the coffee table and handed it to Mom. "This was in the desk, too. I'm assuming it talks about the necklace."

"So where is it?" Mom asked. "I can't wait to see. I vaguely remember her talking about a cameo, but she never wore it or anything."

Her hopeful expression felt like a punch in the gut. "I'm so sorry, but I lost it. I was wearing the necklace the night before Thanksgiving and when I woke up the next day it was gone. I've all but torn the city apart and it's still missing."

"You *lost* it?" Mom asked, looking back and forth between my sisters to see if they were in on it, too. "And why didn't you tell us in the first place?"

"Cate and Gracie didn't know anything. I was afraid to tell you guys because I knew how upset you'd be, but I thought that maybe I could track it down before Christmas and everything would be okay."

"Liz, hon, how on earth did you lose your grandmother's necklace?" Dad said, reaching out to pat my mom's arm in what I assumed was supposed to be a comforting manner. Either that or he was trying to hold her back.

I covered my eyes for a second and shook my head. "I don't know. The clasp must have come loose or something. Trust me, I've been torn up about this for weeks."

"Well, that sucks," Cate said. "Did you try any of the pawnshops or antique stores in the city? Maybe someone tried to make a quick buck if they found it."

I nodded. "I did. No luck. And I'm sorry. I wanted to tell you guys about this sooner, but the cameo became sort of an obsession. I wanted to find out what happened and who Joseph was . . . I felt it was my job to get to the bottom of it since Nan felt there was a reason to entrust me with the necklace over anyone else."

Mom crossed the room to grab a tissue, and Dad followed her. I already felt like crap about the whole situation, but seeing him comfort her while she sobbed made me feel a million times worse.

"Good job, Liz. How the hell do you lose a priceless family heirloom?" Gracie shouted. "Look at Mom, she's sick over it!"

"Oh, and you've been *so* responsible over the years," I said, leaning forward and nearly spitting with anger. "Let's see, was it you who broke Mom's anniversary clock last summer when you were playing catch with your boyfriend in the house? And who sat there acting like a brat while the rest of us cleaned Nan's house from top to bottom?"

"That's different!" she said, looking to Cate for support.

"Enough. This is ridiculous!" Cate said, jumping to her feet. "It wasn't Liz's fault that she lost the necklace. It fell off by accident. The thing was old as dirt and I'm sure the chain wasn't very strong. It could've happened to any of us if we had worn it."

Gracie folded her arms and huffed as Dad strolled back in the living room and put a hand on my shoulder. "Cate has a good point. I know it's easy enough to place blame, but that's not going to bring the cameo back. Can you girls just try not to keep secrets from us in the future? You can come to us with anything."

I nodded, brushing away a stray tear with the back of my hand. I could hear Mom in the kitchen putting a kettle on, and I took the cue to go in and talk to her alone.

"Mom?" I said, peering around the corner. "I just wanted to apologize for everything. I should've told you sooner, but I've been going through a lot myself, too. Besides this."

"Like what?" she said, not turning around, but reaching into the cabinet for five mugs. I took this as a peace offering.

"Just guy stuff. It's not important now. But after I

finished reading the diary, I realized that I didn't want to screw things up with you. Nan and her mother never had the best relationship, and by the time they tried to do something about it, it was practically too late."

Mom turned to face me. "Is that what this is all about? Liz, we've never been best friends. I know you and Nan had a special connection, and I admit I was always jealous of it. But I hardly think our relationship has been like the ones Nonni Gabriella or Nan had with their mothers."

I felt a slight wave of relief. "My grandmother dealt with a lot in her life, as I'm sure you know," Mom added. "That and she was always kind of standoffish to begin with."

I cracked a smile. "I figured that much out from the diary. Nan hardly ever talked about her mother, and now I know why. I just don't ever want things to be like that with us."

Mom sighed and pulled me in for a quick hug. "They won't be. But next time you uncover some sort of family secret, can you give me a heads-up first?"

I laughed and sniffled at the same time. "You got it."

✧ ✧ ✧

THE NEXT DAY was my last one at work before Christmas, and the city was buzzing with people trying to pull their act together at the eleventh hour. I'd just finished ringing up a couple of high school girls who'd bought one of my beaded bracelet watches for their friend (score!) when the shop's bell jingled . . . and in walked Justin.

Addie, who'd stopped by to visit on her lunch break, nearly spit her coffee out, and I shooed her to the back of the shop.

"Hey," he said with a sheepish smile. "I was hoping you'd be here."

I stared at him in disbelief for a few seconds. "Justin, hey. You're the last person I expected to see walk in the door."

"I was in the neighborhood for a meeting and thought I'd take a chance and pop in."

I stepped out from behind the counter, restraining a giggle as the girls looked Justin up and down on their way out of the shop.

"So, a bunch of us are leaving work early and going to happy hour tonight, and I thought I'd see if you wanted to come. I couldn't wait until later to see you."

He looked down, making a show of playing with a display of kitschy cashmere Christmas sweaters, but I could see how red his cheeks had turned.

"Oh, wow. Okay," I said, still surprised at his presence in the shop, not to mention the admission that he couldn't wait a few more hours for me to come over. "If I can get out of here on time, I'll most definitely be there."

He finally stopped twisting the price tag on one of the sweaters and beamed at me. "Awesome. It'll be a lot of fun, I promise. And I might have a surprise for you, too."

"A surprise?" I said, wondering what on earth he had up his sleeve. "And here yesterday I thought you hated me."

"I could never hate you," he said. "Consider this a do-over, okay?"

I smiled. "You got it."

"Crap. Didn't realize it was this late," Justin said, glancing at his phone. "I need to book it back to the office, but text me and let me know if you're coming, okay?"

I nodded, watching the back of him as he left the store. The second the door shut, Addie rushed to my side, along with Kaycee. "Holy shit," Addie said. "I need to come here more often on my lunch break."

Kaycee laughed. "It's like a parade of men in here lately. And I guess that was the famous Justin?"

"Indeed it was. I still can't believe he came here."

"Dude, you're practically shaking," Addie said. "You rearranged that display three times."

I covered my face. "Ad, I haven't felt like this since . . . I don't even want to say it. But you know what I mean."

"Enough said."

"And you are definitely getting out of here on time. I'll see to that," Kaycee said. "What if he ends up making out with some hot coworker under the mistletoe?"

I laughed, but she had a point. Even Lessie knew stranger things have happened during the holidays.

Addie went back to the office, and I got back to work. Customers kept me from checking the time every two seconds, but then there was a lull. I set about cleaning off the register and phone with Lysol wipes, and essentially any other task that helped me avoid thinking about Justin making out with random girls. What if he forgot about me over the holiday break?

Finally, 5:45 rolled around, and what seemed to be the last of the customers left the shop, arms full of bags.

"Just go," Kaycee said, waving me off. "Merry Christmas."

I sent Justin a text saying I was on the way, and took off after giving Kaycee a huge hug and her Christmas present, a pair of silver chandelier earrings with tiny red beads.

Justin said the work crowd was heading to a bar near his office called McGillins, which was about ten blocks away, so I opted for the subway since it was snowing again. Heading underground was *almost* a welcome respite from the weather; it hadn't snowed so often in December in years, and the constant dirty, gray snow piled up along the curbs in the city totally grossed me out.

I emerged at Thirteenth and Market and walked the block or so to the bar, cursing myself for not wearing my Uggs or rain boots. The Action News forecast that morning had predicted a ten percent chance of light snow later in the day, but since I rarely listen to TV meteorologists, my feet were wet and cold by the time I was greeted by the unappealing smell of stale beer and damp wool inside the bar.

I scanned the room for Justin, but the cavernous old pub was not only packed, but incredibly dark. Several large groups of coworkers were scattered around the bar, ties loosened and jackets tossed on barstools, no doubt toasting the last day of work before the Christmas break.

"There's an upstairs too, you know," the bartender said, likely noting how I'd walked past him three times.

I thanked him and stomped up the steps, my shoes making a disgusting squishing sound. Even though none of it was Justin's fault, my patience had left the building by the time I found him sitting at a table in the far corner of the second floor.

"Hey! Over here," he shouted, half standing out of his seat and waving his arms.

There were six other people at the table, all guys except for a pretty brunette sitting to Justin's right, who looked to be about Cate's age, tops. An empty chair sat to Justin's left, and I wondered if he had purposely saved it for me or if it just happened to be the only empty chair at the table. These were the things I analyzed.

The others at the table turned around and waved or smiled as I approached, but the brunette remained stony-faced. *Whatever*, I thought. I was not in the mood to deal with crap from someone who was probably still in college.

Justin poured me a beer from the pitcher in the center of the table and introduced me to his coworkers. Morgan, the surly one, turned out to be the annoying intern he'd texted me about before. She'd just graduated from Drexel and would be starting a full-time position with the company after the holidays.

"So, what do *you* do?" she asked, twirling her long brown hair around one finger and looking as bored as possible while I told her about LM Designs and working at Plaid.

"Jewelry, huh? Good for you. Hey J," she said, putting her hand on his shoulder. "Did I tell you that my cube is going to be right across from yours?"

J? Seriously?

To his credit, Justin seemed as uninterested in where the conversation was heading as I was, and turned his back to her.

"So tell me about your day," he said. "That's cool Addie got to stop by and hang out for a bit."

"Yeah, she comes by once in a while. It was pretty busy all day, but once the snow started again we were dead for a while. "

"Guess the weather isn't exactly conducive to outdoor shopping," he said.

We both sipped our beers in somewhat uncomfortable silence and listened to his coworkers sing along to "Don't Stop Believin'."

"You seem off. I hope you aren't still upset about the other night," he said, leaning in closer and lowering his voice (not as if anyone could've heard him over Morgan trying to hit a high note).

"No, not at all. I'm just cold from walking here in the snow, and I couldn't find you in the bar and looked like an idiot wandering around forever, and I wish you weren't going away for over a week . . ."

He put his index finger against my lips. "I have just the solution."

Justin finished his beer in two long gulps and set the glass down with a thud. "Come with me."

"Where?" I asked, making a face. I'd just started to defrost from the walk; was he seriously already leaving?

"Come outside with me. I promise you'll be glad you did."

I looked him skeptically, but downed my drink and put my coat on anyway. "This had better be good, Miami."

Morgan glared as he threw some money on the sticky table and announced we were leaving.

"I thought we were going to do shots," she said, making an exaggerated pout.

"Sorry, we'll have to take a rain check. Liz and I are going on a top secret mission."

Morgan shrugged. "Whatever. Enjoy freezing your butt off. Nice to meet you!"

"Well, on that note, we're off," I said, making sure to give the intern a big smile while putting my arm around Justin.

We trudged down the steps and out into the cold. The snow still fell lightly, but since it was pitch dark outside, it had more of a sparkly, magical snow quality that even I could find redeeming.

Justin walked like a man on a mission, so I followed behind as best I could in my stupid pointy black boots, feeling a bit like Lessie chasing after Nonni Gabriella.

"So exactly where are we going?" I asked, huffing and attempting to blow my nose in a somewhat ladylike fashion.

"You'll see," he said, waiting for me to catch up and

taking my pink-mittened hand. We walked past City Hall and continued for a few more blocks until I realized our destination: Love Park.

The iconic "Love" statue (the one with the crooked "O" that you see on tee shirts) sat in front of a big fountain, but other than that, the park was just a bunch of concrete. During the day it was usually packed with tourists and the occasional homeless person, but covered in snow and completely empty, other than a lit-up Christmas tree, it felt like a totally different place.

"Love Park is great and all, but isn't it a little cold for this?"

Justin laughed. "Sorry, but I'm all about atmosphere. Don't be mad, but I have something for you. Call it an early Christmas present."

"Seriously? Wow, thank you," I said, confused but intrigued as to what this surprise could be. "But now I feel bad. I didn't realize we were exchanging gifts."

Of course I hadn't bought Justin anything; after all, we'd only been out a few times and had just started talking again. *Addie must be right about him moving fast.*

Justin pulled out a small box, and for a second I thought he was crazy. A million thoughts rushed through my mind. *Who the hell proposes to someone after a couple of weeks? What am I supposed to say? Should I call the cops?*

Fully aware of the "what the hell" look on my face, he assured me it wasn't a ring.

"Just open it."

The lid made a low creaking noise as I lifted it. Nestled inside was what appeared to be Nan's cameo, not a scratch on it.

"Oh my God," I whispered, hands shaking as I pulled it out of the box. "How did you find this?"

"Actually, I didn't. I tried, though. I've been looking for it ever since you mentioned the story. Finally I talked to Addie and she emailed me the picture you texted her when you first found it, so I had a copy made for you."

My heart sunk to the ground; for that brief moment I had thought Nan's cameo wasn't gone forever. The tears trickled down my cheeks before I could stop myself.

Justin's look of pride turned to alarm and he pulled me in close. "Oh crap, I messed up. I'm so sorry if I got your hopes up, I probably should've said up front it wasn't the real one. Please don't cry."

I laughed through the tears, mostly because I couldn't believe he was actually apologizing for doing something so incredible.

"Well, yes, I'm crying because I'm sad you didn't find the cameo, but I'm also crying because I can't believe someone would go out of their way to do something like this for me." I sniffed as he hugged me, still half-laughing, half-crying.

"It's not a big deal," he said. "I just wanted you to have your cameo, even if it's not the real one. Addie told me you couldn't afford to make a copy yourself. Hopefully it's pretty close, although I obviously didn't put the inscription in there."

I raised my eyebrows. "That would be a little weird."

"You never know. Maybe someday you can give it back to me," he said, wiping a stray tear from my cheek. "That is, if you aren't mad at me anymore."

I grabbed his face and pulled him in for the kiss of all kisses. The snow swirled around us, the wind blew, but I didn't care. For the first (and probably last) time in my life, I absolutely loved winter.

EPILOGUE

Two years later

So, TODAY'S THE DAY: New Year's Eve. After all of the planning, shopping and (of course) drama with Mom, I can't believe this wedding is actually going to happen.

Cate's going to be a beautiful bride.

I definitely had my reservations when she and Jesse first got engaged, but both of them have grown up a lot. If they'd gone according to schedule and married when Cate was right of school, they'd probably be divorced by now. Justin disagrees, but then again, he didn't know them back then. He and Jesse have actually become close friends. Jesse even asked Justin to be a groomsman.

It's crazy to think it was two years ago Justin gave me the cameo. When I woke up the next morning and saw my necklace in its little box on his bedside table, it made me realize all over again how dumb I'd been about Adam. He never would've done something like that for me in a million years.

The last time Adam and I spoke was on New Year's Day the next year. He called to wish me a belated merry Christmas and apologize for his behavior at El Vez. I accepted his apology and told him to have a good holiday; he said something along the lines of, "That's it?" I'm not sure what he expected me to do—ask him to come over? Justin came into the room and asked me a question, so Adam got the hint pretty quickly and said he needed to go. We haven't been in contact since then, which is one hundred percent fine by me.

As for my line, Nordstrom never panned out, but it's for the best. I think the buyer was just doing Mrs. Crenshaw a favor, even if she did like my jewelry, because we quickly realized I didn't have the resources or time to make enough pieces to get into their stores. Outsourcing my jewelry didn't feel right, and the more I thought about it, the more I knew I had to follow my real dream.

Earlier this year, I took some of my inheritance money, and with my mother's blessing, used it to open my own boutique, Ella Bella. Helping other up-and-coming designers in the area makes me happy, and my customers love how they can find outfits and accessories that you can't get anywhere else. Mom says Nan would've been my biggest supporter, and I know she's right.

Thanks to the extra income, and the rest of the money from Nan's inheritance, Justin and I were able to buy a condo not far from the shop. Maybe it's not in Addie's (former) fancy building, but it has that artsy feel I love.

Speaking of, Addie's on her way over to pick me up so we can go to the hotel and get ready. Jesse's family paid for the bridal party to stay in suites at the Ritz-Carlton, so we're all pretty excited. Justin is already there, hanging out with the guys and doing who knows what. I'm told there are monogrammed flasks involved: typical groomsmen stuff.

Addie shows up in a puffy white parka that practically touches the ground, waving her arms and cursing at a Septa bus as I get into the car.

"Did you see what that asshole just did?" she asks, pointing at the rogue vehicle that just cut her off, and nearly hitting me with the heart charm on her "Return to Tiffany" bracelet. Although she declared it was "so 2001," Addie has worn it every day since Brad, her new boyfriend, gave it to her for Christmas. He's an elementary school principal, and according to Addie is "adorably clueless" on anything fashion-related that doesn't have a Disney character or superhero on it.

I'm chatting away about the plans for the wedding as we pull up to the valet, and Addie gives me a look. "I'm glad you came around, otherwise this day would be a fiasco with you being a Debbie Downer and all."

I just laugh and shake my head, but if I'm going to be honest, I *am* a teensy bit jealous. Justin and I have definitely talked about marriage, and I assume that it will be the end result for us, but still. You never know.

We walk through the impressive marble- and column-filled lobby and take the private elevator up to Cate's room—the penthouse. She stayed there with my parents the night before and since it's, well, ginormous, the bridesmaids are all getting ready there. Although Addie wasn't asked to be a maid, she's close enough to tag along.

"Holy crap," I whisper, walking into the room. The suite is larger than most New York City apartments and even has a dining room table with a huge arrangement of freshly cut lavender roses in the center.

"I stayed here with my parents once upon a time,"

Addie says, looking a little wistful. There are certainly no penthouse suite stays for them these days. Her parents divorced last year and sold her condo, so Ad moved into a smaller apartment a few blocks away and has to actually pay rent now.

It's just Addie, Mom, Gracie, and me in the room, along with Karen, Cate's best friend from college. Cate decided that having a huge bridal party was tacky, a decision for which I am grateful.

Cate emerges from the bedroom in pale-pink yoga pants and a matching jacket with "The future Mrs. Crenshaw" emblazoned on the back in rhinestones. Just in case anyone mistakes her for someone else.

I give her a hug and hand her a gift bag decorated with silhouettes of brides. "Beep, there you are! Happy wedding day. It's just a little something for you to wear."

She takes a seat on one of the plush burgundy chairs and tears the silver tissue paper out of the bag, pulling out a tiny jewelry box.

"Oh, Liz. You didn't have to do this! This isn't yours, is it?" She holds the cameo up to the light, and I shake my head.

"Of course not. No offense, but I wouldn't give that up for anything." I give the cameo around my neck a loving pat. "We had it made for you; Justin went to the same jeweler who did mine."

Cate wipes a stray tear from her cheek and gives me another hug. "Thank you, I love it. This is the best present I've ever received."

Addie is watching us from across the room, blotting at her eyes with a tissue. We both look at her like she's nuts. "Oh come on! It's an emotional family moment. I *do* cry once in a while, you know."

Tears aside, the rest of the morning goes by smoothly, and before I know it we're helping Cate into her gorgeous Marchesa gown. Personally, I never would've chosen this dress, but the simple, off-the-shoulder ivory sheath gown with a crisscross front suits Cate.

After we slip into our pale-blue satin gowns and matching faux fur shrugs, Cate comes running over with wrapped boxes for each of us. "Just something to wear with your dresses today. I couldn't resist," she says, smiling at me in particular. Nestled inside a small Ella Bella gift box is a pair of silver dangly beaded earrings . . . my earrings. "You do realize I could've made these for everyone for free," I say, shaking my head.

"Whatever. I'm supporting your business!" Cate says, helping Gracie put hers on. "I came into the shop on your day off because I knew you wouldn't let me buy them otherwise."

Addie heads back home to get Brad, and the rest of us spend an hour or so taking photos around the city. We're walking down the art museum steps back to the limo when my tiny satin clutch starts to vibrate. "You'd better answer that," Gracie says. "It might be the crazy wedding planner saying they dropped the cake or something."

I pull the phone out of my purse and notice a 215 number I don't recognize. "This is Liz."

A typical South Philly accent starts talking . . . or in his case, practically shouting. "Yeah, you might not remember me, but this is Joe. From Joe's Pawn and Check Cashing?"

I'm sure the look on my face is pure confusion, and Cate furrows her brow as I sit down on the freezing-cold concrete steps, staring ahead at the skyline in front of us.

"Actually, I do remember you." I'd left him my

business card, as I did at all of the shops I'd visited when I looked for Nan's cameo.

"I kept your number in the drawer all this time. Felt bad since you were so worked up about that necklace. Just wanted to tell ya that a lady came in this morning with a locket that looks like it might be yours."

My heart skips more than a few beats. "Are you sure? Peach, with a diamond chip? An engraving inside?"

"Come and see for yourself, hon. We're open till five."

This can't actually be happening. I say a quick prayer that it's not a false alarm. Not on Cate's wedding day.

"Hold on to it. We're on our way." I end the call and gather my skirt to run down the rest of the steps. Not quite as fast as Rocky could run up them, but hey, I'm pretty good for wearing heels.

Cate and the girls are standing in front of the limo, and accost me as soon as I reach them.

"Is everything okay? Nothing happened with the party rental company, I hope?" Cate's expertly made-up face starts to turn as white as her fur shawl.

"Everything's fine. Get in the limo. Now. We have a pit stop to make."

We climb in and I explain on the way, pouring glasses of champagne for Cate, Karen, and myself.

"OMG. Do you think he's right?" Gracie asks, stealing Cate's champagne glass and slugging back a sip.

"Gracie!" Cate yells, snatching it back.

"What? I need some liquid courage for this fiasco," Gracie says, folding her arms.

I shrug. "Eh, it's a special occasion. Nan always let us have a sip on New Year's Eve, right?"

The limo lets us out at Eighth and Market, and we

get some interesting looks as we run (or in Cate's case, hobble) inside Joe's Pawn and Check Cashing in our wedding finery. Cate's feet rarely make it out of anything higher than Sperry Top-Siders, and I can't help but laugh at the exaggerated shuffle she makes in her silver heels and form-fitting dress.

As we enter the cluttered shop, Joe looks up and shakes his head in understanding. "It's okay. Happens more often than you might think."

"What?" Cate says, and I realize he thinks she's trying to get rid of her ring.

"No, no! She's not calling off her wedding. I'm Liz. Cameo locket Liz?" I'm so worked up that I'm practically out of breath as I lean against the glass case. "Thank you so much for calling me."

He slaps his hand to his wide forehead. "Sorry. Didn't recognize ya with all the makeup. And I never forget a face." He takes a key off a coiled black cord around his wrist and opens a case behind him. "This it?"

Hands shaking, I take the cameo from him, as Liz and Gracie peer over my shoulder. Same size. Same silhouette. There is only one more question. I pry the latch open and a tear slides down my cheek.

Marry me, Ella.

"I can't believe it. This is it." All of the heartbreak and struggle and joy of the past two years comes flooding back at once, and I wrap Cate and Gracie in a tight embrace. I know Nan and Nonni Gabriella have sent us a gift for Cate's wedding day. There is no other possible explanation.

Even Joe coughs to cover up the lump in his throat. "Gettin' me all emotional here, ladies."

After our sister hugfest, I turn to Joe. "I'll never be

able to thank you enough. How much do I owe you?"

He reaches out and squeezes my hand. "On the house, honey. Consider it a Christmas gift."

"Are you sure? This is probably like, really valuable and—"

"Shut up, Gracie," I hiss.

Joe laughs. "Got three sisters myself. Youse guys just have yourself a nice day, okay?"

After thanking him a million times and making a mental note to send Joe one hell of a Christmas gift, I take Cate's new cameo off her neck and give it to Gracie. "Now we all have one."

"What are you doing?" Cate asks, eyeing Nan's necklace as I drape it around her. "I couldn't possibly take this. It's yours."

It was never mine, really. "It belongs to the family. To all of us. And now you have another something old." Her diamond earrings glitter under the fluorescent lights.

"Thanks, Nan," Cate says, looking up at the sky (or in this case, a dingy drop ceiling) with a radiant bride-like smile. This necklace deserved to see at least one wedding, after all.

"Um, guys?" Gracie looks at her phone. "We kind of have a wedding to catch."

✧ ✧ ✧

LUCKILY, THE TRAFFIC is light as we drive out to the posh suburb of Villanova. Paying homage to her favorite movie, Cate and Jesse are actually getting married in his parents' backyard. Granted, they live on a seven-acre estate, so it's a bit of a different story from *Father of the Bride*, but the idea makes her happy.

I've never been to the Crenshaws' home, but I know what to expect from Cate's description (French château-style mansion, indoor pool, screening room, and so forth). However, I'm still taken aback when our limo pulls up to the fifteen-bedroom mansion. Jesse's family isn't just rich, they're *filthy* rich.

We enter an impressive foyer with black-and-white marble floors, where the wedding planner is waiting for us. She's clad in a pink tweed Chanel suit and a headset, along with a clipboard. I give Cate a "what the hell" look, and she just shakes her head.

"Mrs. Crenshaw asked me to show you to the library where you'll be relaxing before the ceremony," the planner says, giving us a "follow me" gesture. We pass at least three sitting rooms, a few gilded paintings, and a fountain with a naked lady pouring water out of a jug before reaching the cozy, wood-paneled library. It looks like something out of Nonni Gabriella and Lessie's day, and I can almost picture them playing cards and gossiping in the corner.

"The guys are already set up in the game room so they won't bother us," the planner says, fiddling with the top of Cate's dress. "Mmm-hmm," I mumble, half paying attention. I'm too busy texting Addie a picture of the room.

Mom walks in and Cate rushes to show her the cameo. I decide to let them have their private moment, but Mom motions me over. "I had a feeling you'd find it eventually. Nan would be proud of you, and so would Nonni Gabriella." She hugs me tightly and then kisses both of our cheeks before running to the powder room to retouch her smeared eye makeup. I have a feeling it won't be the last time one of us has to bust out the Q-tips and tiny mascaras Cate shoved into our purses earlier today.

About twenty minutes later, Mrs. Crenshaw pops her head into the room, letting out an exaggerated squeak à la Lessie when she sees the bride. "I'm just *so* thrilled for you both," she says, dabbing the corner of her eyes with a handkerchief embroidered with a gold "C."

Gracie rolls her eyes and I try my best to shush her in front of Cate's new mother-in-law. I'll give the woman credit; she truly has been making an effort to be friendlier to Cate, although I think Jesse confronting her certainly pushed her in that direction.

"Anyway," Mrs. Crenshaw says, "we're going to get this show on the road! Right, Beatrice?" The wedding planner nods; it's obvious Mrs. Crenshaw is the one in charge of this "show."

We follow Beatrice to the back of the house, out through the glistening solarium and across the courtyard with its cloister-style walkway to see a huge tent set up to the left of the garden. Of course this isn't just any tent; it's a high-tech, heated, hardwood-floored, probably-cost-more-than-I-make-in-half-a-year tent.

I peek my head inside, where about one hundred guests are seated in silver Chiavari chairs. Candles glow from every surface, and flowering trees are set up in silver urns along the aisle, which is scattered with rose petals and embossed with another "C," this one in silver. A towering white arch totally covered with creamy white roses and greenery stands at the end of the aisle, where Jesse and the guys are standing. I have to admit, the whole scene is breathtaking. It might be even more breathtaking if I couldn't actually *see* my breath in front of me. Of course Cate had to be different and get married in the winter.

I pull my furry shawl tighter around my shoulders as the other bridesmaids head into the tent and down the aisle, and then it's my turn. Justin catches my eye and winks as I try to remember to smile and not to run down the aisle. I must take after Nonni Gabriella in the fast walking department.

Soon enough, the vows are said, kisses are exchanged, and I'm linking arms with Justin to walk back down the aisle. "Good job, kiddo. You didn't even trip! I'm impressed."

I laugh. "I might have done some practicing." He opens his mouth to say something, but then stops and just smiles.

The bridal party heads inside for photos and champagne. Justin whispers dirty jokes in my ear as we're forced into stiff formal poses next to the naked lady statue, and I'm sure my face looks absolutely ridiculous.

Soon we go back outside and see the tent has been completely transformed into a winter wonderland theme: silver snowflakes are hanging from the ceiling, even more white flowers cover every possible surface, and trees with their branches painted silver drip with white flowers, lanterns, and crystals. Cate and Jesse's initials are projected onto the dance floor, where the flower girl and ring bearer are already running in circles.

Justin and I make our entrance to a Frank Sinatra song and watch as the new Mr. and Mrs. Crenshaw make their debut. Cate's smile stretches from ear to ear, and I find myself a little teary again.

The night passes in what feels like two minutes; we do shots with Jesse's law school friends, dance to almost every song, and watch as Addie and her boyfriend share their first slow dance together. A few hours later Justin pulls me aside.

"Will you do me the honor of joining me in the solarium?" he asks in an over-the-top fake English accent.

"I'd be honored," I say, "but it's freezing, so let's walk fast." He drapes his jacket around me, and we nearly run across the long stone path to the house.

"So," he says, once we're inside. "It's almost midnight."

"I guess so?" I said, wrapping my arms more tightly around myself. "I haven't been keeping track of time on the dance floor."

He's all fidgety and nearly trips as he attempts to lean against the mahogany bar they set up in the solarium for cocktail hour. The room is deserted now, and all that's left is the bar and a few stray C-emblazoned cocktail napkins.

"You're starting to freak me out," I say. "Is something wrong?"

He looks down. "No, there's just something I wanted to give you before the year is over." He reaches into his jacket, which is still around my shoulders, and hands me a tiny box.

Omg. This is it.

Like Nonni Gabriella, I look up in confusion when there's not a ring inside. In fact, there's *nothing* in it.

"Am I missing something here?"

Justin laughs. "You'll see." His hand brushes against my neck and I feel it tremble as he unclasps the cameo. My heart pounds as he hands it to me. "Open it."

I release the latch on the locket to read an inscription.

Marry me, Liz. Yours forever, Justin

My mouth drops open. I'd been wearing the necklace all day and had no idea that something life changing was hidden inside.

"How on earth did you get this?"

He flashes me a nervous smile. "I took it to the jeweler when you were away for Cate's bachelorette party last weekend."

The crowd outside starts to count down to the New Year.

Justin grabs my hand. "I didn't want to upstage your sister's wedding, but I couldn't wait. We can keep it our secret for tonight if you want."

I nod, still in disbelief that this is actually happening. He laughs, and suddenly I realize I haven't answered the question in the cameo, but then again, he hasn't asked me, either.

Finally he bends down on one knee. "So, Miss Moretti. Will you marry me?"

"Yes," I whisper, and we watch the fireworks explode outside as a new year begins.

ACKNOWLEDGMENTS

A cameo plays a huge part in Liz, Ella and Gabriella's worlds, but in real life this story started in much the same way. I'd been on the hunt for a cameo for some time, but couldn't find anything I liked. A few months later, my husband's grandmother passed away . . . and my mother-in-law gave me an old cameo pendant, brooch and ring she'd found at the house. It seemed like fate.

I'd been working on a novel called "Homecoming" for some time, which was the early version of Liz, Adam, and Justin's story. But something wasn't quite right, and I almost gave up. Hashing out new ideas with my husband, suddenly we started talking about the cameo, and a story about a necklace being passed down through the generations was born. Many thanks to Donna and Mom Mom C. for unknowingly helping to create Ella and Gabriella, and to Tim for being my idea guy.

I want to thank my parents, grandparents, aunts, and uncles for instilling a strong love of reading and writing in me. Whether it was reading crazy stories about Beverly Hills teens during my 90210 phase, or the silly rabbit book I wrote with my sister (hi, Cat), you've always supported my writing. Love and hugs to all of you, especially my mom, Diana, and Mom Mom.

My publishing journey was full of ups and downs, but luckily, it had a happy ending. Huge thanks to Crystal Patriarche and the rest of the team at Sparkpress for helping my dreams come to life, and to Julie Metz for the gorgeous cover.

I'm so grateful for my fantastic critique partners, Jessica Topper and Pat O'Dea Rosen, who read countless versions of this story. I couldn't have done it without you! Thanks also go out to Nicole Lasorda, Tawnie Bailey and Veronica Forand, whose feedback on early drafts of this book was greatly helpful.

My RWA friends are always there to support me, and I'm so thankful I joined such a wonderful community of writers. I've also met many talented and gracious writers in the Women's Fiction Writers' Association, and through reviewing women's fiction for Examiner.com. Special thanks to Josie Brown for your advice and encouragement over the years.

High fives to Lori, Ellis, Tom, Kim, Nadira, the VEO crew, and the rest of my lovely friends for constantly cheering me on. Remember Addie's favorite line, "Stop going back?" Credit for that little chunk of wisdom goes to my friend Gena Groves, who wrote it on a Post-it many moons ago.

And finally, all the hugs and kisses in the world to Tim and Alex. Thank you for always supporting my crazy dreams!

ABOUT THE AUTHOR

KRISTIN CONTINO is a Philadelphia-based freelance writer and editor whose work has appeared in retail, business and parenting publications, as well as a women's fiction review column for *Examiner*. When she's not writing, Kristin enjoys travel, photography, and spending time with her family, and dreams of moving to her favorite city, London. *The Legacy of Us* is her debut novel.

ABOUT SPARKPRESS

SPARKPRESS is an independent boutique publisher delivering high-quality, entertaining, and engaging content that enhances readers' lives, with a special focus on female-driven work. We are proud of our catalog of both fiction and non-fiction titles, featuring authors who represent a wide array of genres, as well as our established, industry-wide reputation for innovative, creative, results-driven success in working with authors. SparkPress, a BookSparks imprint, is a division of SparkPoint Studio, LLC. To learn more, visit us at www.sparkpointstudio.com.

SELECTED TITLES FROM SPARKPRESS

SparkPress is an independent boutique publisher delivering high-quality, entertaining, and engaging content that enhances readers' lives, with a special focus on female-driven work. Visit us at www.gosparkpress.com

The Balance Project, by Susie Orman Schnall. $16, 978-1-94071-667-1. With the release of her book on work/life balance, Katherine Whitney has become a media darling and hero to working women everywhere. In reality though, her life is starting to fall apart, and her assistant Lucy is the one holding it all together. When Katherine does something unthinkable to her, Lucy must decide whether to change Katherine's life forever, or continue being her main champion.

The Year of Necessary Lies, by Kris Radish. $17, 978-1-94071-651-0. A great-granddaughter discovers her ancestor's secrets—inspirational forays into forbidden love and the Florida Everglades at the turn of the last century.

Satisfaction, by Andee Reilly. $17, 978-1-94071-663-3. After discovering her husband's affair, Ginny Martin impulsively hits the road and follows the Rolling Stones from L.A. to Oklahoma, striking up a friendship with Bree Cooper, a free-spirited drifter.

Elly in Bloom, by Colleen Oakes. $15, 978-1-94071-609-1. Elly Jordan has carved out a sweet life for herself as a boutique florist in St. Louis. Not bad for a woman who left her life two years earlier when she found her husband entwined with a redheaded artist. Just when she feels she is finally moving on from her past, she discovers a wedding contract, one that could change her financial future, is more than she bargained for.

CPSIA information can be obtained at www.ICGtesting.com
Printed in the USA
BVOW02s0132210715

409220BV00003B/3/P